ECHOES
OF THE
RAVEN

Ingrid Seymour is a *USA Today* bestselling author. When she's not writing books, she spends her time cooking exotic recipes, hanging out with her family, and working out. She writes fiction in a variety of genres, including fantasy romance, urban fantasy, romance, paranormal, and sci-fi. Her favourite outings involve a trip to the library or bookstore. She's an avid reader and fangirl of many amazing books. She is a dreamer and a fighter who believes perseverance and hard work can make dreams come true. She lives in Birmingham, Alabama with her husband, two kids, and a cat named Ossie.

Instagram: **@ingrid_seymour**
X: **@Ingrid_Seymour**
TikTok: **@ ingridseymour**
Facebook: **/IngridSeymourAuthor**

BY INGRID SEYMOUR

Eldrystone
House of the Raven
Echoes of the Raven

Healer of Kingdoms
A Prince So Cruel
A Cage So Gilded
A Court So Dark

Mate Tracker
The Tracker's Mate
The Tracker's Secret
The Tracker's Rage
The Tracker's Revenge
The Tracker's Dawn

Demon Hunter
Demon Pride
Demon Apathy
Demon Hunger

Wild Packs
Howl of the Rejected
Blood of the Fallen
Cry of the Damned

The Mating Games
(with Katie French)
Rejected Mate
Dark Match

Supernatural Academy
(with Katie French)
Freshman Witch
Sophomore Witch
Disha
Junior Witch
Senior Witch, Fall Semester
Senior Witch, Spring Semester

Dark Fae Trials
(with Katie French)
Outcast Fae
Rebel Fae
Ruthless Fae

Dragon's Creed
(with Katie French)
Luminous
Nebulous
Perilous

Vampire Court
White Pawn
Black Pawn
White Rook
Black Rook
White Knight
Black Knight
White Bishop
Black Bishop
White Queen
Black King
Checkmate

The Morphid Chronicles
Keeper
Ripper
Weaver

Ignite the Shadows
Ignite the Shadows
Eclipse the Flame
Shatter the Darkness

Djinn Curse
Blazing Magic
Dazzling Fire
Burning Darkness

Jewelled Goddess
Godmaker

ECHOES OF THE RAVEN

INGRID SEYMOUR

HEADLINE
ETERNAL

Copyright © 2024 Ingrid Seymour

The right of Ingrid Seymour to be identified as the Author of the Work has been asserted by her in accordance with the Copyright, Designs and Patents Act 1988.

Published by arrangement with PenDreams

First published in Great Britain in this paperback edition in 2024
by HEADLINE ETERNAL
An imprint of HEADLINE PUBLISHING GROUP

1

Apart from any use permitted under UK copyright law, this publication may only be reproduced, stored, or transmitted, in any form, or by any means, with prior permission in writing of the publishers or, in the case of reprographic production, in accordance with the terms of licences issued by the Copyright Licensing Agency.

All characters in this publication are fictitious
and any resemblance to real persons, living or dead,
is purely coincidental.

Cataloguing in Publication Data is available from the British Library

ISBN 978 1 0354 2068 1

Typeset in 11/16pt EB Garamond by Jouve (UK), Milton Keynes

Printed and bound in Great Britain by Clays Ltd, Elcograf S.p.A.

Headline's policy is to use papers that are natural, renewable and recyclable products and made from wood grown in well-managed forests and other controlled sources. The logging and manufacturing processes are expected to conform to the environmental regulations of the country of origin.

HEADLINE PUBLISHING GROUP
An Hachette UK Company
Carmelite House
50 Victoria Embankment
London EC4Y 0DZ

www.headlineeternal.com
www.headline.co.uk
www.hachette.co.uk

To Michael
How many times can I say thank you?
Not enough

Calendar Eras

AV – After the veil
DV – During the veil
BF – Before the veil

I
VALERIA

"I have broken my Tuathacath vows a thousand times. I know not how I shall live with the shame when I return to Tirnanog because, by all the gods, I shall return."

Calierin Kelraek – Tuathacath Warrior and Veilfallen – 21 AV

The dead and the living sleep within the catacombs. Silence hangs heavy in the air, as thick as the dankness of this place. My wrists burn as I continue struggling, pulling, twisting, trying to get free of the ropes that bind me to the cot.

No one has been to check on me in over an hour.

My thumbs hurt as I bend them toward my palms. With one heedless pull, I yank my hands past the tight, coarse ropes. They fall to the side.

Oh, gods! I'm free!

I bite my lower lip to stifle a cry. A layer of skin has been rubbed off in the process, and the raw wounds left behind sting.

Even as my pain flares, I quickly undo the ropes wrapped around my ankles. I stand, and my head swims. Swaying on bare feet, I hold on to the wall, taking deep breaths. A lonely torch burns in a bracket on the wall, warming my face. I close my eyes to the soothing feeling.

C'mon, Val. Get it together.

I will my senses to focus. This is my chance to escape Ríffor and his veilfallen. I may not get another one.

They've been keeping me in a dead-end tunnel, a small alcove that once held bones but has since been desecrated. I've been here for four days. Five? I'm not sure. It's difficult to tell time in this eternal darkness. I still wear the silver-spun dress, my engagement gown. It's torn and doesn't balloon around me like it did that night. While I was unconscious, after I risked my life to save Amira's as she plummeted to the floor, someone must have removed the inner hoop. Now, the beautiful material is ruined, stained black and torn at the edges. At least the many layers of fabric keep my legs warm, even if they drag, which is more than I can say for the revealing bodice.

Taking a few tentative steps, I make it to the arched doorway. Beyond, two more torches are anchored to the wall, their orange glow illuminating a passage flanked by stone walls and a dirt floor.

I see no signs of life.

Crouching, I hurry up the narrow corridor, heart lodged in my throat. At a fork, I look in both directions. I have no idea which way to go. I choose left.

After taking two more left turns and encountering no one, I arrive at another alcove, this one much larger than the last.

I cautiously approach the wall where I notice several hollows. I squint, trying to discern the contents of one of them and jump back when I stare into two empty sockets, the macabre nature of the chamber revealed. More tombs. The hollow is filled with a jumble of bones, a leering skull sitting on top.

A chill races down my spine as I sense the weight of all the forgotten souls trapped in this timeless sepulcher. The dim light flickers, casting eerie shadows that seem to elongate and grasp with bony fingers. The boundary between the living and the dead is thin here, and the past clings tenaciously to the present.

A whispering voice echoes behind me. I twirl to face another hollow, also filled with bones.

You're imagining things, Val. Keep moving.

The whisper echoes again, this time from my left. My breaths coming in a quick staccato, I turn in that direction. In front of me, there's only darkness, another passage without illumination.

I glance back the way I came, wondering if I should go back or keep going forward. The sound of steps from whence I came provides the answer. I remove one of the torches from the wall and rush into the passage ahead.

The darkness seems to swallow the light like a starving monster. I can't see more than a couple of feet in front of me.

Once more, there are whispers.

This time, they seem to come from all around me. I twirl in a circle, the torch flickering.

"It's lonely here," someone whispers, the voice intelligible now.

I take several steps back, and my back hits the wall. "W-who said that?"

There is a long silence without any sound, then the voice again. "Is . . . is someone there?"

I stretch my arm, shining the light further ahead. A gasp escapes my lips when I catch a glimpse of grimy toes peeking from under the hem of an equally grimy dress. I take a step closer, the puddle of light moves with me, creeping forward until it reveals a woman sitting on the damp ground, knees bent, arms tightly hugging her legs.

The grubby-faced creature peers up at me, eyes wide and wet, the bottom of her face hidden behind her arms. Matted blond hair sits in a nest atop her head. She's trembling like a terrified animal.

"Are you all right?" I move closer.

She skitters back, whimpering.

I freeze, put one hand up. "I won't hurt you. I promise."

Gods! Are these endless passages all filled with prisoners?

Blinking, she lifts her head fully. "Va-Valeria, is that you?"

I cock my head to one side, shaken. I don't recognize this person, but she knows me. "Who are you?" I move closer still, making no sudden movements that might alarm her.

On shaky legs, she stands, a hand pressed to the wall for support. "It's me, your mother."

I lean backward, away from her. "You're not my mother. My mother is dead," I say, anger replacing every other emotion I feel. This is no joking matter.

She pushes her matted hair away from her face, revealing pointed ears in the process. "I'm not dead. They lied to you. I'm here. I've been right here all along."

"No, it's impossible. I . . . I saw you die. I was there." I shake my head, pushing away the hope that threatens to fill my chest.

"I knew you would find me. I knew it would be you," she says, walking closer on too-thin legs.

The light from the torch spreads across her face, highlighting her fine features.

I let out a trembling gasp, eyes roving over her high cheekbones, her narrow nose, her perfectly sculpted brow. "Mother?"

She nods. "Yes, it's me, Val."

I throw an arm around her neck and pull her to me. Tears slide down my cheeks as I try not to sob like a child. Somehow, my mother is here. She isn't dead. Orys didn't kill her. My heart stumbles, gripped in a blend of anguish and confusion.

But . . . but . . . her body. It was on the floor of the throne room. We held a funeral, a burial.

Holding her at arm's length, I ask, "How? How is this possible?"

She smiles, her eyes full of the tenderness time dulled in my memories. "My love, there is no time to explain. We have to get out of here."

"I don't know the way out."

Her eyes rove around the chamber, and I can see her thoughts firing rapidly across her expression. "There's only one way." A pause as she searches my gaze. "We have to use the amulet."

I press a hand to my temple, shake my head, and repeat numbly, "The amulet?"

"It will show us the way out," she promises. "It can do anything we asked of it. We can go home. Be a family again. Father, Amira, you, and me. Happy again. Don't you want that?"

The pain of her absence is more vivid as I imagine all of us together like before. She missed so much of our lives, but maybe we can make up for lost time. Except . . . we can't.

My throat hurts as I force the words out. "Father, he's de—"

"He's waiting for us." She caresses the side of my face, such tenderness in her features. No one has looked at me with this much love since . . . since . . .

I pull away, try to clear my mind. Something is wrong. This isn't—

"I need it, my love, my little pixie, please!" Mother begs. "We'll be trapped here forever if you don't give me *my* amulet."

"But I don't know where it is."

"Don't lie, Valeria. I gave it to you. It's the only thing that can save me."

"Save you?"

"Yes, danger lurks. I can feel it in the air."

Those words. Someone else said them to me. Cold fingers slide down my back, and my chest tightens as a terrible feeling of dread saturates me.

"Where is it?" she asks. "Please, I don't want to be here anymore. You have to help me."

"I . . . I . . . It's in the . . ." A knot forms in my throat.

"Find the princess! She escaped!" The order echoes through the long corridors I left behind. They're coming for me.

"They're almost here, daughter. Hurry," my mother urges. "Tell me where it is, and everything will be all right."

"It's in the Re—"

Don't tell them. Don't! a voice screams inside my head. *It's a trick. It's all a trick.*

"C'mon, dear, you can trust me." Mother tries to touch my free hand.

"No! You're not real." My other hand tightens around the torch.

"But of course I'm real." Her face flickers in and out as she says this.

"Liar!" I jump back and shove the flame in her direction.

She screams in pain, covering her face with her hands.

Oh, gods! What have I done?!

"Mother." I reach for her.

She jerks away and reveals her features. Her left cheek is raw, skin melting, only glistening tissue left behind.

I cry out in horror and keep crying until my voice is hoarse, and my throat aches and I wish I could die. I'm thrashing, struggling against rough bindings around my wrists, turning away from a blinding light that pierces all the way into the back of my skull.

"Fucking human!" a familiar voice that I despise growls.

My cries turn to small sobs as I remember where I am, and what is happening. I don't want to give them the satisfaction to see me suffer.

"You're pathetic," my torturer sneers, Calierin, Rífíor's sorceress.

Her espiritu fills my throat, toxic fumes turning the taste in my mouth into acrid ash.

It takes all the strength I have left, but I bite my tongue and go eerily quiet, refusing to let this bitch know how much it hurt to see my mother and believe—if only for a moment—that she was still alive.

Laughter begins in the pit of my stomach and slowly bubbles out of my mouth until I'm throwing my head back, and the tears rolling down my face are of a different, bitter kind. Through wet lashes, I peer up at Calierin, her fae features sharp as blades, and give her a hateful sneer to match her own. She stands over me, menacing, while I sit on the damp floor, hands tied to two spikes staked to the ground at my sides. My arms are outstretched like wings, kept so taut it feels my shoulders will pop out of their sockets.

"*We have to use the amulet. Where is it?*" I say in a high-pitched, mocking voice. Abruptly, I stop laughing and through clenched teeth tell her the only truth that lies in my heart. "I'm never going to tell you where it is. NEVER!"

"*Mallachtdorch!*" Calierin curses. "My hands are tied, Ríf́ior. I've already told you this *shy* torture is a waste of time."

Ríf́ior, my captor, pulls away from the shadows, the scarred side of his face catching the light from the nearest torch, causing the gash that runs across his right eye to look like liquid silver. His raven-black hair gleams in the torchlight. He's so tall the top of his head nearly hits the ceiling of the cramped alcove. I can't help but stare at his pointed ears and sharp fae features. He is Bastien, and yet . . . he is not.

"You need to let me do this my way." Calierin unsheathes a dagger from her belt and places the tip under my eye.

I lean back until my head hits the wall. The blade pierces my skin. A trickle of blood slides down my cheek. My gaze locks with River's—or Ríf́ior, whatever he's called.

"You're a coward," I tell him. "Come do this yourself."

Calierin puts more pressure on the dagger. I feel the strain in my eyeball as it gets pushed back. My exhales come out unevenly, and I hate that they give away my fear.

"Leave, Calierin," Ríf́ior orders.

"Why are you being soft on her? If this amulet is capable of what you say, we don't have time for this."

"Leave," he insists.

"We've been trapped in this godsforsaken realm long enough, and we—"

"LEAVE!"

Her hand trembles, revealing her rage and causing the tip of the dagger to widen the wound it has already opened. A whimper sounds in my throat. It takes her a couple of beats, but she finally pulls away, sheathes her weapon, and leaves the alcove.

Ríffor comes closer. Ríffor . . . this is his true name, not River and certainly not Bastien. It's what Calierin calls him, and I can see why everyone in Castellina mistakes the pronunciation.

I call upon my will in order to hold his ferocious black gaze. By no means will I let him know he affects me in any way. The only thing I want him to know is that I hate him.

"She was beautiful, wasn't she?" Ríffor says. "Loreleia, I mean."

"Get my mother's name out of your filthy mouth, bastardo!" My words are a low growl that makes me sound like a rabid dog. It's what they're turning me into, a feral creature that wants to bite and tear.

He squats, meets me eye to eye. The muscles in his forearms ripple. He interlaces his large hands, elbows resting on his knees.

Only four days ago, I was mesmerized by that gaze, feeling I could willingly fall into its depths. Now, I would tear out his eyes and feed them to Cuervo . . . if I was into letting Cuervo eat garbage.

Moving slowly, he sets one knee on the ground, leans forward, and reaches for one of my bindings. He is close, so close that I can smell him, a combination of sweat and the dankness of this place. Without breaking eye contact, he works on undoing my restraint. I hold his gaze, unflinching.

He glances down at my lips for a split second.

"I hate that I allowed you to touch me," I sneer. "Every time I think about it, I want to throw up."

"You thought quite differently when you were moaning under my weight, little princess." He finishes undoing the rope and sits back on his haunches, putting some much-needed distance between us.

I scoot over toward my still-restrained arm, and nearly sob at the release of pressure in my shoulders.

Hiding my relief, I say, "I was stupid and naïve then. I'm quite a different person now, and I assure you, you inspire nothing but disgust in me. Those memories repulse me."

He shrugs one shoulder. "A shame, really, because if you ever get out of here alive," he twirls his finger to indicate our surroundings, "you would eventually realize it is the best fuck you will ever have."

"Don't flatter yourself. One, I *will* get out of here. And two, my memories of you are so sour by reality that even my hand will be a better fuck than you ever were."

Rífíor throws his head back and laughs. "What a naughty princess you have become, Valeria Plumanegra." His laughter ceases abruptly. "But I'm not here to talk about our little lamentable tryst."

"I know that. Clearly, you're here to get your kicks while your lackey tortures me."

He shakes his head. "I have no interest in your suffering or anything else about you. This entire realm and all its inhabitants can go up in flames for all I care. There's only one thing that matters to me, and it's The Eldrystone."

A small smile tugs at the corners of my mouth as I embrace the certainty of his words. Rífíor would not hesitate to reduce Castella to ashes if it meant securing Niamhara's conduit for himself. Yet, it is precisely this understanding, coupled with my ability to thwart his desires, that makes all the pain worth it—gratifying even.

"That is why," he continues, "I've decided to tell you why it is so important to me, why I need it, and why I did what I did."

"You did it for the same reason as Orys. You did it because you want its power."

He shakes his head. "No. That is not the reason, Valeria. But I understand if you can't see past your own shortcomings, past your own greed."

Rífíor insists on saying that, but greed has nothing to do with my desire to keep the amulet. Only revenge does.

He goes on. "The reason I want it, the reason I *need* it, has nothing to do with a hunger for power. Far from it, and I think it's time I tell you everything."

I hate the part of me that rears its head and stands at attention at his words. I want to remain indifferent to anything concerning this male. He doesn't deserve even the smallest morsel of curiosity from me. But I can't help but crave understanding.

Why has he ordered Calierin to subject me to one nightmarish dreamscape after another: my mother's presence just moments ago, Amira's brutal end at Orys's hands, Father transforming into a monstrous raven intent on devouring me, and more? Why? I want to know.

Why did Rífior infiltrate Nido? Why did he pretend to be someone he is not? Why did he seduce me in order to get his hands on the stupid gem?

I clench my teeth and tighten my fists, hating myself even more for allowing the pain of a broken heart to make me weak.

"So, tell me then, why do you want The Eldrystone?" I ask between clenched teeth. "Lie to me, *Rífior* of the Veilfallen, weave your falsehoods as only you know how."

"What I will tell you next is no lie, Valeria Plumanegra. I only hope that my honesty will appeal to the charity of the woman I first met in Nido."

2
RÍFÍOR

"I stare at the discarded ancient bones on the ground and wonder if my own bones are condemned to join them and forever remain in this godsforsaken catacombs."

Aodhán Utorhán – Veilfallen – 21 AV

She huddles on the floor, one arm tied, the other one free. Her face is soiled, with streaks running down the middle of her cheeks and from the corners of her eyes to the tangle of hair at her temples, the evidence of all the tears she has shed while Calierin tortures her, and while she lies on her cot alone at night and thinks no one is listening.

Calierin would like to use her magic to do more than create harrowing images inside Valeria's head. She thinks that physical pain or the threat of losing an eye would break Valeria more swiftly, but I'm not convinced that is true.

"I'm never going to tell you where it is. NEVER!" Valeria's words are not idle threats. I hear the conviction in her voice, and I know

her well enough to understand she means this to the very marrow of her bones.

If there's one thing I know about the youngest Plumanegra sister, it's that she would do anything for her family. The proof is how, just a few days ago, she was willing to sacrifice her life to save Amira's, placing herself as a shield beneath her sister's plummeting body and the floor, damn the consequences.

So, despite my reluctance to allow Calierin to physically harm Valeria, as it seems like the utmost betrayal of my principles, I fear it will be this psychological torment that will haunt me as my lowest deed in the end.

Ironic, how I thought it would be the most humane way to get the answer I desire.

This is the reason I've decided to tell Valeria the truth—or as much of it as I dare.

"So, tell me then, why do you want The Eldrystone?" she asks me. "Lie to me, *Rífior* of the Veilfallen."

"What I will tell you next is no lie, Valeria Plumanegra, and I hope that my honesty will appeal to the charity of the woman I first met in Nido."

Unbidden, an image of her smiling face enters my mind. I shut it out, denying the weakness that led me to bed her in the first place, a mistake I'll never forgive myself for.

Her glare is dark and unforgiving, but I go on.

"You know well what The Eldrystone is. You found out the truth of it at the library. Did you not?"

She says nothing, just stares at me with that same hatred that seems to burn deep in her soul. She went to the Biblioteca de la Reina with her cousin, and she learned of the amulet's origin.

"You know it is Niamhara's conduit, correct?" I press.

Still, she says nothing.

"Answer me," I demand.

Nothing.

Driven by anger, I lash out, my hand wrapping around her throat as I bear down on her, my nose nearly touching hers. I feel her pulse and warmth in my fingertips. Her gaze is unwavering as it meets mine. She remains steady under my threat, which is more than many valiant warriors I've encountered have managed to do.

She blinks slowly, then licks her lips, the tip of her tongue traveling from one corner of her mouth to the other. I can't help but look down at her shapely mouth and spurn the jolt of desire that runs through me.

With a growl, I shove her to one side, nearly making her topple, and jerk to a standing position. Fury running through my blood, I pace the alcove, doing my best to control myself. This is not why I'm here. I've done enough yelling and threatening and torturing, and none of it has changed her mind.

I need to do this differently. I need to appeal to her kindness because she *is* kind. I saw the way she treats others, particularly those who might be deemed beneath her as a princess. She offers them respect, holds them in high regard, a stark contrast to many so-called nobles I have met.

In truth, I am desperate. I must end this. My kin grow ever restless, and the lies I continue to fabricate in order to hide the nature of *the amulet*—as I simply refer to The Eldrystone—could be revealed to them at any moment.

It is a precarious balancing game I play.

After I changed the plans during our attack on Nido, Calierin and Kadewyn demanded an explanation. They wanted to know why acquiring a trinket had become more important than killing the new human queen, and why kidnapping the snotty princess was crucial after we failed to secure *the amulet*.

I had to come up with an explanation, and after much pondering, I decided that the best course of action was to tell them a partial truth. So I informed them that I had discovered something momentous, that the Castellan monarchy had in its possession a fae-made amulet that could reopen the veil to allow us passage back to our home. As was to be expected, my words had their intended effect. All any of us want is to go back to Tirnanog. It is our priority—more important than making humans understand we are not a plague to be kept under control.

Now, it is time to also let Valeria know the same thing.

With a deep breath, I consciously rein in my anger, determined not to allow her to provoke me once more.

"I know you understand the nature of The Eldrystone," I begin. "I followed you to the Biblioteca de la Reina."

This finally gets a reaction from her. Her eyebrows draw together in confusion.

"That's right, Valeria. If you think you bested me that night, I'm more than glad to inform you that I allowed you to leave, and I took tremendous pleasure in knowing you were wading through shit to a false escape in the sewers. I thought you might retrieve the amulet that day. Instead, I discovered you didn't even know what it was."

Her mouth presses into a tight line, and her chin quivers, a clear sign of her frustration at learning of her failure and naïvety.

"It was enlightening," I say. "I was baffled because you were not using the most powerful tool you had at your disposal to escape your fate and avenge your father. Instead, I carted you off to Alsur to meet your repugnant betrothed."

Her nostrils flare at the mention of Don Justo. "You have nerve. Repugnant? At least he is honest about what he wants. He doesn't slither and lie like you do."

"Fair enough," I say. "But my methods are only on par with those of my enemies. Look at you, for instance, holding on to something that doesn't belong to you, succumbing to the greed in order to become all powerful."

Slowly, she shakes her head. "Don't lie to yourself, Rífior. It's not I who suffers from the greed you speak of. It is you. The Eldrystone may not belong to me, but it doesn't belong to you either. And yet, you have lied, cheated, and killed in order to get your hands on it, while I sit here, innocent of any crime except defending my home and my family."

"I don't pretend to be one of your saints, but the end justifies the means."

"Keep telling yourself that if it makes you feel better about your deceiving, murderous soul."

I go back and crouch in front of her. I want her to look into my eyes as I reveal the truth, and she finally sees reason.

"You know well, after educating yourself, that The Eldrystone belongs to the Theric family. Not to you. Not to your mother. She stole it, Valeria. Loreleia Elhice was a nobody from a nowhere village. She had no business handling a power that wasn't granted to her."

"She wasn't a nobody," she hisses through clenched teeth. "She was the Queen of Castella. You're a nobody, a filthy rebel, invader of my home."

"It is not my fault that I'm here, little princess. I want nothing more than to return to Tirnanog, and so does every other fae trapped in this godsforsaken realm. The only reason we are here, the only person who can be blamed for all this, is your so-called Queen of Castella. It is her fault the veil collapsed."

3
VALERIA

"I bear the literal scars of my encounter with Loreleia Elhice. Her daughter thinks her one of their saints, but she is wrong."

Rifior – Veilfallen – 21 AV

I shake my head as he crouches in front of me, refusing the notion that my sweet mother had anything to do with the collapse of the veil between Castella and Tirnanog.

She wouldn't have done such a thing. She was the kind of person, who would have never brought pain to anyone, much less countless of her kin.

"You're lying," I say, hating him even more than I already do. It doesn't matter what he says. He won't taint the memories of my mother.

"I am not lying. All you have to do is think about it for a moment, and you will see that I speak the truth."

I glance away, breaking eye contact. "I don't have to listen to you."

"But you will because your precious mother is responsible for the pain of thousands. Gods know how many fae and humans are trapped away from their homes—all because your mother lusted over something that didn't belong to her. She used The Eldrystone to close the veil, Valeria. She did it so she could keep the amulet for herself."

I hug my legs, curling up tightly, trying to stave the chills his lies and the dankness in this place drill into my bones.

It's true that the jewel didn't belong to Mother. I did learn of its origin at the library and with Maestro Elizondo. I know The Eldrystone is Niamhara's conduit, which she gave to the Theric family—the royal monarchy—to ensure the balance of magic in the fae realm. Rífíor isn't lying about that.

But the rest? I know Mother would have never done what he claims. She would have never condemned others to live away from their homes and families. She loved Father, Amira, and me above all else. Kinship was the most important thing to her.

Armoring myself with indifference, I recline against the wall and close my eyes. I still feel a chill in my bones, but I'm sure it has nothing to do with Rífíor's claims. No warmth reaches this miserable place, and perhaps I'm growing sick. I feel a fever coming on.

Rífíor exhales deeply, and I know this means he's trying to rein in his anger. He easily loses his temper, and I delight in causing him such frustration.

"What do you really know about your mother, huh?" he asks. "That she was from a small, inconsequential village. That she somehow ended up in Castella and met Prince Simón Plumanegra, no less, and then married him and became queen. Far-fetched for a humble fae female, don't you think?"

My father, before he became king, liked to spend summers out in the country. For weeks at a time, he postponed his normal duties to spend time living like a regular Castellan. He stayed at a friend's farm, worked the fields, and helped with the livestock. He was never the kind to shy away from hard labor. I know this because I witnessed him mucking up his own horse every day after he went for a late afternoon ride.

It was during one of his yearly trips to the country that he met my mother. She had decided to cross the veil and visit Castella. Father was harvesting hay by his friend's homestead, when he spotted someone sleeping under a nearby tree. It was Mother. He used to tell Amira and me how the moment he laid eyes on her, he knew he would marry her one day. This is how they met, and no story anyone else can tell me in its place will supplant Father's own. Certainly not a recounting from a liar like Ríffor.

Despite my indifference, he goes on. "Your father only married her because she had The Eldrystone in her possession."

I huff. "You're pathetic, you know? You're so twisted up inside that you can't imagine anyone loving just for the sake of it. And you're so obsessed with that damn rock that you can't see past your own nose. Father and Mother loved each other very much. But I know enough about you to realize you don't understand how love works. Why is that? Who broke you? Huh?"

Something flashes in his gaze that makes me think I've hit upon something.

"It seems I'm not the only one who doesn't understand," he barks. "We need The Eldrystone to reopen the veil. That is what all of this boils down to. You and your mother and all the Plumanegras don't matter. My people can't stand being in this place any longer."

"And so I'm supposed to give you the amulet? Trust you? One of the most accomplished liars and scumbags I know?"

His mouth opens and closes ineffectually. What sort of argument can he offer to prove he's deserving of all this power when everything about him is deceit and manipulation?

As he stares at me with unbridled resentment, I keep going, hoping to make sure my point gets across. "You say my mother stole The Eldrystone because she was greedy and wanted its power, so if that's the case, tell me why she never used it for anything? You also said the amulet was the reason my father married her. In that case, the same question stands. Why didn't *he* use it either? In fact, this powerful tool you crave so keenly was hidden in an old sewing box for years. After Mother died, Father let me keep it as a toy. So, you see why I don't believe a word you're saying?"

He shakes his head, doubt shaping his expression. His argument doesn't hold water. It's weak and nonsensical, and what else is also weak: the fact that he hasn't once tried to explain where he fits in this convoluted scheme.

I look him up and down with distaste. "If you're going to lie, at least make it make sense, *Rífior*. Also, there's an important piece of information you should've started with. You could have explained who the hells you are, how you knew my mother, how you knew The Eldrystone was in her possession, and how, oh how, did you get the amulet in the first place?"

"Bah! All of that is of no consequence."

"Really?" I turn my mouth down and shrug. "All right,

whatever you say. Though you should know you're putting on a poor show for someone who wants to convince me to betray my mother and my people."

"Betray your mother? She started all of this!"

"Did she?"

His dark eyes narrow, and I can tell he's lying. I know every angle of his face, every twist of his mouth, every tick of his jaw, no matter how slight. Maybe he didn't think I was paying attention when he was pretending to be Guardia Bastien Mora, but I learned to read some of his expressions. He was always so stoic, so corpse-like through his performance that I was forced to acquire enough sensibility to decipher him at times.

"Yes. She did," he spits.

"I can tell you're lying."

"She's responsible for the veil's collapse, Valeria. Hold no doubt about it." He sounds absolutely certain, and something in the depths of his eyes cuts through my barriers and makes me hesitate.

What if she really did what he claims? What if she used The Eldrystone to shut the passage between Castella and Tirnanog? If she did, then there must have been a good reason, something else Ríffor has conveniently failed to mention.

"Let's pretend I believe," I say.

He holds himself very still.

"Why did she do it then? Why would my mother bar her own way back home? Why torture herself like that? She was never able to see her family again. She missed Tirnanog as one misses a limb."

Once more, his cold expression shows a tiny crack. It's no more than a slight flinch, but I recognize it for what it is. There is more.

"Why are you being so stubborn?" he demands. "Wouldn't you be glad to be rid of me? Of all of us?"

"Yes," I say without hesitation. "It would give me much pleasure never to see your scarred face again."

"Then give me The Eldrystone!"

"No," I say. "Because it gives me infinitely more satisfaction to see you squirm, bastardo."

"And you don't care that in the process you're hurting so many others?"

"You said Castella could burn to the ground and you wouldn't care, so why should I?"

"Because you are good, Valeria. I know you."

I nod slowly. "Yes, I *was* good. I wanted everyone to get along. I always argued with Father about giving the fae a voice in the council. He tried to tell me over and over not to be so naïve, not to trust so openly. I thought he was embittered because he lost the love of his life, but I was wrong. What he offered me was wisdom. I didn't learn it in time, and I paid for it."

Legs shaking, I push to my feet, so I can tell him what he needs to hear while standing, holding my head high with what little dignity I have left. He also stretches from his crouching position.

"I'm not good anymore, Rífíor. I'm just as broken as you are, and it was you who did this to me, you who stomped all over what little innocence I had left and crushed it to dust."

He swallows, holding my gaze and looking on the verge of yelling at me to shut up.

"I told you this before," I go on before he can stop me, "but you don't seem to want to listen, so hear me out one more time . . . I will never give you The Eldrystone. Never. I don't care if it has the power to reopen the veil. I only care that you are forever kept from what you want most."

4
RÍFÍOR

"The Eldrystone corrupts everyone. She is not the exception."

Rífíor – Veilfallen – 21 AV

"*I told you this before, but you don't seem to want to listen, so hear me out one more time . . . I will never give you The Eldrystone. Never. I don't care if it has the power to reopen the veil. I only care that you are forever kept from what you want most.*"

Valeria's unwavering words ring in my ears.

I believe her.

I believe that she would rather die and suffer, than give me The Eldrystone.

Calierin could torture her in any manner she wishes, and it wouldn't make a damn difference.

Afraid I would lose my temper beyond repair, I left Valeria after our frustrating conversation, and now I pace the length of my sleeping area. It is a small space with only a cot and a barrel in one corner, which serves as both a table and clothes repository.

I heave a heavy sigh, exhausted. I should rest, but there is too much on my mind.

Ever since the attack on Nido, things have grown increasingly harder for me and my people. Amira is searching for her sister, has vowed to leave no rock unturned until she finds her. To that purpose, Castellina's Guardia as well as the Guardia Real are moving across the capital, searching for the veilfallen who took the young princess. It is only a matter of time before they find us, before someone gives away our location.

I knew this would happen when I decided to abduct Valeria. I anticipated it, but I also thought she would give me The Eldrystone once confronted. At first, I tried talking to her, both rationally and threateningly. When that didn't work, I resorted to lower methods, and as Valeria pointed out, I was too cowardly to administer them myself. Instead, I enlisted Calierin, who is more than happy to take out her pent-up anger on any *human dregs*, as she often refers to our unwilling Castellan hosts.

And now, after all of that, I am down to begging, which also has turned out to be a waste of time.

Damn it all to the lowest hell!

One slip in my resolve, and I ruined everything.

If I hadn't allowed my attraction to Valeria to get through my defenses, none of this would have happened, and my kin and I would already be in Tirnanog. The magic of our ancestral land would be coursing through our bodies, healing our wounds and rebuilding our spirits. Instead, we continue to suffer. We've been here too long and have had enough. Being severed from our realm chips at our will every second of the day, and I fear that, in time, this separation will break us all. I fear the fae in Castella will die out, our magic-bound souls too weak to keep going.

And now, despite all my efforts to persuade Valeria, I'm left with only one recourse to make her understand: telling her the entire truth. But what if revealing even this much fails to sway her? The prospect makes me feel wretched because it would mean that my mistake had irreversibly erased all the good in her.

You are an idiot, the harsh voice of my subconscious hisses in my ear. *If she was ever good, that part of her doesn't exist anymore. She tasted the power of The Eldrystone, and there's no going back from that. She is forever changed by greed. She would rather die than part with the conduit.*

I crack my neck and take a deep breath. Yes, I know this to be true. The Eldrystone corrupts, the way it corrupted Saethara, the way it corrupted me.

Is blaming the amulet how you hope to exonerate yourself from your own wrongdoing? another part of me asks.

Shame and anger mix like poison in my chest. I loathe what I did. I taught Valeria to distrust, but just like her, I also had a teacher who imparted the same teachings. Fate had it that I should be her mentor in that timeless lesson.

Regardless, she will never renounce the power of the conduit. And if she can't have it all to herself, she will make sure no one else does.

That is why I must explore every conceivable avenue to reclaim it. I cannot afford to overlook any possibility, and if partial truths failed to coax her into divulging The Eldrystone's location, then I shall disclose my deepest secret and tell her exactly how I fit into this puzzle.

If that doesn't work, I suppose Calierin will have her way.

5
VALERIA

"Why did I agree to this?"

Gaspar Patrach – Romani Diviner – 21 AV

Riffor walked out of the alcove, his back stiff, his every move deliberate. Anyone else watching him would have thought he was calm, unaffected, but I knew better. I knew by the straight line of his shoulders, and the slight twitch of his fingers that he was fuming.

Maybe I should be afraid. Calierin will probably be back soon to administer a different kind of torture. But despite the possibility, all I feel is satisfaction. I can see he's not impervious to my jabs and insults, though he hides the bulk of his emotions all too well.

I don't know the measure of his wounds and what caused them, but I know they're there. With the full power of my blackened heart, I want to inflict deeper wounds, and then pour salt in them. I wager my refusal is a valiant effort—not that I believe it's enough to even the score. He hurt me to the center of my soul, as deeply as he could.

Father, why did I doubt you?

If I had listened to him, I could have avoided so much pain. Even after Esmeralda's betrayal, I remained a fool. Jago tracked her down and delivered her to me, and in my stupid heart all I could do was forgive her and let her go. I should have known then that no one can be trusted. No one.

But I needed one more lesson to finally learn, and Bastien was the perfect maestro for the task.

I clench my jaw and fists. I want to rage and punch the walls, but before he left, Ríffor tied me to the filthy cot to which I'm confined at all hours unless Calierin pays me a visit.

There's an ache deep in my bones that makes me want to surrender. I've spent many hours fighting my bindings to no avail and eating the scraps they bring me on a bent metal plate. I'm weak and drowsy, and it doesn't take long for a restless sleep to sink its claws into my mind, taking me away into a deeper darkness than the one surrounding me.

Moments later, I'm jolted awake by a sudden scrape near my bed along with the pressure of a heavy hand over my mouth.

"*Shh.*"

Shaking my head from side to side, I struggle, but the pressure only grows more intense as well as the shushing.

"Settled down, niña," a familiar voice whispers.

I blink, willing my gaze to focus on a weathered face, dark beard, and pointed ears. Bright green eyes peer at me, and I finally recognize him.

"That's it. You know who I am, don't you?" he asks.

I nod, uncertain.

"I'm here to help you, so keep those lips tight." Slowly, he removes his hand.

"Gaspar?"

El Gran Místico, the Romani fortune teller who helped me escape Alsur, Don Justo, and Bastien.

"'Tis I," he replies as he works on my bindings, quickly releasing my wrists and ankles.

"How are you . . . ?"

"No time to explain. Let's get outta here before we're found."

Once all the ropes are undone, he helps me to my feet. "Can you walk?" he asks as I sway on my feet.

"Yes."

"Follow me. Quiet . . . like your life depends on it, 'cause it does."

I weakly shake my head and try to muster the strength to do as he says.

He leads me out of the alcove, and we step over a fallen figure and continue down a long dark passage, illuminated by torches sparsely affixed to the wall. I trip on the length of my dress and stumble a couple of times, but I manage to keep my footing. We come to another alcove, this one connected to three other passages.

Gaspar takes the one in the middle, his steps fast but silent. My feet are bare and cold, the heeled shoes I wore to the party long gone. At least it's easier to move stealthily this way.

Wait, no! Something is wrong.

My mind reels with questions. How is El Gran Místico here? Who told him where to find me? Why is he helping me? None of this makes any sense. I come to a full stop, realizing that this is just another trick from Calierin, another espiritu-induced hallucination. Gaspar isn't really here, and he isn't leading me to freedom.

He turns to look at me. "What's the matter, princess? Need me to carry you? I'm not a young lad anymore, but I can try." He attempts to wrap an arm around my waist.

I resist him, glaring at him with suspicion. "You're not really here."

He frowns, and it's clear he thinks I've lost my mind. "Course I am." He takes my hand and squeezes it. "See, flesh and bones."

Shaking him off, I take several steps back. "I'm not going anywhere with you. Your tricks won't work on me anymore."

"What did they do to you, niña?" There is a pitiful look in his eyes.

Tears come to me unbidden at the sight of his compassionate expression.

"I know it may be hard for you to trust anyone right now," he says gently, "but you *have* to trust me. Promise you I won't lead you astray."

No. No. No.

I can't trust anyone. The Romani betrayed me already. Esmeralda turned me in for a bag of gold after acting like my friend. But if Gaspar is the product of Calierin espiritu, how is she able to project him into my mind? She's never met him, has she?

"C'mon." He grabs my elbow and starts pulling me along.

"No!" I try to get free, but I'm too weak.

"Hush, girl!" he admonishes. "They're going to hear us, and then we'll both be trapped in these damn catacombs."

"Who goes there?!" A deep voice comes from behind us.

"Saints and feathers!" Gaspar exclaims. "Look what you've done. I'm getting out of here. I suggest you follow me if you know what's good for you." He turns and hurries down the dark tunnel.

I stand there, frozen, unsure of what to do. I glance over my shoulder and notice the warm light of a torch moving closer.

"Who's that?" the male asks, a veilfallen.

I make a split-second decision. Whether or not Gaspar is real, he is the only one offering to lead me to freedom. I have to follow him. Picking up my dress and holding it in trembling arms, I rush into the darkness ahead. I think I see Gaspar in the faint light of the infrequent torches. As my feet touch down on jagged rocks, the soles tear, and I struggle to muster the strength for the next step.

"Stop right there," the veilfallen calls.

I come to a fork, and I have no idea which way Gaspar went. I look right and left, squinting at the darkness. Suddenly, a hand grabs my wrist and pulls me to the right.

"This way," the Romani hisses.

And then we're running, El Gran Místico pulling me along, nearly dragging me, and it's all I can do to keep up. When my legs finally give out, and I fall to my knees, Gaspar picks me up, throws me over his shoulder, and keeps going.

I bounce up and down as he runs forward, my ribs aching as they hit his shoulder. He is surprisingly fast, a quarter fae if I remember correctly—his talk about not being a young lad anymore merely a jest.

I pick my head up and look back. That veilfallen is still after us, and he's getting closer. A full fae, I'm sure, quite faster than Gaspar, and not encumbered by an awkward load.

Suddenly, the dank walls that have surrounded me for days fall away. A cool breeze stirs my hair.

Gaspar sprints ahead, leading us past a row of trees before veering sharply to the right. The veilfallen isn't fooled though. He stays hot on our heels, closing in with each passing second.

"Set me down," I say. "We need to fight him."

But Gaspar keeps going, runs around a freestanding, broken wall, and screams, "I got her!"

Something slams against my back, driving the air from my lungs. Gaspar topples forward, and we go tumbling over the ground. I roll over him. He rolls over me, and we keep going. When we finally stop, the veilfallen male is also there, the one responsible for sending us sprawling. In one swift move, he springs to his feet and looms threateningly over us, a dagger raised.

"You're not going anywhere," he growls.

The male is as wide as a barrel. He is bald, which makes his ears appear even pointier.

Someone else stands behind the veilfallen. Carefully, he takes a step forward, raising a weapon over the veilfallen's head.

Gaspar lifts his hands and begins to speak louder than necessary, likely to drown out any sounds from what I presume is his companion. "All right, all right, we surrender—"

The veilfallen senses the other man's presence and begins to turn.

Thwack!

The weapon strikes our pursuer across the side of the face and knocks him to the ground. We watch the veilfallen try to stand, but our defender swings again and slams what turns out to be a wooden staff against the back of the veilfallen's head, knocking him senseless at last.

I stare up at our champion with gratitude, and as a ray of moonlight cuts through the canopy above, I realize who he is.

"Jago!" I don't know where the energy comes from, but I jump to my feet and wrap my arms around his neck. I pull away and hold his face between my hands. "Are you real?"

He frowns. "Of course I'm real. But let's go before more veilfallen come." He offers a hand to Gaspar. "Are you all right, man?"

Gaspar takes the offered hand and nods.

Between the two of them, they practically carry me away, cutting through dense trees. My feet barely touch the ground, and I feel as if I'm floating. My head lolls, and my eyelids droop with exhaustion. The forest blurs, and I realize it's all been another hallucination. I'm just a ghost in Calierin's dreamscape.

I'm barely aware of being lifted and placed back on my filthy cot. Jago speaks in a tender voice and wipes my forehead with a wet cloth.

"You're all right, Val. Everything is all right."

6
RÍFÍOR

"Thank all the gods and saints we found her!"

Jago Plumanegra (Casa Plumanegra) – Third in line to the Plumanegra throne – 21 AV

I traverse many labyrinthine passages to get back to the alcove where we keep Valeria. She is hidden well within the bowels of the catacombs, a place few can find even if they're familiar with the tunnels.

As I get closer, I'm still trying to decide how to tell her everything when I perceive something is wrong. The metallic scent of blood hangs in the air as well as the musk of a male I don't recognize.

Hurrying forward under the warm light of the torches, I reach the entrance to the alcove and find the guard on duty sprawled on the floor. I jump over him and run straight into the holding cell to find that Valeria is gone. The ropes that held her are cut loose.

"Godsdammit!" I curse, rushing back out and kneeling to

check on the guard. He has a nasty cut on his temple from which blood seeps profusely, but he's still breathing.

"Incompetent fool," I mutter under my breath, then run at full pelt the way I came.

My nostrils flare as I follow the faint scent of the strange male. It mingles with Valeria's, so it is easy to follow.

Cursing inwardly, I can't fathom who has taken her. No one just stumbles into these catacombs, much less to that far-removed alcove. There are only two possible explanations. It is an inside job, which I'm fairly certain it isn't—every veilfallen knows I will kill them if they betray me—or someone with tracking magic found her. This last possibility is still unlikely, though not impossible. Only my kin possess magic in this realm, and they would think twice before using it against us.

I hear a faint shout echoing in the distance. "Who goes there?!"

That must be them. Someone has spotted their escape. I increase my speed, my shoulders scraping the narrow walls as I twist and turn through the many passages. She's still here. I can't let her escape. Everything we've done will be for naught if she slips through our fingers.

I come to a halt at a fork, disoriented for a moment. I have to close my eyes and will my heart to slow to pick up the scent again. Once I have it, I wait and listen. The right! Hurried steps are echoing in that direction. They are faint, no louder than the patter of a mouse, but I'm sure it is them.

Without hesitation, I sprint that way, arms pumping.

Valeria! Her name is an angry scream inside my head. She can't leave without telling me where that damn bird took the amulet. Like a fool, I have scoured the skies these past four days, trying to spot Valeria's miserable pet, but it is a useless errand. There are too many ravens in the sky to spot the one that matters.

Anger flows through my veins like liquid fire as I veer into a passage that I know leads outside. Whoever came for Valeria has made every correct turn in order to escape. How?! If I get my hands on that damn male, I will strangle him, make sure he tells no one else where to find us.

Several excruciating moments later, I break into the open, the cool night air hitting my sweaty face. I pause only for an instant to reorient myself, figure out exactly which way they went, and start running again.

They headed north into the woods. They can't be far, at least that is what I tell myself.

I crash through brambles, pushing aside broken branches. Their passage is clear, and there is—

With a jolt, I come to an abrupt stop. One of my kin lies on the ground, groaning and pressing a hand to the back of his head as he tries to sit.

"Where are they?!" I demand, dropping to one knee and shaking him by the shoulders.

His eyes roll back into his head as he tries to focus.

"Answer me!"

The male lifts a hand and vaguely points over his shoulder.

With a curse, I sprint past him, doing my best to spot any unusual signs as I go. A bad feeling descends over me. I know there is a small clearing ahead, one that connects to a narrow path, which eventually leads to a dirt road. We often use it when we bring supplies in by wagon.

As I make it to the clearing, I come to a halt and find no one there. My eyes rove around as if Valeria will rematerialize because I want her to, but I know she's already beyond my reach.

I can feel her absence like a void in my chest. The possibility of finally going home which felt so real, so palpable the last few days, has vanished, and once more, I am left with the weight of uncertainty, heavy like an anchor around my neck.

The fury that has been searing my veins as I chased her spills over, and I throw my head back and rage at the heavens above.

For a moment, I forgot myself and grew soft, allowing desire for a woman to taint my purpose, but no more. Valeria Plumanegra and whoever helped her escape will feel the breadth of my wrath. I will not rest until she gives me The Eldrystone.

I'm coming for her and damn everything and everybody else.

7
VALERIA

"San Miguel, protect that sweet child from those awful fae!"

Serena de la Aguila – Royal Governess (Nana) – 21 AV

As I slowly resurface from a troubled sleep, the sound of whispered voices leads me to fight against my drowsiness, compelling me to open my heavy lids.

I'm in a similar cramped space as before, but the difference is the blessed absence of the awful, inescapable dank smell. One more difference, everything is swaying from side to side.

"You're awake." Jago leans over and enters my field of vision. "Hello there, cousin. You need to take better care of your wardrobe. What have you done to that poor dress?"

With difficulty, I push onto my elbows and look around. Two more people are here: Gaspar and the Romani traitor, Esmeralda.

I frown, expecting Calierin to slap me in the face to jolt me out of another cruel hallucination, but the fae female doesn't appear, and the longer I stare into Esmeralda's green eyes, the more I start to suspect this isn't an espiritu-induced dream, after all.

My gaze travels back to Jago, whose eyebrows are raised in an expression that suggests he thinks I'm deranged and expects me to start summoning a flock of singing fairies.

"We rescued you," he says as if speaking to a child incapable of seeing the obvious.

I blink.

Jago glances at Gaspar. "Is she . . . all there?"

"If I were to hazard a guess, I'd reckon they messed with her mind." El Gran Místico rubs at his braided, beaded beard, frowning at me.

"It's all right," Esmeralda says. "You're safe now."

My head whips toward her, and I fix her with a glare as sharp as daggers, half-expecting a swarm of maggots to spill from her lips. Calierin tormented me with visions of Amira's lifeless form overrun by them, crawling out of her mouth, nose, ears, even her eye sockets. I screamed until my throat went raw, all while Calierin laughed and Rífíor watched on, unmoved.

I hug myself and shiver at the thought.

Esmeralda puts both hands up and presses her lips into a tight line.

"Don't be mad at Esmeralda, Val," Jago says. "If it weren't for her, you'd still be deep in the ground. She figured out where they were holding you. And Gaspar . . . he used his pointy ears to infiltrate and his espiritu to guide him straight to you."

I hold my head in my hands and squeeze my eyes shut.

Wake up, Val. Wake up!

When I open my eyes again, Jago, Esmeralda and Gaspar are

still there, peering at me as if I'm made of glass and they fear I'll shatter at any moment.

This is real.

No. It isn't!

I shake my head, feeling on the verge of tears. Slowly, I lie back down, bending my legs toward my stomach and hugging them tightly. I close my eyes and will everything to go away.

"Oh, Val." Jago presses a hand to my forehead. "What did they do to you?"

"You best let her rest. She's been through a lot," Gaspar says.

"Those damn veilfallen!" Jago growls. "Amira will make them pay. Just wait till I tell her where to find them."

"I can make a draught for her. It will help her sleep peacefully," Esmeralda suggests. "I'll see to her feet and that wound by her eye, too."

"Yes, please, do that." Jago squeezes my hand, and I find comfort in his touch.

I try to sleep, but I'm too jittery, my body rippling with intermittent shivers that make my teeth shatter.

Bottles clink, then a moment later, Jago presses a small cup to my lips.

"Drink this, *monita*."

I swallow, surprised and oddly relieved by the moniker. He hasn't called me that in a long time, and there's no way Calierin would have known my cousin used this term as an endearment when we were little. He used to say I was a little monkey who loved to climb trees, that I was born in the wrong body.

You're safe, Val. You really are safe.

It is this thought and perhaps Esmeralda's draught that help me fall into truly restful sleep. Something I haven't had in days.

The softest whisper of fabric travels over my skin. The scent of lavender tickles my nose. There is a *click, click* sound to my right, and I open my eyes to find Cuervo standing on my night table, shifting from talon to talon, his sharp claws tapping against the wood.

When our gazes meet, he bobs his head up and down excitedly.

"Safe, safe, safe," he croaks, his body wiggling from side to side while his head keeps bobbing. I've never seen him this happy before.

"Hey." I reach out a hand and gently pet the side of his neck. "I missed you too, friend."

That's when the realization hits me, I'm in my bedchamber. In Nido. I sit up with a jolt. Jago is slumped in an armchair, snoring lightly, one arm hanging over the side.

Someone walks out of my bath chamber, startling me. The urge to run assaults me, but when I realize I'm naked, I hug the sheets tightly to my body.

"Val!" my sister cries out, runs to me, and wraps me in her arms. "Oh, my sweet sister." She rocks gently, her cheek pressed to mine.

We cry and hold each other without words, and only then I'm convinced that I'm out of the veilfallen's control and out of Calierin's reach.

"As heartwarming as this is," Jago says, "Side boob, Val."

He turns away. I pull apart from Amira and gather up the sheet to my chest. I had let it drop, giving Jago a healthy lateral view of my torso. Good thing the rest of me was squeezed tightly against my sister.

Amira holds my face in her hands and looks deep into my eyes. "I was so afraid I would never see you again."

"I was afraid too, since Fa . . ." I can't finish, can't mention Father for fear I will fall apart. I haven't allowed myself to truly mourn him. My desire to avenge his death and my determination to free Amira propelled me forward, and then . . . then came more pain and betrayal.

Tenderly, Amira caresses my cheek. "I know. Jago told me everything you went through while that sorcerer was in charge. I'm sorry. I'm so sorry."

I shake my head. "No. I'm not the only one who has been through a lot. You . . . Orys . . . what he did to you."

She hangs her head, hiding her gaze from me.

"You know what, Cuervo?" Jago says. "We need to let these ladies talk. C'mon." He gestures toward the open balcony.

Cuervo, normally at odds with my cousin, offers no opposition and flies out of the room, barely making a sound.

"I'll see you in the morning, Val." Jago inclines his head. "I'm absolutely knackered. I haven't slept in days. I'll send in a maid with some tea and food." He exits the bedchamber as silently as Cuervo, leaving me alone with my sister.

"Hold on a second." Amira leaves my side and returns with an oversized tunic, the one I often wear when lounging with a good book. She hands it over. "You were filthy. I had to cut you out of your dress and clean you as best as I could. I don't know what the Romani girl gave you, but you were out cold and didn't seem to feel a thing. You still need a good bath, though."

"You know Esmeralda?"

She nods. "And I'm forever indebted to her."

I slip the tunic over my head, glad to finally wear something comfortable, familiar, and clean.

"What happened?" I ask, fully aware that we are both avoiding talking about Father.

Amira climbs on the bed, gets under the covers, and sits next to me—the way she used to do when we were little.

"After they took you," she explains, "I mobilized the guards and offered a reward for any information that would lead to you and the capture of the veilfallen leader."

"Oh," I say, finally understanding Esmeralda's involvement. "It seems she will do anything for gold."

Amira frowns and shakes her head. "No, she didn't want the reward. Neither did her companion. In fact, she gave me back the coin Guardia Bastien Mora gave her after the Romani helped you escape Alsur."

Esmeralda told me as much the day Jago found her and put her in a dungeon cell at my request, but I didn't believe her.

Amira goes on. "When Esmeralda heard you'd been taken by the veilfallen, she began inquiring amongst her people. Some of them had an inkling of where the veilfallen might be hiding, so she went searching. One of the places her kin suggested turned out to be the right one. She and Gaspar came to Jago earlier today, and they went out to get you. Jago didn't even tell me what he was doing." Amira sounds displeased about this. "But I suppose it was for the better. Castella's Guardia will take care of them. They have their orders."

Her words send my heart hammering. Apprehension takes hold of me, and I can't understand why. I shouldn't care. It's the least they deserve for what they did to me, for invading my home and nearly killing my sister, for all the unrest they have caused in Castella, and for . . . for . . .

I straighten and say, "Good. They need to face justice."

She nods firmly.

I'm quiet for a moment, then a question bursts out of me of its own accord. "Why did they lie to us?"

"To protect us, Val." She knows I mean our parents. "Father thought he had more time. He was going to tell you. Eventually."

"If he had trusted me, he would still be alive. I should've known it was the amulet that helped me vanish Orys after he killed Mother. I foolishly thought that it . . . that it was me. That I had espiritu. I didn't even remember I was wearing the stupid thing that day. If only I'd been able to save Mother, and I had turned that damn sorcerer to ashes." I'm breathing erratically now, feeling as if my heart will give out.

"*Shh*." Amira grabs my hand and squeezes it. "We don't need to figure it all out tonight. I have questions for you, too, but we have time. You need to rest and heal. We'll set everything right. We'll . . . have a proper funeral for Father. We will honor him the way he deserved."

"Yes, that would be . . . nice."

Turning to face me, she runs a hand over my hair. "How about you take a hot bath and wash your hair? I'll help you, and then comb your hair and get all those tangles out."

I nod, and she takes my hand, leads me to the bath chamber, and fills the tub. My injured feet are tender with every step. The water is blissfully hot as I step in. Goosebumps cover my arms and legs as the heat ripples over my skin.

Amira uses a small container in the shape of a seashell and pours water over my head, then begins to soap my hair. It takes several rinses to get all the dirt out, but when she's done, my hair smells of lemons and my scalp tingles. She uses a small brush and runs it over my fingernails, getting rid of the grime encrusted there.

I feel like a child, and I don't mind. My sister is with me. I'm not alone.

There is a knock at the door, and I startle, nearly jumping out of the tub.

"Don't worry," Amira soothes. "There are guards outside. No one can get to you again. It's probably the maid with the food. Wait a moment, I'll be right back."

A niggling sensation starts in the back of my mind, but I can't put a finger on what is causing it.

She leaves, and I try to stay put, but I can't. Instead, I climb out of the tub, legs shaking, and grab a towel. I wrap it around me, go to the door, and peek outside.

"Put it right there." Amira points to a table by the fireplace. "Light a fire, and make sure no one disturbs Princess Valeria."

"Yes, Your Majesty." The maid gets to work by the fireplace.

I pull away from the door, relieved. For weeks, I lived in Nido fearing our enemy was ensconced within the walls of our home and would attack at any moment. In the end, I was right. Orys supplanted Emerito, my sister's closest adviser, and when the sorcerer got tired of playing his game, he struck, nearly killing Amira in the process.

My sister returns. "Oh, you got out. I thought you might like to soak a little longer." She smiles, meeting my gaze through a large, gilded mirror in the corner. "Sit, I will comb your hair."

I watch her, surprised by her fortitude. She has been through so much, and yet she shows nothing but poise, acting like the queen Father raised her to be.

While she retrieves a comb, I sit on the velvet-upholstered stool in front of the mirror. The wound under my eyes is not as bad as I thought. She starts at the tips of my hair, gently undoing the tangles to make sure she doesn't pull on my scalp.

"Are you all right?" I ask, meeting her gaze in the mirror.

"Let's not worry about me."

"But of course I'm worried about you. What Orys did . . ."

She pauses, contemplating the floor for a long moment. Making a decision, she begins to talk. "I don't remember any of it, and I guess that's a blessing. I think he came in posing as a petitioner."

Yes, that makes sense.

She and Father used to split the responsibility to speak to denizens with requests, ranging from charitable requests to help resolving a conflict with a neighbor to asking for a blessing for a newborn. Orys could have infiltrated Nido under such guises without much trouble. After all, he had the ability to assume different appearances.

"The last thing I recall," Amira continues, "is our conversation about the guard detail Father wanted me to arrange for you. And the next moment... I was waking up in the ballroom amidst utter chaos."

"Oh, Amira, I can't imagine how difficult all of this must be for you."

She nods and smiles sadly, the comb running down a strand of hair she has fully untangled. "I can say the same for you."

If she only knew how my foolish desire for a man I scarcely knew ended up complicating things further.

She goes on. "We found Emerito's body in a seldom-visited dungeon."

I gasp, realizing that I hadn't given the real Emerito a second thought—not that I'd had the time or the mental ability to process everything that has happened since the engagement ball. Unbidden, the figure of another person emerges from the recesses of my mind: Don Justo. The last time I saw him he was sprawled on the floor after facing the veilfallen at the ball and losing. Did he survive?

"The poor man," my sister says. "He paid unjustly for being my closest adviser." She pauses and holds my gaze. "I hesitate to bring this up right now, but I have tried to find Guardia Bastien. I have been unable to locate him."

I swallow thickly and stare at my hands on my lap.

"There is no record of him at the Academia de Guardias. Few can even remember him, and I have questioned everyone in Nido. Not even his fellow guards can tell me much about him. Jago... he told me that you and the guardia..."

I close my eyes and inhale deeply, the heat of shame rising from my neck to my cheeks. I don't want to admit to anyone the magnitude of my mistake, but Amira needs to know. I armor myself with courage and speak.

"The . . . the reason you can't find any record of Guardia Bastien is because he . . . wasn't a real guardia. He was an impostor."

"An impostor?" She considers. "Was he working with Orys?"

I shake my head, fighting back tears and the aching knot in my throat.

"Val," she says in a sorrowful breath, "I'm so sorry." She puts a hand on my shoulder for comfort.

Abruptly, I stand and walk out of the bath chamber, my hair only half combed. I don't want Amira's pity. I would prefer her anger, would rather hear her say I was stupid and naïve and had no business sleeping with a guard.

I walk to the fireplace and stand in front of it. The maid is gone, and the logs already glow and warm the room. A tray with food sits on a table surrounded by four armchairs. Amira comes out and offers me the comb. I take it, and she sits in one of the armchairs.

"I don't know what I was thinking," I say. "But it's the most idiotic thing I've ever done."

"Anyone in your position would—"

"No, Amira, you don't know how well he played me. You don't know the enormity of my mistake." I turn and face her, determined to own my blunder with dignity, if that is even possible. "Bastien Mora is Rífíor of the Veilfallen," I blurt out.

She seems unable to wrap her mind around it at first, then her expression twists in outrage. "A veilfallen! Here in Nido. How?!"

"Not *any* veilfallen. Rífíor, the leader."

She frowns, understanding slowly dawning on her. Rífíor. River. A slight mispronunciation of the bastardo's name.

"Now, do you understand?" I ask. "He used me. I fell for his lies. I was reckless and compromised our situation with a person I knew nothing about—only because he was handsome, and I felt . . . I felt . . . *star bursts*." I lay a hand on my chest to show her where those stupid fluttery feelings took root.

I can see disappointment and understanding warring in Amira's expression. She wants to yell at me and console me at the same time, but she can't decide which one should take the prize. I can tell her though. I know what I deserve.

"Somehow," I continue, "he infiltrated our home and fooled everyone. He came with a recommendation from General Cuenca himself and gained access to Father, to you, and me. He could've killed us all if he hadn't been so obsessed with finding The Eldrystone."

Her face is growing red, and her jaw is clenched tightly. I'm tipping the scales, fueling her desire to yell at me.

"He was here for weeks, gaining knowledge that he can use against us," I add, hoping to finally set her off.

Instead, my words defuse her anger, and a smile slowly stretches her lips. "No, he can't."

I frown, unable to understand the gleam in her eyes.

She rises from the armchair and stands in front of me. "You don't have to worry about any of them anymore, my dear sister, because they're all dead by now."

8

RÍFÍOR

"Like Calierin, I begin to doubt our leader."

Kadewyn Zinceran – Veilfallen – 21 AV

I find Calierin and Kadewyn. Rage sings in my veins. The commotion has awakened everyone, including them.

"She escaped," I say, hands trembling as I tighten them into fists.

"What?! How?!" Calierin demands, her volatile temper jumping to the surface.

Kadewyn hangs back, his pale silver eyes gleaming under the torchlight. He looks as puzzled as I feel.

I shake my head, trying to figure out how it could have happened. "I don't know. She had help, but . . ." I shake my head.

"A traitor?" Calierin suggests, then runs with the idea. "Someone here sold us out. I will kill the bhrisconach!"

"Settle down, Calierin," I order. "Our people aren't traitors. I scented a strange male, and I followed his trail outside. They had transport, a wagon or carriage. It was a small effort, though effective."

"We have to go after them!" Calierin declares.

Kadewyn steps next to Calierin. His silver hair makes Calierin's light blond appear positively yellow.

"No," he says calmly. "We have to get out of here. Gather what we can and leave."

He's right. They know where we are now. This place isn't safe anymore. "Give the order," I say.

Kadewyn nods and rushes down one of the bone-filled passages.

"We are just going to let her get away?" Calierin demands.

"No," I say. "We are not."

She grins. "Let us go then."

I shake my head. "I will do this on my own."

"Not again, Rífíor. We can't stand by you if you keep shutting us out of your plans. I can help. Kadewyn can help. We *all* can help."

No. No one can help me, and perhaps my time with the veil-fallen has come to an end. I only became their leader because it served my purposes, but now that I know how I can get to The Eldrystone, they have become a liability. Even if they don't know exactly what the amulet is, the simple fact that they know it can take them back to Tirnanog is enough to make them covet it.

"I don't need help," I say. "I will take care of it myself."

"The way you took care of it before?" she demands with contempt.

"Watch yourself, Calierin!"

"Or what?"

Her fists curl and so do mine. Since our attack on Nido, she has been regarding me with suspicion. She does not believe my tale entirely, and that makes her dangerous. She is the last of the veil-fallen I would trust with more than I have already divulged. She doubts me, but what she does not know is that I do not doubt others the way she does.

I distrust, utterly and entirely.

I open my mouth to respond when a cry of alarm pushes through the path to our left and reverberates against the crumbling walls.

Our heads snap in the direction of the commotion.

"They're already here," Calierin says as she deciphers the words of warning at the same time that I do.

We're under attack. Castellina's Guardia is here. They must have been lying in wait, making sure their princess was safe before they launched their attack.

We draw our swords and run toward what already sounds like a battle.

VALERIA

"W-what do you mean they're all dead by now?" I ask.

Amira's smile deepens. "I told you the guards have their orders. Castellina's Guardia, under the command of the Guardia Real, stormed the catacombs shortly after you were rescued. We couldn't let them get away after what they did. They died in those tunnels like the vermin they are."

My lower lip trembles.

"They were overwhelmed by our numbers," she continues. "And in the end, we flushed the last few with smoke and cut them down as they ran out for fresh air. They're all dead."

As she finishes the last sentence, there's a gleam in her eyes, a flash of the Amira who was possessed by Orys. She sounds cold and . . . not entirely herself.

I don't know how many veilfallen were inside those catacombs, but I can't believe Amira ordered the slaughter of that many people.

Overwhelmed, I turn my back on her and try to examine the strong emotions whirling inside me. At first inspection, I'm not sure what the pressure in my chest is, but I slowly realize it's horror. My sister would never do something like that.

Still, I shouldn't feel this way. I should be glad they're all dead. They've caused unrest for years, and many innocent people have died because of them. They deserved this fate, didn't they? They asked for it.

"I know it's a lot to handle." From behind, Amira wraps her arms around my waist and lays her head on my shoulder. "But Castella will be far safer without them. We should have done this a long time ago. If we had, Father would still be alive."

That isn't necessarily true. Orys was the one who killed Father, and he had no connection to the veilfallen. He shared their philosophy, blamed humans for the veil's collapse, but he was acting alone.

A second wave of emotions crashes into me. The veilfallen are dead.

Rífíor is dead.

I sway on my feet as satisfaction, confusion, delight, doubt, and more flood me and blend into a toxic concoction. I don't understand what I'm feeling. I shake my head forcefully and disentangle myself from Amira.

He's dead. The bastard is dead. He deceived me, tortured me. He got his due. Ríffor of the Veilfallen isn't a problem anymore. His essence has passed into one of the many hells the fae believe in, where he'll pay for his sins.

But if my thoughts on this are unequivocal, why are my emotions tainted by the memories of one night?

I hate myself. I hate myself.

Amira takes my hand and pulls me toward the bed. "I can see this news has upset you. Come. Lie down and sleep. You'll feel much better in the morning. You have been through so much, and it will be a while before you can see everything clearly."

I nod. She's right. I need time. I need distance to set my life to rights. I have to process all the changes and build a new Valeria for a world where Father doesn't exist, and Amira is the type of queen who ruthlessly executes her enemies.

Taking a deep breath, I allow her to lead me to bed. I rest my head down, and she covers me. She rests next to me and wraps me in her arms. She starts humming and unleashes an avalanche of memories inside my mind with the melody. It's a sweet fae tune Mother used to sing for us. It's in Tirgaelach, the old and disused fae language. Neither one of us remembers the words. Many times, after Mother died, Amira and I tried to recall them, even asked Maestro Elizondo if he knew the song, but we never succeeded in recalling it.

Amira smooths my hair. "Sleep. You're safe. No one will hurt you, my little sister."

"I love you," I say groggily.

"I love you, too."

Her tenderness slowly eases the turmoil that rages inside me. My eyelids grow heavier as I start to believe her words of comfort, and the exhaustion of the horrible days I spent in those catacombs descends on me and traps me in its claws.

The niggling sensation I felt in the tub returns, scratching the back of my awareness, but everything slips away. Like leaves caught in a strong wind, my thoughts move further and further away. I want oblivion, crave it. This world feels foreign, and I want nothing to do with it.

Surrendering to sleep is easy after I decide to detach myself from this awful reality.

9
RÍFÍOR

"It's not a fair fight, but these veilfallen took the princess and must pay and serve as an example to others."

Eva Toromayor – Royal Guard Lieutenant – 21 AV

The tunnel is clogged with people. Someone fights ahead, the clash of steel against steel making it obvious. There is no way to push past and help. There are two exits. We've tried both. They are blocked by guards.

I make my way to the front, pushing people aside. They squeeze against the walls to let me pass. Once there, I find one of the veilfallen stabbing an opponent. The guard falls to his knees, and another takes his place. Behind the new guard, there is another, and behind that one, another—more and more as far as the dim light permits me to see.

Here, at last, the humans' sheer numbers will overpower us. We have always been too few to make a difference. It has always been our disadvantage, and today it will be our demise.

The new guard stabs the male in front of me in the stomach. I take the front and make quick work of the human, and then the next and the next and the next. But there is always one more, yet I fight them, unsteady on my feet as I step on the fallen, slipping in their blood and gore.

It doesn't take me long to recognize my efforts are futile. There could be hundreds of Castellina's guards queued up for miles, ready to enter the tunnels. We might dispatch a fair number of them before we tire, but tire we will, and then we'll be nothing but vulnerable prey.

"Retreat," I order those behind him, even though I know there is nowhere to go. We can hide in the bowels of this godsforsaken place, but our meager supplies would run out quickly, and then we would have no other choice but to fight. We must move back, regroup, and come up with a plan that gives us hope.

Calierin's voice rages behind me. "Let me pass. I will blast them to their miserable hell."

"No!" I shout as I slash a man's throat and his blood sprays in every direction, hitting the walls and slicking my grip on the blade. "Hold back, Calierin. You will bury us all."

This place is in shambles. A blast of her magic will bring the earth down on our heads.

"We have to do something," she yells.

"Retreat!" I order again.

I repeat the message to the male behind me as I force my current opponent to take a few steps back with a quick succession of blows. "Everyone, head to the nexus. Now!" We all know this location. It is the largest alcove, which we use for gatherings.

The line of veilfallen behind me starts moving back. It goes slowly at first, and then more quickly until the path is clear.

With a growl, I lunge forward and stab with all my strength. I skewer the first and second man, and leaving my sword in place, I run back at full pelt, knocking down torches as I go, plunging the path behind me in darkness.

Many twists and turns lead me to my destination. The humans won't find us easily. There, we will think of something, figuring out a way to best them.

A group of twenty-five veilfallen surrounds me as I squeeze into the cramped alcove. One lonely torch illuminates their faces, sharpening their features. Calierin and Kadewyn are among them. They all look at me, expectant.

My thoughts trip over each other, all of them futile.

"What now?" Calierin demands in a tone that suggests she anticipates nothing but failure from me.

"We cannot die here," Saoirse says. She's a druidess, trained in the ancient arts of herbalism. She reluctantly became a veilfallen after losing her mate in a tragic mugging perpetrated by two drunken humans.

Calierin thumps her back. "We won't. Our amazing leader will come up with a solution, won't you, Rífíor?"

"This is not the time," I growl.

"This *is* the only fucking time," she spits, her tone contradicting her earlier statement, suggesting she *does* think we will die here, and this is the only chance she has left to air her grievances.

I glare in warning, but it is no use. She points a finger at my face and yells, "This is all your fault."

Calmly, I take a step forward and face her, my nose only an inch from hers. She's as tall as me. "Shut your mouth or I'll shut it for you."

Her violet gaze holds mine longer than most would, but in the end, she looks down and does as ordered.

"Now, think," I instruct her, "is there a way you can use your magic that doesn't involve the earth collapsing on our heads?"

She offers nothing. Calierin is powerful and has good control of her magic, but other than stabbing one guard at a time the same way I did, there seems to be little else she may be able to do.

"That is what I thought," I say, then turn, face the others, and explain our situation in case they have not wrapped their heads around it. "We are outnumbered. I am sure there is a host of guards outside filing in as quickly as we can dispatch them. We cannot fight our way out of here. For everyone we cut down, another takes its place."

I scrutinize their expressions, seeking traces of hubris. Each veil-fallen present boasts the strength of ten guards, a common boast that has led many fae warriors astray since, too often, they overlook reality: they are not worth twenty, thirty, or forty guardias. The sheer numbers of the Castellan forces will always outnumber us as long as the veil remains closed. Yet, the somberness in their faces suggests that this time, they understand hubris will not help them.

"Hiding is not an option either," I continue. "Even if the humans decide not to bury us alive themselves, we do not have enough supplies to last more than a few days. So, everyone, think! We need ideas."

My eyes rove around, trying to find a spark of something in their expressions. Nothing.

Kadewyn shakes his head. "There are only two exits and both of them are blocked."

"Um," Aodhán mumbles hesitantly.

I turn to face him. He's a young fae of eighteen, born here in Castella. He was orphaned when he was twelve, and practically raised by the veilfallen.

"What?" I urge.

He cocks his head to one side, hesitant. "I think there's another exit, but . . . I don't know if I can find it. When we first came here, I got lost and found a narrow opening. Light was streaming in, and I was able to squeeze through it. It put me out by the river."

"Lead us to it then," I say.

Shaking his head, he says, "I really don't know if I can find it again."

I put a hand on his shoulder and shake him slightly. "You have to."

He nods.

"Conall," I point at him, "go to the south exit, fetch those who fight there and bring them here. Hurry!"

He runs out, moving as fast as the wind. We wait for several minutes, no one saying a word. Calierin fumes in one corner, casting angry glances in my direction.

Faster than any other veilfallen, Conall is back. He is breathless and coughing as he speaks haltingly.

"A few are behind me. Most are dead. The humans have started a fire there. Smoke is traveling quickly." Just as he finishes, a gray haze starts to form above his head.

I gesture toward Aodhán. "Lead the way."

Feet leaden, he walks out of the alcove. I follow close behind. Ahead, he pauses, head down. I allow him time to think. After a moment, he veers right toward a tunnel I know leads deeper into the catacombs.

Five others join us as we make our way out. They are coughing and red-eyed, their faces blackened by soot.

"Fucking humans!" Calierin barks. "They're trying to flush us out like rats. They're going to pay for this. Also, that fucking queen and her sister. I will put their heads upon a spike, and *no one* will stop me this time."

I cast a glance over my shoulder. "You try that, and I will gut you. They hold the key for our return to Tirnanog."

"So you say."

Kadewyn pulls on her arm and glares, his pale gaze flicking toward the males and females around us. His message is clear. He's trying to tell her to show a unified front, to respect their chosen leader. And if my goals had not changed, I would make sure to deliver the message myself, but right now, all that matters is getting out of here alive.

Aodhán, who had paused, resumes moving forward. We walk hunched over, trying to avoid the smoke floating above us. The acrid scent burns my nostrils, and a bothersome scratch is building in my throat.

We veer toward a tunnel never traveled. I snatch a torch from the wall and hand it to Aodhán. He holds it aloft and leads the way ahead. Hesitating at a junction, he starts to turn left, then shakes his head and goes right.

I feel impotent and have to control my impatience. Pushing him will not help him think clearer and retrieve his memories of this other exit.

Sharpening my focus, I take mental notes of every turn, every new passage we traverse. I am tempted to ask if we are going in the right direction but hold my tongue.

When we enter a large alcove populated by a massive tomb built from mortar and topped with a long slab of rock, Aodhán looks at me and nods. Not showing my relief, I nod back, my expression letting him know I trust him.

We take many more turns, nearly obfuscating my mental map. A moment later, our guide stops, shining the torch all around at what turns out to be a dead end. He faces me, looking at a loss.

"I knew it!" Calierin exclaims. "This was a fucking waste of time."

Aodhán lowers his head in shame.

I take the torch from his hand and do a second inspection that yields the same results. My jaw clenches. I take a deep breath and address Aodhán.

"Did we take a wrong turn somewhere?"

"I . . . I do not know."

"Think."

"This is the best of my recollection. I genuinely thought—"

"Fuck!" Calierin pulls her tunic over her nose. "It caught up with us."

We'd left the smoke behind for a moment, but it has found us once more. In a matter of seconds, it floats thick under our noses. Saoirse begins coughing and so do some of the others.

"I'm going back," Calierin declares. "If I'm going to die in this hole, I will take with me as many human dregs as I can."

Kadewyn frowns and snatches the torch from my hand. "The smoke," he says, holding the flame toward the dead-end wall. "Look!"

I get closer and squint. The gray haze is slowly funneling out through a small hole in the wall. Kadewyn tosses me the torch, drops to his hands and knees, and starts digging with bare hands.

After a frantic moment of digging, he stops and shakes as a violent coughing fit assaults him. "There is definitely a way out," he manages.

I turn to Calierin, who stands frozen between leaving and staying. "You're welcome to head back and kill as many human dregs as you wish," I say. "Or maybe you would rather use your magic to widen this hole and get us out of here."

Her throat bobs, and I'm quite sure that is her swallowing her pride. Clearing her throat and blinking smoke from her eyes, she comes closer and holds her hands up toward the wall.

"Small blasts," Kadewyn suggests. "You would not want to overdo it and finish the job the humans started."

She sneers but holds her tongue—not an easy feat for her.

As she works, releasing small bursts of magic, we wait, breathing through our tunics and coughing due to the smoke and the dirt that crumbles from above with each thrust of Calierin's hands.

My head swims from the smoke, and my breaths come in short bursts.

After an interminable moment, Kadewyn pushes in front of Calierin. "That's enough." He starts digging again, scooping large handfuls of black dirt and pushing them backward under his legs. "Got it!"

He jumps to his feet, grabs Calierin's elbow and shoves her down into the hole. She grunts in protest but crawls on hands and knees, worming her way out of our would-be tomb.

Kadewyn and I usher out the other veilfallen, one after the other. When we're the only ones left, I get behind him and push him along, even as he attempts to do the same to me. I am their leader for one last day, and as such, I will abandon this sinking ship last.

I crawl out, lungs burning, eyes feeling as if someone poured acid in them. The others have found their way to the river's edge where they splash fresh water on their faces and drink to relieve their aching throats.

Kadewyn lumbers toward them and waves me along. I hold up a hand as I hunch over, hands on knees, and try to catch my breath. Only around thirty veilfallen line the bank. Are the rest dead? Since I joined a year ago, our numbers never surged above fifty. We're slowly dying in this realm, losing our magic, becoming *less*.

Calierin is not wrong. I'm to blame for this attack, and the guilt that cuts through me is deserved. But even if I have lied to them, I have not betrayed them. Everything I have done, and everything I will do from this point on, is to serve the only purpose they care about.

Returning home.

I stretch to my full height, inhaling lungfuls of clean air. Slowly,

I take several steps back and retreat under the cover of trees. Perhaps I owe them an explanation, but I do not have the stomach for it—not when Calierin's rage will take center stage.

It's better this way. They may hate me for a time, but when I reopen the veil, and reenter Tirnanog, I will be the last thing on their minds.

As quiet as a phantom, I walk away, my heading already set in stone.

10
VALERIA

"Simón would never forgive me if something happens to his daughters."

Armando Quiñones – Royal Guard Capitán – 21 AV

Heavy banging on the door jolts me out of bed. Before I know what's happening, I'm on my feet, crouching and ready to pounce. My heart beats as fast as a frightened mouse. Amira is gone, and the fire at the hearth is reduced to embers.

"Princess Valeria," a man's voice calls outside the door. "Princess Valeria, open the door, it's urgent."

"A moment, please."

I glance all around until I spot one of my robes draped over an armchair. Quickly, I slip it on under the faint glow of the fireplace.

"Princess, please hurry," the man calls again.

"I'm coming."

Hands shaking, I search the night table until I find a small dagger in one of the drawers. It isn't the raven dagger Father gave me—someone took it from my luggage when we traveled to Alsur.

However, this one fits perfectly in my hand, which is precisely why I hold on to it.

My heart hammers as I approach the locked door. "What do you want?" I demand.

"It's your sister . . . she needs you," he replies.

"Who are you?"

"Guardia Enrique Palacios. I was with you during your trip to Alsur, at the inn in Las Torres."

I open the door a crack, bracing my foot against it. I recognize the young guardia's face. He's wide-eyed and pale, and so are the three other royal guards who stand behind him.

As I step out of the room, they move back in unison. The young guard notices the dagger in my hand with a quick flick of his gaze, then looks up again.

"You'd best come with us, Princess Valeria." He extends a hand indicating the hall, and it feels more like an order than an invitation.

"What is the matter?" I ask.

"I will explain on the way."

I can't help but be wary. Orys played Emerito's part flawlessly for weeks. Bastien posed as a royal guard for the same length of time. And I walked alongside them without barely a shred of suspicion. I must be careful, even if it feels stupid and unnecessary. I must be brave, too.

Tightening my hold on the dagger, I let my wariness morph into anger. I can't let those two bastardos turn me into a coward, afraid to inhabit my own home. Taking a deep breath, I lift my chin and make my way down the hall. The young guard walks to my right, and the other three behind us.

"What is your name again?" I ask him, examining his black uniform closely.

He wears snug-fitting black trousers tucked into knee-high black boots, along with a black velvet doublet secured tightly by leather straps. A House of the Raven coat of arms—a raven with its wings outstretched over an intricate emblem—is sewn on his left breast. A standard-issue rapier dangles from his waist, completing the ensemble with precision. Nothing seems out of place.

"Guardia Enrique Palacios, Your Royal Highness."

"Tell me, Guardia Enrique, where are we going?"

"The queen's bedchamber."

"Why?" My mouth goes bitter. I know this won't be good.

"There is an intruder in the palace, and he has barricaded himself in the queen's bedchamber, demanding to talk to you."

I stop mid-step and catch my breath.

Guardia Enrique's words are halting and embarrassed because . . . how could the royal guards allow such a thing to happen?!

I don't have to ask who the intruder is. I know. And I also know how he got in. This was the niggling thought that tried to surface earlier when Amira kept saying we were safe. In the back of my mind, I knew we were not, but I was distracted when she said that the veilfallen were dead.

I let my guard down, dared to believe. I should have known better. Vermin like Ríffor don't die easily. This is *my* fault. I should have tried harder to figure out what that niggling thought was, and now . . .

Hastening my step, I resume walking. Soon, I'm running with only the thought of my sister's safety in mind. When I get to her quarters, which reside in the heart of the palace, I run into a dozen guardias, all standing with their swords at the ready.

Capitán Quiñones—a man of fifty with dark chestnut hair streaked with silver at the temples—approaches me as soon as I arrive. He is the leader of the Guardia Real, a towering figure with broad shoulders and chiseled physique that speaks of years spent honing his strength and skill in combat.

"Princess Valeria, this is the situation . . ." he starts debriefing me the way he used to address Father, and I'm grateful for his direct approach, "a fae male infiltrated the palace. We don't know exactly how, but some suspect it was through a secret passage the queen recently revealed to a number of guards. I just learned of its existence a moment ago, and I'm flabbergasted no one thought to inform me of this security risk. Heads will roll, I assure you!" He punches a fist into his hand, cheeks red with anger and maybe shame. "But moving on from this disgraceful oversight, a few guards attempted to stop him. They paid with their lives." He inhales sharply, clearly affected by the loss of life. "I must admit . . . this person must be skilled, Your Highness, and he must have knowledge of the palace to easily evade our posted sentinels and find the queen's bedchamber."

"I suspect you're correct, Capitán Quiñones," I respond, slowly buttressing my spine so I can stand straighter in the face of the capitán and his guardias, who are regarding me warily, appearing unsure of whether or not I'll be capable of handling this crisis.

He nods. "We don't know the situation behind that door. As soon as he stole inside, he barricaded himself. Then the queen spoke and ordered everyone to remain outside and fetch you. She said only you will be allowed inside."

"What do you think I should do?" I ask.

"Let's start by talking," he says. "See if we can accomplish anything that way. The queen is already at risk. Putting you in the same situation is the last thing I want to do."

"All right."

The path opens before me as the guardias move aside. The first thing I notice is blood staining the carpet, the walls. Its coppery scent stings my nostrils, reminding me of the ruthless person I'm dealing with. More people lost their lives today because of him.

Hesitantly, I stand in front of the door. I raise my free hand to knock, then put it back down. Instead, I clear my throat.

Capitán Quiñones nods encouragingly.

"Amira," I call, "I'm here. Can you tell me if you're all right?"

"Val!" she exclaims from behind the door, relief coloring her tone. There's a pause, then she adds, "Yes, I'm all right."

"Who's in there with you?" I ask.

Another pause, then the sounds of furniture being dragged.

"You . . . need to come inside. Only you. No one else."

I grab the doorknob, spurred by the panic in my sister's voice.

Capitán Quiñones shakes his head adamantly. "Tell her you won't come in unless you understand the situation fully."

I do as he instructs.

We wait for an answer. My heart's rhythm intensifies with every passing second. I stare pointedly at the captain.

He mouths, "Be patient."

The hilt of my dagger is covered in sweat. I switch it to my other hand and wipe the sweat off on my robe.

At last, Amira speaks. "He has a dagger to my throat, and he says he'll . . . use it if you don't come in alone. Immediately. No more talking. He says you know he means it."

Ignoring Capitán Quiñones's advice and every instinct in my body, I turn the doorknob and go inside, hastily shutting the door behind me as the captain makes a futile protest.

The scene inside freezes the blood in my veins. Amira's desk sits in the middle of the room, while she stands on the other side, Rífíor holding none other than my raven dagger to her throat. So he was the one who took it. It angers me to see my father's dagger in Rífíor's filthy hands, but that is the least of my concerns.

My sister's eyes are wide, and I know I've never seen her more scared in her entire life. What Orys did to her was much worse than this, of course, but she was barely conscious through any of it. Right now, however, her panic and beseeching expression reveal she dearly fears for her life.

Behind her, Rífíor looks like a mad person. His black hair stands on end, his sharp features are stained by soot, and his eyes are bloodshot. His grim expression makes me more certain that he won't hesitate to take my sister from me. He's clearly beyond reasoning, beyond control.

"You know why I am here," he says in a hoarse voice. "Do not make me explain myself." He tightens his hold on Amira, making her gasp.

I hold a hand up. "Don't hurt her. I'll give you what you want."

The words are out of my mouth of their own accord. I know giving him The Eldrystone is a mistake, but at this moment, I don't care about anything but my sister's safety.

Taking a step back, I take hold of the doorknob and turn.

"No dagger next time, little princess," he says gruffly. "And if anyone but you comes in, she loses her head." He makes my sister gasp again, pulling her head back by the hair.

Facing the door, I squeeze my eyes shut and draw in a shuddering breath, wondering how this male and Bastien can possibly be the same person. Oh, I was so blind.

"As you wish, Rífíor," I say before leaving the bedchamber.

When I exit, Capitán Quiñones's shoulders lower a couple of inches, betraying his relief. "That was very . . . was not . . . I'm glad you're all right, princess. The queen?"

"She's fine," I say. "And everything is going to be all right."

I march down the hall, headed back to my room.

"Where are you going?" the captain asks in confusion.

Glancing back over my shoulder, I say, "I have something he wants. Once I give it to him, he'll let the queen go. I will go and fetch it. In the meantime, you and your guardias must stand by and await my return."

He opens his mouth to say more.

I shake my head. "Have no worries, Capitán. I have this under control."

As I walk away, my steps measured and firm, I hope I've given the impression of someone who knows what she's doing. It's the only way to ensure they don't do anything stupid that endangers Amira.

With each step I take back toward my bedchamber, my resolve begins to falter. A barrage of thoughts and possible scenarios assault me, driving home the absurdity of this entire situation.

If I surrender The Eldrystone to Rífíor, the instant it's in his grasp, he could annihilate us all—not just Amira, but every single inhabitant in Nido, including Jago and Nana. That is all well and good, however, he's using nothing but a dagger to ask me to retrieve a weapon much mightier than any in his possession, a weapon I can use to obliterate him the way I obliterated Orys.

It's ludicrous, except . . . he must know something I don't because he never seemed afraid of The Eldrystone at the engagement ball. He just stood there, his face frozen with cold determination, demanding that I give him the amulet or else his lackey would drop my sister to her death. And now . . . he behaves as though a mere dagger will protect him from the power of Niamhara's conduit. Why?

Doubt fills me, and my fear gorges on it.

Rífior knows more about The Eldrystone than me. I don't know how much more or why, but it's evident he has the upper hand or else he wouldn't be here risking it all.

Once in my bedchamber, I push all of these thoughts aside and run to the balcony.

"*Tch, tch, tch.*" My tongue clicks against the roof of my mouth as I peer into the night, begging Cuervo is nearby and can hear my call. Several minutes pass without the flap of wings to announce his approach.

I call a few more times, but he doesn't come. Just as I'm about to scream his name in desperation, he swoops in from the side and lands on the marble railing. I nearly grab him and crush him to my chest in a hug, which would only make him squirm uncomfortably. Instead, I pet the side of his neck with care.

"My dear friend," I say. "I need your help once more."

His head bobs up and down, and he makes a crooning sound.

"I need you to get me the amulet."

"Treasure," he croaks.

"Yes, treasure."

He lowers his head once, then lunges himself into the sky, strong wingbeats pushing him onward.

"Be fast, Cuervo. Be fast."

I pace the length of the balcony back and forth as I wait for him, murmuring a prayer.

"Please, don't let anything happen to my sister. Please." Of all the gods and saints humans and fae worship in Castella, I realize it's Niamhara who I need to listen to me. "Goddess of Radiance, I don't know why your conduit is here in my realm, why you allowed it to pass to my mother and then to me, but don't let it be the reason I lose my sister. I beg of you."

Cuervo plunges down from the heavens like an apparition, landing on the floor at my feet instead of the railing, and skidding as he flaps his wings. His sudden appearance startles me, and I can tell by the way his small body shivers that he pushed himself hard to get to The Eldrystone's hiding place and back again.

I kneel and cluck a few times in praise. "You're so fast and strong," I tell him. "Thank you. Thank you so much."

He stretches his clenched talon and releases the amulet. Leaving the dagger behind, I snatch it up and run out, my fear swollen, satiated after feasting on my doubts, while one question burns in my mind: Can I use The Eldrystone to break Rífíor the way I broke Orys?

When I get to Amira's chamber, I stop in front of Capitán

Quiñones, breathless and clutching the amulet in my hand. His gaze focuses on the chain dangling through my fingers.

He frowns. "Is that—?"

"Yes. This is what he wants." I cut him off and only pause long enough to regain my breath.

Concentrating on calming my racing heart, I approach the door. Instead of slowing down, however, its beat runs faster. Yet, as I knock and announce my presence, my hand is steady, for which I'm grateful.

Amira bids me to enter. I step quickly into the bedchamber and shut the door behind me. Ríffor and Amira are standing in the same spot as before, my raven dagger still pressed to her throat.

A hungry glint in his eyes, he focuses pointedly on my hand. His hand, unlike mine, shakes visibly. Afraid of the blade, my sister flinches and pushes to her tiptoes.

"Careful," I say, lifting the amulet which rests on my open palm. "Step away from Amira."

He shakes his head. "Place it on the desk."

"Not until you let her go," I insist.

He doesn't bother answering. He simply tightens his grip on the dagger.

My fingers wrap around the amulet. Our gazes hold. I expect fear to bloom in his expression, but other than a hint of avarice, I find little else. Resignation perhaps? As if he's been pushed to the edge of his wits and morality and is now ready to take his chances with whatever may come.

Without making a conscious decision, I will Ríffor's body to collide with the wall. The thought is fierce, yet nothing happens.

No warmth spreads through my chest, and he remains on his feet, the dagger gripped just as tightly.

A rush of breath escapes my lips. Is it relief that The Eldrystone has once again refused to do my bidding? It did the same before, when I attempted to free my sister from Calierin's espíritu as the sorceress threatened to drop Amira to her death.

But what if there's another reason? What if the amulet craves crueler deeds?

You pathetic, weak fool, I chide myself. *You need to end him. It's what he deserves.*

I shake my head. It's not my job to condemn him. He should stand in front of a jury and answer for his crimes. He should hang while all of Castella bears witness. These thoughts are logical, fair even, but most of all . . . they're weak. I showed no mercy for Orys, and Rífíor deserves even less. Yet something prevents me from exerting my full will.

I still see traces of Bastien in him, still feel ensnared in the depths of his black eyes and magnetized by his presence whenever he's near. I can't deny it.

Anger and self-loathing flood over me.

Puta madre, Valeria! Kill him! Kill him!

Clenching my teeth, I redirect the bulk of my emotions toward Rífíor. It is not I who has erred. It is not I who should hate myself.

The darkest side of me awakens, embarrassed at my weak attempt to incapacitate him rather than obliterate him. He doesn't deserve such consideration. He deserves the worst I can unleash.

I let the rancor boil and reach new levels. I think of the way he seduced me. I think of how he ordered his lackey to dangle my sister like a puppet in order to blackmail me, and how he subjected me to torture hoping to break me.

The Eldrystone grows warm in my palm, its power slowly traveling up my arm until it reaches my chest. A smile stretches across my lips, and I flick my hand downward, imagining Ríffor collapsing to his knees, every single one of his bones shattering into countless pieces.

II
RÍFÍOR

"I was wrong. We're not safe."

Reina Amira Plumanegra (Casa Plumanegra) – Queen of Castella – 21 AV

Desperation brought me here, and now it is too late to turn back. For twenty long years, I have searched for The Eldrystone, losing hope so many times, thinking I would never hold the amulet in my hands again, and I would forever be trapped in Castella.

Then I saw Simón Plumanegra's portrait hanging in a cheap tavern. He wore a crown and velvet cape. Never could I have imagined that the man who helped Loreleia Elhice slip through my fingers was the King of Castella himself.

My hope was reborn.

I told myself that even though it would not be easy to get to the monarch, it was only a matter of time until I found a way. It took me an entire year, but I did it. My patience and efforts paid off, and then there it was, right in front of me, between Valeria's fingers—the only thing that can reopen the veil and take me to the place where I can remake my life after Saethara destroyed it.

Except Valeria . . . she got right in my way.

And now, here we stand, reenacting the same tableau in just a handful of days. Me, demanding she give me The Eldrystone. Her, eyes gleaming with the desire for power and the hunger for destruction, while I am left at her mercy, which by degrees dies a slow death as I watch her across the desk.

Surprisingly, for a moment, doubt shapes her features. I should be dead already, broken by her simple will, the same way Orys was, but she's holding back. I see the conflict play in her expression as easily as if she had spoken it out loud. She is a far better person than me.

We stand here, both aware of the futility of my threat against her sister—for what is a man-made weapon against the power of a goddess? Yet, this is my only option. If I'm to recover The Eldrystone, I must place myself at Niamhara's mercy. I must face her judgment and hope she can forgive my blunders for the sake of my kin.

I am willing to face death for them. The road has been long, and I am tired.

Squaring my shoulders, I gaze at Valeria, waiting for her inner conflict to resolve itself. In the end, she is not as good as she would have me believe, and as I expected, greed wins. She wants the power of The Eldrystone for herself. And perhaps she also wants revenge for that night of weakness I shared with her.

Mayhap, I deserve this end.

I did not deserve Saethara's betrayal, but my subsequent actions, following the devastation she wrought upon me, have undeniably led me here.

With no time to even blink, I watch a smile stretch Valeria's lips as she slashes her hand downward.

I wait for the blow, for magic to reduce me to dust . . .

. . .

. . .

It never comes.

Valeria blinks, then flicks her hand again, more forcefully this time. Nothing happens. She attempts a third time. Still nothing.

My hopelessness turns to relief in the span of a breath. The Eldrystone is not responding to her commands. Niamhara is merciful.

Having witnessed Valeria's complete annihilation of Orys, I dared dream the goddess would spare me, but now I realize I never honestly believed it.

Channeling anger and determination through the stone is easy. Only the finer tasks require care and control. I remember well how difficult it was to master subtlety, to weave intricate spells. And since Valeria excelled at the former, it seems I resigned myself to die, and coming here was little more than an act of self-destruction. Deep down, I thought I deserved death, but Niamhara disagrees.

Even after all this time, the amulet is still mine.

I let the dagger cut into the human queen's neck. I feel when the pressure gives and her skin breaks, then the scent of blood enters my nostrils, I do not have to see the wound to know she is bleeding.

"Put. The. Amulet. On. The. Desk," I say, my words bitter shards of ice.

Valeria was willing to kill me and showed no mercy. I shall do the same.

Her lower lip trembles. I deny the relief that seems to flash across her features. It is *not* there. She wants me dead. She can feel no relief at the sight of me still standing, still threatening to end her sister's life.

Taking a step forward, she lowers her trembling hand to the desk and reluctantly places the amulet there.

"Walk back and press your back to the door. Do not make any sudden movements."

She follows my instructions perfectly, keeping her hands in sight.

I force Amira forward, until the top of her legs hit the desk. Once there, I shove her aside and send her stumbling to the floor. With my now-free hand, I snatch The Eldrystone from the desk, my chest nearly bursting with elation.

Finally. Finally. FINALLY.

I doubted so many times, thought this moment would never come. I felt lost without it, felt like a failure, and after all this time, I finally hold it in my hand.

Almost dizzy, I take several steps back, blinking, staring at the amulet, its pale opal appearing so inconsequential, belying the absolute power it channels.

I hear her voice as if through a tunnel. "Go ahead, Rífíor, destroy us."

Drunk from the mixture of emotions assailing me, I glance up at Valeria. She has moved from the door and now stands next to her sister. They hold each other in solidarity, their twin brown gazes full of recrimination and rancor.

Valeria opens her mouth to speak once more, but Amira, the human queen, pulls her back and steps forward, taking control of the situation.

"You . . . have what you came for." Her voice is weak at first, but it gains in strength with each word. "Perhaps you should leave now." She raises a hand toward the door. "I will order them to let you go."

Thoughts and emotions crash against me.

Incredulity, relief, righteousness, fury, and more. Thoughts for Tirnanog, the veilfallen, my family, all the years lost . . . the toxic mixture makes my ears ring and my heart ache and . . .

"You treated us like vermin," I roar, remembering the humiliation, the hunger, the pain.

"Queen Amira, we're coming in," someone shouts from behind the closed door.

I hold the amulet high, a threat of destruction.

"No!" she cries at the door. "Remain outside." Fear trembles in her voice and in her eyes. Turning in my direction and putting both hands up, she speaks calmly. "We can talk about this."

"You sent your men to murder us," I say, spittle flying from my mouth, my grip around The Eldrystone tightening. "Nearly half of the veilfallen are dead. My people have suffered for two decades."

"Your people murdered my mother and my father," she shouts, losing her temper. "You took my sister. I wasn't going to let you kill her, too."

My anger crashes against hers, but fury is all she has, while I hold real power in my hand.

All the pain I have felt since the last day I saw Tirnanog breaks through, and guided by hatred alone, I wish for the destruction of this godsforsaken realm.

As that familiar warmth spreads from my hand to the center of my very being, my gaze locks with Valeria's. Her mouth opens in a silent *no*, but it's too late.

Castella is doomed.

12
VALERIA

"I would take it from her, but it's the only thing she has of her mother. No one will suspect what it really is if they think it's a child's toy."

Rey Simón Plumanegra (Casa Plumanegra) – King of Castella – 9 AV

A surge of panic shoots from the top of my spine and thunders its way down my body. I know something awful is about to happen, and there is nothing I can do to stop it. I reach for my sister's hand and interlace my fingers with her as my gaze locks with Rífíor's.

No, I mouth, uselessly begging him to spare my sister, to spare us all. I know I have no right—not when I wished for his own annihilation just moments ago.

What awful hatred festers between us.

Time slows, and a host of emotions play on Rífíor's face. In the end, a glimmer of regret ignites in his eyes for a split second, then all the emotions are gone, and he falls to his knees, throwing his head back and laughing, laughing, laughing as if he has lost his mind.

Seconds tick by like hours, while Amira and I remain frozen, finding strength in each other. We watch Rífíor in utter confusion and terror. At last, moving as if through thick honey, we turn to exchange a glance.

Rífíor's laugh slowly dies, and the raven dagger and the amulet slip from his fingers and clank to the floor.

Moving with the same agility she displays in the sparring courtyard, Amira swoops down and snatches The Eldrystone from the floor. Pivoting on one knee and bouncing back to her feet, she lands several feet away from Rífíor, who now sits on his haunches, staring blankly at the floor, looking numb.

I'm still trying to process what just happened when Amira yelps, dropping the amulet. She waves her hand about, then holds her wrist, clenching her teeth and hissing in pain. I peer closer to find the imprint of the amulet seared into her skin, raw blisters tracing the shape.

Without thinking, I pick up The Eldrystone.

Amira's eyes widen. "No, drop it. It burns!"

However, it feels cool to the touch, and as my fingers wrap around it, relief floods my chest. For a moment, I worried about what Amira might do with it, but it appears the amulet rejects her.

"Guardias!" she shouts.

In an instant, the door bursts open, and what looks like the entire Guardia Real pours in.

"Throw him in the dungeons," she orders. "I want him guarded every second of the day. Bread and water rations only."

My heart speeds up and sizzling energy ignites my veins, expecting a brawl. Except Rífíor offers no resistance and lets two guards hoist him to his feet. He is limp, absent, as if his spirit has abandoned his body. His feet drag as they push him along, removing him from the bedchamber.

After a moment, only Capitán Quiñones remains. His gaze roves around the space, inspecting every corner. At last, he inspects us, too.

"My Queen, Princess Valeria . . . are you all right?" he asks.

"We're fine," Amira responds in a tone void of any emotion.

The captain's brow furrows, and it's clear he doesn't believe her. "Should I call . . . your physician? Or . . . someone else?"

Amira should have her hand examined and bandaged, but I suspect that isn't the reason the captain thinks the royal physician should be summoned. I'm sure he's more worried about our female sensibilities. I can almost hear him suggesting we drink a nerve-calming tonic.

"No, Capitán Quiñones," Amira says. "I will ring for the chambermaid if we require anything at all."

He inclines his head and clicks his heels. "As you wish, Your Highness. New guards will be posted at your door as well as outside the secret passage through which the intruder infiltrated the palace."

"Thank you. We'll talk later about permanently sealing that passage as well as the guardias' performance."

Capitán Quiñones gives a wince at the latter, but he composes his expression before straightening and retiring from the bedchamber with a few backward steps.

To be fair, the guards weren't dealing with just any intruder. Rífíor is acquainted with Nido. He had weeks to memorize its layout and familiarize himself with every aspect, including guard shifts and placements. Any complaint Amira has about the palace's security may be somewhat misplaced.

Suddenly, my legs go rubbery. I stumble to a nearby armchair and collapse in it. Amira lets out a barely audible whimper of pain and scrunches her face.

"Perhaps you *should* call the physician," I say, gesturing toward her hand.

"I will, just not right this moment." She shakes her head and sits across from me. "I need to sort out what just happened." She's quiet for a moment then asks, "How did that male learn about the passage?"

There's a slight edge of accusation in her voice, as if she suspects I divulged the secret. But it wasn't me. She pointedly holds my gaze, demanding an answer.

"*You* told him," I say at last.

One of her eyebrows goes up. "I did not."

"Well, yes, I mean . . . Orys told him. Before you sent me to Alsur, I tried escaping Nido that way, but you sent *Bastien* after me."

"I see."

I look down at The Eldrystone, relieved by its . . . uselessness, but also confused. It didn't respond to me or to Rífior, apparently. And then it outright rejected Amira. It's as if—

"That thing has a mind of its own," Amira says, reading my thoughts. "Put it away. I don't like it. It's dangerous."

I turn my hand over, concealing the amulet, feeling oddly protective of it.

"Letting you have it was irresponsible of Father," she goes on. "Now it falls to me to take care of it."

"Take care of it?" I repeat.

"Yes, destroy it."

I shake my head adamantly. "I don't think that's a good idea."

"And what would you suggest? You want to keep treating it like a toy the way you have all these years?" There's an edge to her voice that makes me take a closer look. At times, she seems so different from the sister I know, so severe and angry.

But I can't blame her, not after what she's been through, not when I feel much the same way.

"There's power in it, Amira," I say, my voice quiet. "I've felt it. I killed Orys with only a thought."

"Then why didn't you kill *him*?" She points at the spot where Rífíor knelt before they took him away.

"I tried."

"Did you really?" Once more there's an accusatory ring to her voice.

"Yes," I say emphatically. "It didn't work, but it didn't work for him either. He tried to use it. You saw it, but it didn't respond to his command."

"Like I said . . . dangerous. And if those damn fae want it so badly, it will serve them well if we destroy it."

"Something tells me that's easier said than done."

She narrows her eyes. "You don't want to, do you?"

"It has nothing to do with what I want. He said it can reopen the veil."

"Rífíor, you mean?"

I nod.

She shrugs. "More reason to get rid of it."

"What . . . what do you mean?"

"You can't honestly wish to do that?"

I cock my head, confused. The possibility of the veil remaining closed when given an opportunity to open it has never entered my mind. The idea is simply wrong.

"They hate us, Val," she says. "They killed our parents."

"Our mother was fae. Are you forgetting that?"

"Not like you will ever let me."

I was always closer to Mother than Amira. As the future queen, she spent most of her time with Father, learning everything she could about governing Castella, while I happily remained at our mother's side, making jewelry, growing flowers, helping her with charitable work, sewing tapestries, and memorizing anything she ever shared about her life in Tirnanog. I imagine that is the reason Amira doesn't identify with her fae heritage as much as I do.

"There are humans trapped in Tirnanog," I argue. "They deserve to come home."

"It's been twenty years. The ones who would miss Castella are either dead or too old to matter."

I shake my head. "I can't believe you would say that."

"It's reality, Val, and even if it sounds harsh that doesn't make it any less true. Besides, it doesn't appear as if there's anyone who can wield that thing." Suddenly, she turns her face to one side and winces. Grabbing the wrist of her injured hand, she squeezes it.

"You have to get that checked." I point at her wound.

"Yes. It hurts like the devil. I will ring for the maid. She can find a salve in the kitchen, I'm sure. You should go and try to get some rest. There will be much to do when the sun comes out."

I stand and take a few steps toward the door.

"Leave the amulet," she says.

My head jerks in her direction. "What?"

"Leave it." She points at the opal in my hand, then at the desk.

"It's mine," I tell her, even though I sense it's the wrong thing to say.

"It's a security risk, Val. I will make sure it is stored safely until the time we decide what to do with it."

"I've kept it safe for over a decade," I say. "I can manage."

She stands and stretches to her full height, watching me warily.

"Why are you looking at me like that?" I demand. "You don't think I would try to . . . use it against you, do you?"

She doesn't answer, doesn't immediately say, *Of course not, Val, you're my sister. I know you would never do that.*

Instead, she says, "If you won't, you will have no trouble leaving it with me."

I shake my head, a host of bitter emotions filling my chest. "You honestly think I would do such a thing?"

Again, she doesn't answer, but she holds my gaze unflinchingly as I scrutinize her face in challenge.

My first instinct is to tell her I will be the one keeping The Eldrystone safe, but something about her expression makes me pause. Behind her boldness, I see the fear she's trying to hide. Orys took over her mind and used her like one would a soulless marionette. For weeks, she did things she wasn't aware of, and since she regained control, it has been her sole responsibility to repair the fallout.

I have no idea what she has been dealing with since I was abducted, but I can only imagine how hard it has been, doing everything alone. Without Father, without me, without even Emerito—her adviser. The council expressed doubts about her ability to govern Castella while she was under Orys's control, and I'm sure that, after what happened at the ball, their scrutiny has intensified. She already has enough worries without me adding to them, without fearing I might try to usurp her position. It's the most ridiculous notion she could ever entertain, but everything considered, I can't blame her for it.

Besides, the Eldrystone is nothing but a mystery to me, and I wouldn't have the faintest idea how to use it to open the veil. And even if I did, reconnecting the two realms isn't my decision to make—not to mention that doing so may mean more problems than those we faced when the veil collapsed.

"You're right," I say. "It's no trouble to leave the amulet with you. In truth, it's yours as much as it is mine. If it remained with me after Mother died, it was by mere accident."

I walk to the desk and place the opal there, finding it difficult to let it go, but telling myself it's for the best.

"Keep it safe," I add, walking toward the door.

"The vault will serve well for now," she says, looking relieved and offering me a conciliatory smile.

I pause. "That reminds me," I say. "You . . . I mean . . . Orys took my Plumanegra key. I would like to have it back."

"Of course," she nods. "I will find it and return it to you."

"Thank you."

I leave and walk past the four guards Capitán Quiñones left

outside the door. Two of them follow me, and I'm comforted by their presence until I'm reminded of Guardia Bastien Mora and his lies. I always thought of Nido as the safest fortress in all of the realm, but that impression has been shattered. I wonder if I'll ever feel safe in my own home again.

Not with Rifior only a few floors below you, you won't, the most sardonic part of me quips.

13
VALERIA

"Damn Veilfallen! They took my betrothed. She was the prettiest of the two sisters, and I had hoped to make her queen. Now what?"

Don Justo Ramiro Medrano – Master Mason – 21 AV

I get three hours of sleep before my eyes spring open with the first rays of sunlight that slip through the open balcony doors. I'm curled up into a tight ball, the covers gathered around me.

Summer is slipping away, and the nights are becoming cooler—not the time of the year to let the night air waltz into the room. I didn't have the presence of mind to close the balcony before crawling into bed, or even to add another log to the fire.

The only advantage is that Cuervo was able to come into the room and is now perched on the back of an armchair. When he realizes I'm awake, he swoops down and lands on the bed next to me.

"Good morning, friend," I say.

"Treasure?" he croaks, and I swear I see concern in his beady, round eyes.

"The treasure is safe, Cuervo."

He shakes his head, appearing unsure. "Treasure," he repeats and flexes his claws, acting as if he's picking up an imaginary amulet off the bed.

"Safe. I promise." I smile and try to pet his neck, but he jerks his head to the side and hops to the floor. From there, he watches me with displeasure, then takes flight and leaves through the balcony.

I sit up and watch his dark silhouette get smaller against the blue morning sky as he goes far away from here.

"I don't like it any more than you do, Cuervo."

With a heavy sigh, I get out of bed and look around the room. Just hours ago, I was confined to a small, dank underground alcove. I was dirty and hungry and thought I would never see my home again.

Now I'm here, and I feel little to no relief. Father is gone. My sister is unrecognizable and feels leagues away from me, and I have no purpose. Before, I was determined to find Father's murderer. And at the catacombs, I was willing to die without giving Rífíor what he wanted. It gave me strength.

Today, I care about nothing.

I climb back into bed and go back to sleep.

Several days pass in this fashion. I wake up, bicker with Cuervo about the amulet, and go back to bed. Someone brings food and leaves it on the table by the fireplace. I barely touch it.

Jago pounding on the door and shouting my name wakes me up on the sixth day. I drag myself out of bed and open the door, bleary-eyed. A few steps behind him, two guards ogle me.

"What?" I demand.

My cousin's eyes widen, and he pushes his way into the room and shuts the door quickly.

"Now the guards know the lovely shade of your nipples," he says, swiftly finding my robe, tossing it my way, and turning his face to the side.

I glance down and realize my very perky, tanned nipples are visible through my silk gown. I should be embarrassed but find that I don't give a damn. I stand there, arms limp at my sides.

"Well, are you going to put the robe on?" Jago watches from the corner of his eye.

"Fine." I throw it on, tie it, then collapse into an armchair by the fireplace. There is a cup of cold tea accompanied by pastries.

Hands on hips, he peers at me down his nose. "It's past noon."

"And?"

"Um, aren't you hungry?"

"No."

"Thirsty?"

"No."

"Bored?"

"No, Jago. I just want to sleep."

He has come to visit me every day, though I turned him away half the time.

Kneeling in front of me, he takes my hand in his. "Are you . . . dispirited? I think you are."

"I'm fine." I extricate my hand and stand.

Thrown off balance, he falls back on his bottom and looks up at me, outraged.

I ignore him and walk out onto the balcony. There's a chill in the air, but the autumn sun still manages to warm my skin. Castellina stretches from the foot of the palace, an intricately woven tapestry of vibrant colors. To the east, the Realta Observatory's immense broken shards sparkle, reflecting rainbows in all directions. Hard to believe the fae were once our friends and bestowed such beautiful gifts upon us. Why do we forget so easily?

Jago joins me. "I know it's been awful for you, but maybe staying busy will help you get through this."

I say nothing, barely registering his words like buzzing, annoying bees.

"I know you, Val. You do best when you—"

"He's in the dungeons, did you hear?"

Sucking on his front teeth, he ponders for a moment, then asks, "Who exactly are we talking about?"

Ah, so even after six days, the news hasn't spread through the palace. Amira must have ordered discretion. Smart. Nido has suffered enough breaches, one more and Castellans will start to question how we could ever protect them when we can't even protect ourselves.

I face my cousin. "Rífíor."

"He was apprehended?" He sounds incredulous. "I was sure everyone died in those catacombs."

"Not him. The bastardo made it out, then came straight here. Got in through that secret passage you and I tried to use to escape."

"Saints and feathers! We should've thought about that. In all the commotion, I forgot."

"Me too."

"So what happened?"

I tell him everything, barely mustering the energy for more than a few words.

Wind whips our hair around, presaging the blustery nights to come. When I finish recounting what happened, he pivots away on one foot and grabs his head. He walks into the bedchamber, pivots again to face me, and throws his hands up in the air.

"I just . . . this is . . . The Eldrystone . . . the . . . what in the fuck is going to happen now?" he asks, his eyes roving all over as he considers his own question.

"I have no idea, and I don't care." I drag my leaden body back to the bed and climb under the covers.

"Of course you care. You can't go back to bed. C'mon, get dressed and we'll find out more." He pulls on my arm, but I bat him away.

The bed dips as he sits behind me. "Valeria, please. This isn't good for you."

I sit, and we're eye to eye. I consider doing what he says, but I simply don't have the energy for it. "Just let me be."

"Do you want to talk about it? It might help."

I collapse onto my pillow and throw the covers over my face. "Go away."

There is no way I'll voluntarily relive what I went through. I never want to think about it again, and the best way to do that is to sleep.

Jago lingers for a few minutes, but in the end, he leaves me alone, and I surrender to the oblivion of sleep.

The next time I wake up, it's to Amira's voice. She's talking loudly, urging me to get out of bed. I throw a pillow over my head to muffle the sounds, but she snatches it away.

"You don't think I want to stay in bed all day, too?" she demands. "Of course I do, but I'm a Plumanegra, and there are a million things to do around here. Get up and be of use."

"Not today," I protest, hoping that the promise of a tomorrow will drive her away. I can play this game forever.

"You're going to let one asshole male do this to you?"

I glare at her. "You think this is about Ríffor? You're wrong."

"Am I? Because I went through worse than you did, and I'm still here, making Father and Mother proud."

My mouth opens and closes as I search for an appropriate response. Calierin mentally tortured me for four days, and Orys possessed Amira's mind for much longer. But who can measure these things?

Finally, I say, "I'm not you, Amira."

"That's correct. You're stronger. Much stronger."

This takes me aback. She's the oldest, raised to be stern and disciplined by our father. Raised to be a queen. I'm not stronger. I grew up not wanting anything to do with the duties of this place. Father died knowing this. I'm a disappointment and a failure.

"You avenged Father," she goes on. "You freed me and saved us all from that cruel sorcerer. You fought the veilfallen and never gave up."

I shake my head, the backs of my eyes burning. Amira sits on the bed, pulls me to a sitting position, and wraps me in a tight embrace. Tears spill onto my cheeks. I try to stop them, but they keep coming and coming and coming.

My sister simply holds me, rubbing circles on my back and letting me cry until my tears are spent. Slowly, the knot of tension

I've been carrying inside my chest unravels, and suddenly I can breathe again.

She holds me at arm's length and offers me a sisterly smile. "Father would be proud of you."

I shake my head. The notion seems ridiculous.

"Truly, Val. I don't know what I would do without you." She lets me go and picks at the bandage around her hand.

Returning her smile, I say, "Thank you."

"Don't thank me yet. I have an unpleasant task for you."

A ball of dread forms in my stomach. "What task?"

"Remember your betrothed?"

"Oh, no!"

She nods empathetically. "I need you to talk to him."

So he survived the engagement ball attack. *Maldición!*

I've barely spared him a thought and expected he was dead. The last time I saw him it was prone at Rífíor's feet, but it seems he survived, unfortunately. I chide myself at the thought. I should be glad—for him, not for me—that he's not dead, that Rífíor didn't manage to kill another Castellan.

"Um," I hesitate. "You don't expect me to . . ." I can't finish the horrible thought.

She shakes her head. "No, Val. I don't expect you to marry him."

"Oh, thank the gods!" My shoulders go limp with relief.

"But I do expect you to talk to him, explain *why* you won't marry him. Also, I hope you can convince him to continue helping us hold Los Moros' threat back in the south. We really need his help."

"And how am I supposed to do that?"

"I don't know, but I'm sure you'll think of something." She pats my hand and walks to the door. Glancing over her shoulder, she says, "Renata Suárez is my new adviser. She has your Plumanegra key. Find her, and she'll give it back."

I slump back into bed, dreading a conversation with Don Justo. I almost miss the catacombs. I thought I was rid of the insufferable man, but apparently, his ambition knows no bounds.

Gods, help me!

14
VALERIA

"Them fae folk can pull off miracles. Seen it with me own two eyes. Like their espiritu talks to the saints or something."

Bonifacio Gómez – Human Vagrant – 1 DV

"Traitor!" I call when I see Jago descending the steps across the mezzanine on the second floor of Nido's center building.

He stops mid-step and looks up, giving me a huge smile. "You have rejoined the living, I see."

We meet halfway.

He looks me up and down. "And you even took a bath."

I grab his arm and lead him aside as a group of guardias passes by. They carry a large, folded flag—the Plumanegra standard, from the looks of it—and march in unison, their movements as precise as clockwork.

"I know you told on me. Now, thanks to you, I have to talk to Don Justo," I hiss.

He presses a hand to his heart. "My condolences."

"I thought he was dead, or at least back in Alsur."

"Dead? Why would he be dead?"

"It doesn't matter." I wave a hand in front of his face. "Since this is your fault, you have to help me."

"I don't think I—"

"Shut up and let's go visit Nana. I want to see her."

On our way to her quarters, I explain that Amira wants me to keep Don Justo as our ally, sans royal wedding.

"You might as well ask an elm tree for pears, or a turnip for blood," he says.

"Stop saying such motivating things and start thinking of how we can convince him."

We don't find Nana in her bedchamber, which is unusual. The only other place where she normally goes is a small dining hall next to the main kitchen. There is a large fireplace there that helps keep her bones warm and allows her to visit with the cook, her friend of many years. We find her there, sipping creamy soup from a small bowl. The savory scent hits my nose and awakens my appetite.

"Nana!" I rush to her and hug her from the side.

"Oh, mi niña!" she exclaims, her voice nearly breaking with emotion. "I was worried sick about you."

"You had no reason to worry, Nana," Jago says. "I told you I would get her back, and I did."

As Nana squeezes me and kisses my forehead, I look up at Jago, a well of gratitude filling my chest. I don't even remember if I thanked him. I wouldn't be here if it wasn't for him. Of course, there are also Esmeralda and Gaspar to consider. I must thank them as well.

Nana composes herself. Her gray hair is up in a neat chignon, and she wears a high-collar dress trimmed with lace, simple but stately.

"Sit, child. Sit." She gestures toward the chair to her right. "And you," she points at Jago and to her left, "sit here."

This dining hall accommodates no more than twelve people, and it's mainly reserved for impromptu, informal meals. Still paintings of vases and flowers in shades of blue decorate the wall. The upholstery and the carpet are also blue, which might be another reason Nana likes this dining hall. That's her favorite color.

We do as she says as she rings a small bell. A servant appears right away, and Nana instructs him to prepare a feast for three, including Tarta de Santiago, my favorite dessert.

When the food comes, I can't eat much—my stomach wants me to go slowly—but I try a bit of everything, especially the tart.

"Your mother's necklace is truly The Eldrystone then," Nana asks, after sipping from her teacup.

I nod. "It is."

"What an amazing wonder," she says.

It turns out Nana always harbored suspicion about Mother's necklace, noticing the way Mother would sometimes gaze at it with a certain reverence. Then when Maestro Elizondo mentioned my curiosity about the jewel *and* The Eldrystone, she immediately sensed that my intuition was on the mark. Now, I can't help but wonder if there was more to her suspicions.

"Nana," I say, "what exactly made you so sure Mother's necklace was important?"

She sets down her tea and thinks for a moment. "I honestly

don't know. I suppose I always had many questions about your mother."

I lean in closer, eager to hear what she has to say. An aura of mystery surrounded Mother at all times, and I used to think it was because her fae heritage had to be kept secret from everyone, but now I know the aura extends far beyond that.

"She came to Nido with your father," she continues, "after one of his habitual journeys to Leonesa, on the very eve of the veil's collapse."

I was aware of this, of course, but the knowledge never carried the significance it carries now. The fae blame humans for the collapse of the veil, which I always thought was wrong.

"The only reason we are here, the only person who can be blamed for all of this, is your so-called Queen of Castella. She is the reason the veil collapsed."

Mother was fae, so the blame may be misplaced unless Father was involved somehow.

But is it possible Rífíor's telling the truth? Is it possible Mother took the amulet from him and somehow used it to cut off access between the realms? And if so, why?

There has to be a reasonable explanation, something that led Mother to such a decision.

Regardless, it all starts with Rífíor. He stole the amulet in the first place. It doesn't belong to him either, and I bet he bears the full responsibility for what happened between him and Mother and is only trying to shift the blame.

Jago frowns, pondering. "What are you saying, Nana?"

"Well, it's not a tremendous leap of logic to think that if Queen

Loreleia was in possession of The Eldrystone, and her arrival in Castella coincided with the collapse of the veil, that she had something to do with it, is it?" Nana says, voicing the very words I'm trying to deny.

Jago exchanges a glance with me, looking shocked. He blinks and glances back at Nana. "But why close the veil?"

"That is anyone's guess." Nana dabs her lips with a lace-trimmed napkin.

"What do you think would happen," I begin quietly, tentatively, "if the veil were to reopen?"

Both Nana and Jago contemplate my question, brows furrowed, but neither one of them offers an answer.

"Would it be good or bad?" I press.

"That is a difficult thing to predict," Nana says, her voice tired.

"I think it would be bad," Jago says at last. "The fae who are trapped here hate us. If they go back, they might return here with an army to retaliate for twenty years of less-than-stellar treatment. Imagine an army of agile fae who in addition are loaded with espiritu invading Castella."

"The fae were always peaceful," Nana says, "but I wonder how their realm is faring without the conduit Niamhara created to help curb their *magical* prowess."

I frown at Nana, surprised by her comment. It seems she has put a lot of thought into this. She gave emphasis to *magical* because we have never called those innate abilities *magic*. When fae first came to Castella two thousand years ago, our ancestors viewed that type of power as a manifestation of the inner spirit, a unique energy that must come from the saints. In a way, they were right.

Espiritu comes from a higher entity: Niamhara. They say she created fae in her image, which therefore granted them her abilities to control the elements. Who knows? Maybe magic does come from our spirit.

"Marco and I have talked about this at length," she adds as she notices my confusion.

That explains it. Maestro Elizondo loves nothing more than to expound and analyze every topic from every angle.

"But don't those people trapped on either side deserve a chance to return to their homes?" I argue.

Nana nods slowly. "Certainly, but what if in the process, it brings suffering to a greater number of people? What if it brings war as Jago suggests."

Jago shakes his head. "I'd say we leave that wasps' nest alone. I like things the way they are."

I can see the logic in their words, but I can't help but feel it is wrong to condemn so many to a life of exile.

Nana reaches across the table and puts her hand over mine. "Don't fret, mi niña, I'm sure Amira will devise a way to make things better for everyone."

As I nod, a small smile stretches my lips. Yes, Nana is right. Amira will figure something out.

15
VALERIA

"Craft a similar key for my youngest daughter, except smaller. She should match her sister yet know her place."

Rey Simón Plumanegra (Casa Plumanegra) – King of Castella – 2 AV

After sitting with Nana and Jago, I meander through the palace, thinking about our conversation. More than once, I have to pause and shake myself as flashes of the different dreamscapes Calierin put me through flood my vision. It takes much effort to push them away. I must conjure images of happier times, when my family was whole.

It works, and I hope with time those awful few days will be erased.

However, there is another thought that keeps intruding and proves harder to dismiss: Rífíor is here, in the dungeons.

I tell myself I'm unable to stop thinking about him because he's the only one who has the answer to all my questions, but I fear, deep inside, that there's more to it, and I hate myself a little more for it.

Determined to keep my mind clear of him, I go in search of Renata, Amira's new adviser. In my opinion, she's a major improvement over Emerito—Renata used to serve as Father's scribe, and she was always nice to everyone. I would never tell Amira that, though. She had a soft spot for the little man, and I should not disrespect the dead.

I head to Amira's study and find guards posted at the door, a new development since Nido's core rooms were always considered safe due to its concentric design, which traditionally only required protection in its outer ring.

When I enter, I still expect to see Father sitting behind his desk. The sight of Amira is incongruous in his place, and I suspect it will take a long time to get used to it.

My sister looks up from a document she's reading. When she notices me, she sets it down, signs it with a flourish, and offers me a smile. Standing behind her, Renata takes the document and sets it on top of a large pile of parchments.

"Val, I'm glad you're here." *And not in bed*, her expression seems to add.

"I came for my Plumanegra key," I say.

"Oh, yes, Renata will get it for you. I have a meeting with the council, and I'm already late." She glances at the large clock in the corner and stands. She comes around the large desk in a hurry and pats my shoulder on the way out.

Renata offers me a sincere smile. "I'm so glad you're home safe, Princess Valeria."

"Thank you, Renata."

She has beautiful brown skin as flawless as polished wood. Her eyes are the color of honey and her hair a mass of curls that frames her face and defies gravity.

"Let me get your key," she says, though she remains by the desk, making sure all the documents are perfectly aligned and the quill is returned to its proper place. Once done tidying up, she walks to a tall cabinet with many drawers, a relic that has sat in this room for who knows how long.

I approach Renata, distracted by a portrait of Mother and Father on the opposite wall. It depicts their wedding day, portraying the immense joy of a couple destined to be united by fate.

"That is one of the loveliest portraits in all of Nido," Renata says, pulling me back into the moment. She's holding my Plumanegra key in one hand, the drawer from where she got it still open.

"I agree." I extend my hand, and she offers me the necklace with the feather-shaped key hanging from it.

The key opens my nook in the family vault, which holds nothing at all. It's not the contents of the strongbox that matter, though. It is the necklace itself. Father gave it to me.

"Thank you," I say, inspecting it.

"Adviser Suarez," someone calls from the door.

Renata turns to the door, back straighter than any royal guard. "Yes?"

"The queen asked me to deliver a message. She says she needs the summer ledgers right away."

"Certainly!" She rushes to one of the bookshelves, retrieves a hefty volume, and hurries out. At the threshold, she stops and glances back over her shoulder. "My apologies, Princess Valeria."

I wave a hand. "Not to worry. I'll show myself out."

Renata is out the door with the messenger quick at her heels. I don't envy either of them. Amira can be as demanding as Father. I smile fondly and begin to turn toward the door, but the contents of the still-open drawer make me pause. Frowning, I pull the drawer out a few more inches to reveal a row of Plumanegra keys held in velvet-lined boxes.

With a painful pang in my chest, I notice Father's key. I recognize it immediately. It's bigger than mine, the shank and bow carved into the shape of a raven's claw. Tears blur my vision as I examine the other keys and read the names scrolled in their respective boxes. Julián Plumanegra, Jago's father. Vicente Plumanegra, my grandfather. Margarita Plumanegra, my great-aunt. The names keep going. Some boxes bear multiple names, indicating that more than one person held the key at various times. It's a customary practice. When someone passes away, and the key is no longer needed, a new Plumanegra infant can inherit it.

On closer examination, I notice there are two more layers of boxes underneath the first one. In fact, there are more drawers, and I suspect they hold more keys. How didn't I know about the contents of this cabinet? I guess I always took it for granted, another ancient piece of furniture among many.

I return my attention to the open drawer. The only empty box is the one with my name. Next to it, I notice Amira's name and her key sitting there. It looks a lot like mine. The shank and bow are shaped like a feather, except hers is slightly bigger than mine. She doesn't wear hers all the time like I do. She claims it's clunky, and it doesn't match all her dresses.

Amira said she would put The Eldrystone in the vault, the rogue thought resonates inside my head as loud as thunder.

Slowly, I lift a hand to touch the key and instead end up slamming the drawer shut and turning away.

"You have *your* key," I murmur under my breath. "That's why you came here. Now, leave."

The document Amira was signing when I walked in sits on top of all the others. Without meaning to, my eyes rove over the parchment, moving quickly over words that seem to jump off the page.

Proposal, safety, internment, fae, walls, guards.

What?! I read again, more carefully this time and can't believe my eyes, can't believe that is Amira's signature at the bottom of the page, except I saw her penning it there myself.

It can't be. She can't possibly intend to build a holding compound to detain all the fae, a place where they'll be confined behind guarded walls in order to keep them apart from Castella's citizens.

I shake my head. *She can't. This is . . . horrible . . . a crime against innocent people.*

Without making a conscious decision, I turn back to the cabinet, open the drawer, take Amira's key out, and replace it with mine. Quickly, I hang the new key over my neck, close the drawer, and march out of the room.

What are you doing, Val? What are you doing?!

I hasten down the hall, the weight of my sister's key feeling utterly wrong around my neck. Yet, I understand why my instincts drove me to take it. If Amira truly intends to imprison the entire fae population living in Castella, I may need The Eldrystone, after all. I don't know exactly what I would do with it. All I know is that it would give me leverage.

Before I lose my courage, I head down to the first floor and make my way to the vault. My heart hammers out of control as I walk past the two guards that flank the wide entrance. They click their heels and bow their heads, saluting me. I barely acknowledge them, too nervous to even wave.

Inside the circular vault, an eerie quiet envelops me. Two columns hold matching fire bowls, kept lit at all times. In the center of the floor, the Plumanegra coat of arms is fashioned out of pieces of broken ceramic that reflect the firelight. The place is fortified by layers and layers of stone, the heavy steel portcullis kept open during the day and lowered at night. Only members of the Plumanegra family are allowed inside—some more easily than others. It all depends on whether or not the guards on duty recognize them.

I remove the key from around my neck and turn in a circle, trying to remember which of the nooks belongs to Amira. It's been a long time since we used to play here, and she pointed out her strongbox to me.

Luckily, they all have a symbol of their respective key etched in their doors. Despite the fact that there are over six hundred nooks, it only takes me a moment to spot Amira's. It's in the fifth row, third column.

With a shaking hand, I insert the key into the lock. I stand frozen for several beats, worried that I'll open the small door, and The Eldrystone won't be there.

Holding my breath, I turn the key and pull.

When I lay eyes on the amulet, a surge of air escapes my lips, carrying a wave of relief more acute than I care to admit. Though I try to convince myself that I want The Eldrystone solely to aid the fae if need be, shame flushes my cheeks as I reach for it.

The instant my fingers make contact with the cool gem, a sense of rightness washes over me, as if the world has been set straight and nothing can go awry from this point on. I hang the chain around my neck and draw in a deep breath. My eyelids flutter closed, and something like peace washes over me. I should have never given it to Amira. Only the gods know what she intended to do with it.

A quick perusal of the contents of her box reveals a collection of trinkets. Locks of hair, rocks, a kerchief with Mother's initials, and a pair of raven earrings. A pang of guilt hits me. I made those earrings, and it seems she considers them valuable enough to keep them under lock and key. Yet, my guilt is not enough to stop me from taking the amulet and risking the loss of my sister's trust in the process.

"I'm sorry, Amira," I whisper softly, closing the small door. With a twist of the key, I seal the vault and leave with the most powerful object in existence.

Yet, as I depart, I have the distinct impression that I've done both the right thing *and* the wrong thing.

16
VALERIA

"I must think of something to protect us from the fae before they invade every home in Castella."

Reina Amira Plumanegra (Casa Plumanegra) – Queen of Castella – 21 AV

Nerves tingle all over my body, making me restless. I need a release, so I go in search of Jago. I find him in his room, sprawled on the floor atop a mountain of cushions.

"Hey, how about a sparring match?" I ask.

"Not in the mood." He yawns.

"I need the exercise and not to mention the release of sword-to-sword combat." I bite my tongue, fighting the urge to tell him I'm a thief.

"Wine can have the same effect."

I raise an eyebrow. "Did you miss the part where I said *exercise*?"

Getting up from his comfortable nest, he tips an imaginary glass to his lips five times in a row. "Need I say more?"

"But—"

He stops in front of me and presses a finger to my lips to silence me. "I've been thinking about how to get Don Justo off your back, and I think I came up with something."

"You did?! I knew I could count on you. What should I do?"

"I can only discuss this if we *exercise*." He tips an imaginary glass again.

I roll my eyes and sigh. "Fine then."

We leave his room, take a sharp right, and head to the main cellar. There are three, one in each wing and one in the central building. We're headed to the latter, the biggest one of them.

When we get there, Jago uses his Plumanegra key on the lock. To the right of the door, a shelf contains an array of candlesticks in brass holders. I grab one and light the candle in one of the gas lamps attached to the wall. The lamps are kept lit around the clock for this very purpose.

After pushing the door open, Jago grabs his own candlestick and lights it too, then descends the steep steps into the cellar.

"I know just the bottle I want to open," he says.

A shiver climbs up my arms as the temperature drops. When we reach the bottom, Jago proceeds to light candles arranged on a table situated in the center of the elongated chamber.

"I'll get the wine. You get the rest." He walks down one of the many narrow aisles that extend into the darkness, carrying his candlestick.

I procure a corkscrew, glasses, and pristine white napkins from a well-stocked hutch, then arrange two places for us at a tall table.

"Get some cheese, why don't you?" Jago's voice echoes from

down the aisle. All I see is his face illuminated by candlelight as he searches the shelves.

Before I fulfill this request, I retrieve a coat from a rack on the wall and slip it on. It's slightly big, but the fur-lined collar promises the right amount of warmth. All the cellars are provisioned and maintained properly, supervised every day by one of the *ama de llaves*—mistresses of keys—and I must say, they think of everything.

I find the customary three small wheels of cheese in the rack. I cut a few pieces of Jago's favorite, Manchego, and my favorite, Roncal.

Jago returns with the candlestick in one hand, a wine bottle in the other, and a huge smile on his face. "1789 DV Xérès Oloroso. I've been working my way back through the different vintages, and this is next. I've heard it's exquisite."

He expertly opens the bottle and pours it into the glasses. We both swirl and smell the wine, then take a small sip.

A moan sounds in the back of Jago's throat, and he closes his eyes, savoring. He smacks his lips. "It doesn't disappoint."

"Agree," I say. The taste is wonderfully nutty with lots of depth.

He pulls a stool closer to the table and sits, one leg on the stone floor and the other hooked over the footrest.

Once he appears comfortable, I get to the point. "So what's your idea? How do we deal with Don Justo?"

"We kill him," he announces.

I almost choke on my wine. After coughing a few times, I clear my throat. "You can't be se—"

He laughs. "Of course I'm not serious. The man is a dolt, but he did fight valiantly during what, from now on, shall be known as," he holds his glass up, "*The woes of the whimsical and witty Princess Valeria Plumanegra and the stolen fae amulet.*"

"Don't you think that's a tad too long?"

"No, it's perfect."

"If length doesn't matter then you—" I begin.

Jago interrupts me. "Speak for yourself. I think *length* does matter, almost as much as girth."

I laugh, and I think it's the first time since I've been back.

He winks, satisfied with himself.

I take a sip of wine, then say, "All I was going to say is that you should add your name to the title. You also played a part."

"*Pshaw*, all I did was fetch Cuervo, and even that chicken played a bigger role than me."

I shake my head. "You're my partner in crime. Without you, I would be lost."

He considers for a moment, then nods. "True." He refills his glass and clinks it to mine. "Here's to my partner in crime, my cousin from another dungeon! Together, we've committed acts so legendary, even the bards can't sing their glory. We navigate the treacherous waters of mischief like a pair of swashbuckling pirates—except our treasure chests are filled with laughter and our swords are . . . er . . . made of cheese." He pops a piece of Manchego into his mouth.

I laugh once more, this time more heartily, then clear my throat and do my own toast. "To the one who always has my back, even when we're running from angry bastardos in disguise. May our schemes be as endless as the excuses you come up with . . ."

"Hey!" he protests.

I go on. "And may our adventures be as wild as the time we

convinced Nana that we didn't injure our fingers while juggling daggers. Here's to us, allies in absurdity!"

We laugh, holding our stomachs and pounding the table. It almost feels like old times, but I sober up too quickly, fearing I have no right to merriment—not when I consider what Amira is planning to do to our fae neighbors.

"It'll get easier," Jago says, noticing my change in expression. "Memories will fade."

I don't know exactly what he's referring to, Father's death, Bastien's betrayal, the fact that I killed someone, or the torture I endured in the catacombs, but maybe I've quickly made my peace with all those things because I'm more worried about what's to come than what lies behind.

"So what's your real plan to get Don Justo off my back?" I ask, knowing I have to get this one problem out of the way before I tackle any others.

"All right," Jago begins. "You might've noticed all the attention he was getting during the ball. The bloke is good-looking. You have to admit."

I move my head from side to side, considering this. It's hard to be objective because when I consider Don Justo in his entirety, his abrasive personality overshadows whatever good looks he may possess. His every dashing smile becomes chilling, and the sparkle in his blue eyes seems malicious.

Jago bats a hand. "Even if you can't admit it, every other woman present at the ball noticed. Many looked positively green with envy."

"So?"

"So one of them was Gran Duquesa Sara Plumanegra."

I narrow my eyes, thoughts speeding and tripping over Jago's insinuation. "Are you suggesting that supercilious Sara should marry Don Justo?"

He gives me a huge smile and nods, looking proud of himself.

"She would never agree to marry a man without a title. Or any man, for that matter. She thinks everyone is leagues below her."

"Except you and Amira. She has always been jealous of you two. You're the only ones she's ever nice to."

"That's not true. She is never nice."

"Like I said, she's jealous of you and might love the thought of breaking you and Don Justo up."

"All right, but it's a big leap to assume she'll marry him, *and* that he'll agree to take a grand duchess over a princess."

Jago smiles wickedly. "Who said they would have to agree?"

Still smiling from ear to ear, he explains what he has in mind, and when he's done telling me everything, I feel sullied.

"We can't," I say. "It's not right."

"If you want something that feels *right*, you shouldn't have asked *me* for ideas, Dear Val."

I grab my head and rub circles into my temples.

"If you can think of another way, I'm all ears."

Sighing, I say, "I'll just have to talk to him. Appeal to his conscience."

"Good luck with that. I don't think the man knows how to take *no* for an answer. He's accustomed to winning."

"I have to try."

He pours more wine for himself. I wave a hand at my glass when he tries to do the same for me.

He shrugs. "More for me."

"There's something else you should know," I say.

"Oh, saints! Do I even want to hear it?"

"Amira is planning to create a holding compound for the fae," I blurt out.

He stops, glass halfway to his mouth, and stares at me, slack-jawed. "Is that a joke?"

I shake my head.

"She told you this?"

"No. I accidentally read the proposal when I was in her study."

"That's wrong." He pauses, then adds, "Cruel, even. What is she thinking?"

"I . . . I feel as if she's become a different person, Jago. As if Orys . . ." I search for the right words, "*tainted her* and he's still coloring her every decision."

"What are you saying? That she's still possessed? Or . . . not in her right mind?"

I stare at the bottom of my empty glass. "I . . . I don't know. It's not like she doesn't have the right to be angry, but I don't think she's seeing clearly, and I'm afraid of what the council will do with this idea of hers."

"Oh, I know exactly what they'll do," he says. "They'll run with it."

Abandoning the wine glass, I begin pacing along the table. "I know the idea of reopening the veil won't fix all our problems, but it has to be better than what she's planning."

"I'm not so sure about that. Only the saints know what has happened on the other side of the veil these last twenty years, but one thing I'm sure of . . . when the fae go back to their homes, they won't have anything nice to say about us—on the contrary. I still think opening the veil will invite a war we can't win."

"What if . . . what if . . . we close it after they go back?"

He contemplates quietly for a moment, then says, "Assuming the amulet will oblige, you would have to open it and close it more than once. It would take time to get the message out across Castella to all of those who were displaced."

I nod, considering. "We could send a notice and set a few dates throughout the year to allow them to cross."

Pushing the cheese around on his plate, Jago shakes his head. "I don't know, Val. The Fae King is going to want his amulet back. The moment he realizes what's happening, he'll send his army to retrieve it."

I let out a frustrated exhale. Jago is right. "Then we set one date, send the message out, and only open the veil once."

As soon as the words are out of my mouth, I realize there is a big problem with both of these ideas. The fae don't trust us.

"Do you think the fae would believe such a message?" he asks, echoing the same thought that just sprouted into my head.

I sigh. "No. They won't come. In fact, they'll probably go into hiding."

They live among us now, but the moment they hear we're trying to round them up, my idea won't sound any better than Amira's.

Mind racing, I pace the length of the table several more times before I propose my next idea. "I open the veil, cross to Tirnanog, shut it again, then talk to King Theric and broker a peaceful solution."

"San Miguel protect you, cousin. I doubt you'll get a warm reception."

"Maybe I will, if I hand him Rífíor on a silver platter."

Jago's gaze flicks from side to side as he considers. "It's risky, but it might work. Our family always had good relations with the Therics. But do you think Amira will allow it?"

I consider for a long moment. My mind tells me that she will. Amira is reasonable, logical. But my gut tells me something completely different.

"Your survival instincts are in your gut," Father told me more than once. *"If you don't listen to them, you're inviting disaster."*

Even as Father's words echo inside my mind, I try to convince myself that my sister's heart remains unchanged, that it still harbors goodness. If I'm wrong, the fate of Castella may be in jeopardy.

17
VALERIA

"We can't have two incompetent women in charge of Castella. Good thing I'm here to do something about it."

Don Justo Ramiro Medrano – Master Mason – 21 AV

"Treasure!" Cuervo exclaims happily that night on the balcony of my bedchamber when I call him and give him back the amulet. Odd how The Eldrystone feels safer in his care than in my sister's.

"Hide it well, my friend. I may need it again."

Bobbing his head, he hops across the railing, then leaps into the sky, flying in the direction of the observatory. He quickly disappears into the night, and I go inside and lay my head on the pillow, tempted to remain there for another week.

The realm will be fine without me. Won't it?

Morning comes too fast. I don't bother to put on a dress for my impending meeting with Don Justo. I asked Renata to arrange it, knowing I can't put the task off without angering Amira. Instead,

I wear my most comfortable, well-loved leggings and tunic—my recovered raven dagger strapped to my side.

I stare at my image in the mirror and smooth my hair into a braid, then plump my cheeks in order to look alive, not attractive.

My complexion is dull. I spent nearly all night tossing and turning, thinking of what to say to Don Justo and how to talk to Amira about her proposal for the fae. Needless to say, I didn't get much sleep.

For hours, I considered both conversations, imagining what they would reply back, then adjusting my words based on their likely responses. Deciding how to approach Don Justo—a man I barely know—should have been the hardest of the two, but it was my imaginary conversation with my sister that took strange turns and left me feeling at a loss.

Maybe it's wishful thinking, but in the end, I've come to believe that the proposal is just that. She's toying with the idea. Once we talk, and she understands what a betrayal to Mother a holding compound would be, she will see things differently.

To my shame, I would be lying if I didn't admit it wasn't my sister or Don Justo who truly kept me awake. There was someone else on my mind occupying more space than he deserves.

Rifior.

Bastien.

Bastien.

Rifior.

Both separately, then together, merging into one perplexing figure I can't seem to eradicate from my thoughts.

Every time I closed my eyes, Rífíor's scarred face and pointed ears morphed into the human semblance of a man I decided to trust, a man who made me feel so much.

The memories of the night we spent together, the way he touched me, kissed me, and looked at me are carved into my mind as if in stone. And being here alone—on the bed where he was mine for the briefest moment, and I felt nothing but the exquisite rightness of it all—I'm weak, so weak that if any trace of Bastien lingers in Rífíor, I'll be lost.

In those feeble moments, anger rises, and I hate myself. Rífíor is a monster. Anyone capable of torturing another can't possibly be any good and deserves to rot in a dungeon for the rest of their life.

Shaking myself and pushing all these thoughts and worries aside, I leave my bedchamber and head to my meeting.

I still have an escort that follows me around wherever I go, but I hope that soon, as things return to normal, their presence won't be necessary anymore.

My meeting with Don Justo is in the largest, most impersonal waiting room I could think of. When I enter, asking my guardias to remain outside, I find him inspecting a portrait of my grandfather, Rey Vicente Plumanegra. In this particular painting, he's in his early thirties, surrounded by four pointers, a bow held casually in one hand, and an empty quiver hanging from his back. A dozen rabbits hang from a pole to his left, displaying his hunting prowess.

Don Justo turns to face me, a forced smile plastered on his face. Slowly, his intense blue eyes scan the length of my body and pause at my scuffed boots. His smile falters. In contrast, he wears a tailored doublet of rich velvet, its deep hue catching the light with a subtle sheen. Beneath, he sports a crisp linen shirt, the collar adorned with delicate embroidery.

"Princess Valeria?" he says in the tone of a question, as if he thinks they have sent an impostor in my place.

"My grandfather loved murdering innocent creatures for sport." I gesture up at the portrait of the exacting man.

Don Justo is clearly displeased by my comment—no doubt he likes murdering little creatures for fun, too.

"I hear your favorite dish is cochinillo," he replies, sharp with his verbal swords.

One cannot feast on meat without murdering an innocent creature. My preference for suckling pig is a detail I shared with his mistress of keys in Alsur, and I'm surprised he's aware of this. He must have thoroughly interrogated her about me.

"Touché," I say, allowing him a win since I'm about to cause him a loss.

He smiles, self-satisfied, then takes a step closer. "I'm so relieved you're all right."

I take a step back to ensure he stays at a safe distance. "Thank you."

"If those responsible weren't already dead, I would make sure they met the end of my sword."

The possessive tone in his voice makes me want to say something rude, but I restrain my temper and, instead, reply in the friendliest tone I can muster. "You're a very *protective* man, Don Justo, a valued denizen of Castella. We appreciate everything you do in the south to defend the realm from the threat of Los Moros."

"I do no more than a man who loves his realm would do." He inclines his head as if he were doing it all for honor and not personal gain.

"The whole of Castella thanks you, including me," I say, running a finger over the back of a gilded sofa as I meander further away from him. "I also thank you for fighting so valiantly during the veilfallen's attack on Nido."

Yesterday, Jago told me that the exact details of what occurred have not been made public, for obvious reasons. It wasn't hard to come up with a lie. No one can possibly guess that Orys had the queen under his spell for weeks and was working to undermine not only the Plumanegra rule but also the human rule. Therefore, the official report states that the sorcerer infiltrated the palace, tried to supplant the queen, but failed.

"No more valiantly than you, my dear princess. I'm rather impressed by the fact that *you* ended the sorcerer. You must tell me how you did it." His eyes narrow with interest.

Only the veilfallen and my sister bore witness to my confrontation with the sorcerer, and the report excluded any mention of the amulet and the espiritu it lent me to accomplish the deed. It's only natural for Don Justo to be curious.

I gesture vaguely with one hand. "He exhausted his powers, and I saw an opportunity. That is all."

A sound in the back of his throat expresses his enduring skepticism. Yet, I'm not here to address his doubts. He has no business asking questions that only concern my family, so I swiftly come to the crux of the matter.

"Before my father died," I say without preamble, "he and I were contemplating your proposal. However, we never arrived at a final decision. After his death, Amira was overwhelmed and a little distraught. She wasn't clear about Father's intentions regarding my autonomy in determining my own future."

Don Justo's eyes narrow, an edge of displeasure tainting his features as he begins to suspect where this is going.

"I'm sorry to say," I go on, "that she refused to listen to me and sent me to Alsur against my will. That is the reason I left shortly after arriving at your villa. My sister wasn't happy and ordered me to go on with the engagement. But then the veil-fallen took me, and her fear for my life caused her to see things more clearly. I—"

"She cannot break our agreement," he interrupts, his words firm and spoken between clenched teeth.

"You can't fault the queen for wishing for her sister's happiness. Though I want to make clear that I bear full responsibility for the final decision." I pause so that my next words have the desired effect. "I do *not* wish to marry you."

His nostrils flare, and his hands tighten into trembling fists. "If you deny me, you may find our southern enemies soon knocking at your very door."

"Whatever happened to your love for Castella?"

He comes around the couch, trying to reach me, but I move to the other side, keeping the piece of furniture safely between us.

"Your sister will bear the blame," he says, "and her reign will be deemed weak. Many already feel she isn't a worthy replacement for your father."

Instantly, anger reaches a boiling point in my veins. "Amira

Plumanegra is Simón Plumanegra's eldest daughter, raised and trained by him to be the best queen any realm could wish for."

"Debatable."

"You're out of line!" I say, my words charged with red-hot fury. "You were politely welcomed into Nido as a faithful denizen of the realm, but perhaps you aren't what you portray yourself to be. Your words about our queen and your threats to the realm are nothing but treasonous. I could have you arrested."

His left eye twitches as he realizes his mistake. He takes a deep, calming breath. "You are right," he says in what seems to take a monumental effort. "I'm out of line, but I hope you will understand my disappointment. My apologies." He inclines his head.

I don't believe him, not for a second, but I can't make an enemy of this man. I have to offer an olive branch.

"I do understand," I say, my effort as monumental as his. "Your contributions deserve appreciation. I'm willing to provide funds for your army."

He presses a hand to his chest. "You offend me, Princess Valeria. It isn't riches I seek. I have enough gold to last me many lifetimes."

"Forgive me." I incline my head and lower my gaze to the floor.

He turns toward the door, and for a moment, I believe he will walk out, and I'll never have to see him again. But it's all a show, and he turns on his heel, smiles, and says, "There *might* be a way you can help me, however." A pause. "I'm still an unmarried man in search of a *regal* wife."

18
VALERIA

*"Wouldn't you know? With Simón Plumanegra dead,
I'm fourth in line to the throne."*

***Gran Duquesa Sara Plumanegra (Casa Plumanegra) – Fourth in
line to Plumanegra throne – 21 AV***

I hate the need to placate that awful man. Don Justo is a villain if I've ever seen one. But I have to put the future and peace of the realm ahead of everything else, and if that means trying to find him a wife . . . so be it. I can only hope that any respectable woman I steer in his direction will see through his façade and run far away from him.

It's ironic how Jago's idea to thrust Don Justo at another royal ended up being the outcome of our conversation. I guess I was too naïve to expect Don Justo to simply walk away without a prize for all his troubles. Perhaps we will need to go with my cousin's plan and introduce him to Sara.

Taking two steps at a time, I hurry down the staircase in search of my sister. As I round a corner, I'm staring at the floor and have to come to a sudden stop to avoid a collision with what looks like a walking bolt of yellow silk and lace.

"Apologies," I blurt out at the voluminous dress.

"Valeria," a syrupy sweet voice says, making me cringe. "Are you well? After what happened, I've been concerned about you." Fake concern colors her tone.

I would recognize that voice anywhere. It's as genuine as those beauty marks Emerito fancied. Reluctantly, I meet the woman's gaze and try to match her smile. I almost succeed, except my face feels stiff.

"Sara, it's good to see you," I say, avoiding her question.

Gran Duquesa Sara Plumanegra. Fancy running into her. It's as if my thoughts conjured her. Could the gods be sending me a message?

She's my second cousin, granddaughter of Teresa Plumanegra, my grandfather's sister. In our tradition, the Plumanegra surname is passed down through both male and female lines, a custom uncommon in Castella, which is the reason we bear the same last name. She is fifth—no, now fourth in line to the throne, following Amira, myself, and Jago—as she keenly likes to point out whenever given the chance. Unfortunately, her mother passed away last year due to a tragic fall from her horse, and with her father also deceased and being the eldest of three siblings, she inherited the title of grand duchess and moved up the line of succession.

Like many other Plumanegras, she lives in Nido—somewhere in the west wing. I seldom see her, though, a testament to how big the palace is.

She looks like a sunlit cloud in her voluminous yellow gown, her chin held up imperiously. Cascading blond curls frame her slender face, flowing past her shoulders.

"You look," her cold gray eyes scan me from head to toe, "the same as always, so you must be all right."

"I could be better."

"Glad to hear. Glad to hear."

What? Is she even listening?

She pulls out an elaborate fan and waves it around her face. "I was just talking to my brother about the council meeting this morning and told him how surprised I am to discover that Amira has a backbone, after all."

I frown, curiosity overtaking my anger at her backhanded comment about my sister. Sara holds a seat on the council, like her mother Ana Plumanegra and her grandmother Teresa Plumanegra before that.

With cold calculation, she examines my reaction, then delivers her venom as I knew she would. "The taint of the fae shall soon be removed from our streets."

I feared this was where Sara was going, yet the words cut me deeply. I convinced myself that Amira would not dare present the proposal to the council and wash her hands of our heritage.

Somehow, I manage to keep my feelings hidden from this viper and say, "I'm sure I don't know what you're referring to, Sara." I sidestep her and walk away. "My apologies, I have somewhere to be," I add as an afterthought.

She huffs, then throws her words at my back. "You and Jago could have benefited from a proper governess. A horse has better manners."

I stop and do my best to bite my tongue, but this battle was lost many years ago when Sara and I were little girls, and she taunted me with jokes about my dead mother.

Calmly, I turn, push my face close to hers, and say in a soft voice, "I believe you're wrong. A horse would have already stomped on your snake head."

She gasps audibly, pressing a hand to her chest.

As I step back, I wink. "And your governess can't hold a candle to Nana. At least she taught me to respect other people's dead parents, so I'll refrain from making jokes about yours. Have a good day, Gran Duquesa." I curtsy with exaggerated deference, then turn on my heel and leave.

It takes me several passes up and down an empty hall to calm down and gather my thoughts. When I feel capable of facing Amira, I head toward her study.

Rolling my shoulders, I knock on the door. Renata peeks out and offers me a smile.

"Does Amira have a moment? I wish to talk to her," I say.

The adviser is gone for a moment, then returns and lets me in. "She can see you now." After I enter, she closes the door behind her, leaving me alone with my sister.

Amira is waiting for me with her arms crossed over the desk.

My gaze darts toward the cabinet where the Plumanegra keys are kept. I wait for her to demand where The Eldrystone is, but it appears my sleight of hand remains unnoticed. An urge gnaws at me to swap my key with Amira's before my luck runs out.

"Renata told me you met with Don Justo just now. How did it go?" she asks.

"I'm handling him."

She narrows her eyes, and I think she will press me further, but she lets it go. "Good."

I know this means she has decided to trust me. I wish I could do the same, but I think she's making a big mistake.

"I ran into Sara," I say.

Amira says nothing. She simply holds my gaze.

"You can't," I manage.

"I have to. We need to quiet the unrest, and this is the best way."

"It's . . . not right."

Fluidly, she pushes to her feet, hands flat on the desk. "And what they did to our family . . . is that right?"

"Orys is dead, Amira."

"And what about Ríffor and the veilfallen who escaped? What about those fae still out there who will continue to do harm to our denizens?" She points vaguely in the direction of the city, her finger shaking.

"They can be punished for their crimes, but the innocent shouldn't have to pay for the mistakes of others."

"Well, you and I are paying. Regardless."

"Amira, please, you must think this through. This . . . action can't be part of your legacy."

"That is not for you to decide," she says, fixing me with the same unyielding gaze as the other night, when I hesitated to relinquish The Eldrystone.

By all accounts, it seems Orys made her distrustful, even of me. But how can she feel threatened by her sister? I've never given her a reason.

She won't think that when she discovers the amulet is missing, a rational voice chimes in within my head.

"I know it isn't my decision," I say. "I only fear for what you still have to lose."

Her eyebrows knit together, and at her silent, questioning expression, I see my chance to go on.

"Orys took much from you and me. I regret not ending his life the first time, so that he never had the opportunity to harm you. What he did to you was awful. I see the toll it takes in the shadows beneath your eyes. You're not sleeping well. I know you're scared, and I understand why."

Tears glint like silver in her eyes, and no matter how hard this is to put into words, I have to keep going, have to get through to her.

"You don't want to disappoint Father. You don't want to fail as a queen. You're scared you may lose me and want to keep me safe. You're also worried that anyone around you can turn out to be a traitor, an impostor, so you're unwilling to trust."

Her tears spill, cutting twin paths down her cheeks.

"But you can trust me. I'll help you. We'll get through this together."

"Will we?" she asks.

"Yes."

"You're certain?"

"Yes."

She swats her wet cheeks with the back of her hands, drying the tears with the bandages around her injured palm. After several calming breaths, she comes around the desk and heads for the door.

"All right, come with me then," she says, and without glancing back, she walks out, expecting me to follow her.

19
VALERIA

"What is wrong with me? I feel like I can't even trust my own sister."

Reina Amira Plumanegra (Casa Plumanegra) – Queen of Castella – 21 AV

At first, I have no idea where we're going, but when she walks deep into the palace and heads straight north of the central building, the realization hits me.

We're going to the dungeons.

"I don't want to see him, Amira," I say.

"You said we could get through this together. Have you changed your mind so quickly?"

I shake my head, and she hurries her step, her dress billowing behind her. It's red and seems to leave a trail of despair behind her. She descends the steps of the dimly illuminated passage toward the dungeons with the determination of a member of the Guardia Real. I follow, feeling anything but determined.

Two guards stand at attention and click their heels when we appear.

"At ease," Amira says, and the guards relax. With a commanding air that I feel would crack under the least amount of pressure, she takes a ring of keys from a metal hook on the wall, turns to one of the guards, and issues an order. "Give me your rapier."

He blinks in surprise, as do I, but I don't dare contradict her in front of these men. Hastily, he unsheathes his sword and hands it over, exchanging a wary glance with his partner.

"Remain alert," she commands. "I will call you if the need arises. Otherwise, don't bother us."

"Yes, Your Majesty." They hold their heads high and click their heels again as we pass under the arched doorway and find Rífíor's cell all the way at the end.

Torches, instead of gas lamps, illuminate the dank passage. No one else is here, but the veilfallen leader sitting on a narrow stone ledge, a statue with his gaze set on infinity. He doesn't look in our direction as we appear, doesn't even acknowledge our presence in the smallest of ways. It's as if his body is an empty shell.

There is a bowl with untouched bread on the floor. The smell of urine and sweat clog the air, making me wince.

"How many people have you killed, Rífíor of the Veilfallen?" Amira asks, tapping the bars with the rapier. "How many of them human?"

He continues to stare into the distance, seemingly oblivious to our presence. Despite his despondent attitude, his posture is straight, regal.

"Too many to count, I imagine," she says. "I shudder to think how many more you would have killed if The Eldrystone hadn't a mind of its own."

Still no reaction.

Amira glances at me sidelong, appearing disappointed at the lack of answer. At last, she thrusts the rapier into my hand. Frowning, I take it, and she proceeds to unlock the cell.

"What are you doing?!" I demand.

She doesn't answer. She just throws the cell door open and steps aside.

My heart skips a beat. I raise the sword, ready to defend my sister, but he remains impassive.

"Kill him," Amira says, pointing at the male.

"What?!"

"Kill him, Val. Do this with me?"

I shake my head. "No. This isn't how we do things. There should be a trial."

"Why? We already know what he did. Why waste time and resources on this *hijo de puta*." Her curse shocks me. She never uses such words.

"Because Castella stands for justice," I say.

"Few know he's here. None care."

"I care, Amira. I—?"

"You care about him?" she interrupts.

At this, Rífíor blinks and lowers his chin to his chest, the first indication that he isn't a piece of frozen meat, but a hot-blooded male.

"That's not what I was going to say," I reply.

"You love him, don't you?" She throws the words like an accusation.

"It has nothing to do with love. I hate him for what he's done to me, for teaching me to distrust people the way Orys taught you, for making me afraid of my dreams at night. I. Hate. Him."

"Then kill him!" Spittle flies from Amira's mouth.

I stare at Rífior, the rapier trembling in my hand. His lids lower, and he shuts his eyes as if resigned to die in this moldy cell.

His defeated attitude perplexes me. This isn't the male I know. Rífior is full of determination. He's intense and driven. That's why he found The Eldrystone, except . . . the amulet wanted nothing to do with him.

Rejected and without his quest, he appears to be nothing but a broken male. Why is Niamhara's conduit opposed to him now? Presumably, he wielded it successfully in the past—if not, why else search for it so desperately?

Seeing him like this does something to me. Slowly, I lower my sword. I don't know what lies in his past, what made him do all the terrible things he has done, and how it all connects to my mother. I don't know if he suffered, if he lost something precious, and that means I can't judge him.

Pain has turned Amira—my sweet, compassionate sister—into a person I barely recognize. Pain has also changed me. I can feel it even now, urging me to use the sword and end another life in the pursuit of vengeance, but I have no right to take away that which I didn't give. I'm not a god and don't intend to act like one. Not again. Orys deserved what I did to him, but that doesn't mean the weight of my actions is easy to live with. No matter how much Rífior deserves the same fate, my load is heavy enough already.

I have to think of my sister, too. If I don't show her there is another path besides anger and bitterness, might she become a blind, single-minded tyrant like Rífíor?

No. I can't let that happen.

"Kill him!" Amira orders me again.

I shake my head. "I'm not a cold-blooded murderer, Amira, and neither are you."

"I will show you otherwise."

Lurching forward, she goes for the sword, one hand gripping my wrist and the other attempting to pry my fingers away from the hilt.

I take several steps back, tightening my hold and turning sideways, away from her.

As we struggle, she drives me against the wall, slamming my shoulder hard. I have enough presence of mind to glance in Rífíor's direction, fearing he might take advantage of the scuffle to attack us. He could easily use one of us as a hostage in order to procure passage out of Nido. But my quick glance reveals he has no interest in us. He's still sitting motionless, head lowered, eyes closed—either oblivious to his fate or resigned to it, I can't tell which.

As I free my sword arm from Amira's grip and hide the rapier behind my back, using my body to keep her at bay, I entreat her, "Please, sister, you're better than this, better than him and Orys. Remember Mother's love and gentleness toward everyone. Remember all the things Father taught you. He was a good king, and you will be as good for Castella as he was. Don't let evil change you."

Relinquishing her struggle, her body goes limp against mine, and she begins to cry, her shoulders shaking as she sobs. I wrap an arm around her and hold her tight. I dare to think I've gotten through to her, but then she pushes away from me with a frustrated growl and glares at me.

"No!" she hisses. "I will not be weak."

"It's not weakness to aim for peace."

She bares her teeth and points at me. I wait for her to argue further, but instead, she whirls and marches down the corridor, disappearing around the bend.

For a long moment, I remain slumped against the wall, the backs of my eyes burning as I wonder if I have lost her forever.

"In the frailty of the soul, hatred finds its breeding ground," Ríffor's deep voice echoes from within the cell.

I startle, head whipping in his direction. I had forgotten he was there and can't help but shudder at the truth behind his words. Chest heaving, heart beating out of control, I cautiously approach the cell door, push it closed, and turn the key.

He doesn't look at me and still appears indifferent, but clearly, he's not as oblivious as he would have us believe.

I take several steps away from the cell until I can't see him anymore. The rapier trembles in my grip as an idea enters my mind. I shy away from it, try not to let it take shape, but it takes root without my permission, driven by the force of fear for my sister.

Shaking my head, I try to hide from the notion. It would mean going against Amira, and I don't know if I have the courage, if I'm willing to prove to her that she's right to distrust me. She is the queen whether or not I like it. The gods didn't choose me to lead Castella and make the difficult choices required of a leader. My sister was given that task. I have to let it go. I have to stand down. It's the right thing to do for someone in my position.

But if that is true, why can't I push away the certainty that if I don't intervene to alter Amira's chosen path, the entire realm will suffer the consequences? Why do I feel that inaction will condemn me to a life consumed by regret?

RÍFÍOR

Echoes of their voices linger, crashing between me and the damp walls.

"Kill him!" the queen ordered Valeria.

I wish she would have.

Nothing makes sense anymore. The Eldrystone refused its power to me, and without it, my entire purpose for being is gone. It makes no difference if I am here in this cell or elsewhere. I am stranded in this godsforsaken realm regardless. It makes no difference if I live or die.

My kin and I will forever be trapped in Castella. It is worse than a death sentence.

This realm and its people are of no importance to me.

Valeria was a misstep. Nothing more.

She might have been useful if she slit my throat. Maybe their senseless laws will do the job. A walk up to the gallows cannot come swiftly enough.

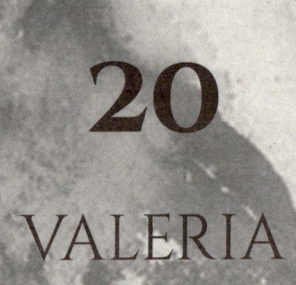

20
VALERIA

"She's the best sister I could have ever wished for."

Reina Amira Plumanegra (Casa Plumanegra) – Princess of Castella – 19 AV

The lives of Nido's residents can be as different from each other as the sides of a coin.

There are the guards, who live under military rigor, waking up before the sun comes out, marching and doing drills, mucking up horses, and guarding the palace at all hours.

The servants—scullery maids, laundry maids, kitchen boys, housemaids, lady's maids, valets, nursery maids, cooks, and more—with tasks ranging from preparing meals to scrubbing floors to applying makeup.

Clergy conducting mass in the many chapels. Courtiers attempting to gain favor with Amira and other family members. Council members attending meetings, shaping policy, stabbing each other in the back, anything in order to gain more power.

There are also stable boys and their masters, librarians, teachers, nurses, physicians, spies, and informants. The list is endless.

At one point or another, I have been part of all these people's lives, especially when I was small and at the mercy of my parents. Father used to drag me to many events involving the clergy, council members, and this or that Don and Doña. But as I grew older, I slowly distanced myself from most of the court's affairs, finding many of the people involved too superficial for my taste. Instead, I began to find enjoyment in the simple joy of doing crafts, the company of those closest to me like Father, Amira, Jago, Nana, Maestro Elizondo, and Cuervo, the release of sparring with a worthy opponent, and the rush of freedom whenever I managed to get on the other side of Nido's imposing walls.

One aspect of Nido's life that I particularly despise is the constant gatherings organized by one court member or another. They always involve elaborate food and music, ridiculous dances, women parading around in the latest fashion and hungry men who refuse to be satisfied solely by the appetizers—one and all attempting to gain advantage through learning or revealing a secret, making or breaking alliances, or seducing one another.

For a long time, I managed to stay away from all of this, and maybe that's the reason this particular event is teeming with too many people. Not only because I'm in attendance, but because I organized it. They are curious to see what the prodigal princess has in store for them.

The event was put together at a moment's notice, and I feared few would attend, but I shouldn't have worried. Word traveled like a speeding arrow, and though many of the Dons and Doñas who live outside of Castellina were unable to attend, I trust that won't be an issue. Surely, Don Justo can find a wife among all these overpowdered ladies.

My stomach churns with displeasure as I walk into the reception hall arm-in-arm with Don Justo Medrano. He is wearing a jacket in a blue hue that complements his eyes. It is adorned with gold thread embellishments and accentuates his broad shoulders and slender frame. His tall frame and imposing comportment command the room, and his gold-spun hair shines with the light spilling through the large windows. His cerulean gaze holds an unshakable confidence that seems to entrance every lady in the room.

For my part, I also wear blue, although not by design. The satin fabric of my dress shimmers and flows like ocean waters as I move. The seamstress did a wonderful job despite the haste.

The cancellation of our engagement hasn't been announced yet. I will have to do it here, citing—per Don Justo's request—his desire to find a wife less inclined to masculine behavior. The man thinks he's being mean-spirited. He doesn't realize he's doing me a favor.

Jago tips his glass from across the room. He's surrounded by a group of women, who would like nothing better than to take his Plumanegra last name. They have no idea he has sworn off marriage. I don't blame him. He has as much in common with those women as I do with—my gaze sweeps the floor—Conde Salvador Almolar, for instance. He asked for my hand in marriage once. The pudgy man is fanning himself and holding his wine glass with his little finger sticking up, the frills of his shirt hanging down nearly ten inches. He has one of those beauty marks Emerito liked to wear, and of course, his dog's tail mustache.

He acknowledges me with a flourish of his fan when he notices my gaze. I return the gesture before shifting my attention to the appetizer table. I swiftly select a glass of wine and a piece of silverware to tap against it. No point in delaying the inevitable.

I'm about to clink the glass and call everyone's attention when the Gran Duquesa Sara Plumanegra approaches, her chin held up so high it almost points to the ceiling. Wearing a slanted smile, she puts out her hand and extends it toward Don Justo. He takes it and kisses her knuckles, gaze set on her bosom as his lips linger a moment too long.

As much as the two deserve each other and despite Jago's original idea for the couple, Sara is the last one who should marry this man. I've had time to think about it, and I fear their greed would compound into something dangerous.

"It is such a relief to find you are well after that terrifying ordeal at your engagement party," Sara says. "You fought bravely, I'm told. I was fortunate enough to make a quick exit. Others weren't so lucky."

"Indeed," he replies. "I was only bested by a veilfallen who could wield espiritu. That can hardly be called a fair fight. Before she attacked me, I took out a sizable number of those *bastardos*."

Sara lets out a little squeak at his inappropriate language. Her eyes dart around as if to make sure no one heard. There is a delighted little smile on her lips, however, as if the edge of danger glinting in Don Justo's eyes excites her. She was raised more sheltered than Amira and I ever were. She was never around guards, learning how to sword fight, witnessing their sometimes-crude behavior and foul language. Her mother cared only about tea parties, elaborate dresses, and gossip. Undoubtedly, she did an excellent job passing her values down to her daughter.

I must intervene and not allow whatever this is to go any further.

Just as I open my mouth to say something, the doors to the room open wide and Queen Amira's presence is announced.

My heart leaps. Amira isn't supposed to be in attendance. This whole affair with Don Justo is my responsibility. Has she realized I took The Eldrystone? Has she come to demand it back?

She greets a few people on her way in but heads in my direction as soon as she spots me.

I try to put on a smile, but it proves an impossible task.

"Your Majesty," Don Justo, Sara, and I say in unison, respectfully inclining our heads.

"I am sorry to interrupt, Valeria," Amira says, "but I need to discuss an urgent matter with you."

I swallow thickly. I'm certain she has discovered my deed and wishes to make me atone for my betrayal. Without waiting for me to say anything, she turns on her heel and walks out. Everything else forgotten, I set down the glass and silverware and rush after my sister, a million useless excuses running through my head. If only I'd had an opportunity to switch our Plumanegra keys, but every time I've been by her study she or Renata have been there.

Whispering prayers under my breath, I trail behind her. She halts a cautious distance from the party in the long, empty hall.

As I stop in front of her, my face feels cold, drained entirely of blood. "What is it?" I ask, nearly out of breath.

"There has been an attack on the Biblioteca de la Reina. The veilfallen are claiming responsibility."

There is no time for relief. This is nearly as bad as Amira

figuring out that I took The Eldrystone from her. Despite the attack on the catacombs, it seems there are enough veilfallen left to still create chaos. This won't help the fae's cause. My sister will interpret this assault as further justification for her plan.

And the Biblioteca de la Reina? I know I shouldn't care about the location, but I worked hard alongside Father to make the project a reality in honor of my mother. As I imagine the possible damage, my chest grows tight.

It takes me a moment to gather my thoughts and wonder why Amira felt the need to interrupt the party to tell me this. I doubt it was only to make me aware of the disturbing news.

"I need your help with your Romani friends," she says.

I blink in confusion. "Why?"

"For years, our spies failed to find the veilfallen's hiding place, but your friends accomplished it in only a few days. I want to use all the resources at my disposal in order to eradicate this threat once and for all. Please, enlist their help. They will be compensated generously, of course. That's all they care about anyway, right?"

I shake my head. "You shouldn't say things like that, Amira."

"Things like what?" She raises an eyebrow in challenge. "The truth, you mean?"

"You're the queen, and those are *your* people. I don't remember Father ever —"

She raises a hand to quiet me. The gesture is imperious and demeaning. "I'm not Father and don't ever try to draw comparisons again." She turns to leave, then looks over her shoulder. "I will always fall short."

I walk back toward the party, head down as my thoughts race. My legs propel me forward, and I'm barely aware of entering the room. As I step inside, everyone grows quiet and stares at me. I search for Jago. He winces, looking sympathetic as if I've suffered some sort of injury.

My gaze immediately flicks to Don Justo. He's looking satisfied, pleased with himself even. From the way everyone is peering at me, I have a feeling he just dragged my name through the dirt.

I try to muster the energy to care, but it would be easier to get Sara Plumanegra to eat dessert with her salad fork.

"He told them that Uncle Simón practically forced him into accepting your hand in marriage," Jago explains as we walk back to my bedchamber at the end of the gathering. "Said that from the moment he met you, he knew it wouldn't work out, that he couldn't stand your foul mouth, and he wants to marry a lady not a . . . manlike hellion."

I huff and roll my eyes.

"Sara stood by his side the entire time," Jago says. "She was nodding so hard I thought her head would fall off. I was extremely disappointed when it didn't."

"Oh, well. I doubt anyone thought he was delivering some sort of obscure news. No one in their right mind has ever seen me as marriage material."

"That's the spirit." He punches my shoulder. "It's what I've always said anyway."

I glare at him.

"I mean . . . that marriage is a troublesome scheme. Not for smart people like you and me."

"Ah-ha, sure." I shake my head and sigh.

"I told you Sara would be all over Don Justo." He sounds pleased.

"An alliance between those two is the worst thing that can happen. I've thought about it, and I don't like it."

"I don't entirely disagree, but it was an easy way to get him off your back, which is what you wanted. Sara will probably find out that Don Justo hates poetry readings, and it will be the tragic end of their romance."

I laugh. "I hope you're right. Anyway, at the moment, we have bigger problems."

He frowns. "We do?"

"Whatever's left of the veilfallen must've reorganized because they just attacked the Biblioteca de la Reina."

"Oh, shit. So that's why Amira came to fetch you? To tell you that?"

I nod. "That and she wants me to talk to Esmeralda and Gaspar. She thinks they can help us find the veilfallen's new hiding place."

Jago makes a sound in the back of his throat that expresses doubt. "The veilfallen are going to be more cautious than ever. I doubt even the Romani can help us find them this time."

"I agree, but I'll talk to them regardless. I haven't had a chance to thank them for helping me, so . . ."

He nods. "Do you want me to ask them to come?"

"Yes, that would be great. In the meantime, I'll attempt to mitigate the damages however I can."

"Good luck with that." He sounds as skeptical as I feel. "I'll go find Gaspar and Esmeralda right away."

"Thank you, Jago."

He waves a hand to let me know there's no reason to thank him, but he has no idea. I would be lost without him.

Once in my bedchamber, it only takes me a moment to change out of my dress and replace it with a comfortable outfit. After that, I rush across the east wing and make it to the center area in record time. I must make another attempt to return Amira's key.

There are no guards in front of her study's door. A good sign. I knock. No answer. I knock once more, louder this time. Still nothing. I exhale in relief.

Looking right and left, I try the knob. The door is locked. But that's not a problem—not with Amira's key hanging around my neck. Pulling the chain over my head, I quickly key the lock and slip into the room. I breathe slowly, trying to calm my nerves. Everything is tidy, tidier than when this was Father's domain. A pang of sadness assaults me as I imagine him stroking his beard. I push the image away and march toward the heavy cabinet.

Swiftly, I open the drawer and make the switch. I ensure Amira's key rests perfectly in its velvet-lined box, then hang my own key around my neck—its weight instantly feeling right and reassuring me. Amira may still find out what I did, but at least a casual peek into the cabinet won't send her running to the vault.

The sound of steps outside the door sends me into a panic. My eyes rove around, trying to find a hiding place, but that's only my first instinct. Hiding would be ridiculous. Instead, I throw myself into a corner armchair, my posture slumped to make it appear as if I've been waiting in boredom for some time.

When Renata opens the door, using her key, she blinks at me in surprise. My sister pushes past her adviser and also stops in her tracks.

She frowns. "What are you doing here?" She glances at Renata. "Didn't you lock the door?"

"I . . . I thought I did, Your Majesty." Renata stares at the floor, her eyes moving from side to side as she searches her memories. She seems uncertain, which helps my case.

I let out a huge yawn and straighten. "I'm sorry, I let myself in. You know social gatherings exhaust me. It was nice and quiet here. Just what I needed."

Amira appears unsure for a moment, then seems to push her concern aside and walks to the desk.

Straightening and stretching like a lazy cat, I say, "Um, I came to tell you that I talked to Jago about enlisting the Romani to help us. He's trying to contact them as we speak."

"Good," she replies, barely acknowledging me. Clearly, this isn't one of the most prominent items on her list of worries.

I stand and approach her desk. "Is there something else I can help you with?"

"There isn't," she assures me, barely sparing a glance my way.

"Are you sure? I could—"

"You already made it clear you disagree with my plan to relocate the fae, so unless you have changed your mind, I assure you there's nothing you can help me with."

"Amira, perhaps you should reconsider. There are—"

"I don't need another lecture, sister. There's nothing you can say that will make me change my mind. So please leave. I have important things to do."

I lower my head and take a few steps back. "I'm sorry. I will let you know if I learn anything from the Romani."

She only grunts in response, and as I close the door behind me, I can't help but wonder about the path ahead of her. What comes to mind looks nothing like what I used to imagine before Father died. I always envisioned her as a fair queen, happily married to a good man, and mother to a few bright kids, who would promise an even brighter future. Now, I see none of those things.

Instead, I perceive darkness and unrest. I picture her as a bitter woman, always distrustful, even of those who love her most and have her best interest at heart. I want nothing more than to take this burden off her shoulders, want to erase the possibility of that gloomy future, and I only see one way to do it—the same one that occurred to me in the dungeons and has been plaguing me every moment of the day.

Gods, but what if I'm wrong? What if I make things worse and my actions only guarantee the bleak future I've imagined?

I would never forgive myself. There has to be a way to dissuade her. I have to keep trying.

21

VALERIA

"I wish she would show more interest in official matters. Perhaps with time."

Rey Simón Plumanegra (Casa Plumanegra) – King of Castella – 19 AV

The next morning, I wake up to Cuervo's croaks out on the balcony. The door is closed due to the fall chill, and he hates that. Yawning, I get out of bed and walk outside. A shiver runs up my arms when the air hits me.

"Good morning, Cuervo." I kiss the top of his head, and he preens and sways from side to side. "You're so flirtatious today."

"Treasure safe," he reports, as if he clearly understands how important this knowledge is to me.

"Thank you, friend."

Cuervo jumps off the railing and flies away. He looks like a bird with a purpose, and I feel a bit jilted by his abrupt departure—not that I can blame him. I have been too busy to pay much attention to him. Before all of this started, I used to spend a lot of time with him, exploring the city, playing, and feeding him. Now, I wouldn't get to see him if it weren't for his morning visits, however short.

Hoping I can make time for him soon, I take a quick bath and dress in black leggings and a gold-embroidered burgundy tunic. They are the nicest set I own, formal enough for a council meeting. I finish the look with a tight braid.

After much thinking about what I should do to help Amira, I decided it's time to stop skirting my duties, even the most loathsome ones. I had hoped to live a carefree life, where I only had myself to worry about. I never wanted to be responsible for the welfare of others. An obstinate bird was as far as I was willing to go, but just as my sister's future looks nothing like what I imagined, mine is morphing as well. I don't like it, though my decision to take up my spot in the council as Father always wanted is not entirely selfless. If I'm able to put Amira's life back on the right path, perhaps mine will be set straight, too.

Walking with purpose, I leave my bedchamber. Yesterday, I checked the schedule and know there will be a meeting in one hour. This gives me enough time to visit Nana and enjoy breakfast by her side, next to the warm hearth in her bedchamber.

Like usual, she's up early, warming her old bones by the fire. Today, there's a cart topped with hot tea and honeyed rolls next to her rocking chair. Depending on how she feels every morning, she makes her way to her favorite dining hall by the kitchen or requests breakfast in her room. Today, it seems, her joints aren't cooperating, and she's staying in.

There are extra teacups and rolls on the cart—enough for four. Amira, Jago, and I visit her whenever possible, especially around mealtime, and she ensures there's always enough food for everyone.

After kissing the top of her head, I serve myself tea and sweeten it with three sugar cubes, then place a roll on a small saucer and sit across from her. She smiles at me and sips from her cup, rocking gently.

"You look smart this morning." She scans me, focusing on my polished black boots. "There isn't even mud on your soles."

I take a large bite of my roll and mumble, "I'm attending a council meeting this morning."

She sets her teacup down. "Did I understand you correctly, dear? Council meeting, you said?"

I nod.

Calmly, she sets the teacup back on the cart, pondering the news. By her confused expression, I assume that Amira's plan to confine the fae hasn't reached her ears.

"Amira is trying to do something I don't agree with," I say.

"Child, are you sure it is wise to oppose your sister? She's only beginning to get her sea legs as queen. She will not appreciate her younger sister undermining her authority."

I'm glad for Nana's immediate disapproval. Now I know exactly why I came here this morning. I need her opinion, her judgment. She'll be my guiding force today. If she still thinks I'm wrong after I tell her what Amira is planning, I will relent.

Choosing my words carefully, I say, "She has changed much

lately, Nana. Sometimes, I don't recognize her. Father's untimely death was a huge blow to her, and I think the attack from Orys Kelakian warped her perception of the fae."

Nana doesn't interrupt. She simply nods, encouraging me to continue, so I do.

"Because of this, she has developed a plan to *relocate* the fae. This is what she calls it, but in truth, her plan means their extrication from society and their imprisonment behind secure walls."

As she takes everything in, her gaze drifts to the burning logs in the fireplace. She twists her hands together, rubbing her aching knuckles, and as she digests my words, her expression slowly shifts, inviting deep grooves of worry to her forehead.

After a long moment, her rheumy eyes meet mine again. "She must indeed be tremendously changed if this is her plan. I haven't seen her but a couple of times since your father died. I must admit she seemed haunted, but I attributed it to the demands of her new role. You're not in an easy position, Valeria, but I certainly understand your desire to act now. We must fight to uphold our values, and I know well what yours are."

"You and Mother always taught us to respect everyone, to treat all as equals, no matter their race or creed. Why has Amira forgotten that?"

"Perhaps she hasn't," Nana says hopefully. "Perhaps all she needs is a reminder. Have you tried talking to her in private?"

"I have. More than once."

"I guessed that much." She shakes her head.

"She refuses to listen, Nana. She's hurting so much, and she keeps pushing me away. I don't want to oppose her in front of everyone, but I don't know what else to do."

"It seems to me you're at a difficult crossroads, mi niña. All I can advise you to do is to follow your heart."

Does listening to my heart mean the same as listening to my gut? I wonder as I make my way to the council meeting. If it does, that means that Father's advice would be the same as Nana's, and I should completely ignore the nauseous feeling in the pit of my stomach.

When I get to the double doors leading to the meeting, I stop and take a deep breath.

Gods, help me!

I push the door open and walk in. Several faces turn in my direction, each one expressing surprise. Inclining my head in greeting, I move further into the room. Amira isn't here yet, but I find my way to the head of the table, where a chair larger and more elaborate than the rest presides.

When Amira and I attended with Father, she sat to his right and I to his left. There aren't any additional chairs next to the leading seat anymore, but an attendant standing in the back of the room quickly finds one and sets it to the right of my sister's, sparing me the embarrassment of appearing clueless and out of place.

Sara shoots me a glower from across the table. She's not the only one. Ministro Flores and Ministro Covarrubias do too. The rest seem indifferent, and only Ministra Eva Aquina, the minister of war, offers me a welcoming smile. She was one of Mother's few friends. We used to see her often when we were little, but not so much after Mother's death. The Ministra and Father never seemed to see eye to eye on most important policies.

I don't take a seat. Instead, I stand next to my chair and wait for Amira to arrive. When she does, it doesn't take long for her to notice me. Her expression hardens, and it's obvious she knows why I'm here.

"Your Majesty," all murmur as they stand and nod their heads in greeting while she makes her way to the head of the table.

She stands in front of her chair, and the attendant pushes it in when she takes a seat. Everyone else sits down, including me.

Taking advantage of the rustle of chairs and clothes, she hisses out of the corner of her mouth, "What are you doing here?"

"Trying to help you avoid making the biggest mistake of your life."

She turns to face me and leans closer. "Have you stopped to think it is you who is making a mistake?"

I blow air through my nose and smile sadly. "Trust me, I have. I don't want to do this. Please reconsider."

"Oh, Valeria, always so naïve." Calmly, she straightens and sets her hands flat on the table. "The main topic of our agenda pertains to *The Haderia*."

What? They even have a name for it? *Hada* means fairy in our old language, so Haderia would mean a place where fairies live, or in this case . . . a place where they're *kept*. They can't be serious.

"Every proposal has been presented," she continues, "including financial information of how the project will be funded. I trust you have read each page and every painstaking detail I've put together with the help of some of you. Are there any questions?"

Everyone has a stack of documents in front of them, except me. I realize how woefully unprepared I am, but I have a feeling Amira wouldn't have facilitated a copy for me if I'd asked beforehand.

Ministra Aquina is leafing through the pages, wearing a frown. "I have a question as a matter of fact."

"Why am I not surprised?" Sara says, her mouth twisted to one side.

The Ministra ignores her. "Funds from our efforts against Los Moros in the south are being diverged into this ... unnecessary endeavor."

So she is against the project. I wonder who else. My gaze travels quickly around the table, trying to judge everyone's mood. Some are hard to read, while others like Sara are nothing but open books.

Amira opens her mouth to speak, but Sara puts a hand up and demurely asks for permission to speak. Amira grants it.

"Our alliance in the south isn't as precarious as we believed it to be only yesterday. Other members of the family may not care or be willing to make sacrifices for Castella, but I'm certainly not one of them." Her gray eyes flash in my direction for a split second. "I have secured an alliance with Don Justo Ramiro Medrano. He will continue to make his resources available in support of our sovereignty."

Oh, gods!

So Sara's ambition proves greater than her haughtiness, after all. An awful turmoil stirs in my chest, emotions clashing, the biggest one . . . apprehension. This doesn't bode well. Yet, I can't focus on their so-called alliance now. That's a problem for another day. I'm here for a different reason.

"Thank you, Sara," my sister says. "We value your . . . sacrifice."

I know Amira well, and I can tell from the tone of her voice that she realizes the danger of this partnership too. She casts a sidelong glance in my direction, and I can't tell whether she's angry at me for allowing it to happen or grateful that, for now, it facilitates her plans.

Bishop Benedicto, the religious viewpoint of the council, clears his throat. "I apologize for not being in attendance during previous meetings," he says, hands interlaced in front of him, the sleeves of his robe hanging wide. "I know I've missed much of the discussion, but I would like to take a moment to contemplate the humanitarian aspects of this project."

I sit straighter in my chair, eager to hear what he has to say.

"In the history of our proud nation," he continues, "with all due respect to Queen Amira, we have never endeavored to curtail the freedom of others."

My sister's fists tighten under the table, but she doesn't interrupt him.

The bishop goes on. "Based on the church's charitable enterprises, we estimate that there are over twenty thousand fae in Castellina alone. A holding compound for that number of people will be a challenge and will quickly become a burden to the crown."

"Bishop Benedicto," Amira says, "yes, your absence from previous meetings has certainly hindered your understanding of the council's commitment to this project. We are more than willing to confront these issues in order to guarantee the safety of our people, including all citizens, members of the court," at this, she pauses and glances toward Father's portrait on the wall, "as well as *the clergy*. It is only a matter of time before they make you their next target."

"If the financial burden isn't of concern to the council," the bishop says, "I must appeal to your sense of compassion. No good can come of this, Queen Amira. Such an action will only brew animosity between our races. Moreover, an internment camp will inevitably create harsh conditions for its residents."

The bishop is expressing my exact thoughts. Expectantly, I peer at Amira's face, hoping to see a glimpse of understanding in her eyes, but she only seems to harden her resolve.

"No harsher than what they have created for our citizens with their unwarranted attacks," she says. "They live in constant terror, always wondering if they will be next."

Bishop Benedicto presses his hands together as if in prayer. "Those attacks are perpetrated by a small number of rebellious fae, Your Majesty. The vast majority are peaceful creatures, who toil every day to feed their families and contribute to our society."

"I never took you for a batracio lover," Ministro Eliseo Flores says. He is the minister of agriculture, a man with jowls the size of beehives.

The cleric's gaze slowly swivels to Ministro Flores. "I love all creatures equally, good don."

Ministro Flores rolls his eyes upward to express his skepticism.

"We have been trying to eradicate that *small number of rebellious fae*, as you call them, for a long time," Amira says. "We thought we had succeeded in destroying them, but the attack on Biblioteca de la Reina reminded us they're unrelenting. They have regrouped and easily recruited new members. Every fae out there," she points a hand beyond the walls that surround us, "is a potential enemy of our country, a future murderer."

"Queen Amira, please. I—"

She lifts a hand. "We've heard your opinions, Bishop Benedicto, and they will be taken into account as we make our final decision. I think it's time we vote."

I sit there, my stomach in knots. Bishop Benedicto has spoken better than I ever could. He also carries the authority of the church, and Amira was unmoved by anything he said. What could I add that would help change her mind? I've already tried and failed.

But her vote isn't the only one that matters. Every minister present and every Plumanegra in attendance has to cast a vote. Maybe there's something I can say to the others that will sway them in the right direction.

"Let's proceed—" Amira starts, but I clear my throat, doing my best to control my nerves.

"I would like to address the council," I say, my voice firm despite everything.

Beside me, Amira takes a deep breath, as if trying to draw patience from the air. "Much as Bishop Benedicto, you have been absent from crucial discussions. We don't need to waste any more time dealing with those who are uninformed and unprepared."

"As a council member, I have the right to address my equals," I say, citing one of the main rules of the council, which she knows well.

She turns her hands over in a gesture of surrender, her expression signaling that it won't matter what I say. No one will change their mind. I hope she's wrong.

"We have to find another way," I say.

Bishop Benedicto has tried to appeal to our coffers and compassion, but that didn't work, so I have to try a different angle to approach the topic. I also need to wisely use what little time my sister might allow me.

"Many of the fae have espiritu," I continue. "They will find a way to escape any security measures you place around them."

Ministro Flores scoffs. "Good! Let them. Those are the ones we will take care of first."

Bishop Benedicto's eyes open wide and Condesa Juana Clavel lets out a little gasp behind her heavily ringed hand.

Amira interjects. "There aren't many who still possess those abilities, and this document," she places her hand on the many pieces of parchment stacked in front of her, "outlines procedures that will help with those eventualities, should they arise. Perhaps you should read it, Valeria."

"Yes, I haven't read it, but I still don't think it is what Castella needs," I say. "If we do this, it isn't something we can take back. A year from now, we can't say *oh, sorry, we made a mistake, go back on your merry way.* Those who don't hate us now will surely hate us then."

My eyes rove around the long table, holding everyone's gaze for an instant. I'm met with more hostility than I would like. It seems few are opposed to Amira's plan.

"If we do this, we might be committing to years upon years of oppression, a burden we may have to pass on to future generations."

I stare squarely at Amira at this. She may be willing to let hatred shape her life, but what about her children? Has she considered what their lives would be like growing up with this kind of burden?

I notice a slight tightening of her eyes, and for a moment, I think I've said the right thing, but then her expression hardens once more.

"At least," she says, "the chance that we'll be there to advise them and support them will be higher."

In those words, I perceive the brunt of her pain, the fierce way she misses Father. And for the first time, I realize that she must mourn him far more deeply than I do. It's not that our love for him is not the same. It's that ever since Amira was old enough to sit still and listen, she was by his side. It was her duty to learn and grow into the ruler Castella needed. Wherever Father was, Amira could be found, taking notes, whispering reminders in his ear, sharing meals and tea breaks, laughing at a joke only they understood.

Then one day, she woke up from a nightmare of Orys's making and found Father gone, unable to offer the advice and support she now needs.

Desperately holding on to my last bit of hope, I glance around the table once more. I perceive no change in anyone. I've done too little . . . too late.

"Now that you've had your say," Amira smiles condescendingly, "may we proceed?"

I sit back down, defeated.

Even before the votes are tallied, I know the result. What I didn't count on was the weak opposition the council offered.

There were only four votes against Amira's proposal, and it's obvious who casted: Bishop Benedicto, Ministra Aquina, Condesa Clavel, and me.

Gods! How did we get here?

Perhaps this was the way it would always turn out. Perhaps two fundamentally different races living in harmony is an impossibility. Our differences were never meant to be surmounted. Compromise was never an option. Clearly, I've been fighting the wrong battle, and there is only one solution.

The fae must return to Tirnanog.

22

VALERIA

"The wind of fate blows all ships, but the captain steers his own course."

Old Castellan Proverb

As we leave the council room, Amira grabs me by the elbow and pulls me aside. She waits for everyone to walk out of earshot then hisses in my face.

"How dare you oppose me so publicly?" she demands. "We talked about this, and you knew my position well."

"I'm sorry, Amira, but I felt it was my responsibility to speak my mind."

"For what little good it did. All you've managed to do is let everyone know you don't stand with me. I thought we could do this together. I thought we could be a family, but since Mother died, you always set yourself apart from Father and me. You always stood on the wrong side of who we are."

I yank my elbow from her grasp. "Who we are?" My chest starts heaving. "There are no sides."

"Of course there are. You live in Castella, not Tirnanog.

Mother filled your head with nonsense. That realm is out of our reach, and it will forever remain that way, so it would serve you right to embrace what is real—not some fantasy land you will never see."

I shake my head. She's wrong. I *will* see Tirnanog. I have always believed that. My every daydream growing up started with the miraculous reopening of the veil. Countless times, I imagined espiritu flowing back into Castella and reigniting the shifting skills passed down to our family from our fae ancestors. And in those dreams, Father, Amira and I conquered the sky together, black wings beating at the rhythm of our hearts, the thrill of who we really are coursing through our veins.

Amira scans my face, then snorts with forced amusement, likely seeing my hopes etched in my expression.

"You have always been a hopeless dreamer." She shakes her head and takes a few steps back. "I hope you will come around. If you want to sit by my side to help me create a better future for Castella, I will be glad to have you. I dearly hope you will reconsider your position."

Golden brown hair and olive dress whipping, Amira turns and walks away, her back straight, her steps firm. Renata waits for her down the hall and immediately pushes a stack of papers into Amira's hands, rattling instructions about the rest of the day.

I walk away, temples pounding, feeling the weight of my responsibilities pressing down on me like an anvil atop my head. Amira already sees my dissent as a betrayal. What will she think when she finds out I've taken The Eldrystone?

Of their own accord, my feet veer in an unintentional direction, and I find I'm heading toward Nana's bedchamber once more. She's still in her rocking chair, needles in hand, attempting to knit.

"What are you doing, Nana?" I ask. "You know that isn't good for your hands."

She sets her work down on her lap and looks up. "Two visits in one day. I would say I'm glad, if not because I know the circumstances."

I sit across from her and stare at the gray ball of yarn on the floor. She taught me to knit while Mother passed down her embroidery skills.

"I'm making some mittens for Jago," she says. I know what she's doing: using small talk to get me to calm down and open up to her. She knows me so well.

"You shouldn't be," I say. "Your hands will hurt tomorrow."

"They always hurt, niña. But not to worry, I'm taking my time. I started this a month ago, and I'm yet to complete the first one." She laughs at herself, glancing down at her knobby fingers and flexing them a few times.

In one of my many daydreams involving Tirnanog, I find a powerful healer who uses their espiritu to alleviate Nana's pain and maybe even cure her—not to mention help her live forever.

"Why can Amira only think negatively?" I find myself asking.

Nana narrows her brown eyes. "Negatively, you say?"

I nod.

"I don't think that's exactly what I would call it. Perhaps I would use a different word like . . . vigilantly."

A frown cuts across my forehead at this.

"You see," Nana goes on, "she's like a parent now, and the citizens of Castella are her children."

I have no idea where she's going with this.

"You can't deny that there are dangers in the realm—many of which can enter our path. The way children travel down the road is often careless, oblivious to strife and injury. Therefore, it's a parent's job to foresee these things for them. Hold them back before they fall into a pit. Pull their little hands away if they mean to touch the flame. Keep them from the morsel of food that might choke them. It's only by anticipating what may happen that parents keep their children safe from harm."

"I understand your analogy, Nana. I really do. But Amira is Castella's Queen, not her mother. And its citizens aren't her children."

"That may be so, but that doesn't mean she doesn't feel protective of them, that doesn't mean she isn't trying to clear the path for them so they can live safe lives."

"But what if she's wrong?"

Nana inclines her head to one side. "I didn't say she was right, my dear. I was simply trying to explain what might be driving her decisions, her negativity as you call it."

"So you believe she's wrong," I ask hopefully.

"I didn't say that either."

My shoulders slump. Sometimes talking to Nana can be exhausting.

"I'm afraid, in this instance, only time will tell."

"What if . . ." I don't know how to ask this question, so I stop and stare at the floor.

Nana waits patiently for my thoughts to take shape. They don't. I'm afraid to reveal my intentions to anyone. And what if she tells Amira?

Her rocker creaks as she begins to move gently back and forth. She picks up her knitting again, and the needles click together, a sound that I find soothing for some odd reason.

I think of the patter of rain, of sitting quietly waiting for the sun to drive away the gloomy weather—Mother, Nana, Amira, and I sitting by a cozy fire, all of our heads down, working on one project or another, the progress slow but deeply satisfying. I remember waiting for the rain to ebb, so I could go outside and play. Now, I long for nothing more than one of those afternoons with them.

"Do you think there's such a thing as fate?" The question springs from my mouth fully formed, but uninvited.

"Do you?" she asks back.

"Um . . . I don't know."

"What does your heart tell you?"

Leave it to Nana to throw my question back at me. I shrug. My heart, my gut, my brain . . . they all seem useless at the moment. I have no idea what to do.

"Well?" she presses.

I shake my head forcefully. "I really have no idea."

She finally sets aside her work for good, placing it inside a woven basket sitting next to her chair. "I think it's nonsense," she answers, surprising me.

I peer at her curiously, waiting for more.

"Why would the saints put us in this realm so we can follow a path they already chose for us? It would only make for boredom for everyone, don't you think?"

I smile despite myself. She's only joking—not taking me

seriously. I can't blame her. She's probably not in the mood for such a conversation. For a long while, Nana's only pursuits have been peace and quiet. Her own words, not mine.

She winks. "Do you want to know what I truly believe?"

I nod.

"I think fate does govern the lives of some, though not all. But for certain individuals, it is destiny that matters."

"Aren't they the same thing?" I frown, never having given much thought to the difference between the two.

She shakes her head. "Destiny is what we make of ourselves—not what someone else decides for us. A person with a purpose shapes their own path, taking actions that bend the trail toward their goal, their vision. However misguided your sister might be, she's trying to shape Castella into what she thinks will be a better place."

"But she isn't only crafting her own destiny. She will affect so many people."

"Those affected by her decisions believe it is their fate, and there lies the difference."

I push to the edge of the armchair. "The fae don't have a choice, Nana."

"There is always a choice."

"I'm sorry. I'm not sure I believe that."

"Perhaps because you anticipate a choice between good and evil, but reality isn't always so clear cut. At times, our options are limited to the unfavorable, the extremely unfavorable, or the downright dreadful. Nonetheless, the choice remains."

"What would be their other choice? Death? They're already exiled, for all the gods' sake! That isn't fair."

"I believe your father schooled you well on the fact that life and fairness are mutually exclusive."

Indeed, he used those exact words. He said them often enough that even Nana can quote him.

"I believe *you* have a choice to make," she says.

I blink, looking up at her and wondering if she suspects what the choice is. Her gaze pierces mine so intensely that I feel as naked and vulnerable as a babe. And even though her lips remain sealed, I sense her unspoken words echoing in the air.

"Now, niña, will you be ruled by fate? Or will you forge your own destiny?"

23

VALERIA

*"They think I'm greedy because I want gold.
I want gold because I have none at all."*

Esmeralda Malla – Romani Healer – 21 AV

My steps are firm and purposeful as I make my way to my bedchamber, the plan that has been brewing inside my head quickly refining itself.

"At times, our options are limited to the unfavorable, the extremely unfavorable, or the downright dreadful. Nonetheless, the choice remains," Nana said.

There is no doubt in my mind that Amira's choice fits the last category, and I can't let that be the fate she dictates for those less fortunate. She will bend the fae to her twisted vision because their choices are few and all bad, but mine show a glimmer of hope, and I now understand I must act because I'm fortunate to have a better choice than they do.

In my bedchamber, I swiftly gather a rucksack with warm clothes and a few supplies. I hide it under the bed, then go in search of Jago. I find him only moments later, turning the corner down the hall and heading in my direction.

"There you are. Been looking for you," he says.

"I was with Nana. I need to talk to you."

He stops in front of me. "Esmeralda and Gaspar are here. I finally tracked them down."

I had forgotten he was still trying to locate them.

"That was no easy task," he continues. "They moved their settlement, and the troop was getting ready to leave Castellina. Caught them just in time."

I hesitate for a moment, thinking I should let Amira talk to them while I handle my own plan, but in the back of my mind, something locks into place.

"Where are they?" I ask urgently.

"In one of the waiting rooms in the central building."

"Who saw them come in?"

Jago frowns. "Just a few guards."

"Good."

He cocks his head. "Um . . . why?"

"There's a slight change of plans." I grab his arm, whirl him around, and start walking back toward my bedchamber.

"And by slight, I take it you mean major." He gives me a raised eyebrow in question.

I say nothing.

"Vaaal?" He stretches out my name, begging for an answer.

"You know me too well."

He throws his head back and groans. "Bugger me sideways! I knew the peace couldn't last. What now? Do we leap off the battlements and hope we finally can shift and fly? Or do we steal the crown?"

I slapped his arm. "Don't even talk about that."

He puts his hands up. "So what is it then?"

"I can't tell you right now."

"Great." He slaps both hands to his cheeks and drags them down, looking as if he's done with life altogether. "Now I'm really afraid."

"You have a choice as always," I say.

"No, I don't."

"Yes, you do. You can craft your own destiny. I'm sorry if I made you a victim of mine."

"A victim?" He narrows his eyes. "Didn't you say you were just talking to Nana?"

"I did."

"Figures. Don't let that old crone get inside your head," he warns. "She may look like a sweet doña, but she has some strange philosophies like that one about fate and destiny. I've heard it before. '*Give purpose to your life and shape your destiny, or succumb to fate's whims*'," he says in a high-pitched tone meant to sound like Nana. "*Pshaw*, I'm not a victim of your destiny. If anything . . . I'm part of it." He looks around. "Where are we going, anyway?"

"Back to my bedchamber?"

"Why?"

"I need currency."

He thinks for a moment, then makes a face, indicating he has an idea of what I intend to do with said currency.

After visiting my bedchamber, we hasten back to the waiting

room where Jago left Esmeralda and Gaspar. Following a slight knock on the door, we walk in and find Esmeralda standing in front of a large tapestry hanging from the wall. It depicts a battle-ready regiment beneath a graying sky.

Esmeralda and Gaspar look out of place in the austere room, their vibrant traditional garb clashing against the muted backdrop. But despite the contrast, they exude an air of dignity and grace, their presence a reminder of the rich world outside these walls.

Esmeralda's fierce green eyes scan me up and down. "Glad to see you have recovered, *princess*."

I thank her despite the antagonizing tone of her voice at the last word. Gaspar is more respectful, inclining his head and offering a soft greeting.

Matching his deference, I also incline my head, then walk closer and offer him my hand. He looks at it hesitantly for a moment, but in the end, he takes it. I cover it with my other hand and look him straight in the eyes.

"I want to thank you for your help in the catacombs," I say.

At the mention of the catacombs, an image of damp walls flashes before my eyes, and a sharp scream echoes in my ears. I take a deep breath, pushing the memories away. It takes effort to keep them at bay, but I won't allow them to grow and fester. I need to focus. I can't let anything distract me.

"It was the least I could do for a . . . friend," Gaspar, El Gran Místico, says.

"Oh, please," Esmeralda tosses her black curly hair behind her shoulder, her large array of bracelets tinkling. "We got offered money to find her. She's not our friend."

I turn to the Romani woman. "Which you did not take, I'm told."

She shrugs as if it means nothing.

"I believe it's only fair that you should be compensated for your efforts," I say, "and such compensation wouldn't preclude friendship, I assure you. I have much to thank you for. Twice, you have helped me."

"Once, I have betrayed you," Esmeralda replies.

From the way she's looking at me, I can tell she's remembering sitting inside that cell, the day I intended to make her pay for said betrayal. She was contrite then, but she is back to her feisty self.

Danger lurks. Ready yourself," she said to me—a warning from Gaspar that matched Bastien's . . . Rifíor's, and that presaged Orys's attack.

"All's well that ends well," I say.

"Is it?" she asks, eyes flicking toward Gaspar.

"Pardon me, princess," the bearded Romani says, "but I sense not all is well."

Of course he does. Perhaps his cards told him things are about to change. Perhaps that is why their troop is leaving Castellina.

"Your *perception* proves right once again, El Gran Místico," I say.

Jago clears his throat and glares at me, the question *what are you doing?* stamped all over his face. I give him a slight nod to indicate I know what I'm doing. He frowns and shakes his head in disagreement. Still, I decide to confide in them.

"We need your help," I say.

Gaspar's expression hardens.

One of Esmeralda's dark eyebrows goes up, betraying her interest. "What is it this time?"

Placing a hand around Esmeralda's elbow, Gaspar starts guiding her out of the room. "Your cousin said something about thanking us for our help. We consider ourselves thanked. Now, we have to be on our way. The troop's heading north, lots of dirt to kick on our first day. C'mon, Esmeralda."

"Please, hear me out," I beseech them.

Gaspar shakes his head, his mind made up. But to my relief, Esmeralda pulls out of his grasp, digging in her heels.

"I want to hear what this is all about," she says.

"Trust me, chavé, you don't. Let's get outta here." Gaspar attempts to grab her again, but Esmeralda takes a step out of reach.

"No harm done in lending an ear," she argues.

The man sighs heavily, looking resigned. Esmeralda is stubborn and willful. I learned that much after interacting with her for only a few days. It seems Gaspar has experienced a lifetime of her obstinacy, however, and he knows when fighting is futile.

"Well . . ." she places a hand on her waist and juts her hip out, "we're waiting."

I offer her a smile, then another one to Gaspar, who I fear will need more convincing. "Jago, me, and a . . . companion would like to join you in your travels. However, we would like you to head west."

"Wait, what?!" Jago demands. "What companion? You don't mean—?"

I cut him off with a glare.

Gaspar and Esmeralda exchange a glance. Jago makes a

restrained sound in the back of his throat. His lips are pressed tightly together as if he is fighting very hard not to say anything else, but in the end, he loses the battle.

"Val, would you mind stepping outside for a moment, so we can discuss this in private?" He gestures toward the door.

"No, Jago," I say. "There's nothing to discuss. My mind is made up. I've thought about it carefully."

"But—"

"It's all right. Remember you always have a choice."

He rolls his eyes but relents.

"Sorry, Princess Valeria," Gaspar says, "but our lot never goes west. It isn't worth the trouble." He turns to Esmeralda, who makes a face, mouth twisted to one side and nose scrunched up, making it clear that west is definitely not her preferred route.

"Ready to go now?" Gaspar asks her.

"I'll make it worth your while," I blurt out, taking a hold of the leather bag attached to my belt. Its contents clink together, leaving no doubt as to their valuable nature.

Gaspar shakes his head. "No disrespect, princess, but our plans are set in stone. There's no changing them."

Esmeralda laughs. "Set in stone? We're Romani, old man. You think she's going to believe that?"

"Hush, chavé! I'm trying to save our hides here," Gaspar's voice is several octaves deeper, the perfect timbre for scolding one's child. Father used a similar tone with me many times. My heart aches a little at the thought.

"Stop calling me *child*," she protests, then asks, "Save our hides from what? Traveling on dirt roads? It's what we do."

"Don't be such a fool! Why don't you ask her why we need to head west? Or, more importantly, who is this *companion* she's dragging along, huh?"

Esmeralda turns her fierce gaze on me, expecting an answer to Gaspar's questions.

I know I can't expect them to help me and change their plans without an explanation, but that doesn't mean I want to tell them everything—not to mention that revealing my plan is dangerous. They could go straight to my sister and tell her what I intend to do in exchange for a bigger bag of gold and no risk to their lives, still I have to be clear, make sure they understand the perils involved.

"What I intend to do constitutes treason," I say.

Both Jago and Gaspar grab their heads in unison and look up at the heavens—the former looks vexed by my straightforwardness, and the latter outright horrified. Their synchronized movements would be funny under other circumstances, but at the moment, I couldn't muster a laugh if my life depended on it.

"Treason?" Esmeralda echoes. "The kind that sets Castellina's Guardia on your tail? Is that it? You're crazy, princess. In case you haven't noticed, we're into surviving. You were right, old man. Let's get out of here."

They start toward the door, but I step in front of them. "Please, allow me to explain. After that, you can decide whether or not to help me." They hesitate long enough for me to entreat them a little further. "Sit down. It's a lengthy conversation. I can have some tea and pastries brought in." I rush to the cord hanging in the corner and pull on it, then nod to Jago to help me take care of the refreshments.

Almost immediately, there is a knock at the door, and my cousin takes care of giving instructions to the servant without letting them in. In a matter of minutes, tea and pastries are set on the long, low table in between the sofa and two armchairs where Jago and I sit. Esmeralda and Gaspar have taken their place across from us on the sofa, and despite their reservations about what I'm about to tell them, they're not being shy about the treats in front of them.

"These are really good," Esmeralda mumbles through a mouthful of honey and walnut buns.

Jago nods. "Yes! They're my favorite. I like them with extra honey."

"Umm, I love honey." Her lips glisten with the sticky substance, leaving no doubt in anyone's mind that she actually does.

For his part, Gaspar seems to prefer the savory empanadas, and in no time, he's on his second cup of tea, a heavy dash of cream mixed with it.

In hopes their nerves will ease, I let them enjoy everything and try to wait until they've had their fill to begin talking. However, the day is wearing on, and I intend to get out of Nido today. The more time I wait, the more likely Amira is to discover The Eldrystone is missing.

As I explain everything about the Haderia, Esmeralda and Gaspar listen without interruption. I begin by describing what my sister intends to do with the fae. I tell them I tried to stop her, but that the council voted for her idea almost unanimously. I make it clear that there is no stopping this from becoming a reality.

"That's absolutely horrifying," Esmeralda declares, "but what does it have to do with us? We're Romani, not fae. We're citizens of Castella, not foreigners."

Gaspar shakes his head and looks sadly in Esmeralda's direction. "Oh, chavé, I know you're smarter than that." Without offering her further clarification, he shifts his attention to me, narrowing his eyes. "You say your sister and all her people want to do this."

I nod.

"And going west with your *companion* will help? You're not just running off?"

"For me, running away stopped being an option a long time ago," I answer.

Before Father died, fleeing my life in Nido had seemed like the only way to be happy. Now, the world Amira promises to create doesn't even seem like the type of place where anyone would be able to find joy. If I'm ever to live the life I want, I have to fix this first.

"I still don't see how any of this has anything to do with us," Esmeralda complains. "Your sister wants to fuck with the fae? She can have at it. The veilfallen brought that on themselves. Us?" she turns to Gaspar, "I say we hurry back and get out of this accursed city. We've wasted enough time here."

Gaspar doesn't move even as Esmeralda stands and glares at him. Instead, he begins to explain what he and I both see very clearly.

"It'll begin with the fae, but it won't end there. At first, they'll check for pointy ears. Long as ya got them, they won't give a fig if you're Castellan or some foreigner. But once they've rounded them all up, who's to say they won't look further. I'm a quarter fae and have a bit of espiritu in me. Most Romani are mixed. No, chavé, this has *everything* to do with us."

"So what are you saying? That they'll come after us next? That's ridiculous," Esmeralda protests. "How will they prove any of it?"

"When has proof been needed to find us guilty of anything?" he asks.

A pang of shame travels across my chest. I've never done any Romani harm, not directly, but I guess that doesn't matter when, in my privilege, I would always receive the benefit of the doubt, and they would be condemned without question.

Next to me, Jago also appears chagrined by the implication.

"You can't be serious?" Esmeralda points a finger directly at me. "She's a half-fae. Same as the queen. It would be hypocrisy."

"It's often the ones with the dirty hands pointing fingers," Gaspar says. "The scales of justice tip unevenly for the Plumanegras and their likes. Absence of proof is enough to damn us while evidence sets them free."

"Hey!" Jago pushes to the edge of the armchair.

I place a hand on his knee to calm him down. "He's not wrong, cousin. Not in this instance."

Jago is red in the face, ready to defend our honor. "We're not criminals." The words are a hiss between the cage of his teeth.

"Can you attest for every damn royal?" Gaspar asks.

"Of course not! I'm responsible for myself only, so don't lump me in with everyone else."

Gaspar shrugs. "Fair enough, but I still doubt you'd spend a day inside that Haderia if it came to it."

Jago opens his mouth to keep arguing, but I intervene.

"That's enough. We don't have time for this. We have to act. Tonight. Please help us."

"You've got nerve to ask us for help," Esmeralda says. "You two live right here with her. Stop her."

I sigh, suddenly feeling exhausted. "Like I said, I tried, but she's determined."

"Try again."

"That path is closed to me now." I really would like the Romani's help, but I'm doing this with or without them.

"We best get moving, Gaspar." Esmeralda tugs on his sleeve. "The further we are when this mess kicks off, the safer we'll be."

Gaspar doesn't budge.

I take the money bag and spill its contents on the table. The coins spread over the surface, clinking and sliding over the smooth wood. A few of them fall to the floor and glitter on the dark rug.

Esmeralda's eyes grow wide, her pupils shrinking to pinpricks in a sea of green. She sits back heavily, looking defeated, the sight of gold eclipsing all of her concerns as I anticipated. Her mother's health is poor, and Esmeralda is responsible for taking care of her. Of course coin can be used to manipulate her. I feel low for doing it, but I'm desperate.

"You've told us why you want us to help you, and maybe there's more than just gold that makes it worth our while," Gaspar says. "But if we're to help you, you need to tell us everything."

I was hoping the why and the gold would be enough. I fear that if I say more, they'll run out the door. But I suppose I have no other choice.

Swallowing my doubts, I nod. "You must promise me not to tell anyone what I'm about to say."

"Promise," they both say in unison.

Jago looks at me sideways, his expression asking, *Can you really trust their word?*

The answer is *no*. The truth is I wouldn't trust anyone with this information. If I'm being honest, I'm only ready to tell them because if they don't agree to help us, my only choice will be to leave them locked up in a cell with orders to release them only after we have left Nido without their help.

"I have a way to open the veil," I say without further preamble.

They both blink and comically cock their heads to one side.

"Truly?" Gaspar asks.

I nod.

"And what is that?"

"I'm afraid I cannot share that information," I say.

He's quiet for a moment, considering. At last, he says, "You talked about a companion, one other person besides yourself, who is it?" he demands in a tone that lets me know our conversation is over if I don't reveal the identity of the third person.

I come clean. "The leader of the veilfallen, Ríffor."

"Saints and feathers, no!" Esmeralda exclaims. "You really are crazy."

Gaspar leans back on the sofa, his eyelids opening and closing at a fast rate.

"What's wrong with him?" Jago asks.

Esmeralda presses a finger to her lips and mouths something unintelligible. The fit passes so quickly that I almost dismiss it.

She places a hand on his shoulder. "What is it? What did you see?"

The man shakes his head, his face draining of color.

"What is it?" Esmeralda insists.

"That male is dangerous," Gaspar says at last. "But . . ." He trails off, looking confused.

Esmeralda peers at me as if I'm the stupidest person she's ever met. "Didn't we just get you out of that mess? And now you want to get tangled up with him again? You must have a death wish." She turns back to her friend. "Gaspar, we better steer clear of this. Even with the gold, this smells bad."

"There are many forces at play, chavé," he says. "I can't see straight, but I got a feeling if we don't help, this won't turn out well for no one."

"Danger lurks. Ready yourself," those words, that message that he once delivered through Esmeralda, ring inside my head, and for some reason, his expression right now seems to carry the same dire warning. Whatever his skills told him just now was grim enough to scare him. I don't like it, even if this might turn out to be the reason they decide to help us.

"What are you saying?" Esmeralda asks. "That we're getting involved in this mad business?"

They exchange a loaded glance, then he nods slowly.

Esmeralda stands up abruptly. "Not even for another bag of gold!" she exclaims. "No, count me out."

Gaspar looks down and rubs at his temples.

"How about two more?" I ask.

"Two more?" Esmeralda looks down at the gold on the table. "Same as that one?"

"Same as that one," I answer.

"We'll do it," Gaspar says. "Lay out what you need us to do, clear as crystal."

So I do, and after I finish explaining everything, Jago and I walk them out of Nido through seldom-traveled passages to evade detection.

As we watch them walk away, Jago ruffles his hair. "I don't know about you, Val, but I think we just got majorly fucked. Three bags of gold?" He whistles. "They played us just right."

"I know, but I don't care."

"Gaspar is good at what he does, but I'm sure they're used to conning smarter people than us."

Gold doesn't matter to me. The amount I promised them will keep their troop for a number of years, and I can't regret the immense difference it will make for them. Yet, I don't believe it was all a show meant to con us.

"I believe Gaspar saw something that truly made him afraid," I say.

"Nah, don't be so naïve, Val. He's just *that* good."

"I've been around him more than you have. I've seen him do things. He warned me once before, and he was right."

He shrugs. "I suppose he's bound to be right half the time. Don't you think so?"

"For all our sakes, I hope, this time, he's wrong."

That afternoon, I spend hours in one of the libraries, reading all I can about Tirnanog and its king. A meeting with Korben Theric may lie in my future, and the more I know about him, the better.

24
VALERIA

"Would to the gods I had never met you, Saethara!"

Rifior – Veilfallen – 21 AV

Later, as I make preparations to leave, I run into Amira and Renata. Though I try to relax, I stiffen as they approach. It takes a big effort to put on a smile when we meet in the middle of the hall.

"I was told the Romani were here," my sister says. "Did they agree to help us find the veilfallen's new hiding place?"

I swallow thickly before responding. Lying to my sister doesn't come easy. "They . . . did. They'll let us know right away if they discover their location."

"Excellent. I will see you later. I have some matters to attend to." She and Renata make their way down the corridor, barely concerned with me.

I keep going and glance over my shoulder as they turn down a passage that leads to the vault. My heart skips a beat.

The vault is not the only thing in that direction, Val.

There's no reason for Amira to retrieve The Eldrystone—not when she can't wield it, not when her hand is still wrapped in a bandage. I have to repeat the same mantra several times until I believe it. I'm tempted to follow them to make sure I'm safe, but I have too much to do.

Over the next hour, I go about with my heart in my throat. I expect to see guards charging in my direction with orders from Amira to apprehend me. But once a suitable amount of time passes after our encounter, I relax. It's only then that my hands grow steady as I gather rope, a tinderbox, and other things for our packs. It is only then that I can return to my bedchamber to go over my plan one more time.

One important piece of the puzzle is for me to talk to Cuervo and get him to understand that tonight, we will be leaving Castellina. One thing that weighs heavily on me is that Father hasn't had a proper funeral.

Forgive me, Father.

He would disapprove terribly of what I'm about to do. He would want me to stand behind my sister, no matter what. But I also know that Mother would feel differently. I have a duty to her, too. It's no easy task, but I push these worries away and focus on the path ahead.

A few times I'm tempted to ask Cuervo to retrieve the amulet, but in the end, I decide against the idea. It's too risky to carry the jewel with me as we exit Nido. We might be discovered as we make our escape, and Amira might take it back. There's also the possibility that Rífíor might see it and be tempted by it. He gave it up before, but time in a cell might have changed his mind about that.

No, I need to keep The Eldrystone away from him for as long as possible.

When I call Cuervo, he flies around in circles sweeping over Nido's battlements above me. From a distance, we must look like nothing but grains of rice atop a huge gray mountain to him. The palace's sheer size is a testament to the Plumanegra's power and wealth. It took over a century to build this place, to mine the huge rocks and transport them here, to place them atop each other and shape them into what they are now: the most massive building in the entire realm.

At last, my friend alights upon the balcony railing. His ebony feathers glisten in the fading sunlight, displaying iridescent hues of blue and purple that surpass any painter's palette. He skips from talon to talon, head bobbing.

"We travel tonight," I tell him.

We've traveled many times, so he knows what this means. His wings spread wide as he flaps them a few times. He hovers over the railing for an instant. It's his way of telling me he's excited about the news.

"Make sure to follow me," I say.

I know he'll vigilantly watch the palace's perimeter to make sure he doesn't overlook my departure.

"One more thing, Cuervo. You have to bring the treasure with you. Do you understand?"

He inclines his beak, and it touches his chest as he bows. He understands.

"But keep it safe." He can hide it when he's not flying and following us. "Safe, do you understand?"

Once more, he bows.

"You are the best of friends, Cuervo." I bow back, feeling the utmost respect for him.

Sometime after midnight, I quickly make it to the dimly illuminated steps that lead to Rífíor and, perhaps, my doom.

When I get to the bottom, I discover both guards on duty peacefully asleep, just as intended. A part of my plan entailed discreetly administering a sedative into their evening meal, a job well done by Jago. He knows the young woman responsible for distributing dinner to numerous guards throughout the palace—they had a fling at some point. Jago's role involved intercepting her en route to the dungeons and engaging her in conversation to divert her attention while he slipped the soporific into the food.

I remove the keys to the cell from the hook on the wall and walk sideways between the two slumped guards. They snore and appear content and lost in pretty dreams. I mean to keep walking with firm steps, but I come to a sudden halt, my breaths growing rapid and my heart hammering behind my ribs. I hate that the thought of seeing him makes me feel this way. I hate that I need him in order to do this. I want to leave him behind bars to rot for all his crimes, including those against me.

After a few deep breaths, I get my emotions under control and keep going. Even though I walk lightly, my steps echo across the cavernous space, surely alerting Rífíor to the presence of an untimely visitor. Yet, when I appear, he makes no attempt to glance in my direction.

He still looks like a literal statue, sitting motionless in that way that only the fae can. In the dim light, with all the colors muted, it truly appears as if he's made of stone, an imposing sculpture chiseled by a master. The sight is unnerving and sends a shiver running down my spine.

My hand is firm as I place the key to the lock, turn it, and pull the door open. Rusted hinges whine, setting my teeth on edge. In fact, my entire body is on edge. I wrap my hand around the hilt of the raven dagger at my belt.

"You're coming with me," I say.

No reaction. He simply stares at the wall across from him.

I know I have to say something to shock him out of his stupor, something to rattle what he thinks he knows. Otherwise, we'll sit here all night.

"I need your help to reopen the veil." I speak the words quickly, enunciating every syllable to make sure he hears me correctly.

I wasn't wrong. I get a reaction right away. His head turns slowly, the surprise in his expression undeniable.

Moving like a mountain waking up from a dream, he rises to his feet and takes two long steps to the threshold. There, he stops, his inscrutable black eyes fixed on mine.

First, he scans my face, and next the area around my neck. I know he's searching for The Eldrystone. I wonder if solitude has renewed his desire to possess it. Nothing in his features tells me one way or the other.

"Why?" he asks simply, his deep voice a rumble that skitters over my skin and makes me think of whispered words . . .

Lies.

"I don't have time to discuss that," I say. "All you need to do is come with me." I extend a hand, inviting him to walk down the hall.

He glances in that direction, and I look at his profile. It's made of sharp dark shadows and cruelty. Slowly, he turns to look at me to appraise me once more. His nostrils flare as a million thoughts seem to cross behind the barrier of his eyes. I can't fathom any of them. He's worse than a blank canvas. He's the deep darkness between the stars. Unreadable.

After a moment's thought, he says, "You really intend to do this."

It's a statement, not a question, so I offer him no reply. If he remembers anything about me, I hope his memories are of a woman who isn't afraid to act when necessary.

He stands there a little longer, and I want to ask him if he thinks it'll be possible to reopen the veil, but I hold the words back. If he says it is, I won't believe him, anyway. That's the only answer that will get him out of here, after all, so he might lie in order to go free. Even with that knowledge, however, I know I would embark on this journey and hold on to whatever hope he offers me. Any kind of hope is better than the nightmare in Amira's plans.

With a flick of his eyes, he glances down at the dagger and my hand wrapped around its hilt. Not too long ago, he and I fought on Nido's rooftop, and I bested him. The difference was he was pretending to be human. Now that I know he's Fae, that he's Rífíor of the Veilfallen, I realize I wouldn't stand a chance against his speed. The threat of my weapon means nothing. If I take him on this journey, it won't be at the point of a dagger. He'll come of his own accord and do everything in his power to make my goal a reality. Returning to Tirnanog is what he wants most in the world, after all.

I let my hand drop, and I would be lying if I said I don't feel as vulnerable as a child in front of a rabid wolf.

One of his dark, perfect eyebrows goes up as he stares at my now-empty fingers. Without blinking, I lift my chin to show him I'm not afraid of him. Yes, I know he would best me in a fight, but I wouldn't shy away. I would make sure to leave my mark—maybe one to match the scar in his right eye.

"As I told you, I didn't close the veil. Your mother did," he says, "so I don't exactly know how to reopen it."

Something about the evenness of his tone makes it sound like the truth, but that only means he's a good liar. The best.

"But The Eldrystone can be used to reconnect our realms, correct?" I ask.

He nods without hesitation, a lock of midnight black hair falling forward. "Yes."

"And you know exactly where to go?"

"Yes."

"Then we must go. Here," I remove the cloak I'm wearing, "put this on and let's get out of here."

"What made you change your mind?"

"Like I said . . . no time for explanations."

He hesitates, and for a moment, I think he might remain at the threshold, unsure and maybe even afraid. But at last, he takes the cloak, throws it over his shoulders, and follows me.

Giving a cursive glance at the guards, we walk out of the dungeons. At this hour, Nido sleeps, and few walk the corridors. Those who do are guards, and we're careful to avoid them. I know the palace better than anyone, so it's easy to find the right hiding spot to escape their notice.

We're in the process of crossing a wide vestibule into the west wing when Rífíor suddenly stops, cocking his head to one side and listening.

"What is it?" I ask.

"Steps. Many."

His fae hearing is sharper than mine, but it only takes a couple of beats for me to notice what he's talking about.

Shit!

So many marching steps—which I immediately recognize as the Guardia Real—aren't common at this time of night. Someone, or more precisely, numerous someones are headed in our direction.

25
VALERIA

"La Matadora is yours now, son. See that you kill many enemies with its sharp blade."

Rey Vicente Plumanegra (Casa Plumanegra) – King of Castella – 1981 BV

We stand frozen under the gently swaying banners that hang high above us. The vestibule is open, with balconies running all around it on the second level. It's a wide-open area, the worst possible place to get caught. There is nowhere to hide. Our only hope is to slide behind one of the columns that hold up the balconies.

"Here!" I urge Rífíor.

As I slip behind the thick pillar, I stand sideways and make sure to stay out of sight of the approaching steps. A moment later, Rífíor stands directly behind me, so close that I can feel his warmth. I stiffen, feeling a heated blush go up my neck.

As the guards move across the vestibule, I take small steps forward, rounding the column to make sure we remain hidden. The entire time Rífíor is right behind me, matching my movements.

I feel his breath near my ear, and I want to scream. This proximity is painful, a reminder of all his lies and the way he used me.

It seems like forever before the guards pass and move on. I'm about to step out of our hiding place when Rífíor takes hold of my waist and yanks me back, and I end up flush against his torso, his long fingers circling my waist.

For an instant, I'm confused and think of Bastien pulling me tightly against him, wanting something I can't give him. But when I hear more steps accompanied by my sister's voice, I realize there's more than the guards to worry about.

"Why would she take the amulet, Renata?" Amira asks in a pained tone. "What does she intend to do with it? By the saints! I never thought she would betray me like this."

"She's only misguided, Your Majesty," Renata says. "I'm sure she thinks she's doing the right thing."

"No. We talked about this. She knows what going against me means."

Her words cut me deep. I don't mean to betray her. I mean to save her from making a terrible mistake. I only want what's best for her and Castella. I don't want her throne, which is what she seems to be implying.

I take a step forward without even thinking. I want to tell her once more what a terrible mistake she's making. Maybe if I find the right words, I will be able to change her mind this time.

Rífíor's hands tighten around my waist and keep me in place as Amira and her adviser rush across the vestibule after the guards. They're headed to my bedchamber, which they'll find empty. After that, Amira will send her guards all over Nido and

Castellina, and if we're not out of here already, Rífíor will end up back in a dungeon cell with me as company.

Once everyone is out of earshot, I jerk away from Rífíor and throw him a nasty glare over my shoulder.

"Keep your hands off me," I sneer.

He inclines his head. "As you wish, princess."

"Besides, you reek," I retort, hoping to embarrass him.

He shrugs as if it's all the same to him. "Not through any fault of my own. You really should treat your prisoners better."

I would give him a detailed list of all the ways I'd like to treat him and depriving him of a bath is the least of the nasty afflictions he should suffer. But we don't have time for that, so I hurry across the vestibule and dash down the passage from where the guards and my sister emerged.

We have to hide a few more times before we make it to the small library. We find more guards than normal rushing through the corridors, likely on their way to join the first group we encountered. Regardless, we get there unnoticed.

I hate that I have to let Rífíor know about another secret passage in Nido. We already had to seal one, and this one will have to follow the same fate. Luckily, there are others. I'll just have to safeguard their existence and location more fiercely from now on.

Reaching behind a bookcase, I retrieve the gas lamp and the two rucksacks I stashed there earlier and toss one to Rífíor. He catches it one-handed and weighs it up and down.

"Just a few supplies and coin," I say by way of explanation.

My rucksack also contains my Plumanegra key, which may come in handy to prove my identity.

Next, I pull out Father's fae-made sword: La Matadora. The blade is immune to espiritu. It's been hanging on a wall for a long time, but if I'm going to Tirnanog, it will be more useful than a rapier—even if I can't wield it as dexterously. I hang it across my back.

Frowning, he peers at La Matadora. "Where is *my* weapon?"

I shrug. "I didn't think arming you would be wise."

"I beg to disagree." He looks around the room, his dark eyes quickly alighting on a sword inside a display case. There are too many in Nido, I realize in frustration. With firm steps, he walks to it and takes it out.

Puta madre!

"This is the only type of supply I need," he says, effortlessly twirling the weapon with a mastery that seems as natural as drawing breath.

I stare at the blade warily. I should have foreseen this. I want to tell him to leave it, that it doesn't belong to him, but the sword is also fae-made, a forgotten gift one or another Plumanegra received a long time ago from our once-allies. I can only hope it'll serve us better in hand than behind glass.

"Don't worry, princess," he says with a smirk. "You are safe with me."

"As safe as I was in those catacombs?" I sneer.

"You are alive, aren't you?" He scans me up and down as if to indicate no harm came to me.

But there's harm that can't be seen, and sometimes that's the worst kind. I have managed to keep the nightmares at bay, but it's not easy. It requires constant effort and vigilance. I miss the days when I could close my eyes and drift away to sleep, surrounded by happy thoughts and memories. Now, thanks to this male, I'll never have that again. He doesn't need to know that, though. He and his damn sorceress didn't break me.

"You're an asshole, Rífíor of the Veilfallen, but I'm sure you already know that." I turn, face the bookshelf at the end of the room, and brace my hands against its sides. I push it with all my weight, but it doesn't click as it's supposed to.

Annoyed, I turn to Rífíor and say, "You do it."

With incredible ease, he pushes on it and causes the desired click. One end of the bookshelf swings open like a door, revealing a gloomy passage. I light the gas lamp and charge in, slicing the darkness in two. Rífíor sets the bookshelf back in place without me asking, leaving only the small flame to illuminate our space.

I'm reminded of going through a similar passage with Jago not so long ago. Too bad it isn't my cousin who accompanies me now. Instead, it's a male I despise, someone who might slice my throat for the fun of it.

All the questions that have been plaguing me since this plan took shape come back in earnest. What if he escapes and rejoins the veilfallen? What if he takes The Eldrystone from me? What if we fail and I make an enemy of my sister for no reason?

Shaking my head, I dismiss all those thoughts. It's too late to second-guess myself. From now on, I must be committed and do everything within my power to reach the border and open the veil.

At first, the passage is surrounded by man-made walls, but as we progress, they suddenly transition to natural stone, giving way to the caverns I know rest beneath Nido. The passage grows tight, and Rífíor has to hunch down to avoid hitting his head. Progress is sluggish as we navigate through what could easily be labeled as the palace's bowels. The passages are narrow and twisted enough to warrant such a description.

It is only thirty minutes later that the path ahead opens up, and we're able to walk unencumbered. We sit at a crossroads, and I remember well I must walk up the middle slope to reach the exit. Father drilled Amira and I many times about all the secret passages in the palace. He made sure we knew how to traverse each one of them without getting lost. It's amazing how sturdy the memories still feel inside my mind.

When we reach the end of the slope, we encounter two narrow ledges extending to our left and right. They're barely wide enough for a single adult to sidle along.

Hanging the rucksack from my neck and repositioning it to my front, I press my back to the wall and take the ledge to the left, arms out for balance. Rífíor gives me a narrowed-eyed look but doesn't question my actions. Instead, he follows, the tips of his boots protruding from the ledge by about an inch. A thirty-foot drop looms below.

I focus my gaze on the concave ceiling, determined not to think of myself broken and dead at the bottom. Slowly, I shuffle my way to a recess big enough for two. Before I can say anything, Rífíor steps into the space with me, once more pinning me against his body.

Saints and feathers! Really?

"I fear you have driven us into a dead end, princess," he says, the rumble of his voice directly behind my ear.

"I have not, and you must step back onto the ledge if you want us to get out of here."

He grunts but doesn't argue. Once he's out of the recess, I locate the footholds and handholds embedded in the wall and begin climbing up the vertical channel that extends overhead. It isn't easy to ascend while holding the gas lamp, but I manage.

Once at the top, moonlight seeps through a metal grate and fresh air whistles down the tunnel. Pressing one shoulder to the grate, I push. It takes a moment to dislodge the obstacle—it's been in place for a long time without disturbance—but eventually, it comes loose. Relieved, I push it out of the way with my free hand.

Setting the lamp outside, I climb the rest of the way and crawl to a patch of grass where I sit to catch my breath. A moment later Rífior emerges from the hole and crouches next to the lamp. Quickly, he puts it out and replaces the grate, making as little noise as possible. Tall grass surrounds us. He stretches his neck to look over it, surely to determine our position.

"We're a good distance from Nido," he points out.

"Let's keep going." I climb to my feet but remain in a crouch.

"I hope you have some sort of plan. Your sister seemed mad and is sure to send guards after *us*."

He sounds slightly amused. No doubt it delights him to find that I'm at odds with Amira.

"Shut your mouth, and follow me," I bite out the words. I have no patience for him.

Gods! If it were up to me, he wouldn't say another word until we reached the veil.

A thought occurs to me, and I smirk. Maybe some binding rope and a gag will appear in his near future—I'm the one in charge of this expedition, after all.

My smirk dies when he says, "Watch how you talk to me."

Losing my patience, I whirl on him. "Or what? You have no magic to torture me, and your friend isn't here to do your dirty work for you."

Before I realize what's happening, Ríffor is on me, using the weight of his body to push me against the trunk of a tree, caging me in.

"You're infuriating," he rumbles, his nose practically touching mine. "I should . . ."

My insides tremble with instinctual fear, and my mind offers reason to combat it . . . *He won't hurt you. He wants the veil reopened. I'm his only hope.*

But logic has no power over the gut-wrenching certainty that he'll eat me alive. He looks feral enough, his sharp fae features amplified by the shadows, his black eyes swallowing all the light, threatening to suck me in and leave me adrift in a sea of darkness.

I clench my teeth to stop my chin from quivering. I don't want to give him the satisfaction of knowing he scares the shit out of me. This bastardo's intention is to intimidate me, and I can't let him know that a mere glance and a growl in that deep voice are all it takes. No, I need to establish boundaries and make it clear that he should fear *me* instead.

"Should what?" I demand. "Beat me? No doubt you would manage wonderfully since you're a big brute. But you don't scare me."

"Are you sure about that, princess?" His gaze falls to my mouth, and quickly comes back up.

"Absolutely," I reply. "And you know why? Because I have power over you, Ríffor of the Veilfallen. Because without me, you'll never make it back to Tirnanog, and you'd still be rotting in that cell, feeling sorry for yourself. The Eldrystone burned and branded my sister, but for you, it didn't care enough to muster even a hint of espiritu. Honestly, I think Niamhara couldn't care less whether you live or die."

A growl sounds in the back of his throat, and I know I got to him. It's time to press my advantage.

"So, from now on, you'll keep your offensive presence away from mine. Five paces, at least. Is that clear? If you don't, I'll make certain you never walk across the threshold between Castella and your realm. I swear it to all the gods."

True fear—terror, even—enters his expression for a split second, but it's gone so fast I have to wonder if I imagined it, especially because when he speaks, his voice is as firm and intimidating as ever.

"You're playing with fire, Valeria Plumanegra."

"It doesn't concern me. If you're fire, then I'm water."

What? Did I really just say that? Oh, gods! That sounded as dramatic as something Emerito would have said.

"Water, huh?" he says, his teeth flashing a condescending grin. "You don't even have The Eldrystone with you right now. Is it still in the possession of that abominable bird? How can you be so careless with such power?"

I shrug. "True, so do your worst while you can. I dare you. Kill me if you will. That will only ensure you never get out of here. Hit me, and you'll ensure the same fate. Either way, lay a finger on me and see what happens." I lift my chin up, unintentionally bringing my mouth closer to his. I realize my mistake too late, but I don't back down. I'm not afraid of his physical threats, no matter their nature.

He flinches at my words. "I am not an animal, Valeria. I would never lay a finger on you. Not like that, anyway." He smiles sadly, then, very slowly, takes several paces away from me. He stops, exactly at five. "You have nothing to fear from me. As you well understand, my most ardent desire is to return to my home. In over two decades, this is the first time a real possibility has presented itself. I will not throw it away. I will make one thing clear, however, I am not your friend. I am your enemy. Do not ever forget that."

"It's you who should never forget it," I sneer. "I'm not doing this for you. There's another reason, a good reason that doesn't take into account the motivations of a selfish bastardo like you. You're only here because you're necessary. If there was anyone else who could help me, I would have left you behind, rotting away. What you have done can't be forgotten, much less forgiven. I'll forever consider you my enemy. I will forever hate you."

"Hate me all you want, little princess. It means nothing to me." He whirls on his heel, and I can't see his expression as he finishes his declaration. Maybe I imagined it, but there was a certain hitch in his voice when he said it meant nothing to him.

Perhaps there was, but either way, it doesn't change how *I* feel.

26
VALERIA

"She's still young, but I can already tell. She will be a great queen."

Rey Simón Plumanegra (Casa Plumanegra) – King of Castella – 6 AV

We walk uphill for an hour. From our vantage point, we're able to monitor all activity around the palace. Four times, mounted guards have left Nido, each group galloping in different directions. Two of them headed into Castellina, while the others broke ranks and dispersed on outbound paths. They'll be monitoring the main roads out of the capital, no doubt, acting as scouts that can later inform of our position.

We'll be on one of those roads along with the Romani troop, which the guardias will spot without a problem. I'm counting on them searching the wagons. I'm also counting on Gaspar's protective espiritu to hide us from their prying eyes. His skill kept me safe before, and it'd better do it again.

Our advantage lies in cutting across the hills behind the palace. It's a steep route, and my thighs burn as I push up the rocky terrain. My heart beats fast, and my lungs pump at an accelerated pace. I'm fit, but Ríffor makes me look like Nana walking up a short flight of steps. His thighs are twice as thick as mine, all lithe muscle with a dusting of dark hair. What in all the hells? I shake my head to erase the uninvited image.

Not soon enough for my taste, we crest the hill and start our descent on the other side. I breathe a sigh of relief, as do my legs. Going down, it gets easier to navigate the slope and keep up with Ríffor.

The westbound road out of Castellina meanders across the city, avoiding the hills to create a smooth passage for carriages and the like. In doing so, it adds several miles to the journey, miles that we have shortened by tracking over the rocky terrain. It will take any guardias headed that way at least twenty more minutes to catch up to the Romani troop, which got a head start and now waits for us.

When we reach the bottom of the hill, it takes no time to spot the silhouette of Gaspar's wagon sitting under the shadows of a heavy tree. A dark shape pulls away from the trunk at our approach. Ríffor, who has been holding the sword he took from the library in his hand, lifts the weapon.

"No need," I say. "They are here for us."

As the dark shadow approaches, it resolves into my cousin. "Thank the saints you're here!" he exclaims. "The wait was driving me out of my mind." He envelops me in a tight hug. When he pulls away, his honey-colored eyes flick to Ríffor. They're full of contempt as well as a warning. Jago hates him as much as I do for what he did to me.

"You better behave yourself, fae, or I swear I'll kill you and bury you under Castellan soil that I'll then turn into a latrine for every human to shit in."

Rífíor seems more amused than anything else. Clearly, he doesn't think my cousin would stand a chance against him, but he shouldn't take him for granted. Jago trained at the Academia de Guardias, raised by my father for a military career and the post of Capitán de la Guardia Real—whether or not Jago wanted it.

Jago returns his attention to me. "The rest of the troop has moved ahead . . . at a slow pace, so we'll catch up to them quickly. Um . . ." He scratches his head. "I feel like there's something else I'm supposed to tell you but . . ."

I wait.

He shakes his head. "I forgot. It mustn't be important. At any rate, let's get going." He walks up to the wagon and opens the back door, which groans on its wooden hinges. El Gran Místico's painted sign sits above the door.

A gas lamp much like the one we left behind illuminates the interior, which seems a lot smaller than I remember.

Odd. I frown.

Climbing after me is a disgruntled-looking Rífíor. It's clear he doesn't like to turn his back on anyone, much less a man who just threatened him with an eternity of shit upon his grave.

Jago climbs in last and closes the door, latching it securely. He knocks twice on the ceiling, and the wagon starts moving. Sitting next to me on a narrow side bench, he ends up directly in front of Rífíor. They stare at each other, and the tension inside the small space quickly mounts to a deadly level, making me wonder if we're going to make it to Tirnanog's border in one piece.

We sit quietly for a long time. I stare at the wood planks at my feet, praying. I wish it were possible to ride on separate horses, but we need to remain hidden. Either one of us would be recognized by the guardias when they inevitably stumble upon us.

A sudden sound of wood sliding against wood startles me. I jump back, while Jago and Rífíor attempt, but fail to draw their long swords inside the cramped space. Through instincts alone, my dagger finds its way into my hand, and I hold it up, ready to attack.

A wood panel in front of the wagon finishes sliding to one side, and none other than Gaspar climbs out of a makeshift compartment.

"Ta-da." He strikes a pose worthy of El Gran Místico.

"What in the name of all the gods?!" I blink repeatedly, watching him stretch, though not to a full height—the wagon isn't tall enough for that.

Jago snaps his fingers. "That's what I was supposed to tell you, that Gaspar modified the wagon and made a hidey-hole."

I blink some more as if that will clear my hazy thoughts, but it accomplishes nothing.

Rífíor looks at Jago and me as if we're a couple of idiots with the sense of two nails. He looks Gaspar over, nostrils flaring. "I recognize your stink."

"Much obliged." Gaspar smirks.

"You were in the catacombs."

"The princess needed my help."

Slowly, as I try very hard to wrangle my scattered thoughts, I begin to remember *we* asked Gaspar to create a hiding place in his wagon. But it seems we forgot. Why? The answer strikes me . . . Gaspar's espiritu! I never quite understood how it works, but it seems it addles your mind and makes you forget and not notice whatever it is he wants you to overlook.

In Alsur, the day I was running from Don Justo's villa, I stumbled upon El Gran Místico's wagon and climbed inside without an invitation. While I was there, Bastien searched for me right outside the door and never thought to look inside.

"Surprise," Gaspar says with a wink. "It'll be tight in there, especially for this one," he eyes Rífíor sideways, "but it'll do."

"What is he talking about?" Rífíor asks in his deep voice and that tone that assumes everyone should stop whatever they're doing to answer him. It's infuriating.

"Big, but not too bright, eh?" Gaspar wrinkles his nose, and I love him for the comment because it clearly infuriates Rífíor, though he tries to hide it.

Jago snorts, which only adds to Rífíor's aggravation.

To disguise his annoyance, he cocks his head to one side and narrows his eyes as he examines Gaspar's ears. "Your glamour is weak. Your ears are showing."

"Bah," he bats a hand in the air, "you can see it 'cause you're fae. Human eyes never see past the spell. Me, I'm just a quarter fae. That's where my espiritu comes from, along with these fancy points." He gestures to his ears, then switches his attention to me. "Did you make it out smooth-like?"

"Not as smooth as I would have liked," I say. "Guardias were alerted about us sooner than anticipated."

Gaspar scratches his beard. "That isn't good. I was hoping we'd have a chance to put some ground between us and Castellina."

"I know." I nod. "But I guess it's all the same. They would've come after us one way or another, and sooner or later, we would be making use of . . ." The words slip away, and it takes me a moment to wrangle them. "Um . . . your hiding place."

"What hiding place?" Rífíor asks.

I glare at him in the same way he did earlier, suggesting that he's an idiot, dumber than a nail.

"That one, right there." I point out the sliding panel, which is still open.

Rífíor rubs the back of his neck, a deep frown cutting across his forehead. He's surely wondering how he forgot about it so quickly, and I see the moment he understands the way Gaspar's espiritu works.

Proving he's no dumb nail, Rífíor asks something I hadn't thought about. "How are we going to know to hide when we keep forgetting the place even exists?"

"That's why you have me." Gaspar taps his chest.

Rífíor looks skeptical. "Who is to say you are always going to be around?"

"You better hope I am."

"Esmeralda can help, too," Jago puts in.

"And so can everyone else in the troop, once they catch wind that you three are here. My espiritu is trained to not affect the troop," Gaspar says. "I reckon it's time for you to slap on that glamour, Rífíor of the Veilfallen. Best keep it hush-hush that we're sheltering Castella's most wanted fae."

There is a slight change in Rífíor's expression at the mention of his glamour. Is it because he thinks seeing him as Bastien will send me into a fit of hysterics?

"Also, hide the scar," Gaspar adds, pointing at the right side of Rífíor's face.

We all wait for him to don his glamour, but as we stare, nothing happens.

"Oh, so you're going to be difficult?" Jago asks. "Fantástico!"

Reluctantly, Rífíor opens his mouth to speak. "I can't put on a glamour. I have no magic."

We all exchange confused glances. Fae always have enough magic for a glamour. Besides, we already know he can disguise himself. What's the point of lying?

"What kind of bullshit is that?" my cousin asks.

"I *don't* have magic, all right?" Rífíor growls, loud, angry. "Calierin used her skill to round my ears and make my scar disappear."

"Who the hell is Calierin?" Jago asks.

"His torturing bitch," I reply.

My cousin's hand tightens into a fist, making his leather glove creak.

Gaspar shakes his head. "I'm only part fae and still got enough espiritu to pull off a glamour and more. Never heard of a fae without the knack for changing their looks."

"Well, now you have." Rífíor's tone is final, indicating he's done with the subject.

"What is wrong with you?" Gaspar sounds truly puzzled.

"Nothing is wrong with me." Rífíor's glare makes the Romani whither visibly.

It's clear this is an extremely touchy subject for Rífíor. Curiosity sinks its claws into me, and I want to know the reason for his inability to conjure a glamour.

My mother didn't have much espiritu. She could communicate with plants, knew what they were feeling, what they needed. It wasn't a strong sort of skill, and yet she was always able to conjure a glamour. In fact, she was able to keep her glamour on all day long without effort.

So why is Rífíor unable to change his semblance? Does he really possess no espiritu at all? If it's true, it might explain why he stole The Eldrystone from the Fae King. The lack of a skill common to all fae would certainly become a sore spot for anyone, perhaps even a source of shame.

We sit in silence for a long time, the rocking motion of the wagon luring me into uneasy drowsiness. I feel bone tired. The last few days have been full of stress and sleepless nights as I fought with the decision to betray my sister. And now, it's done, and I know I've broken her heart into a million pieces. I heard the pain in her voice as she asked Renata why I took the amulet.

"By the saints! I never thought she would betray me like this." Her words echo in my lethargic mind.

I'm exhausted now, and sleep will be possible because my body demands it. In nights to come, however, I'm not so sure my festering guilt will allow me such luxury. It doesn't matter how logical and worthy my intentions are, reason can't override the deep shame I feel in the center of my soul.

A ringing in my ears yanks me away from the edge of sleep, and I snap my eyes open. My heart is beating fast for no apparent reason. Rífíor is tense and listening intently, his head cocked to one side.

"What is it?" Jago asks.

"Horses," Rífíor replies. "At least seven of them."

"I hear them too," Gaspar says. "It's time for you three to disappear." He stands and starts gesticulating toward the hiding place he created for us.

Rífíor lifts a thick black eyebrow, looking as though he has no intention of squeezing into the confined space.

"If you don't," I threaten, "you'll find yourself back in a dank cell for the rest of your miserable life, so get your haughty ass in there."

A muscle ticks in his jaw, and I can tell he wants to give me a piece of his mind, but maybe our earlier conversation had the desired effect. He restrains himself and rises slowly to his towering height. Hunching to avoid banging his head on the low ceiling, he scrutinizes the compartment with a critical eye. The space is approximately four feet tall, with a depth of no more than three feet.

Irritation etching his face, he climbs inside the space, setting his back against one side of the wagon and gathering his legs to his torso.

Gaspar closes the sliding panel to hide Rífíor, then opens a second one on the other side and points at Jago. "You're next."

He gets in the same way Rífíor did, and the tips of their boots end up only a few inches apart. There's no way I will fit in there.

"Curl up tighter," Gaspar says. "Make room for the princess."

"This is it for me," Jago says.

"How about you, Rífíor?"

His only answer is a grunt that makes it clear he can't make himself any smaller.

"Shit, *I* can hear the horses now," Jago says. "We need to hurry!"

"Saints and feathers!" Gaspar exclaims. "Um . . . um . . . Jago, get out."

My cousin scrambles out. "Now what?"

Gaspar says, "Rífíor, stretch your legs."

He does, his boots appearing and reaching all the way to the wall.

"All right, now Jago, sit on top of his feet."

Jago makes a face. "That won't be comfortable for either one of us."

"Getting snatched up and having our journey cut short before it even starts won't be no better," Gaspar points out.

"I must say, for the record," Jago puts in, "that this goes against every fiber in my body."

He climbs back, and his backside ends up on top of Rífíor's ankles.

"Stretch out your legs, too," Gaspar tells Jago. "And Val, sit on your cousin's lap. With any luck, you won't be cooped up in there for too long."

I certainly hope not. I might have gotten the better end of this deal by ending up on top, but being in such close quarters with Rífíor will still be unpleasant. In the scheme of things, it's a small price to pay to gain the freedom of the fae folk trapped in Castella.

A moment later, when angry voices order the wagon's driver to a stop, this narrow hiding place is the least of my worries.

Please, Niamhara, don't let them find us.

27

RÍFÍOR

*"No one can be trusted. I will extricate her from my heart,
no matter how much it hurts."*

Reina Amira Plumanegra (Casa Plumanegra) – Queen of Castella – 21 AV

The weight on my legs hardly registers as a concern. I could bear it indefinitely without any problems. But this proximity to Valeria is truly unsettling. I want to rip apart the flimsy panel enclosing us and flee. I would bolt from the wagon and vanish into the forest, never to be found again. It's a tempting idea, though an impossible one—not when the chance to reopen the veil lies so close at hand.

My jaw is clenched, and my eyes are closed. I intend to keep them that way, but as her scent—a blend of lemon and lavender—fills my nostrils, they involuntarily slide open, and I have to curse my heightened senses.

Despite the darkness, I see her clearly. She sits with her head hanging low, eyes directed at her lap. One of her thumbs worries at the other, picking at a hangnail. Her lips move as if in prayer, though I hear no sound escaping from her.

Jago's hands are around her waist as she sits on his lap. The heat of anger climbs up my chest, and I have to remind myself that he's her cousin.

Her tongue darts out, and she licks her lower lip.

As angry voices reach us from outside, her head tilts to one side to better listen. Chin trembling, she breathes through her mouth, chest rising and falling. It's obvious she's terrified of being caught. No harm would come to her if we're discovered, but it seems she really wants to reach the veil and reopen it. I am terribly puzzled by her apparent determination. What happened that brought her to this decision and made her go against her sister? Whatever it is, it can't be good, and I have to bite my tongue not to ask at that very moment.

"Search all the wagons," someone orders.

Gaspar throws the door open and steps outside. "What's the matter?" he asks in the groggy voice of someone who was rudely awakened.

If we're discovered in this ridiculous hiding place, I will not be responsible for what happens to those guards. I'll kill them all before Valeria even has a chance to remind me they are her kin.

"Shut your mouth and get out of the way," the same guard barks.

Murmurs reach my ears. The other troop members, I assume. They sound scared, and I don't blame them. The Romani are treated nearly as badly as us fae folk. It's a disgrace, one that Simón Plumanegra should have never allowed to fester and propagate. Any good king would have uprooted such tendencies.

Abundant trampling of horses and boots follows as they search for us. Our wagon tips slightly from one side to the other as someone climbs in.

In front of me, Valeria sits entirely frozen, but for that slight trembling of her chin. My hand twitches as the impulse to reach out and caress her cheek overtakes me.

Damn all the gods!

Every bit of logic in all the realms tells me I should despise this creature, but since the very beginning, my body has had a will of its own when it comes to her. She is as water to a parched body, a beacon to a sailor, chains to a prisoner. Inexorable.

Gods, erase her from my mind!

I squeeze my eyes shut and clench my jaw, doing my best to ignore her delicious scent.

"Anything?" the person in charge calls from outside the wagon.

"Um, no, Teniente Coronel." He sounds unsure. "Uh . . . only a bedroll, I guess."

"You guess?"

"I mean, only a bedroll, ma'am," he calls with added confidence.

The wagon rocks again, and the door slams shut. We are safe. At least, that is what I tell myself. I don't feel at all safe in Valeria's presence.

28

VALERIA

"We have to leave. Quick. I don't know where we are going, but my magic tells me something very bad is about to happen."

Ciara Vron – Fae Outcast – 21 AV

After we hid, Gaspar produced a bedroll and spread it over the wagon's floor to make it appear as if he had been sleeping.

Clever distraction on his part, I think, until I realize he means for us to actually use it. Physically, it's possible, though only if we were willing to rest right next to each other, like arrows in a tightly packed quiver. That may be how he and his troop do it, but there's no way I'll lay my head down anywhere near Rífíor. Hiding in that compartment is as far as I'll go.

"Have it your way. Good night," Gaspar says, lying down right in the middle of the floor, Jago and my feet bracketing him on one side, and Rífíor's on the other.

Normally, the troop stops for the night, leaving the road and setting up camp under the blanket of the dark sky. There, everyone sprawls out with abandon and unleashes their dreams without a care in the world. I witnessed some of their customs during my journey with them from Alsur to Castellina. It was the first time I ever felt free in my life. I doubt I'll feel the same way this time around.

Soon enough, Gaspar is snoring, oblivious to our discomfort. But it isn't so bad. I have Jago, and reclining against one another, we find enough relief to catch a few hours of sleep.

I wake up sometime later with a burning ache in my neck. Groggily, I rotate my head to ease the tightness. Jago is leaning heavily on me, which causes its own set of aches and pains. He's sound asleep. At least one of us deserves some rest.

When I finish rubbing sleep out of my eyes, I find Ríffor staring directly at me. He makes no attempt to disguise his scrutiny, those black eyes as harsh and impenetrable as ever. His sharp cheekbones match the slope of his pointed ears.

"You snore," he says.

"No, I don't." *Oh, gods, do I?*

He shrugs as if it makes no difference to him whether or not I believe him.

"So . . . why are we here?" he asks, his voice quiet, never disturbing the others. "What made you decide to open the veil?"

I bite my lower lip. I don't want to tell him. Amira's scheme is shameful and admitting that any member of my family is capable of such a terrible idea is difficult. Moreover, I know he'll be furious, and he's threatening enough as it is. But he's going to find out one way or another, and by all the gods, I refuse to let fear dictate my actions. So, without a preamble, I tell him the truth.

"My sister and the council plan to relocate all the fae to a guarded section of the city."

"You're talking about internment," he says, eyes wide and nostrils flaring.

"Yes, internment," I repeat, doing my best to take whatever responsibility I must for the turn of events. "I tried to stop her, but I failed. I couldn't make her or the council listen to me. I don't agree with what they're doing, and though my sister will forever see my actions as a betrayal, I believe reopening the veil is the only solution. That's why we're here."

He's quiet for a long time, then seems to take a moment to dispel his anger. When his expression relaxes, he says, "I must thank you, Princess Valeria."

I do a double-take. "Did they switch you with someone else in the dungeon?"

"You may think me a senseless savage, but everything I have ever done is to protect my people."

I sneer. "How do you figure chaos and destruction do that?"

Too many times, Calierin used her powerful espiritu to blow up buildings, while the others caused further terror and stole whatever they could in the turmoil. Innocent people often died in those attacks.

"The big majority of the fae trapped in this realm live in poverty," he says. "They try to find jobs, but few do, and you know well why. If we destroyed your fancy buildings, if we stole, it was to provide for them."

I shake my head in denial. He's lying. He *must* be lying. Everything that comes out of his mouth is a falsehood. They sowed terror because they hate us.

"I can see you don't believe me." He shrugs. "It doesn't matter.

I won't deny that I was also searching for The Eldrystone. I thought I might find it hiding in the safety vaults used by your nobility. I hoped your father had confined its safekeeping to one of these places. Though, deep down I knew, I would have to infiltrate Nido to find it."

And did that include seducing the naïve princess? I want to ask, but I have to leave all of that in the past. I can't let what happened between us cloud my judgment and actions from here on out. It won't be easy. He stirs so many emotions in me, hatred and anger the strongest of them, but there's also . . . desire, which I fear.

"I thought I would be able to use it for this very purpose," he continues. "To guide my people back to their homes, to save them from living their long lives as pariahs."

"Do all those lies help you sleep better at night?" I ask. "You wanted to destroy us, not save your people. The moment you laid your hands on the amulet, you tried to use it against us."

I hold his gaze, expecting him to deny my accusation. He keeps eye contact for a few seconds, then looks down, a sure admission of guilt. If The Eldrystone had responded to him in Amira's bedchamber, I fear the entirety of Castella would be a pile of rubble right now.

"You're a monster." The whispered words are out of my lips before I can stop them.

He doesn't try to deny it. Instead, he looks up at me, and in that moment, I understand I'm not the only one who believes it. He does too.

"Why?" I ask.

His already hardened expression grows even more stern.

Whatever events shaped him into who he is . . . he clearly doesn't want to talk about it. Despite his youthful appearance—perhaps around twenty-seven or twenty-eight—his dark eyes, unchanged by any glamour, betray a different story. He could be a hundred, two hundred years old. More? Only the gods know what trials and tribulations he might have endured over such a lengthy existence. Still, I don't think anything can justify his desire for destruction.

"The *why* doesn't matter," he says at last. "I am who I am."

Closing his eyes, he reclines his head and crosses his arms, acting as if he's finally decided to go to sleep. I sit there quietly, my mind turning with possibilities. I don't sleep, and I know he doesn't either. It's easy to see he's wide awake, his own thoughts whirling after our conversation.

If I could take a glimpse into his mind and read all his secrets like a book, would I understand him? Would I forgive him?

Inevitably, I turn the question inward.

To Amira, I'm a traitor. Would it change her mind if I were laid bare before her? I'd like to think so.

But if you want Amira to give you a chance, shouldn't you do the same for him? the voice of fairness asks within my mind.

29
VALERIA

"If only I'd persuaded Esmeralda's ma to join us. She might not be safe if what I've foreseen for Castellina comes to pass."

Gaspar Patrach – Romani Diviner – 21 AV

A series of loud knocks startles me into a sitting position, jolting me from uneasy dreams. Jago also seems alarmed and as disoriented as me. Only Rífíor is calm, though I have the feeling he was already awake.

"Get up, you lazy fucks, if you want to break your fast," a familiar voice calls from outside the wagon. Esmeralda.

I feel drunk as I strap La Matadora on, open the small door, and place a foot on the first step. I wince at the bright sunshine seeping through the canopy of a large oak. Birds chirp overhead and bright green moss pads my steps better than a Catalunyan rug. Taking a deep breath of fresh air, I marvel that the world is still this beautiful when everything else around me feels like decay and rot.

Jago and Rífíor follow, stretching like cats. Though in the latter's case, the analogy might work best with a lynx. He appears more ferocious and intimidating, while Jago makes me think of a cuddly kitten. I smile inwardly at that. Jago wouldn't like this comparison at all, but he doesn't have to know.

"You can't be smiling after that miserable night of sleep," Jago says.

I shrug and follow Esmeralda. Her hips sashay, and her collection of bracelets tinkles as she goes. She's dressed in a layered, tattered skirt of green, yellow, and purple—her feet bare, leaving dainty indentations in the moss. Jago's eyes follow her, tracking her every move with a frown.

She guides us around the oak tree, where Gaspar sits next to a crackling fire, tending to what appears to be a pot of oats cooking over the flames.

I glance around, searching for the rest of the troop. "Where is everyone else?"

"Up the road." Gaspar drops a stick of cinnamon into the porridge, breaking it into smaller pieces. "They know we're carrying precious cargo . . . they just don't know who yet. We would rather keep it that way for as long as we can."

"I see."

The oats roil, releasing the sweet scent of cinnamon, making my stomach growl. Esmeralda passes around mugs of tea. I raise my cup to my nose and inhale deeply, enjoying the smell of chamomile.

"Fancy us putting cinnamon in porridge," Esmeralda says.

"Food supplies from the princess's kitchens," Gaspar points out. "She even got pepper and saffron. Not sure how to use that last one."

"I'll tell you how," Esmeralda puts in. "We sell it."

Rífíor looks at me sideways, and it feels like a reproach. I instructed Jago to gather supplies that might be useful for the trip. It seems he let his stomach do the thinking. Spices didn't even make my list.

We all sit around the fire, except for Rífíor who stands aside, reclining his back against the tree. He braces one foot against the trunk and sips his tea almost carelessly, eyes surveying our surroundings. When offered food, he dismisses it with an absent hand gesture.

Angry at myself for being so focused on his presence, I tear my eyes away from him and stare into the distance. The terrain is flat and covered by thick trees. The underbrush is dense and undisturbed, except for the area that marks our passage. I focus on a bug flying overhead, then a bird, which turns out to be Cuervo.

Good bird, I think, meeting his inquisitive gaze and inclining my head in greeting. He doesn't appear to have The Eldrystone with him, but I have to assume it's somewhere nearby, well hidden.

I clear my throat. "Excuse me, I need to . . . relieve myself."

Heading in the opposite direction of where Cuervo sits, I push through the brush, ensuring the wagon remains a barrier between my companions and myself. I walk a safe distance away to make sure no one sees or hears a thing. I wait and start to worry when Cuervo doesn't appear after a long moment. Swirling, I peer up at the trees, trying to spot him.

"Where are you, Cuervo?" I say under my breath.

A rustling sound makes my head jerk to the left. I squint, scanning the heavy foliage. Wings flap on my right, and I turn to watch Cuervo land at my feet, the amulet clamped tightly in his talon.

I squat next to him. "Hello, friend," I coo, happy to see him, wishing I only had him and Jago for company on this journey.

He releases the amulet so I can retrieve it.

"Thank you." I pick it up from the ground and quickly hang the chain around my neck, hiding the gem under my tunic. "And thanks for being here." I smile as he preens, pulling on one of his iridescent feathers. "Stay close, all right? Don't be a stranger."

He flies away, likely to find himself a delicious breakfast.

I return, take a seat, and sip my tea, trying to act normal. Gaspar hums as he spoons oats onto a battered metal plate and bangs the spoon against its edge.

Before long, my attention returns to Rífíor, drawn as if by a magnet. I feel his presence like a thorn in my side, a thorn I wish I could extricate and cast away.

He's a bad male, Valeria. Kick him out of your mind then burn the memories to ashes.

It doesn't matter what he said about helping his people, about doing all those things for them and not for selfish reasons. I can't trust him. He deceives like a spider spins its web. Expertly.

"Why do I get the bottom dregs?" Esmeralda demands. "Give them to him." She points at Rífíor.

"In case you didn't notice, he didn't want any of it," Gaspar replies. "Besides there's nothing wrong with it. I didn't burn it this time."

She sneers and stares at her porridge. "I see burnt bits in here."

"Here, you can have mine," Jago says.

Without hesitation, Esmeralda exchanges her plate for Jago's.

Gaspar shakes his head. "Don't you go pandering to her. She'll strip you bare if you let her."

"I don't mind the burnt bits. I like them," Jago says.

What? What is he talking about? He doesn't even like oats. I look between my cousin and Esmeralda. Jago stares at his plate, swirling the spoon, and looking chagrined. What is going on here? My cousin has never looked chagrined in his entire life. Does he like her? I know him well enough to recognize the signs of his attraction to someone, but I haven't seen any of them. Typically, it all begins with flirting and making his intentions known from the start. Instead, he's behaving as he did when he was ten and had a crush on one of the chambermaids.

Saints and feathers! Does this mean he really, really likes her and doesn't only want to get under her skirts?

The thought makes me almost giddy inside. Jago seems to have a real crush on someone! It's endearing except . . . my giddiness vanishes right away. Esmeralda is the last person Jago should have that kind of crush on. She is shrewd, and I get the impression she's very experienced in matters of the heart. Or should I say *loins*? Either way, this can't bode well—not to mention this is the wrong time for such complications. We have enough troubles as it is. I'll have to talk to him about it when we have a moment of privacy.

"So how long will it take to get to the veil?" Esmeralda mumbles between bites.

"At our current pace, I would say about a fortnight," Gaspar responds.

Rífíor grunts.

"The tree trunk doesn't approve," Gaspar says.

"I don't," Rífíor responds. "Give us two horses and Valeria and I can get there in half the time."

Jago huffs. "Are you forgetting about the guardias?"

"We can outrun them," Rífíor says.

"Maybe, maybe not. Secrecy is our best ally."

"You've waited this long, veilfallen," Esmeralda says. "You can wait a little longer, don't you think?"

"It may seem that way to you, human, but every day in this godsforsaken realm is untold misery," Rífíor retorts.

"This godsforsaken realm, as you call it," I say, jerking to a standing position, "has provided you with shelter and food, and everything you need to survive for two decades, so show a little gratitude." I don't think my argument is sound, but anger is the sole force guiding my words at the moment.

"Don't worry, princess, the days I spent with you weren't so bad."

"You fucking bastardo." I start toward him, ready to kill him. I'll teach him not to ever bring up the biggest mistake of my life.

I've barely taken a step in his direction when my ears start ringing and my heart beats out of control. I clutch at my chest.

"What is it? Your heart cannot resist the sight of me?" He grins crookedly.

"No, asshole! I . . . I don't know. Something is wr—"

A whistle sounds to my left. A violent pain in my left arm follows as an arrow nicks me, and my legs go weak. I fall, grabbing hold of the aching spot. Something warm and sticky coats my fingers. Blood! I stumble and nearly fall but manage to steady myself. Another whistle follows, and another arrow embeds itself in the oak tree, mere inches from Rífíor's face. He jumps into action, unsheathing his sword and dropping to one knee by my side.

He presses a hand to my shoulder. "Are you all right?"

There is concern in his eyes. I recoil from it, from him.

He snatches his hand away and glances at Jago. "Take cover!"

Jago doesn't question the order and starts pulling me behind the oak tree. I hiss in pain as he tugs me along.

Shit! The guardias found us. I thought we'd managed to leave them behind, but—

A blinding blast strikes the base of the tree. Gaspar throws an arm over his eyes as he rounds the trunk, followed by Esmeralda. The acrid smell of charred wood fills the air. Espiritu? The guardias don't have espiritu—not unless they hired a sorcerer.

"Devils! I told you we should have never agreed to this," Esmeralda says.

Gaspar looks affronted. "*You* told *me*? You were grinning ear to ear over the gold."

"Quiet!" Jago hisses as I scramble to extricate myself from his hold.

"Let me go. I'm all right. It's just a scratch." Pushing my cousin away, I get to my feet and peek around the tree trunk.

Rífíor stands in a crouch, the sword he took from the library positioned right in front of him. Lucky the thing is fae-made! Lucky he took it!

Another ball of espiritu comes flying our way. Quick as the wind, Rífíor moves into its path and cuts it in half, angling the blade just so.

The attack disintegrates into thousands of miniature fireworks that fizzle harmlessly to the ground.

"Drocháin," Rífíor curses, followed by a name I despise. "Calierin!"

She's here? How did she find us? My entrails tremble as the memories of what she did to me rise like phantoms inside my mind. I press a hand to my stomach, feeling sick.

"I would know your magic anywhere, you harpy. Show yourself," Rífíor shouts. "Fight me like a real warrior."

"What? Is he crazy?" Esmeralda pulls at her dark hair. "We need to get out of here."

"And how are you going to do that?" Gaspar asks. "On your flying horse?"

"Ha, you're so funny. At least the others are safe," she spits. "I should've stayed with them."

"Fucking traitor!" Calierin's voice resounds across the forest. "You sold us out."

"Then come and kill me . . . if you can," Rífíor taunts, twirling the sword to the left, the right, the front. The blade goes so fast it seems nothing but a blur.

Bushes rustle across the way, and Calierin strolls out, hands raised and throbbing with espiritu. I clench my teeth and let hatred eat away my fear. I came to dread the sight of her, the gleeful glint in her eyes, but I've been fighting to erase her face from my nightmares, and I won't allow her back in.

Calierin's not alone. The male named Kadewyn is behind her—Rífíor's second. His silver hair reflects the morning sunlight that filters through the thick canopy. I met him in the catacombs. Well, *met him* is a stretch. I laid eyes on him and heard his name. That's all. He holds a drawn bow in his left hand.

I touch the wound in my arm. *Bastardo! He tried to kill me!* Or did he? Perhaps I only deviated the shot when I stood up. Perhaps he meant to kill Rífíor instead. From the way Kadewyn glares at his former leader, that seems to be the case.

Calierin and Kadewyn cut an intimidating pair. I don't blame Esmeralda for wanting to run. The sight of them makes my insides turn to water. My history with the sorceress isn't helping, but I'm determined to give this female no power over me.

I reach behind my back, and slowly, my hand wraps around La Matadora's hilt. Taking a deep breath, I step from behind the tree, my weapon *zinging* as I draw it out of its scabbard.

30
RÍFÍOR

"Calierin is right. Rífíor is a liar and a traitor."

Kadewyn Zinceran – Veilfallen – 21 AV

"Damn you to Talrocht," I curse. Has she lost her mind? Valeria is a good fighter. Very good, in fact, but she is no match for the likes of Calierin.

"Retreat," I order her.

She gives me a sideways glance that tells me exactly what she thinks about me and my order.

"You are going to get yourself killed," I retort. "But what do I care?"

"Exactly," she shoots back. "So shut your mouth." I bristle at her tone. She's infuriating.

Calierin and Kadewyn come to a stop a few feet away from us. They both wear hateful expressions I have often seen on their faces though never directed at me.

"Did you think we wouldn't find you?" Calierin barks her question.

I only stare at her, my sword in a white-knuckle grip.

"I knew we never should have trusted you," Calierin says. The magic in her hands pulses with every word she utters. "Do you know how many of our people died in those catacombs?" A pause. "Walverdin, Preesah, Janeer, Stohehk. Do you want me to keep going?"

Every name sends a stab of pain into my chest. I did not mean for any of them to die. We were safe in those catacombs for a long time. I never suspected they would find us. But I say none of these things. I only wait, ready for whatever she throws my way. If only Valeria would get out of the way, I would have one less thing to worry about.

"Why did you do it?" Kadewyn asks.

Leave it to reasonable Kadewyn to ask that question, to try to understand. Would he change his mind about me if I told him the truth? It matters not. I do not owe either of them an explanation. However, for the safety of my travel companions and our quest, I will tell them our goal and hope my reasons convince them to leave us alone.

"I only have one purpose," I say, "and it is to help our people."

"Bréagah!" Calierin curses.

"I care not if either of you believes me, but we are on our way to reopen the veil."

Valeria shoots me a warning glare.

Calierin cackles. "Do you expect us to believe that?"

I did not expect anything but her pigheadedness. It is Kadewyn's expression I concentrate on. There is a slight tightening of his white eyebrows, and I almost sense my words drilling a hole through his anger and letting a bit of reason in. He has a wife and a daughter in Tirnanog, two big reasons to hope.

"It is true, Kadewyn," I add.

"And the little princess is helping you now? Just like that?" Calierin asks in a mocking tone. "Is that why you are so cozy with her all of a sudden, huh? You must think we are really stupid. You are lying about that amulet. There is something else going on here."

I ignore her and continue focusing on Kadewyn.

"Valeria Plumanegra can wield the amulet, Kade," I say. "And she *will* usher us home."

"Is this true?" Kadewyn addresses Valeria.

But she never has time to answer because Calierin lifts her pulsing hands. "I'm done listening to lies."

"Wait!" Kadewyn shouts as a blast of magic explodes in my direction.

I raise my sword, but the attack never arrives. Instead, Valeria jumps in front of me to defend me, using her own fae-made sword. Surprise floods through me. Why would she . . . ?

She provides the answer. "You and I have a score to settle, bitch."

Of course, Valeria isn't trying to defend me. Her motive is revenge. I lean forward and whisper in her ear, "What do you think you're doing? She is going to wipe the forest floor with you."

She grunts in disagreement and takes a step forward to put some distance between us.

"Valeria, let Riffor take care of this," Jago suggests, stepping from behind the tree, his own sword in hand, though he does not look as certain as Valeria. In fact, he looks like he wants to hide again. I would call him a coward if we were not dealing with Calierin. Instead, I believe he is smart, much smarter than his cousin.

"Shut your mouth, the both of you," Valeria snarls. "This is between me and this bitch."

"Listen to your cousin," I insist.

"No!" Calierin barks. "I am going to kill your little precious princess, Rífíor, which is what I should have done from the beginning."

Calierin cuts a hand through the air, and a shaft of light in the shape of a knife flies forward, boomeranging toward Valeria's head. Both Jago and I move forward to intervene, but Valeria is much faster, and with an upward swing of her sword, she cuts the attack in half.

I frown and so does Calierin. Valeria's movements were fast, her steps firm, her parry confident. I know she's well-trained. I learned that much when I was pretending to be Bastien, and we sparred on Nido's rooftop. But it seems I underestimated how well her tutor taught her. Yet, I find no comfort in the fact. I need to take care of Calierin myself before my only chance to get back to Tirnanog dies before my eyes.

I move to attack but once more Valeria is there before me. I frown, confused. What is happening here? There is no way her human speed can match mine.

The answer comes to me an instant later. She has The Eldrystone now. Seeing her use it once more renews my hope that she *will* be able to use Niamhara's conduit to guide me home.

Calierin channels all her anger and energy into undoing Valeria. The palpable hatred emanating from her consumes her focus, blinding her to the fact that Valeria is, in this moment, a vastly different opponent than she should be. Kadewyn, however, the more perceptive of the two, notices it. He can tell that Valeria's movements are not completely human.

"What the?" Jago mumbles, his expression etched in confusion as he exchanges a glance with me.

"It's The Eldrystone," I whisper.

Understanding dawns on him, and relief replaces some of the worry in his expression.

As the fight continues, Valeria's footwork is an expert dance.

A Tuathacath warrior, Calierin is nothing but excellent, which means Valeria is just . . . superb. It strikes me that her prowess is not all due to the magic in the stone, though. Her skills are inherently impressive, with the amulet merely enhancing her speed. Nothing more, nothing less.

Calierin deals magic like a volcano spewing lava. Flashes of violet fly through the air, creating mesmerizing patterns that blind the eye. She hurls spells overhand, underhand, twisting her wrist to add a spin to them. But it doesn't matter how creative she gets with her combinations; Valeria and her blade are always there to stop the magic.

There is grace and precision in the princess's movements, and I cannot help but be in awe of what she can do.

It is only when Calierin nears exhaustion that she begins to comprehend something is amiss. Soon the colors of her magic become pale and her speed subpar. Breathing hard, she stops, fists trembling at her sides. Undeterred, she pulls out her sword with a *zing* and takes a step forward, beginning her charge.

Kadewyn, always the more sensible of the two, puts a hand out and stops her. "Something is wrong here," he says. "She fights with fae speed. How is that possible?"

Calierin cocks her head to one side.

"It could be the amulet," Kadewyn says. "That or . . . she has fae blood in her veins."

Kadewyn is not wrong about that. Although the latter is not the reason Valeria's performance has outdone Calierin's, but this could be risky. They don't need to know Valeria's parentage.

I position myself to Valeria's left, with Jago flanking her on the right, and calmly remark, "I believe you are outnumbered."

For the first time, they appear wary. I can tell Kadewyn knows they miscalculated their odds. If I had to take a guess, I would say they were propelled here solely by Calierin's fury. She can stoke a good fire in anyone's gut with promises of death and revenge. Just like any good Tuathacath warrior, her tongue can weave an intricate tapestry of rage that will only be unraveled by death. It is a skill sometimes necessary in war, but it can also be a hindrance when a level head is needed.

I open my mouth to tell them they need to leave, but before I can say anything, Valeria throws her sword to the ground and takes out The Eldrystone from under her tunic, pulling the chain over her head, and dangling the amulet in front of them.

"This is what your precious leader has always wanted," she says. "It's about time he tells us all exactly why."

31
VALERIA

"I will have that amulet one way or another."

Calierin Kelraek – Tuathacath Warrior and Veilfallen – 21 AV

My heart knocks hard, making it difficult to breathe. I know I'm taking a huge risk by doing this, but I find it necessary. I inhale deeply several times in order to calm down.

Fighting Calierin was exhilarating. I felt the amulet enhancing my speed enough to match hers, enough to give me the agility I should have inherited from my mother. My blood still sings with the thrill of it all, and I must gather my will to preside over this moment, to let my mind take over the physicality of the battle.

Amidst the intense focus demanded to fight the sorceress, I saw an opportunity to leverage Rífíor's former allies to gather information. I've embarked on this journey with little knowledge of him, and no idea of his true motives. For all I know, he wants to destroy Tirnanog. He has refused to give me answers, but maybe he'll talk to his own kind. He was willing to tell them where we're headed. That shows a level of trust.

"Valeria," Rífíor snarls, "what are you doing?"

I ignore his question. If he didn't want me to talk to them, he shouldn't have so casually revealed our destination to this lot, possibly jeopardizing our plans. Perhaps he was trying to avoid a confrontation or hoping they would join us, but whatever the case, he should have thought better of it. I don't want Calierin anywhere near me. Impossible as it seems, I hate her more than I hate him.

Calierin regards the amulet dangling from my hand with distaste. "So that is what you betrayed us for, Rífíor? You made us believe we could have it and then you abandoned us and let your people die like moles underground."

Rífíor turns his attention to the sorceress, though I still feel his disapproval radiating in my direction. "I have always looked at the bigger picture."

"The bigger picture, eh?" the sorceress sneers. "And by that you mean what exactly? I always suspected you had ulterior motives. You keep secrets and you scheme on your own."

"I owe you no explanations," Rífíor bats a hand at the air, "so if you are done with your pathetic display of power, we must be on our way."

"No." I shake my head. "For once, I'm with your lackeys. I would like to know more."

"That is not my problem. I am not here to satisfy anyone's curiosity."

"You see . . . that is what is wrong with you," Calierin says. "You act as if everyone should follow you, trust you, and why? Because you are special? Nah, you are no better or different than any of us. You are just another stranded fool, trying to survive in this awful place."

A muscle twitches in Rífíor's jaw, suggesting he has taken offense. It appears he truly believes everyone should unquestioningly trust and obey him by virtue of . . . what? His good looks? I hate to agree with this bitch, but I've always had the same impression. Maybe the time he possessed The Eldrystone turned him into a narcissist. Except now, he's no different from any other fae. In fact, he's less. He doesn't even have enough espiritu to conjure a glamour.

Rífíor sheathes his sword carelessly. "Gaspar, Esmeralda," he calls, "let's pack and get on the road."

Jago crosses his arms. "Who put this one in charge?"

"No one," I say. "I'm the only one who gives orders here."

Rífíor shrugs. "Whatever you say, princess. If you don't mind the guards catching up with us."

Once more, he refuses to come clean. I seethe in frustration, but I'm not the only one. Calierin's face is so red, she appears ready to explode.

"What the fuck do you mean you are on your way to reopen the veil with *her*?" Calierin demands, pointing at me.

"Just what I said," Rífíor retorts, his perfect composure lending him a striking air. "Were my words not clear enough?"

"You fucking bastard," she shouts. "You better not ever let your guard down because I am going to slaughter you. Not even your mother will recognize what is left of you."

Rífíor returns to the tree and reclines, nonchalantly examining his fingernails, appearing as bored as Jago does during mass. "You already tried and failed—unless you want to try again. This time only your sword against mine." He gives her an inquiring sidelong glance.

Calierin says nothing. She just fumes, literal smoke coming out of her pointed ears.

"Is that . . .?" Jago points at the smoke and squints. "Yes, it is. Smoke's coming out of her ears."

"What?" Calierin takes a step to one side and looks up. Her hands fly to the sides of her head. "What the fuck is this?"

Behind me, Esmeralda giggles. "She's boiling mad."

What in the . . .? I frown. Rífíor stares at me, then his eyes flick to The Eldrystone, which still hangs from my hand. Is he trying to tell me *I* caused that? I glance back toward Calierin, wish the smoke to stop, and, to my surprise, it does.

Saints and feathers! I only had the thought that she was fuming. I didn't mean to do that. This makes no sense. Back in Nido, the amulet refused to do what I wanted, and now . . . I have to be more careful with this thing. I shake my head and put the chain back around my neck, the weight of the amulet offering more comfort than I would like.

Kadewyn doesn't miss my interaction with Rífíor. Suspicious, he peers at the dissipating smoke with a sneer on his handsome, pale face. "You are lying. There is no reopening the veil with that thing."

"Of course he is lying." Calierin rolls her eyes.

Rífíor is looking at me, a request etched on his features. I have no trouble deciphering it. He wants me to tell them he isn't lying. I suppose he's done it often enough that his word means nothing to them. But why should they believe *me*? I'm just a human they hate, a member of the family who, in their minds, has kept them subjugated for twenty years.

The question is . . . do I want them to believe Rífíor? Is there any benefit to having them on our side despite the way I feel about Calierin? I don't want her anywhere near us, but maybe she and Kadewyn can serve as lookouts for us. They've been following the troop since we left Castellina, and they did so unnoticed. They're good trackers and fighters, so it wouldn't hurt to have their help, if it came to it. Yet, that's logic talking. My instinct of self-preservation, however, is saying something completely different. If I'm to heed Father's advice, I should listen to my gut and stay away from them. But unless I kill them, they'll continue following us.

There is a part of me that would relish flattening Calierin like a bug. I can almost conjure the image of her body bending at my command, blood soaking the ground as broken bones protrude from her skin. It would be so easy. All I would have to do is wish for it, and it would happen. It's tempting, so tempting.

Calierin lets out a groan of pain, a hand flying to her ribcage.

Oh, gods!

I'm doing it.

Stop, Valeria.

I take a step back, recoiling from the glimpse of evil my soul has revealed.

Rífíor raises an eyebrow, aware of my intention, but there's no judgment in his expression.

Clear your mind, Valeria. You're not a tyrant.

One death on my conscience, no matter how deserving the

victim, is enough. I won't be like these fae. I'm better than that. With a deep breath, I clear my mind.

Calierin sidles toward Kadewyn, a hint of fear in her features. She also seems to know why her ribs felt ready to snap.

"Yes, Rífíor, you're right. We're wasting our time," I say tiredly. "Let's go."

I'm starting to turn toward the wagon when the amulet heats up under my tunic. It's only a momentary flash, but it makes me stop. Hesitantly, I take a step toward the wagon. The same thing happens. As I stand there, puzzled, the chain tugs, pointing in Calierin's and Kadewyn's direction.

Is the amulet trying to tell me something?

To make sure I'm not imagining things, I press a hand to my chest and force the amulet down. Once it settles, I try to leave once more, but the same thing happens.

Yes, The Eldrystone does seem to have a mind of its own, which means Niamhara wants me to heed logic over my instinct of self-preservation. As I ponder, it seems to me that I need more than Father's voice and lessons inside my head to guide me. And why couldn't that be The Eldrystone? It wouldn't lead me astray, would it? Besides, I'm trusting it to save my sister from making the worst mistake of her life.

All right, Goddess. I shall listen.

Taking a deep breath, I face Calierin and Kadewyn, my expression stern. "Rífíor isn't lying," I declare. "I *can* reopen the veil."

Calierin laughs. "You two are really made for each other, huh? What sort of bréagah is this? Did you bring her to the catacombs as a decoy to lead her guards to us? Were you party to that plan?

Was it all a scheme you two came up with to get rid of the veilfallen?"

"Paranoia will be your downfall, Calierin," Rífíor says. "Believe what you will. It doesn't matter, and it doesn't change what Valeria and I are going to do. With time, you will know the truth. And you will thank us when you are able to cross back into Tirnanog. This is what I have been working hard to accomplish since I joined the veilfallen. I have never lost sight of the real goal. You, on the other hand, care more about castigating humans than anything else."

I wince at his choice of words, but they aren't wrong. Calierin takes pleasure in inflicting pain on my kind. She was gleeful every time she had the chance to torment me, and always harbored the grim expectation that she'd be allowed to do worse the next time.

It suddenly occurs to me that if Calierin goes back to Tirnanog she might come back with an army of people just like her. I shiver at the prospect, which Jago has seen more clearly from the beginning. What if reopening the veil is a mistake?

If you can open it, you can close it again, a small voice says inside my head. Yes. I need to keep this possibility in mind. I can't lose sight of what's right due to fear.

Rífíor goes on. "It's up to you. You can either go back to the capital, or you can help us get there and witness the miracle we have been praying for all this time."

Kadewyn's brow furrows. "Castellan guards are after you." His words are thoughtful. "We saw them on the road. They seemed . . . desperate. That's why you need our help."

Rífíor nods in assent. "Yes, and I feel it is only a matter of time before they get clever enough and find us." A pause. "What do you say then?"

Kadewyn thinks for a moment, his pale eyes roving over the ground as he seems to ponder every aspect of the situation.

"Are you seriously considering going with him again?" Calierin demands. "After the way he betrayed us? Have you lost your mind?"

Kadewyn shrugs. "Why else would he be traveling west with her?"

"The hells if I know, but we did not come here to fall into one of his traps again."

"Given that your original goal failed," Rífíor puts in, "perhaps you should reconsider." He puts on a crooked grin.

"Fuck you!" Calierin spits.

"Hate me all you want, Calierin, but you can't afford to dismiss me—not when you are already trying to remember if Tirnanog really smells as sweet as in your memories."

"Think about it, Kadewyn," Calierin says, "if she can really reopen the veil, it means her family was the one responsible for its collapse in the first place and every single one of them must pay for all we have suffered."

"My family had absolutely nothing to do with the veil's collapse," I say. "I think you have been barking up the wrong tree all along," I direct a pointed glance at Rífíor, "and the person responsible for all of it has been cleverly hiding amongst you all along."

Rífíor blows air through his nose, unamused. "Such an overactive imagination."

"Why would she say that, Rífíor?" Kadewyn asks.

Ríffor sneers. "Your guess is as good as mine."

Kadewyn doesn't say anything else, but his expression tells me he sees merit in my words. Unlike Calierin, he seems like someone who uses his brain. After a long moment, he makes up his mind. "All right, I'll go with you. I'll help." He starts walking in our direction.

"You cannot be that stupid," Calierin insists.

Kadewyn glances over his shoulder. "Like Ríffor said, if there is the slightest chance that this is true, I cannot afford to doubt him. I care not about revenge, Calierin. All I care about is seeing my wife and daughter again, and I would not forgive myself if the veil reopens, and I go one more day without them."

"Those heartstrings of yours have always been your weakness, and one day, they will be the death of you." Calierin is all resentment and taut muscles, while Kadewyn only looks resigned.

"Perhaps," he says, "but following my heart has never led me to regret anything in my long life, and I am not about to turn a deaf ear when such a chance presents itself." Turning his pale countenance to Ríffor, he says, "I'll get my horse."

"Kadewyn," Calierin chides in one last effort to make him change his mind.

He glances over his shoulder. "What do you have to lose? You saw what that amulet did for her. Your magic was no match for it. Do you not want to find out what has the power to easily best you?"

The sorceress's expression changes, and I can see curiosity taking over. She will come. I have no doubt about it.

Niamhara, I hope you know what you're doing.

32

VALERIA

"My only hope for survival is leaving the realm."

Loreleia Elhice – Mate Rite Candidate – 1999 DV

Hours later, we find ourselves on the road. To my relief, Rífíor was of the same mind as me and thought it would be better for Calierin and Kadewyn to follow us at a distance, unnoticed. They're to be our scouts and keep an eye on the road ahead as well as behind us.

Despite the sorceress's presence, knowing that we're guarded eases my mind a bit. We will have proper warning if guards come searching for us again. This allows us to leave the stuffy wagon to walk alongside the horses when we slow or take a rest. Another advantage is not having to be cooped up with Rífíor in that cramped space. He prefers walking most of the time, even when the pace intensifies. He seems tireless, able to keep up thanks to his fae speed.

As Jago and I exit the wagon for one of our walking stints, he braces his hands around his waist and arches his back, stretching and causing his joints to pop.

"I swear I would be willing to walk all the way there," he says. "I hate that wagon. It reeks of unwashed Rífíor."

I chuckle. He isn't wrong. It really stinks in there.

We walk for a few minutes in silence. Cuervo flies overhead. I watch him catch the currents, easily gliding through the air, not a flap of his wings needed. A pang of longing hits my chest as I imagine flying alongside him, a warm breeze caressing my face. So many times I've wished to know if I inherited Father's abilities, if I would be able to shift were the veil still connecting us to Tirnanog, and espiritu still flowing between the realms.

Jago's question pulls me back to reality. "What do you think he's hiding?"

"Rífíor, you mean?" I ask.

He nods.

I shake my head. "I don't know for sure, but I think he had something to do with the veil's collapse. He says my mother did it, but—"

"Your mother? That's crazy."

I have avoided the conversation with Jago for fear of where it might lead. "That's what I thought at first, but now, I believe him."

He frowns. "You're joking, right?"

"Like Nana said, my mother *did* have The Eldrystone in her possession, Jago. Whether she took it from Rífíor or the Fae King, she had something that didn't belong to her—not by a long shot. I'm sure she had a good reason. I *do* believe that. The question is . . . what role does Rífíor play in all of that? He was aware that Niamhara's conduit was in Castella, and that my mother had it. That means they knew each other. Something happened between them."

Jago makes a face. "You mean like . . ."

"No! Not like that."

Gods! I hope not.

This turn in the conversation is what I was afraid of.

"Um, hey, you looked impressive back there," he says, quickly changing subjects. "Almost like your mother's daughter. The amulet did good by you this time."

"It did. I wasn't sure if it would work, but I had to confront her, Jago. I had to prove to myself and to her that I'm not afraid of her."

"I'm glad it didn't hang you out to dry then. I wouldn't like a fried egg for a cousin."

"Ha ha."

He winks, lifting my spirits.

After another quiet moment, I say, "The sight of her still makes me sick to my stomach, though. All that she did to me, all she made me see, it's so hard to keep it all locked inside."

He comes close and wraps an arm around me. "I'm sorry, Val. You can talk to me about it."

I shake my head, unable to go on.

"It's not because you're embarrassed, is it? Because you shouldn't be. You know you can tell me anything."

"I know. I know. It's just . . . I'm trying to keep it all out of my mind, so talking about it defeats the purpose."

"And that's working for you?"

"For the most part. At least the nightmares stopped." I give him a wry smile. "But seeing her . . . I don't know . . . it brought some of those emotions back up."

"I can't even imagine how you must feel. I'm sorry you had to go through all of that."

I swallow hard.

"Hey, you confronted her." He gives me a squeeze. "She has no power over you. You were absolutely amazing."

I smile, knowing it was all thanks to the amulet. Without it, I would probably run and hide.

"And same as I'm here if you need to talk, I'm also here if you need help kicking her ass again, all right? Just name the time and place and I'll come."

We both laugh, and he bumps his hip against mine.

"Have I told you how lucky I am to have you?" I ask.

"Maybe."

"Well, I am. If it weren't for you, I would be alone in all of this."

"And if it weren't for you, I would be napping in my room or enjoying the next vintage in the cellar."

I push him, and he staggers away, laughing.

We go around a bend in the road, and I'm startled by someone's presence, sitting on a fallen log. It's Rífíor, chewing on a blade of grass. His legs are crossed at the ankles, and the way he is looking at me lets me know he heard everything Jago and I were talking about.

Damn fae hearing!

I need to remember that out of sight shouldn't mean out of mind with him. I hated that he heard how vulnerable Calierin makes me feel, how the torment they put me through sits on me like a stain I may never get rid of.

"*Bastardo!*" I whisper as we pass, sure that he also heard that.

"No worries. I don't think he overheard," Jago pauses. "*Pshaw*, who am I kidding? Of course he did. But don't worry, we'll be rid of him soon."

Rífíor stays behind, while Jago and I continue walking behind the wagon. We're quiet for a long time before Jago starts a new conversation.

"So . . . tell me about Esmeralda."

I glance at him sidelong, arching my eyebrows and putting on a teasing smirk.

"Don't look at me like that," he says. "She's beautiful. I'm smitten." He clutches his heart, trying to sound carefree, but it doesn't work. His natural state is already nonchalant, so trying to act as if he doesn't care makes him look foolish. It's as if Cuervo were trying to don a cloak of black feathers.

I open my mouth to tease him about it, but then stop myself. I don't want to deter him from what could be his first real crush in a long time. Though maybe I should. It's Esmeralda we're dealing with, after all. She's as shrewd as they come—not that Jago might not benefit from a little of his own medicine. Ever since he developed into the handsome man that he is, he has broken countless hearts, never apologizing for any of his actions. Honestly, I'm torn. I don't want him to get *his* heart broken, but I'm afraid he will never learn to be a better man if he doesn't meet his match, and maybe Esmeralda is exactly that.

"What can you tell me about her?" he asks.

"I don't know much about her besides what I learned during the brief time I spent with them. She travels with the troop and sells poultices and draughts. She learned the trade from her mother. I met her, too. She doesn't travel and stays back in Castellina because she's sick. I can tell Esmeralda worries about her a lot."

"Any siblings? A dad?" he asks.

"I don't think so."

"What about a . . . boyfriend?"

"I don't know. She didn't mention one."

He smiles, looking satisfied.

"Um, I think she's a pickpocket," I say.

"What? Are you serious?"

"Yes. On our way back from Alsur, we stopped in a small town. She pretended to bump into a man, and the next thing I knew, we were running. He called us thieves and yelled for the guardias. It turns out she took his money bag."

Instead of looking concerned, Jago seems amused. "I guess I better hold on to my valuables." He laughs.

"I don't think it's funny. I think it's dangerous, and one day she'll get caught."

"And then she'll hang, unlike you and me, no matter who we murder." There's sarcasm in his tone, but we both know it's not far from the truth.

In our realm, not everyone gets what they earn, and not everyone gets what they deserve. I wish I could change that, but it's unrealistic, given our greedy human nature. I smile sadly to myself. It seems I might grow up to be a philosopher.

That day, we don't stop for a midday meal. Instead, we ride until late afternoon, then find a place off road to eat dinner and sleep. The sun hasn't fully gone down, and the sky is tainted in beautiful colors that soothe my mood. A river runs nearby, the sounds also calming my senses. Once more, we stay away from the rest of the troop. Riffor tends to the horses, making himself useful.

Gaspar seems grateful for the help, and immediately starts cooking, claiming a hunger big enough to eat a dragon.

When I offer to help Esmeralda chop the vegetables for Gaspar's soup, Jago, who only enters a kitchen to pilfer freshly baked rolls, promptly volunteers to lend her a hand instead.

Stepping aside, I find myself idle, my attention promptly ensnared by Rífíor's lithe, graceful movements. The muscles in his forearms flex as he removes the horses' harness and pats their necks. His trousers tighten over his backside as he bends to check their hooves. When he catches me looking, I pretend disinterest and bend down to tie my already tied boots. I mumble curses under my breath.

Calierin and Kadewyn are supposed to be keeping an eye on the surrounding areas, ensuring no guardias are near, but I don't fully trust them—no matter what Niamhara thinks. I wouldn't put it past Calierin to betray us.

Planning to do my own reconnaissance, I glance around, searching for an easy-to-climb, tall tree. After a quick scan of the woods, I spot the perfect one across the clearing. I pass in front of Rífíor as I make my way there, but I keep my gaze straight ahead. I feel his attention on me, almost like a touch.

Doing my best to ignore him, I reach the tree and begin climbing, easily finding handholds to pull myself up higher and higher. If there is a tree within Nido's walls that can be climbed, I have climbed it. When I was little, it was one of my favorite pastimes. I could outdo anyone, including Jago, who was very careless and willing to try anything just to beat me. However, he simply didn't possess the skill. He used to joke that Mother's ancestors were monkeys. I whacked him in the head with a stick for being so rude and spent an hour kneeling in a corner because I drew blood. Nana's punishments were ruthless sometimes.

Before long, I find myself at the top of the tree about forty feet off the ground. From my vantage point, I can see everything. I see the skyline, dancing with different hues of orange and pink. I see parts of the road we've been following, meandering around patches of forest and steady heading west. I see the rest of the troop some distance away, busying themselves with their own tasks to procure dinner and care for the horses. I see the river we heard earlier. It gurgles with clear water and runs across the land in very much the same way as the road.

What I don't see is our friends, Calierin and Kadewyn. Not that I expect to. They're meant to stay hidden, unnoticed. So I guess that's a good thing, as good as the fact that I don't see any guardias either.

After I'm satisfied with my surveillance, I find that I don't want to get back down to earth. I'd rather stay here closer to the clouds, the fresh air caressing my face and stirring my hair. Inevitably, my thoughts steer toward Amira. I grab a hold of The Eldrystone and wonder how she's doing, what she's thinking. My chest tightens with a mix of emotions.

Will she let me explain myself when all of this is said and done? Will she even want to see me? Will she think of me as a friend or an enemy? Will her eyes hold the same sisterly love it always has? Perhaps I'm being too hopeful with these questions. Perhaps a better question would be . . . will she allow me to live, or decree my execution?

I shake my head, trying to chase the thoughts away. I shove them in a separate corner of my mind and draw the curtain closed. I've shoved many things in there lately. For the longest time, that room only existed to hold memories of Mother's death, but recently, there's been no shortage of troubling matters that also need to be stored away.

Turning my back on that hidden room, leaving behind the horror of my parents' deaths, Bastien's betrayal, Calierin's torture, and all the questions about my sister, I focus on nothing else but the peaceful swaying motion of the trees and the distant gurgling of the river.

After some time of quiet contemplation, a splashing sound captures my attention. I glance in its direction to find someone bathing in the river. No, not just someone, Rífíor. He has jumped in, clothes and all. I can tell it's him even from up here. His jet-black hair and wide shoulders are unmistakable.

"About time," I murmur. The smell of dungeon inside the wagon was getting unbearable.

From the safety of my perch, I watch him swim to and fro. He seems at ease in the water. In fact, he seems to fit right in with nature, as if he couldn't possibly belong anywhere else.

After a good soak, he rubs vigorously at his clothes without taking them off. After thoroughly scrubbing them, he walks to the shore and removes his shirt. Twisting it, he expresses all the water, then hangs it from a branch. The perfect lines of his chest ensnare my gaze, and I find myself admiring the expanse of smooth skin, and the ridges and valleys of his abdomen that narrow down to his waist, where a trail of dark hair disappears under his trousers. I catch my lower lip between my teeth, telling myself I should look away.

He proceeds to remove his pants then.

You definitely should look away now, Val.

But I can't. I'm hypnotized and suddenly reliving that night we spent together. The tip of his tongue running along my upper lip. The press of his body on top of mine. The silver scars across his chest.

"Damn, is there anything about you that won't make me lose my mind?... This is not about altruism, princess. I want to fuck you. This night, you are mine."

He twists his pants in the same fashion as his shirt, but I'm barely aware of this. Instead, I'm mesmerized by the way water sluices down his strong thighs. The way his hip bones jut out. The way his powerful shaft hangs between his legs.

A hot jolt strikes my core, and warm moisture seeps between my legs.

Gods! What's wrong with me? Why does he make me feel this way? Why does my body want him when my mind easily finds a million reasons to hate him?

Suddenly, Ríffor goes still.

I stiffen, fearing he has perceived some sort of danger. He's attentive for a frozen moment, head cocked to one side, then his dark eyes flick directly to mine.

A second jolt of desire hits my core, followed by the heat of a blush.

Gods! Smite this tree and take me down with it.
No such luck.
Cheeks burning, I climb down the tree and, when I reach the bottom, sink to my haunches and hide my face in my hands.
For the love of all the gods, what is he going to think now?

33
RÍFÍOR

"It has started. A dark shadow falls over Castellina."

Gaspar Patrach – Romani Diviner – 21 AV

The river feels frigid under the light of the moon above. While everyone else in the camp sleeps, as I should be doing, my mind remains restless. Despite my efforts, I can't quell the hunger within me. It's been present all along, but it intensified earlier when I sensed someone watching me while I bathed. It took me a moment to spot her—a little raven perched at the top of that tree, hunting for a meal. But I found her.

She was a fair distance away, but I saw her more clearly than she may realize. Desire flickered in her expression—her pupils dilated, her lower lip caught between her teeth as she trembled. It was this unguarded display that did this to me.

I'm submerged up to my neck, and this icy water should quiet my instincts, but this want is unlike anything I have ever experienced . . . even with Saethara.

Valeria has done a convincing job of making me believe she hates me, but her face told a different story.

A story that sets fire to my blood.

Cursing under my breath, I walk out of the river, water dripping down my body. I crack my neck and don my now-dry clothes. Sleep will be impossible tonight. *Curse all the gods!*

Once dressed, I sit on a rock and stare at the flowing current. Moonlight silvers its surface, which I disturb with a handful of rocks as I search for yet another distraction. I try everything to get her out of my mind, but images of that one night we spent together keep parading in front of me, blinding me to everything else. Her naked skin glowing in the lamplight, the peaks of her firm breasts, the column of her neck as she threw her head back in ecstasy. I can almost taste the sweetness on her skin in my mouth and feel the warmth at her core as I entered her.

I jerk to my feet, growling in frustration. My cock is so hard it throbs uncomfortably. Lust clouding my every thought, I whirl and march back toward the camp. With every step, reason fights valiantly against my desire, but it loses every time.

The clearing is quiet, only the chirp of insects and the occasional hoot of an owl disturbing the peace. I stand at the edge of the clearing, chest falling and rising as I survey the camp. Tonight, everyone sleeps under the stars, except for Valeria. She opted for spreading her bedroll inside the wagon. It couldn't be more perfect, especially because she left the door open, and I've convinced myself it is an invitation for me to come in.

On bare feet, I cut across the clearing and gently step onto the wagon. It lowers with my weight as I watch Valeria's prone shape stretched along the length of the planked floor. She is sound asleep. Her rhythmic breathing tells me that much.

I hesitate only for an instant, thinking there's still time to turn around and take another dunk in the river. She is not waiting for me. She is lost in a dream, judging by the way her eyes revolve under closed lids.

But who am I trying to fool?

I ease the door closed, shutting out most of the moonlight. However, I can still discern her silhouette illuminated by the faint rays filtering through a small window carved at the highest point of the front wall.

Doing my best not to scare her, I kneel at her feet, then crawl on hands and knees up the length of her body, never touching her. I feel her radiating warmth, and it is like a salve that promises healing and maybe even salvation.

When I am face to face with her—my arms and legs framing her body—I inhale her scent, impossibly getting more aroused.

"Valeria," I whisper, her name a guttural growl deep in my throat.

I wait for her eyes to open and her sleep-addled mind to clear and realize I am here. It requires all of my will not to take her right away without even asking. When her gaze locks with mine, I wait for her answer. I hope she will say *yes*.

If she does not, I will beg if I must.

VALERIA

My eyes spring open as a low rumble, like a caress, travels over my skin. I nearly scream when a feral gaze locks with mine, but a callous finger to my lips makes me hold back.

"*Shh*, it's me," Ríffor says. "I am not here to hurt you, unless you want me to."

"Get off me," I manage in a trembling voice. He could be here to steal the amulet.

"Are you sure that's what you want, princess?"

"Of course I'm sure."

"The way you were looking at me earlier makes me think otherwise."

The hunger in his eyes tells me he's not worried about The Eldrystone right now. I press my hands to his chest, ready to push him away, but the effort is feeble, and instead, I find myself enjoying his solidity.

He chuckles, a sound as deep as the darkness in his eyes. "You want me."

"You want me more." I toss the words like a challenge.

"Yes, I do." He cups my face with one hand and starts lowering his mouth to mine.

"No!"

He stops, frowning.

This time, I do push him away. Reluctantly, he sits back. I slide my legs out from under him and sit.

A combination of annoyance and disappointment shape his features. His lips part to say something, but no words come out. Shifting my legs, I kneel, which brings me closer to him. I can't help it. My body takes the reins from my brain when Ríffor is this close. My nose is inches from his. His chest rises and falls at a faster than normal rhythm.

"Was that all it took, veilfallen? A look from me?" I ask, chest brimming with satisfaction.

His nostrils flare. "That was more than just *a look*. Maybe it was an invitation."

I lean closer still. His breath is warm. Gently, I lay a finger across his lips at the same time that I press my lips to his jaw and begin to kiss him.

He groans, and his hands wrap around my waist.

"You may kiss me, just remember one thing," I say, pulling away but leaving my finger across his lips. "*Not* on the mouth."

There's a glint in his eyes, come and gone in a second, but I interpret it for what it is. Relief. He agrees with what I'm asking.

Sex but not intimacy.

We are adversaries, pieces sitting on opposite sides of a board with a clear dividing line across the middle. There can be no intimacy when such a chasm lies between us, when betrayal has been the fuel to this fire between us.

He nods, then lowers his mouth to my throat and begins to kiss the very spot where my pulse beats out of control.

"I shall kiss you everywhere, milady," he says, his tongue tracing a circle under my earlobe as he easily lays me back down and settles on top of me again.

He takes his place between my legs, his hardness pressing deliciously against my middle. I groan and throw my head back as he continues to dispense kisses along my neck and collarbone.

Expertly, his hands pull my tunic over my head and discard it to the side. Just as quickly, he removes his own shirt, and then his heated skin settles over mine. We both sigh, enjoying the silky pleasure of it.

Trailing kisses lower and lower, he places his mouth on my left nipple, over the fabric of my binding. His hot breath filters through, making me quiver with need.

Abruptly, he pulls on the binding and rips it apart. My breasts fall free, and he growls deep in his throat, hooded eyes roving over my naked torso. Hungrily, he lowers his mouth again and begins to suck, whirling his tongue at the same time. The sharp points of his teeth scrape my skin, and my core thrums, hot and wet.

I suck in a breath as his tongue whirls and flicks. Greedily, my hands travel down his muscular abdomen. He thrusts his hardness into me as I pull on his waistband, fully distracting me from my goal.

"This is my moment," he rasps, then pulls down my leggings along with my undergarment before I have time to realize what he's doing.

He leans back and kneels for a better look. I feel both shy and exuberant under his dark gaze.

Tugging on my legs, he places me exactly where he wants me. I gasp as his right hand travels down the inside of my leg. He stops just short of his target and begins to trace the outer lips with his forefinger. He stops again, this time right in the very center. Holding my gaze, he slides in, making me moan.

His finger curls as he dips it in and out. I'm lost in ecstasy and miss the exact moment he lies next to me, but now he's there, kissing my breast, sucking on my nipple, all along reaching deep inside of me. I buck my hips, desperate for all he has to give.

As I tremble, he slides another finger inside me, then moves to kneel between my legs again. Slowly, he lowers his mouth to my apex and laps once. My eyes fly wide open in surprise.

He smiles in satisfaction.

I stare at him intently, asking for more. He obliges, lowering his head and circling my most sensitive spot with the tip of his tongue. His hand thrusts harder, and I accept the offering by lifting my hips.

My body tenses with ecstasy as he simultaneously sucks and flicks his tongue against my tender nub.

Undone, I moan in rapture, my body assaulted by tremors as release washes over me, leaving me feeling boneless and in awe of all the amazing sensations he can easily coax from my body.

Gods! Why does he have such power over me?

34
VALERIA

"Rífíor of the Veilfallen asked for it. The pay is too good to turn down. I'm going after him."

Galen Síocháin – Fae Sorcerer – 21 AV

I spend the next week hating myself and regretting my actions. *I hate him* is a mantra that repeats itself over and over.

I hate myself and this irresistible attraction I feel for Rífíor. It's an infection, an incurable one at that. Every time the memory assaults me, shame burns in my cheeks.

Today, as I sit alone inside the wagon, it's no different. We're heading steadily west on our journey to the veil. I'm grateful to be alone while Gaspar sits with the driver, and my cousin and Rífíor walk outside.

Jago asked me to come out and get some fresh air, but if he keeps seeing my distracted expression, he will interrogate me until he figures out the reason. Instead, I made excuses and stayed here, hiding like a coward, the way I've been doing all week.

As much as I try to condemn my weakness, however, I can't

help but relive the exhilaration of that night every day without fail. The way Ríffor knew exactly where and how to touch me, the way his supple mouth dispensed kisses along my jaw, tantalizingly close to my lips, while his daring fingers reduced me to nothing but a bundle of sensations that promised to light up my world, then promptly *and* thoroughly delivered on that promise.

The only redeeming aspect is that I didn't allow his mouth to touch mine. At least that's what I keep telling myself since I did allow him to reach more private places. Except it does mean something, doesn't it? Because his dark eyes glinted at the request. He wanted sex as much as I did, but not more. So my request was evidently welcome.

You're a fool, Valeria.

A fool in need of a jolt to the head that will make me stop hoping he'll come to me again as I've been expecting every night since then, just to feel great relief when he stays away.

At the brink of pulling on my hair and screaming, I opt to exit the wagon and join Jago. Remaining inside, allowing my thoughts to fester, feels even more unbearable than enduring Jago's abnormally astute questions.

Throwing the door open, I set La Matadora behind my back. I'm poised to step onto the ground when my ears start ringing and my heart hammers like a giant fist, erasing all the nonsense from my mind. What's happening? This is the third time I've felt this way since we left Castellina. The first time was when I woke up as guards approached the wagon, and the second time was right before Calierin and Kadewyn ambushed us. It seems like every time there's danger I—

Rífíor suddenly emerges from the side, brandishing his sword. Assuming a menacing stance, he positions himself in the middle of the road with his back to me. The muscles of his wide back ripple as he twirls the sword.

"What is it?" I jump off the wagon, my razor-sharp survival instinct kicking into action.

He answers, without glancing back. "Hooves. Many and fast. Twenty horses or more."

Oh, shit!

"Not Calierin or Kadewyn then?"

"No."

Just as the word comes out of Rífíor's mouth, Kadewyn suddenly arrives from the side, riding in a thunder of motion. His horse leaps over the thick brush and skids to a stop.

"Royal guards!" he shouts.

"What the fuck?" Rífíor demands. "Why did you let them—"

"I didn't let them *anything*," Kadewyn cuts him off. "They have magic and hid their progress. I didn't spot them until they were too close."

Rífíor curses, using words I don't understand.

Jago is there in the next instant. "Hurry, Val, let's hide." He starts to climb onto the wagon.

Rífíor growls in frustration. "If they have magic, they will find us. We might as well hand ourselves over if we trap ourselves in there."

"Then what do we do?" Jago asks just as the beat of hooves reaches my ears and sends my heart into a matching gallop.

"Use your amulet," Kadewyn says. "Only magic will hide you from them."

Swiftly, I reach for it under my tunic, expecting to feel its warmth, but it's cold to the touch, unresponsive like before. *Dammit!*

I shake my head. "It's not working."

"What?" Jago punches the air.

"Then ride with me." Kadewyn extends a hand in my direction. "Quick, come on!"

I hesitate.

"No!" Jago protests. "We have to stay together. Try it again."

I squeeze the amulet tightly. *Please, please, work!* They all watch me intently, but Niamhara has decided to abandon us again.

"Nothing," I say.

"*Puta madre!*" Jago curses.

"We need to ride then, catch up to Calierin." Kadewyn offers me his hand again. "Her magic is the only thing that can save you now."

Rífíor lets out a frustrated growl. "Valeria, Kadewyn is right. Ride with him. I will run alongside and keep up until we reach Calierin."

"Val." Jago puts a hand on my shoulder, his expression conflicted.

"Jago."

I see the logic in what Rífíor and Kadewyn are saying, but I can't leave my cousin. They'll bring him back to Castellina, and there's no telling what punishment Amira might devise for him in her state of mind.

He must see something in my expression because he squeezes me and gives me a resigned nod. "Go, I'll be all right."

"Amira is out of her mind," I said. "She might . . ."

"I'll be fine. She wouldn't hurt me. I'm her favorite cousin, remember?" He smiles sadly.

"You're her *only* cousin, you idiot."

"Exactly."

"Hurry!" Rífíor growls. "They're close."

Jago gives me a tight squeeze. "Go get them. Fix this mess. Go, go!" He pushes me toward Kadewyn, whose hand is still stretched out in my direction. "Wait!" He jumps into the wagon and tosses out our rucksacks. "Take these." We both catch them.

"Thank you," I mouth.

Brimming with fear and guilt, I take Kadewyn's hand. With one swift pull, he yanks me onto the horse. I throw my leg over the animal's hindquarters, take the mount, and wrap my arms around his waist.

"Ya!" He spurs the gelding forward.

The horse bucks, then takes off at full gallop. He steers us back the way they came. We leap over the bushes and dash through the forest, weaving in and out through the trees. I glance to the side and see Rífíor. He's running, arms and legs pumping fast. It's a sight to behold. I had no idea he could produce this kind of speed. Looking over my shoulder, I see nothing but the trees we've left behind—no sign of my cousin or the troop.

Gods, please let them be all right. Protect them from Amira's anger.

I would never be able to forgive myself if something happens to them, to Jago.

The gelding huffs and jumps over a dead log. I hold on to Kadewyn for dear life. Rífíor still follows, but he's falling behind the further we go. It seems he can only maintain top speed for a short while. We keep heading west, the woods thickening, making the terrain harder to navigate. Soon, Kadewyn urges the horse back toward the road.

"Faster," Ríffor shouts. "They're coming." He releases another burst of energy and catches up with us. His lips are peeled back as he exerts himself to the fullest.

Looking back, I catch a glimpse of our pursuers. I see at least five of them. One of them, the one in the lead, lifts a hand, holding a cloud of red magic.

"Shit! Where's Calierin?" I shout.

"She'll find us. She won't miss this racket," Kadewyn shouts back.

I guess she won't, but she'd better hurry.

An orb of lethal espiritu hits the tree to our left. It bursts into flames, causing the horse to shriek. The animal careens as Kadewyn steers it into the road. For a precarious moment, I fear we'll topple over, but the gelding rights itself. Without stopping, we keep galloping, the open road stretching in front of us.

I glance back, waiting for Ríffor to break out of the woods, but he doesn't. *Where is he?* A part of me is worried, but I know he's all right. It's safer for him to keep running through the woods. He can avoid the trees more easily than the horse can. He's not lying dead on the ground, reduced to an espiritu-burnt piece of charcoal.

He's fine. He's fine.

He'll be there to help me figure out how to reopen the veil. That's the only reason I'm worried about him. If Amira's sorcerer-for-hire did hurt him, I couldn't care less if it weren't for our mission.

"Calierin, where in the hells are you?" Kadewyn shouts to the winds.

As if summoned, she comes around the bend, her horse skidding and nearly falling into a ditch. She takes a moment to assess the situation, violet eyes homing in on our pursuers. She must spot danger because she braces her legs against the saddle, rears up, and shoots a veritable fountain of espiritu. It flies over our heads.

Instinctively, we both lean forward, making ourselves smaller. After it passes, I look back and watch the shimmering force collide against a vicious attack that was spiraling directly toward us. There's a loud *boom* and sparks fly out in a circular pattern.

Saints and feathers! They're willing to kill us, willing to kill *me*. Are these Amira's orders? I can't believe they are. The guards must be taking liberties. If I die, they'll tell her it was an accident and call their mission to stop us accomplished.

Our horse reaches Calierin's and throws its head back, letting out a loud whinny.

Expertly, she pulls on the reins and maneuvers her mount back the way she came. "Follow me," she orders, then guides us around the bend. Quickly and taking advantage that we're hidden from view, she veers into the forest. "This way."

The animals break through the bushes, leaving obvious signs of our passage. However, a stream of Calierin's espiritu smooths the vegetation over, erasing any trace of the disturbance.

"Where's Rífíor?" I demand.

"I'm right here." He appears as if out of thin air from behind. "Worried about me, princess?"

"Of course I was worried," I spit. "Your expiration date isn't until we open the veil."

"*Shh.*" Kadewyn puts a finger to his lips.

Is this the plan, to hide so close to the road? I glare at Calierin, is she not going to use her espiritu to hide us? Panic mounting, I reach for The Eldrystone once more, but its power eludes me still.

Puta madre!

We're all as still as statues. Even the horses are still. My heart beats in my ears, and though I strain to listen for our enemies' approach, all I hear is its incessant pounding.

Rífior stands in a crouch, sword in hand. He looks ready for anything, even if his expression betrays no worry. Does he have that much confidence in Calierin's espiritu? I felt the ravages of her cruelty inside my mind, and I've used my blade to block her potent volleys. But can she be one with the gentle hand of nature? Can she help us blend in with the swaying foliage and let the birds' song be the only sound of notice?

Hooves thunder in their approach. I bite the inside of my cheek and hold my breath. Our pursuers streak by. Relief begins to take shape. My shoulders relax a fraction.

Someone shouts, "Hold!"

The horses come to a sudden stop.

"This way," the same voice calls.

Rífior doesn't wait. He darts into the road and charges, sword raised to mow down whoever stands in his way. Kadewyn and

Calierin jump off their horses, matching Rífíor step for step. My hand flies to the hilt of Father's sword at my back, but it freezes there.

No. No more death.

The guardias aren't really our enemies. They're *my* people. I can't let this happen. I remove my hand from La Matadora and reach into my rucksack. Straightening and putting on an air of command, I follow the others, an irrefutable order issuing from my lips.

"Stop in the name of the Plumanegra Dominion," I say, holding up my Plumanegra key.

There is enough force in my voice that it carries through the ranks. Fae and human alike halt in their tracks. Their gazes turn to me in a moment of hesitation I must take advantage of. I place the Plumanegra key in my pocket and take hold of The Eldrystone next, begging it to do its job . . . if it comes to it.

"I am Valeria Plumanegra and demand to know who's in charge?"

Next to me, Rífíor lowers his head and tilts it in my direction. "This will not work," he murmurs.

I ignore him.

A woman I've never met urges her horse forward from the back of the line. Four others accompany her. She cuts a formidable presence atop her sleek mount, flanked by a retinue of guardias and a figure clad in a heavy cloak, presumably the hired sorcerer. With a steely gaze fixed on me, her features betray nothing. Every line on her stern face speaks of resolve and duty.

"It is I," she says.

"State your name and rank." The bars on her left arm give me the answer, but it's the customary question.

"Teniente Coronel Eva Toromayor, here on Capitán Armando Quiñones's orders and by extension the queen's," she responds in the clear tone inherent to her military training.

I open my mouth to issue an order, but she cuts me off.

"In the name of Queen Amira Plumanegra, you are under arrest."

"That's ridiculous," I burst out. "Under what charge?"

"The charge is treason. Punishable by death."

I nearly gasp. Is this what she's been instructed to say to scare us? Or is it true? I hate that I don't know the answer, that I fear my own sister wants me dead.

"Surrender your weapons or face the consequences," she says.

I examine the faces of all those present, there are a couple that look familiar. Yet, there isn't a shred of sympathy in their expressions. On the contrary, they appear irate.

The sorcerer slowly lifts his hands.

Rífíor tilts his face upward to meet the male's eye and recognition widens his eyes. "Galen?"

The sorcerer's eyes flick toward Rífíor. As if time has slowed, I watch his expression morph from determination to utter shock. He lowers his hood and blinks as if trying to wake up from a dream.

"It can't be," the sorcerer says in a rush of breath.

Before I can blink, Rífíor leaps, propelling himself off the ground as if on springs. Stuck in a time bubble, I watch him fly through the air, sword poised to cut the sorcerer down.

Calierin springs into action next, followed by Kadewyn.

Gods!

I can't let this happen. If I do, there's no telling who will be dead or alive in the end. Gripping The Eldrystone so hard my fingers ache, I pour all of my will into a command.

"STOP!"

The guardias, who have only begun to draw their swords, halt mid-maneuver. The horses freeze, their mouths open in a silent cry as spurs dig into their sides. Mouth falling open in horror, I watch as the skin of our pursuers begins to change color, turning gray.

I shake my head, convinced I'm imagining things. This isn't—

As if he's hit an invisible wall, Rífíor plummets to the ground with a heavy thud, his forward trajectory coming to a sudden stop. He growls and twists in pain, the sword falling from his hand.

"Mallachtdorch!" Kadewyn curses and rushes to Rífíor's side. "What is wrong? Gods, your arm!"

There's no answer from Rífíor, only more growling.

Kadewyn glances up at me, an accusation in his expression.

Still clutching The Eldrystone, I take two steps closer, afraid of what I'll see. Rífíor's teeth are bared, his strong features twisted up in agony. With monumental effort, he moves his arm to show me what I've done.

From his elbow to the tips of his fingers, his skin is gray and rough. As I stare, the color travels upward, reaching for his biceps. He twists and groans like a wounded beast. I don't know what to make of what I'm seeing. My mind stutters as my eyes dance between the frozen guardias and Rífíor.

I fall to my knees next to him.

"You turned them to stone," Calierin says in awe, poking one of the horses' snouts.

Kadewyn curses, sounding angry rather than shocked this time. "Do something!"

Jolted by his cry, I swiftly take hold of Rífíor's stiff hand and squeeze it in mine. I close my eyes and think of his fingers, moving and healthy. An image of his hands caressing my body surges in my memory. The heat of shame rises up my neck, and I start to suppress the memory.

Rífíor's eyes roll in the back of his head as his entire arm turns gray.

"You are killing him!" Kadewyn stomps a foot, lashing out.

In desperation, I let the memories of the other night flood me, reliving, in my mind's eye, the way his rough, calloused hands brought me to ecstasy with their gentle touch. My eyes close of their own accord. The Eldrystone grows warm, and in the next instant, Rífíor's hardened fingers turn supple.

His groans of pain stop, and a natural color slowly returns to his skin. Wincing, he holds out his hand and flexes his fingers.

Overwhelmed, I push away from him, standing and fearfully lifting my eyes to the petrified guards. Teniente Coronel Toromayor's blade is only halfway out, and her mouth is open in a mute cry. The sorcerer—Galen, Rífíor called him—has his hands up, twisted in the weaving of an incomplete spell.

Each face is carved in stone, grimaces and cries frozen . . . Forever?

Gods! I look at Rífíor, at his now-functional hand. No . . . not forever. I can undo it.

I take a step toward Teniente Coronel Toromayor. "I can . . . fix this."

Rífíor steps in front of me and shakes his head. "You stopped them. Now, we can keep going."

My head spins, and I let go of the amulet, horrified by what I've done. "I didn't want to hurt anyone."

"You could have fooled me," Calierin says, her violet eyes watching me with interest and cunning.

For some reason, I suddenly think of Jago saying we should stay together. Why did I leave the troop? I shouldn't be with these three. One of them lied to me for weeks, another one tortured me, and the other did absolutely nothing about it.

"We should go back to the troop," I say.

Rífíor shakes his head. "We cannot. We have to go before the other guards catch up."

"But why?" Calierin asks in a mocking tone. "It seems we have nothing to worry about." She glances sidelong at the mounted statues. "I mean . . . if Princess Valeria is capable of doing this, why are we worried?"

I lunge forward, ready to strangle the bitch. "I don't take pleasure in hurting others."

Rífíor holds me back while Calierin grins, looking pleased with herself.

"Valeria," Rífíor says softly. "We cannot go back." A pause. "Think it through, we will get there much faster and end this once and for all. We shouldn't take any chances."

The fight drains out of me, turning my bones to sand. I go limp in his arms. He holds me up, but I quickly regain my senses. I can't lose my resolve now. I must finish what I set out to do. Now more than ever.

"All right," I say.

Rífíor nods, and we walk back to the horses—two of them, which means we will have to ride in pairs. There's no way I'll ride with Calierin or Rífíor, so I stick with Kadewyn, which doesn't feel much better. Rífíor, however, has something else in mind. Quickly mounting Calierin's horse, he offers me a hand.

The sorceress's mouth twists in displeasure, but she doesn't say anything. I don't want to ride with him, but at least I know we have the same goal. I left Nido with him, after all. Resigned, I take his offered hand. He pulls me up, and somehow maneuvers me and the horse so I end up in front of him, his torso flush against my back, his arms caging me in as he holds the reins.

Before I can protest, he urges the horse forward, while Calierin and Kadewyn argue about who will control their horse. Rífíor doesn't wait for them, he charges forward, guiding us west and further away from the troop. My heart hurts at the thought of Jago left behind, the threat of treason hanging over his head. I hope they were able to get away from the guards. I hope he isn't on his way back to Castellina to face Amira's wrath.

Calierin and Kadewyn finally catch up with us a mile down the road. The former won the argument, and the latter seems resigned to ride in the back.

Without the troop, we cover more distance as we ride late into the evening. I try to ask Rífíor who that fae sorcerer was—Galen, he called him—but his response is an ineloquent grunt. I think of

Jago and Cuervo, who must have been hunting and will find me gone when he returns. Will he try to come after me?

We finally stop for the night, and only then, I realize there is no wagon to sleep in, not even a bedroll. Do we even have food? There are saddlebags on both horses, but they don't look like they hold much.

In the end, my worries about food are unfounded. Calierin ensnares four rabbits using her espiritu, and within a couple of hours, the delicious scent of roasted meat wafts through our small camp.

I eat because I know I have to. I even drink their cheap wine and welcome the burn as it goes down my throat. Once I've eaten my share, I lean back against a tree, my eyelids drooping with exhaustion.

Images of the day unroll before my eyes: Jago's worried face, a burning tree, horses and people made of stone. It all blends together, promising a night of restless sleep.

Despite the images, I drift off, but something rouses me. Blinking drowsily, I open my eyes. Through the thin plume of smoke rising from our fire, I spot Rífíor and Calierin standing some distance away. They face each other, their gestures sharp and jerky, indicating they're engaged in an argument.

Frowning, I watch them with interest, trying to catch what they're saying, but their words are unintelligible. As their exchange grows more heated, Rífíor makes a pacifying motion and gestures in my direction. Whatever he says seems to placate Calierin, and she nods as if they've reached some sort of agreement. An uneasy feeling climbs up my spine, suspicion settling in the pit of my stomach.

As Rífíor walks away, he looks in my direction. Swiftly, I close my eyes and pretend to be asleep again. I remain that way for several long minutes before I find another place to rest, one far away from Calierin, though close enough for me to still keep an eye on her. I don't plan on sleeping.

I will be watching her closely.

35
VALERIA

"Radina, my beloved mate, I pray to Niamhara that I shall embrace you and our daughter soon."

Kadewyn Zinceran – Veilfallen – 21 AV

A hand covers my mouth, and something sharp and pointed digs into my neck.

"Make a sound and I will bleed you," Calierin hisses.

I inhale sharply, a cry stuck in my throat. I stayed awake well past midnight, but at some point, exhaustion won the battle. I curse inwardly, angry with myself.

"Make a sound," she repeats, "and I swear I will give you a second smile, a very bloody one." Slowly, she removes her hand from my mouth and starts patting my pockets. She comes up with my Plumanegra key and regards it, cocking her head.

"What is this?" she demands.

She pockets the key in a heartbeat, and I almost yell at her to give it back. It's mine. Father gave it to me. In that instant, I want to turn her to stone, but a shiver runs through me remembering the guardias' faces and the way Rífíor screamed in pain. I'm not like her. That doesn't mean I'm helpless, though.

I take a deep breath and strike her wrist, sending her dagger flying.

"Drocháin!" she exclaims.

Growling, she wraps both hands around my neck and begins to choke me. But I know well how to get out of this situation. I don't need espiritu for this. From under her grip, I stick my hands between her arms. At the same time, I buck my hips and jerk her arms apart. Her grip loosens somewhat, and that's when I'm able to turn on my side and push her away with my legs. Free, I scramble away from her. She quickly crouches and lunges, hands glowing with espiritu. She is so fast I have no time to think, and before I know it, she's on me, her hands clasped around my neck once more. This time, I do reach for the amulet's power and . . .

A crimson sun bleeds over me, casting long, twisted shadows from the many skeletons of buildings that choke the horizon. The air thrums with a relentless buzzing, like a million angry hornets trapped in my skull. I'm adrift in the ruins of a city, my body a hollow shell echoing with desperate screams. Each one claws for dominance, a chorus of agonizing memories not my own—the chilling isolation of total darkness, the sting of a lash, the searing agony of a pyre. I turn and take in the desolation, the destruction. This can't be. This is not Castella.

My home can't be gone!

I'm screaming, my throat bare to the night as my blood-curdling cry rents the night.

"It's over, it's over." Rífíor is kneeling over me, shaking me. He slaps my face, not too gently. I turn away and see Calierin, unconscious, her face right next to mine. Panicked, I push away from both of them and jump to my feet. I startle when I notice Kadewyn off to one side, watching. I warily put some distance between us, too.

"You," I say in a rush of breath. "You sent her. This was your plan all along."

Rífíor doesn't say anything. He simply looks at me with a frown.

"I should have listened to Jago. I should have . . ."

For the first time, I notice The Eldrystone is in his hand, the chain wrapped tightly around his knuckles. Fear works itself into the marrow of my bones. He may not be able to use the amulet, but what about Calierin and Kadewyn? Of course, Rífíor would trust them more. And the other night? It was just another betrayal, a way to seduce me, so I would let my guard down, and like a fool, I did just as he expected.

A voice in the back of my head is trying to tell me something, but the mixture of anger and fear that suffuses my veins leaves little room for more.

He lifts his hand, raising the Eldrystone toward me. I step back, terrified that, this time, Niamhara will lend him her power to break me the way I broke Orys.

I brace myself for the worst.

Rífíor's dark eyes grow darker still as he lowers his face and his strong brow casts shadows over them.

My mouth goes dry.

Moving so close that I see the silver line of his scar cutting across his eye, he takes my hand with his free one and lifts it, palm up. My fingers tremble, and I'm embarrassed by the terror that has overcome me. Without a word, he presses the amulet into my hand, closes my fingers around it, and retreats.

Numbly, I stare down at the jewel, then back at Rífíor. My fear turns into a tangle of emotions that I can't comprehend. I try to speak, but my lips are sealed shut. No matter . . . I'm sure only nonsense would come out.

I glance all around. At Kadewyn standing behind Rífíor and Calierin lying on the ground. Rífíor's expression is unreadable despite his actions. For a long moment, I stand unmoving, unsure of what to do.

"I can't," I say. "I have to . . ."

I can't trust Calierin or Kadewyn anymore—not that I ever did.

Slowly, I back away, my grip tight on the amulet, and head toward the horses, picking up La Matadora on my way there.

Rífíor catches up with me. "Where are you going?"

"I can't stay with them. You know that."

He nods, looking resigned. Pressing a hand to his chest, fingers splayed, he asks, "Can *I* join you?"

I thought he would take it for granted that he was coming along, so I'm surprised by his willingness to leave the decision up to me. But I guess he knows I can't do this without him.

I nod.

He turns to Kadewyn. "I'm sorry, but we must leave."

The male narrows his pale eyes, which flick angrily toward Calierin. "I didn't do this."

Rífíor glances sideways at me, and I know he's asking if I can let

Kadewyn join us, but I have my hands full with one of them. It's all I can take.

"No," I say. Just one word, irrefutable.

"I understand," Kadewyn replies. "But I hope you will also understand that I'll still be heading west. I'll give you a head start." He pauses and points at Calierin on the ground. "I'll try to make sure she doesn't interfere, but I can't guarantee anything."

"Thank you." Ríffor bows, then joins me.

He saddles Calierin's gelding with practiced ease. When he's done, I reach for the reins, mount the beast, and settle gingerly in the saddle. One of Ríffor's dark eyebrows arches up. I stare at him blankly. He sighs in resignation and—in one fluid motion, more agile than any human could ever manage—leaps onto the horse and takes his place behind me.

I need to forge my own destiny and that requires me to stop letting others take the reins.

36
RÍFÍOR

"Niamhara, why have you stopped listening to our prayers?"

Vivan Aster – Fae Outcast – 21 AV

We ride nonstop, Valeria holding the reins and keeping the horse at a considerable trot. The first few hours she is relentless, but after some time, exhaustion gets to her, and we slow down. I know Kadewyn is fair and will remain behind for some time before he finally follows us. Valeria does not have to worry about him.

Moreover, there is a different route that can lead us to the veil—one neither Kadewyn nor Calierin are likely to follow if we carefully cover our tracks. I will tell Valeria about it, just not yet. She is in shock and needs to feel in control again.

The moon shines overhead, and a light breeze blows from the west, pushing Valeria's scent in my direction. Her sweet combination of lemon and lavender is fainter after days of travel, but it is still there. She is so close, I long to bury my nose in her hair and take her scent fully, but I resist, keeping my hands on my thighs as the gelding's movements rock us back and forth.

Damn Calierin!

I feared she might try something, so I made her promise to behave. I thought her word as a Tuathacath warrior might be worth something, but I was wrong. Still, despite my need for rest, I tried to keep an eye on her, only halfway sleeping. I was nearly too late, which is unforgivable.

Valeria's hands fall limp at her sides, and the horse slows. I'm about to say something when she slides off the saddle. I catch her just in time, my hands circling her waist.

I shake her lightly. "Valeria, wake up."

There is no answer. I shake her again, still nothing.

Something warm and wet slicks my right hand. I stare at my fingers and find them stained with sticky blood.

"Drocháin!"

I jump off the horse and help an unconscious Valeria lean forward until her torso lies along the horse's neck. Blood blooms over her tunic, looking as black as the night.

"Valeria, wake up!" I slap her cheek, but her eyes remain closed.

Grabbing the reins, I guide us to the side of the road, ease her off the animal, and lay her gently on the ground. Her face is ghostly pale from the loss of blood. Lifting her tunic, I examine the wound. She didn't escape Calierin unharmed. The dagger pierced Valeria's side. Yet, she said nothing, more concerned with getting as far as possible from those she can only regard as her cruel enemies.

This is my fault.

"Valeria, please wake up!"

I shake my head, puzzled as to why I didn't notice the scent of blood earlier. I should have detected it. Now, she has been bleeding for hours, steadily losing her life force. It makes no sense. Frowning, I peer at the chain around her neck. There's only one explanation. The Eldrystone hid her injury from me, but why? Never before has it acted with a mind of its own, but now it seems to have some sort of plan.

I press my fingers to her neck. Her heartbeat is weak.

Pulling on the amulet's chain, I snake it out and stare at the jewel.

"Heal her!" I command it, the way I have done a thousand times.

I peer at the wound, expecting it to knit itself, but nothing happens. The amulet does not obey me. Instead, she seems to grow paler, her lips turning a terrifying shade of blue.

"Heal her, *dammit*! Why won't you listen to me?!"

No result.

My eyes rove in all directions, concern mounting.

I have no healing skills, none that would help her at this point, anyway. If it were a small wound, I could bandage it, and it would help, but for this . . . she needs a real healer, a fae one even. But where?

Attempting to quiet my mind, I take a deep breath, mentally retracing the roads we have traveled, trying to pinpoint our exact location. I know this land like the back of my hand. For nearly twenty years, I wandered these parts aimlessly, harboring anger toward life and shunning company, until I eventually journeyed to Castellina and discovered the truth about Simón Plumanegra's identity.

It doesn't take me long to figure out we are close to Badajos, a small town only a mile east of where we stand. Wasting no time, I tear my sleeves off, tie them together, wrap them around Valeria's middle, and pick her up. She is solid, fit as any sword fighter and tree climber—all the things a proper lady should not be. Yet, she feels light in my arms, small, and it takes little effort to put her back on the horse and leap behind her.

With a jerk of the reins, I urge the animal forward. I go as fast as I dare, afraid that too much jostling will intensify her bleeding. It seems an eternity before we ride into town. It is late, the streets quiet, but I remember an inn with a tavern that stays open day and night.

There will be people at the inn, and they will be able to direct me to a healer. I will accept no other possibility. When I arrive, I carry Valeria in my arms, bursting through the thick wooden door. The chatter quiets as I step inside. Several sets of eyes turn my way, immediately filling with distrust.

"She is injured," I announce. "I need a healer. Now!"

No one moves. They just continue staring. I walk further into the inn, weaving through the tavern's tables, pushing all the way to the back counter, where a burly man with a dark mustache stares at me with the same disdain I am used to.

"She is human," I say, hoping this will make a difference. "She needs help, or she will die."

The innkeeper lowers his eyes and examines Valeria closely.

"She's probably wearing one of those glamours," he says.

I want to reach out across the bar and strangle him, but not yet.

"I'm not trying to hide anything," I say. "If I were, I would be wearing a glamour myself. Please, she is dying. We will pay for your services and for the healer. A fae one." I suspect only magic can save her at this point.

I knew it would come to this, so I am prepared with gold from her rucksack. Before he comes up with another excuse, I slap five gold coins on the bar top.

"Five now. Five more later," I say.

His eyes grow wide. I doubt he has ever seen one gold coin, much less five. The thought of ten seems to be scrambling his brain.

"No?" I ask. "I guess we will take our coin elsewhere." I make as if to take the gold back.

He beats me to it. "No, no. We can help." He picks up the coins and slips them into his pocket. "Go upstairs," he instructs. "First room on the right is clean. Take her there, and I'll send for the healer. He's one of your folk. They say he's good. Only reason we keep him 'round." He laughs at this.

I remind myself that I am going to strangle him *later*, not now. Instead, I nod and rush Valeria upstairs.

The room is small with a narrow bed, a chair, a dresser, and a table. The furniture is rough-hewn, but the space is clean as the innkeeper said. I leave the door open to allow light from the hall to spill in, then set her down on the bed and check her pulse. It is weaker still.

I throw our rucksacks and swords on the floor. Cursing repeatedly under my breath, I remove her boots, unsure of what else to do to make her comfortable. In the dim light, her cheeks look hollow and her eyes sunken. Kneeling at the side of the bed, I watch her and wonder at the edge of fear in my heart.

If she dies, the veil will remain closed. It is the only reason for my worry.

"Oh, dear, she looks frightful," a heavyset woman comes in, carrying a tray with a water bowl, rags, and a lit candle. She places the tray on the small table by the bed and proceeds to soak one of the rags.

"Are you the healer?" I ask, confused. She is not fae.

"No, just that fool's wife," she responds as she begins wiping Valeria's face.

I infer she means the innkeeper.

"She's so cold," she says. "Worse than I thought. My daughter is making some tea, but now I doubt she'll be able to drink it." She looks up at me. "What happened?"

"Knife wound," I say.

She folds back Valeria's tunic and, with practiced hands, cleans the wound, removing all the blood and revealing the extent of the damage. Carefully, she palpates Valeria's stomach, a trickle of blood oozes from the wound.

"It seems she's bled a lot," she says, "but I don't think there's damage to any vital organ. If there was, she'd be dead already. If they find Thoran, I think he can help her. Pray that they do."

I close my eyes, and for the first time in many years, I find myself invoking Niamhara's name.

Please, Goddess, let them find the healer, let him come and help her. I have not asked anything of you since . . . I shake my head. *Please, Valeria does not deserve this.*

When I open my eyes, I find the woman peering up at me.

She nods and offers me a gentle smile. "A prayer is the best thing right now. The girl needs it." The woman presses a hand to Valeria's forehead. "San Rafael keep her safe. She's young, and it's yet too early for her to enter the heavens. Guard her and spare her life for she may yet have much to do."

I swallow thickly, unsure of what I am feeling. My chest is tight, and I think it is anger, but I do not know anymore.

Her hands move over Valeria's hair, one finger tracing the streak of white hair. Peering back at me, she has a questioning expression on her face. Does she know that the youngest Plumanegra sister sports such a defining mark? If she does, I am not about to confirm any suspicions she may be harboring.

There's a small knock at the door, and I dash to open it. I expect it to be the healer, but a young girl comes in with the tea the woman mentioned. She rushes in, places it on the table, and leaves in the same hurried manner.

The woman tries to make Valeria drink, but liquid spills down the sides of her mouth, proving a useless task. She straightens and turns to me. "No luck, but keep trying. See if she'll drink a little. It should help her with the pain. I'll go see if they have word from Thoran."

She walks to the door, and halfway out, glances over her shoulder. "My name is Francisca, by the way."

When she leaves, I grab the teacup and sit at the edge of the bed.

"Drink," I urge. "It will be good for you." I press the teacup to her lips. Her mouth remains closed. "Do it for me."

To my surprise, her lips part. I tip the cup and allow a little tea to dribble in. She closes her mouth again.

"Swallow, Valeria."

Her throat works, and she swallows.

My breath catches as her eyes open for an instant, meeting mine. It happens so quickly that I think I have imagined it.

Hope, that terrible betrayer, glimmers in my chest.

She will be all right. She will make it.

A part of me does not think so. Not without the healer, anyway.

I stare at the door, willing it to open and let this Thoran in, but it remains shut. He is not coming and without him . . .

I don't dare finish the thought.

Setting the teacup down, I am determined to try again in another moment. My hand moves of its own accord, and I caress the side of her face. I whisper her name, hoping the sound will anchor her to this world.

Several moments pass, my impatience building and building. I try the tea again, but this time she doesn't drink it.

"Look at me, Valeria," I entreat her.

But her eyes remain as tightly shut as her lips.

My desperation quickly switches back to anger—a more familiar emotion, and I am at the brink of going downstairs to demand someone bring me that damn healer when the door opens.

Francisca rushes in with a wart-covered dwarf, carrying a satchel slung across his chest.

Hells devour me! This is no fae healer, and if he is a healer at all, he must be a Nightmend, a savage with the worst kind of magic.

37
RÍFÍOR

"A touch of magic is a scar on the soul."

Nightmend Proverb

I rise to my feet, letting go of Valeria's cold hand. "What is this? I asked for a fae healer. Not this."

The dwarf rumbles, tugging at his thick, braided beard.

The innkeeper appears at the threshold. "And I brought you one. Now, pay up."

I step forward, ready to do the strangling my hands have been itching for, but his wife bars my way.

"The girl's the priority. You can square your accounts later." Over her shoulder, she throws her husband a nasty glare. He huffs, but there is no question as to who runs this household. She turns to me, and with the same stern expression, adds, "And you, you should know better than to look down on Thoran. Haven't your kin been mistreated enough? Must you also mistreat others the way they have done unto you? Is that all you've learned during your time stranded here?"

Her tone makes me bristle. I do not let people talk to me this way, even if their words ring true. Yet, I swallow my displeasure because Valeria *is* the priority.

I am still unsure about the healer, however. Nightmend dwarfs have crude healing methods that are as likely to kill the patient as to make them better. But what am I to do? Valeria will die if nothing is done.

Since that fateful day Loreleia took The Eldrystone from me, the powers that rule the realms have been against me. Why would today be any different? It should not surprise me that I am left at the mercy of complete strangers. Unable to do anything else, I take several steps back and incline my head.

Francisca grunts in approval. "Thoran, would you kindly help the girl? I did what I could, which wasn't much. She's in a weakened state."

With a grunt and a sidelong glance at me, the dwarf approaches the bed and regards Valeria with his small beady eyes. His skin is weathered as if he has spent countless hours out of doors. He is stout, with a protruding belly and bowed legs that march unevenly over the wooden floor.

His people form a small population in Tirnanog, so small that he is the first of his kind I have ever encountered in Castella. In fact, I thought none of them had been stranded here. Clearly, I was wrong.

They inhabit a region known as the Shadowed Glen, which is nestled deep within the heart of a mountain range named The Shadow Peaks. Their land is shrouded in perpetual twilight, thanks to the mountains themselves and the dense woods that stretch across the landscape. Holes carved into the mountainsides serve as their homes, while the lush, wild forest provides ingredients for their remedies, and only the gods know what else. The scant few who have ever visited this land say the air is tinged with magic and whispers of ancient energies that echo through the towering peaks. Nightmends rarely venture out, and those who do peddle their healing skills to the desperate . . . like me.

Stretching out his hands, Thoran lets them hover over Valeria's body, his stubby fingers wiggling.

There is no evidence of magic, no color or disturbance in the air to indicate that any power is emanating from him. Yet, Valeria winces and a weak sound breaks through her blue-tinged lips.

Thoran grunts, his mouth turning upside down as he speaks in a deep voice. "The blade cut deep, but all that is vital is well. Lots of crimson wasted, easily replenished by food and drink and rest. What is left to do is close the wound, and for that there must be payment." His small eyes swivel in my direction, twin mud pits of distrust and resentment.

"We have gold," I tell him. "I have already said we will pay." I dig a hand in my pocket but freeze when Thoran speaks again.

"Not that kind of *payment*." He says the last word as if it leaves a sour taste in his mouth.

"What kind then? No price is too steep to save her."

"We shall see."

He gestures toward the table, prompting Francisca to swiftly remove the tray, which she places on the dresser. Thoran then reaches into the satchel slung across his barrel chest and retrieves what appears to be a leather scroll, thick and musty. Setting it on the table, he proceeds to unroll it. A myriad of unsightly tools is stored in individual pockets, looking as if they would serve better in torture than in healing.

Quickly, he pulls out what looks like a fishing hook and line and threads the two together. Next, he pulls out several bottles filled with murky liquids that might have been siphoned from a dirty pond. A deep frown cuts across his forehead as he cranes his neck to peer up at me.

"Remove your shirt and lie on the floor," he instructs.

I look around confused. "What?"

"Well, there ain't no other bed, is there? So the floor it is."

"But why do I—"

He cuts me off. "Your girl has little to no time. You want to waste it sitting here, interrogating my every move?"

Grinding my teeth against every fiber of my body, I do as he says and remove my shirt. When I lie on the floor, I welcome the cold on my back. It is the only thing that feels real in this entire situation.

"Align your middle with your girl's," the dwarf says.

It is a strange request, but I scoot down until my waist is parallel with Valeria's.

Thoran comes around and stands on my right side, in full view of the bed. He uncorks one of the bottles and dips his finger in it. Eyes flicking back and forth between Valeria and me, he seems to calculate the exact spot of her wound. Carefully, he lowers his muck-covered finger to the right side of my abdomen, marking the exact spot. At his touch, a stab of pain runs me through. I clench my teeth, and my growl of agony hisses out.

"A warning would have served me right," I spit, lifting my head to look at the spot he marked. I expect to find a wound, but there is only a small blemish made of the brown liquid he pressed onto my skin.

"Interesting," Francisca murmurs, watching from the corner.

The stark pain slowly morphs into an acute throbbing sensation deep in my gut. I settle back down, my doubts growing. How will he save Valeria by hurting me?

At least if she dies, I will soon follow.

Forming a circle with his thumb and forefinger, he hovers his hand over my side and aligns the circle with the brown muck. Murmuring words I do not understand, he begins to recite the same chant over and over again, while he makes the circle of his finger smaller and smaller.

The pain on my side fluctuates as if someone is repeatedly stabbing me.

Digging my nails into the wooden floor, I watch Valeria's face through bright flashes of pain. Her features tense with each fresh wave that assaults me. Her body spasms, betraying her anguish.

Thoran's chants stop when the circle of his fingers closes. I dare hope it is all over, but then he picks up the fishing hook and line, pinching them between the same two fingers.

Sweat slides down the sides of his weathered face.

Heating the tip of the hook in the candle flame, he warns, "'Tis going to hurt."

I glare at him.

"More," he clarifies. "But if you care about your girl, you will bear it like a proper male." He cocks his head in question.

I nod to let him know I can take it. I have been through worse, after all.

Without further ado, he stabs the hook into my skin and proceeds to sew me as if I am nothing more than a tattered rag doll. Every stab of his curved needle feels like a thousand daggers mercilessly tearing at my insides. I claw at the floor until my nails feel ready to rip from their beds. My vision wavers, but I manage to gaze at Valeria, who shares the same agony. Her body trembles uncontrollably, and sweat pours down her brow. Her face is covered in a glistening sheen, illuminated by the flickering candlelight.

An eternity seems to pass as I silently plead for each stitch to be the last, yet there is always another, and another, and another.

All the while, Thoran murmurs under his breath, this time a different chant that sounds like gibberish to my ears. When I think I cannot endure it any longer, he stops and casts the needle to the floor.

The ping of metal reverberates through the air, as loud as the pounding of my heart, my harsh exhalations, and Valeria's feeble whimpers combined.

Abruptly, Valeria sits up, her face ghostly pale, her eyes sunken hollows. A blood-curdling scream erupts from her lips. Time seems to stand still for a moment, before she collapses back down, her features slack and devoid of her normal vitality.

Groaning, I roll to my side and crawl toward the bed. Grabbing the mattress, I pull myself up and peer at her face.

"Valeria. Valeria!" She is deathly still. I turn back to the dwarf. "What have you done? You killed her!"

He is slumped against the wall, looking as if he has run for leagues without stopping. "I have done what you asked," he replies, words choppy and breathless. "I saved her, and we both paid. Nothing is free in this world. There must always be balance."

A small exhalation comes from Valeria. My gaze flicks back to her, and though she is quiet once more, I notice her pulse beating lightly at her throat. It is still weak, but her brow has relaxed, and her expression seems peaceful.

My head slumps on the mattress. Gingerly, I press a hand to my side, the ache of the dwarf's ministrations still festering deep in my gut.

The innkeeper pokes his head through the door. "Is it done? Did he pay up?"

Francisca swats him, and he vanishes once more. My eyes drift closed as I watch Valeria's chest rising and falling. I am suddenly tempted to press a kiss to her lips. The feeling is unwelcome, not unlike the lust that drove me to the wagon the other night. There should be no room for sensibilities left in me. I shut that door a long time ago.

Even when life seemed to offer me a perfect opportunity for happiness, the façade unraveled to reveal a rotten core. It would be ludicrous to expect anything different from whatever this is between Valeria and me, a relationship born of my deceit and laced with her greed for The Eldrystone.

No. That door must remain closed.

The dwarf puts his tools away. Wiping his brow with his sleeve, he shuffles toward the door.

"Thoran," I call.

My eyelids barely pried open a sliver, I watch him stop at the threshold, silhouetted by the hall light. He throws a glance over his shoulder.

"Thank you." My words are sincere.

He grunts and nods, then leaves.

Exhausted, I slowly slide back onto the floor, my consciousness shrinking like an echo until nothing remains.

38

VALERIA

"Fancy that! A princess of Castella staying in my inn."

Francisca Martinez – Castellan Innkeeper – 21 AV

I grunt as I move and pain blooms in my abdomen. A rush of memories hits me. Calierin attacking me, her dagger piercing my side, the frantic urgency to escape, the searing jolts coursing through my bones with every beat of the horse's hooves.

And then . . . nothing.

My hand flies to my neck. Relief washes over me when my fingers wrap around the amulet. The opal feels cool to the touch, comforting.

Slowly, I open my eyes and see Rífíor's face resting mere inches from mine. His eyes are closed, the fringe of his black lashes swooping upward toward the corners of his eyes. His breathing seems labored. There is no color on his cheeks. His olive skin is actually sallow, making him appear ill. I search my addled mind for a reason, but I can't remember anything past the pain and my quiet prayers to Niamhara. I asked her to heal me, and perhaps she listened, eventually.

I glance around, examining the small room we're in. It seems Rífíor found us a place in some sort of inn. It isn't much, but it appears clean and tidy. Sunlight spills through a small window, illuminating the simple furniture, well-polished by time and use.

Pushing the covers down with a trembling hand, I inspect my wound. I'm weak and even lifting my head to see better takes a toll. I collapse back down, wondering who mended me. All that is left is a silver scar, the size of an acorn, so I'm certain espiritu was used.

Was it Niamhara or someone else? Did Rífíor find this inn and a fae healer? Did his actions save my life?

I glance at him once more, the curve of his black eyebrows, the thick line of his lashes, the stubbled line of his jaw that I yearn to caress.

Arg, Val! Don't be an idiot. If he saved you, it's because he needs you.

He stirs. I shut my eyes for some stupid reason. Maybe because I don't want him to catch me staring at him like a fool. Besides, I'm tired, so very tired. He lets out a quiet groan as he stands, his clothes rustling. Maybe Calierin stabbed him too, and I just didn't realize it. Either way, it doesn't matter. We're here now, and it's all right to rest. It's all right to . . .

I startle awake. I must have fallen asleep. I don't know how long I've been out, but maybe it was a long while because no light filters through the window anymore.

At first, I think I'm alone, but then Rífíor peels away from the shadows in the corner, where he sits on a chair that groans as he stands. The light from several candles illuminates his angular face, clinging to the dark perfection of his hair like stardust on midnight velvet. He seems better than he did before, not as haggard.

He stares at me, saying nothing. I wish I could close my eyes and pretend to be asleep, but . . .

I swallow. The simple action sends me into a coughing fit that makes my side smart. He walks to a small table and pours a glass of water from a metal pitcher. Coming close, he tips the glass to my mouth, holding my head up with his free hand to help me drink. The water is cool, a blessed relief to my heated body.

"You still have a fever," he says, "but you are improving."

After a few sips, he rests my head back down. I think of what to say, but my mind is foggy.

"It was stupid what you did," he says. "You should have told me you were wounded. You could have died."

"I . . . had to get away from her." My voice is scratchy, barely a croak.

"I could have bandaged your wound," he goes on, "put pressure on it so you did not bleed out. It might have spared us all of this." He gestures around the room.

Naturally, he's furious about the time wasted. Without my blunder, he might already have reached the veil—or better yet . . . Tirnanog—and would finally be free of this wretched realm and its inhabitants, including me.

"Like I said," I clear my throat, "I couldn't wait to get away from your . . . *friends*."

He runs a hand through his hair, looking tired. "It is all the same, I suppose. I keep thinking I should have been able to smell all that blood, but I did not. It makes me suspect Niamhara's hand."

Saints and feathers! Even I was able to smell my own nauseating descent toward death. Rífíor, with his keen senses, should have as well. That is indeed strange. Suddenly, I remember something.

"Calierin took my Plumanegra key!" I say.

"Not to worry, I took it back. It's in one of the rucksacks."

"That's a relief." I pause. "Do you really think Niamhara hid the scent of my blood from you?"

"I do. I have a feeling she has been interfering *for some time.*"

His tone hints at a *for some time* measured in decades, far exceeding the mere weeks I've envisioned.

"What precisely do you mean?" I ask, though I doubt he will answer my question. Ever since I met him, he has been more impenetrable than the Plumanegra vault.

To my utter astonishment, he sighs with resignation. "I believe it is time to talk. But first, you should eat something. You have to regain your strength."

What? He's finally ready to talk, but he wants me to eat first. Seriously? I couldn't care less about food right now. I think I would gladly starve to death while he tells me all his secrets. I can't even count how many nights I've stayed up inventing conjecture after conjecture about his past.

"I will go get the broth Francisca offered and be back shortly."

"Wait! Forget about the stupid broth." I sit up, holding my side and wincing. "We can talk now."

He leaves anyway, and as he shuts the door behind him, I clench my teeth in frustration. With difficulty, I prop the pillow against the wall and fully sit up. The pain around my middle brings tears to my eyes, but once I get comfortable, it returns to a dull ache. I wait, picking at a hole in the sheets to distract myself. Every minute feels like an hour, and I imagine some catastrophe befalling him, keeping me from ever learning the truth.

I'm irrationally relieved when he comes back. He carries a tray with a ceramic bowl and a piece of bread. The bowl steams as he sets it on the table, and the scent of seasoned broth wafts in front of my nose, awakening my hunger. He tears the soft parts of the bread and drops them into the bowl, then attempts to feed me with a wooden spoon.

I pull back. "Um, what are you doing? I can feed myself. I'm not *that* helpless." I'm taken aback by his behavior. I never imagined Ríffor as the nurturing type.

He sets the spoon down and puts his hands up. "I'm glad. I'm not accustomed to treating adults like infants."

I glare at him. "I'm not an infant."

"No, you certainly are not." He grins.

I hide a blush by lowering my head as he places the tray on my lap. I begin to eat and find the broth mild in taste, perfect for my convalescent stomach.

"It's good," I say.

He nods, pleased for an instant, then his stern, unreadable expression returns.

"Well? I ate. Are you going to talk now?"

"You hardly had a taste."

I shove three more spoonfuls into my mouth. "Happy now?"

He grunts to indicate he isn't, but I'm done with this game. "Don't try to back down. This conversation is overdue."

"Very well." He pulls the chair from the corner closer to the bed and sits, interlacing his fingers. "Let me start by saying that my life is my own, and I don't owe anyone any explanations. So this is not that. This is only a necessity. Understood?"

I arch an eyebrow, thinking about his words and trying to decide whether or not they're true. After some pondering, I come to the conclusion that they are not.

"I disagree," I tell him. "I think that, after everything you've done, after the way you've treated me, the least you owe me is an explanation. From the beginning, I've been nothing but a pawn to you, a means to an end. Nothing justifies treating anyone like that. Nothing except, perhaps, a terribly, *terribly* good reason. So, if you want me to understand you and maybe one day forgive you, you *will* explain yourself."

His response is a grunt.

I wait expectantly for him to begin but instead, he says, "You're sitting up. The healer said that once you were able to do that, you should walk. So, get up." He takes the tray away and puts an arm out, crooking his elbow.

"Puta madre, Rífíor. I'm not walking anywhere until you—"

"This will be done on my terms," he says categorically.

We stare at each other, his dark eyes holding the resolve of who knows how many years of stubbornness. I know I'll never win.

Defeated, I take his arm, and with his help, stand. As I stretch to my full height, my bones creak, and every inch of my body hurts. I think this is how Nana must feel, her joints ready to split in two at the slightest movement.

My legs tremble as I try to look stoic, but I don't fool him. He turns and wraps an arm around my waist, offering me the support I need—in truth, bearing most of my weight. He guides me to the other side of the room, then back again. It only takes a few steps, but I'm utterly spent, catching my breath as if I'm not accustomed to exertion.

"One more time," he says.

I don't feel as if I can possibly take another step, but I won't let him use my lack of effort as an excuse not to talk, so I turn and, gritting my teeth, do it one more time. Once back, I'm ready to collapse on the bed, but he doesn't allow it. Instead, he practically picks me up and deposits me on the chair.

"There," he says. "That should give the housekeeper time to change the sheets." He heads for the door.

"Where are you going now? How many excuses are you going to come up with to postpone the inevitable?"

He glances back over his shoulder, one eyebrow arched. "My excuses got you this far, didn't they?"

Bastardo! I try to make a flourish with my hand to let him know he has won, but I'm so weak, the effort is wasted since it looks as if I'm waving at imaginary flies.

He's gone and back in under a minute. As he waits for the housekeeper, he stands in the corner, arms folded over his chest, one foot crossed over the other.

"I never imagined you to be such a . . . dedicated caregiver," I say sarcastically.

He doesn't take the bait. He just continues to stand there with his corpse-like expression, the same one I grew familiar with when he played his role of royal guard.

A moment later a friendly, heavyset woman comes in, followed by a younger girl.

"I'm so glad to see you so recovered," she says as the girl begins working on the bed, quiet and demure. "We thought we would lose you."

We? I glanced questioningly at Rífíor.

"Francisca was very helpful last night," Rífíor says, "and I have no doubt her generous efforts played a big part in your survival."

"Oh," I manage. "Thank you."

"Don't thank me. Thank him." She hooks a finger toward Rífíor. "You were near death when he burst in here. It was late, but he wouldn't take no for an answer from my stubborn husband and convinced him to fetch the healer. After Thoran took care of you, this one wouldn't leave your side." She smiles at Rífíor. "You found you a good one, girl. Hold on to him."

Rífíor stares at the floor, and I find myself suddenly fascinated by the rafters overhead.

"But never mind all that." Francisca bats at the air. "You will be right as rain soon. Thoran's espiritu is still at work." She turns to the girl. "Almost done? By the way, this is my daughter, Lina."

I incline my head. "Nice to meet you, Lina."

The girl blushes as she curtsies, then continues working, smoothing the sheets. They are nice enough people, and it seems I owe them a great deal, but I'm impatient to talk to Rífíor, so I'm glad when Lina finishes the bed at last, and they leave, promising to return with a savory supper that will finish restoring my strength.

"Want to lay back down?" Rífíor asks.

"No, I want to sit here." I point to the bed. "And you, sit there and fucking get started."

"Such language, Little Princess."

"Don't call me that." It's what Bastien called me when he broke my heart.

The smirk on his face dies gradually, swiftly replaced by a stern expression unlike any I've seen on him before, which is saying a lot. My own mood shifts, becoming as solemn as his. I fear that whatever he's about to tell me will be more dire than anything I've learned about him so far, which is also saying a great deal.

I steel myself, wondering if the impending revelation will shatter me beyond repair.

39
RÍFÍOR

"Garras is a good name. Only you would befriend a bear."

Venancio Rincón – Castellan Farmer – 1998 DV

Where to begin? They always say from the beginning, of course, but I simply cannot. There is so much pain, so much I cannot bring myself to confess, that I must start elsewhere.

The end, I suppose.

The time is here to divulge everything. In the next two days, we will arrive at the veil, and I have no doubt Valeria will reopen it. I have seen what she can do with The Eldrystone, nearly as well as I did in the past when its power belonged to me.

Moreover, the goddess clearly favors her in a way I never personally experienced. Niamhara seems to be guiding this quest, her power working in Castella as easily as it ever did in Tirnanog, the collapsed veil no obstacle for her influence.

So yes, soon, I will be in Tirnanog, home, and I cannot curtail my hopes, no matter how hard I try. Once there, I will need the amulet back, and the only way Valeria will agree to give it back without a fight is if I tell her the entire truth.

She waits patiently, her expression wary. I am loath to admit that confessing everything scares me. I should not care, but alas, I do. She will despise me when she learns what I did.

Pushing through my reserve, I begin.

"Let's talk about Loreleia Elhice," I say, because that is the beginning of the last two decades here in Castella—never mind the true beginning when Loreleia and I were still in Riochtach, Tirnanog's capital. I cannot go that far. Not yet, perhaps never.

Her eyes open wide, and I know she will not begrudge my backward storytelling, not when it commences with her mother, not when Loreleia also left Valeria in the dark about the past, just the way I have.

Measuring my words, I continue. "She stole The Eldrystone from me, Valeria. I know you doubt it, but it is the truth. It happened not far from here. It was the day she met your father, the day she made her escape from Tirnanog."

At the word *escape,* Valeria opens her mouth as if to protest, but no words come out. Mayhap she has decided to listen without interruption.

"Yes," I say. "She was escaping, and I was pursuing her. She took The Eldrystone from me in Riochtach, and with help from an unexpected ally, she thought to find refuge in Castella. Of course, I was determined to stop her, and I suppose I would have succeeded if not for your father. He was taken with her as soon as he laid eyes on her, as if she had put a spell on him."

For the first time, I wonder if The Eldrystone had something to do with their instant connection, if Niamhara was already working on whatever plan she seems to have laid out for us, her pawn pieces.

"He was quite willing to give his life for her. He gave me this scar, you know?" I say, vaguely gesturing toward my face. "And he's also responsible for the scar on my chest."

I regret the words as soon as they cross my lips. She has seen me naked as well as I have seen her, but it hardly bears reminding her at this moment. But that worry may be misplaced as she appears astounded by my revelation. Her father is responsible for my disfigurement.

I clear my throat. "He did not inflict the chest wound himself. That one came from a *friend* of his, a bear . . . of all things." I pause, remembering the fierce creature and how it jumped to Simón's defense.

"Garras," Valeria whispers.

I cock my head to one side.

"That was the bear's name," she says. "Father told me stories about him. He told me he raised the bear from a cub and that an enemy he despised killed him."

"Indeed, I slew the animal defending myself," I admit, glad to see that she possesses some knowledge that will help corroborate my story. She will not willingly believe what I am yet to reveal, so I am grateful for any help I can get.

"Your father and I fought when I tried to take the amulet from Loreleia," I go on. "To my surprise, he shifted into a raven. I knew then he must have fae blood, though I truly had no idea who he was, the future King of Castella," I add bitterly. "How could I have suspected that Loreleia had met such a powerful figure upon arrival."

I remember how fiercely he fought for someone he had only just met, and how impotent I felt without The Eldrystone. I had grown used to its power, used to relying on it rather than my own skill.

"I was determined to get the amulet back. No matter the cost. Never in my wildest dreams did I imagine that Loreleia would be able to wield it against me."

I stare into Valeria's face. She hangs from my every word, riveted.

"She used The Eldrystone to curse me. I don't think she intended more than that, but it was the curse that slammed the veil shut."

Valeria gasps, understanding dawning on her.

I nod. "It was her words, her curse, that caused all of this. So yes, *she* trapped us here."

She shakes her head, shunning my words.

"She hated me," I add. "She would have said anything to hurt me, and she knew that condemning me to a life away from Tirnanog would be the worst type of punishment. She also took away my magic. It's the reason I can't conjure a glamour."

The words of Loreleia's curse echo in my ears.

You are a monster. You deserve what Saethara did to you and worse. I curse you to live without magic. I curse you to never be able to return home, to always be alone, and to never find love. So be it.

I cannot bring myself to tell Valeria more, and the lie of omission—the reason why Loreleia did not want me to go back to Tirnanog and condemned me to a life without love—burns in my throat.

I sit quietly, scanning Valeria's face, trying to find the smallest indication that she believes me. It is crucial that she does, though as she speaks, I am reminded that it will not be an easy task to convince her.

"No," she protests, shaking her head. "My mother would have never cut herself off from her home. She missed her family deeply, every day, every hour. She longed to go back."

"No more than I do, I assure you."

Anger etches Valeria's features, and I know I said the wrong thing, so I quickly amend myself.

"The words of her curse were not precise. They were vague. She wanted *me* to suffer. She wanted to bar *me* from my home—not bar herself and others as you point out. Nonetheless, this is what happened. From the day that I . . ." I trail off, unable to bear it all. "The Eldrystone seems to have a mind of its own. Loreleia might have not meant to strand us all here, but I am beginning to suspect Niamhara has a different plan."

She does not argue about this point. It is clear, she has noticed how temperamental the amulet has been. She lowers her eyes and stares at the floor. I can tell she's thinking, her sharp mind quickly and efficiently pondering every detail I have provided, weighing each against what she already knows.

In a moment, her mind will be full of questions, questions I do not want to answer, even though I told myself I was ready to do so. I am not.

I am not!

Abruptly, I stand, burdened by the weight of countless years spent evading my past. I have never run from a battle. I have always faced the sword with equanimity and valor, but Valeria's judgment . . . I cannot face. Like a coward, I march out of the room, ready to drown these awful memories. I never should have unearthed them.

40
VALERIA

"Tonight, I will dance the night away around the bonfire."

María Salazar – Badajos Resident – 21 AV

"Wait! Where are you going?" I reach out a hand toward the door as Rífíor exits, leaving me alone in the room with a thousand newly sprouted questions that demand an answer. "Come back," I call as I attempt to stand, but pain brings me short.

I press a hand to my side, groaning. It takes me a moment to get to my feet and walk to the door. Holding my wound gingerly, I peer into the hall, but there is no sign of Rífíor.

It's evident it was hard for him to dredge up the past. I've never seen him so upset, never thought he could look so vulnerable—not when strength and indifference are his defining characteristics. This was not the person I know. This was someone else entirely.

And it's the main reason I'm inclined to believe him.

The whole story seems ludicrous, even as I recall his strained expression as he related it to me. Mother wasn't a vengeful person.

The idea that she devised a curse seems nothing but far-fetched. Unless . . .

Unless there was an exceptionally good reason.

The very thing that Rífíor doesn't want to talk about, which is what I've suspected all along.

Holding my side, I take several steps back and sit at the edge of the bed, wondering if *I* want to talk about it, if knowing what drove Mother to curse Rífíor will also push me to my limits.

My mind races, attempting to piece together the puzzle. Rífíor stole The Eldrystone. Could he have taken a life to accomplish it? Perhaps he even murdered the rightful owner, the Fae King. I shake my head, overwhelmed by the possibilities. Maybe he didn't commit a murder, but surely only a grave transgression could have provoked Mother's drastic measures.

If he killed someone, I have no right to judge him. I've killed, too. And after all this time, it's possible that he has had time to reflect and regret his actions. Perhaps Mother's punishment had its intended effect.

No, not Mother's punishment. Niamhara's.

I agree with Rífíor. Her influence is unmistakable. Even now, I sense her hand at work, shaping our path toward an objective that eludes my understanding. I'm afraid of where she may be leading us, but what other choice do we have?

Outside the window, I hear excited voices, people going about their lives without a care in the world.

For an hour, I wait for Rífíor to return, but he doesn't. Without thinking, I start pacing the room from one end to the other, so preoccupied that I don't notice how quickly the pain in my side is subsiding. Gingerly, I press the spot and find that there's only a small ache. Nothing I can't handle. Francisca was right. The healer's power is still at work, steadily mending me.

Finding my clothes clean and folded on top of the dresser, I change quickly and leave the room in search of Rífíor. The noise from the tavern on the first floor grows louder as I approach. I'm surprised to find people dressed in costumes, wearing masks and moving about in excitement. I quickly make some mental calculations and realize that La Feria de Zafra takes place around this time of the year, and the farmers and livestock owners of Leonesa—the western-most region of Castella—come together for trade and other festivities. The latter seems to be in full swing.

As I come down the steps, the man behind the counter notices me and points with his chin in my direction. His wife's eyes widen, and she quickly approaches, weaving through the crowd.

"I'm so very glad to see you on your feet," she says. "May I help you in any way?"

"Thank you. Um, yes, have you seen Rífíor, my companion?"

She gives me a rueful smile. "Yes, unfortunately. He's drunk." She points at a far corner in the back, where Rífíor sits slumped on a chair, three bottles in front of him. His head lolls to one side.

"Fantástico," I mumble.

"Maybe he's letting out steam," she says. "He paid the price to heal you. It couldn't have been easy."

I want to ask her what she means by that, but she walks away before I can. I approach Rífíor and nudge his boot with mine. He doesn't stir. I do it again, this time harder, more of a stomp on his toes than a nudge. He deserves it.

Groaning, he pulls his foot back and squints at me. At first, he doesn't seem to recognize me, but then his mouth turns downward, as if the mere sight of me causes him pain. He sits up and glances around at the masked revelers.

"What in all the hells?" he slurs.

"It's La Feria de Zafra, I figure. It's that time of the year. We're in the Leonesa region, after all. Badajos, right?"

He grunts in response, then stretches to his full height, picks up one of the bottles, and drains it to its last drop. Setting it down with a *thud*, he pushes away from the table and heads for the door, stumbling.

"Where are you going?" I demand. "We need to finish our conversation."

Weaving precariously, he makes it outside, where the noise is considerably louder than it was just an hour ago. The residents of Badajos are starting to come out in full force to celebrate.

Standing on the narrow wooden porch in front of the inn, Rífíor makes a face of disgust at the sight of all the happy people. Swaying only slightly, he runs stiff fingers through his silky hair. It's standing on end, and the maneuver makes it worse.

"Damn, useless human wine," he complains. "If I only had some feyglen."

The three bottles he drank could easily knock a large man out, but it barely seems to have had any effect on him. The fae process alcohol a lot faster than we can.

"Are you backing down now?" I ask. "Will you not tell me what I need to know?"

"You don't need to know anything. Leave me alone."

Under other circumstances, I would probably yell at him and demand that he does as he promised, but something about his harried expression makes me feel sorry for him. There are things in my past I can't bear to talk about, so I understand how he feels. Of course, this only makes my curiosity bigger, for what could affect him so? Still, I feel like the right call is to let him be and allow him to tell me on his own terms. Besides, he did save my life and watched over me all night. He has earned a break.

Even if I understand, I don't need to show him I've decided not to be hard on him. He never makes anything easy for me, so why should I?

I step off the porch and onto the road with the revelers. "You're a coward."

Holding my side as I walk, I blend with the crowd, following the sound of distant music. At the end of the street, I reach a plaza where a bonfire burns in the center and people dance. Some of their sequin masks blink in the light, dazzling the eye. The music is lively and makes me want to dance. Odd, considering everything.

Out of the corner of my eye, I see a cart with masks for sale. Their intricate design draws me closer. I pick one up. It's black with golden filigree, and black feathers lining the top. That's probably the one I would buy, if I had any coin with me.

"That one would look pretty on you," the seller says. "Would you like to try it on?"

I consider putting it on just for fun, then decide against it. "No, thank you."

The seller looks at me with narrowed eyes, focused on the white streak of hair hanging in front of me. His mouth opens and closes, and my heart picks up its beat. Is it possible that he recognizes me? No, we're far from Castellina. There are no portraits of me here, are there?

"Aren't you—?"

"We'll take two." Rífíor appears behind me, picks up two masks, and throws down more coins than necessary in front of the man. He pulls me aside by one arm, his strong fingers digging into my skin.

"Hey, that hurts. Let me go!"

Seemingly recovered from his drunkenness, he says, "It doesn't take you long to find trouble, does it? If he has not figured out who you are by now, he soon will. Here, put this on." He tosses the black mask in my general direction, and I catch it before it hits the ground.

I tie the silk ribbon behind my head, the smooth material gliding between my fingers. Rífíor does the same with his mask, dark eyes glancing back at the vendor.

"He is still looking this way," he grumbles, then seizes my hand and pulls me into the throng of dancers, effortlessly twirling me around before drawing me into his embrace as the crowd swirls around us.

The next thing I know, he's guiding me dexterously to the rhythm of the music. I fall easily into the movements, letting him take the lead, enjoying the subtle strength of his arms and the sturdy pressure of his chest against mine. My breath catches as I inhale his delicious musk. This was definitely not in anyone's predictions, not even El Gran Místico's.

At first, he's focused on looking over the crowd, his eyes narrowed, his face etched with suspicion and distrust. But at last, he seems to relax, and once he's sure we're out of trouble, he starts releasing me.

Unwilling to let the moment end, I hold on tighter, squeezing his hand and pulling him closer. His perfect, thick eyebrows go up.

"Dance with me a bit longer," I say. "It's been a long time since I've had such a reprieve."

"We're not here to enjoy ourselves, princess. And what about your wound?"

"It barely hurts," I lie; moving around is making it smart uncomfortably, but nothing I can't handle.

Despite his gruff tone, he secures his grip around my waist and leans into the dance with more enthusiasm than I would have expected.

His movements are graceful and practiced, which makes me wonder about his life in Tirnanog before he became a stranded pariah. When the song ends, he twirls me one last time, then pulls me close. My chest hits his, and one of his hands slides from my waist to the middle of my back, fingers splayed.

He gazes down at me, our noses nearly touching. His lower lip trembles, and I see the moment his resolve breaks. Possessive and hungry, he kisses my neck. His tense body feels wild and full of desperation, as if time is running out, and this is the last time we will be this way. I want to pull away from him and search his expression, but I can't because I also want to stay, kissing him, lost in his embrace.

Breathless, he tears away from me, and I cling to his shirt, trying to keep him in place. He seems lost for an instant, but finding his resolve, he picks me up, turns away from the revelers, and takes me past a line of trees in the back of the plaza.

All around us, I perceive the silhouettes of several couples, tangled in each other's arms, letting the euphoria of the festivities warm their blood the same way it has warmed ours.

Ríffor takes me deeper and deeper into the woods until we're utterly alone. There, he pushes me against a tree and traps me in the cage of his arms and the delicious weight of his body. One of his hands wraps around my throat as he looks me over with unbridled hunger.

"What did you do to me, Valeria Plumanegra?" he demands. "This is not meant to be. This cannot be."

"What cannot be? Tell me?"

Without answering, he kisses my neck again. His body is solid against mine, and the heat of his desire suffuses my skin the way the sun's warmth does. I pull on the silk ribbon of his mask and release it. It falls to the ground. I do the same with mine. I don't want anything between us.

As he leans back, his gaze tracks up my body, stopping at my mouth. "Do you want me to touch you, Valeria?"

Yes. Yes. I do. I can't bring myself to say it, though.

At my lack of response, his eyebrows go up. A tight smirk on his lips, he removes his hand from my neck and, with a shrug, steps back.

"I do," I blurt out, without thinking.

"Do what?"

I swallow my pride. "I want you to touch me."

He chuckles and comes closer, his hands landing on my waist, then traveling upward until he cups me. His thumbs press against my nipples. A shock of pleasure leaves me breathless. His mouth comes closer to mine. He licks his lips. I hold his gaze. I still haven't changed my mind about my no-mouth policy, but I can't tell whether or not he's still glad about it.

When he kisses me, his lips come dangerously close to the corner of my mouth. My eyes flutter closed. He trails kisses along my jaw as his thumbs move in lazy circles over my nipples, fueling my desire.

He pulls away as something in the air seems to change. All around us, the forest is muted as if a curtain has come all around us.

"What . . .?" My heart skips a beat, fearing an attack, though my senses haven't warned me of anything.

As if in answer, The Eldrystone lets out a dim glow, like a firefly blinking in and out.

"It seems we have been offered some much-needed privacy," Rífíor says.

"So it seems."

It's as if Niamhara is pushing us closer.

He lifts my tunic over my head and discards it on the moss-covered ground. With expert fingers, he relieves me of my binding and proceeds to kiss my breasts. I pant as a wave of ecstasy rolls over me. His tongue darts out, skimming over my nipple. I sink my fingernails into his shoulder, and he makes a sound of satisfied approval in the back of his throat.

What game is he playing? Does he think he's the only one with power over me?

Hells no!

Gathering my will, I push him away. His dark eyes go wide. On impulse, I lick his neck, tracing a hot path to his stubbled jaw. At the same time, I *accidentally* rub my forearm over his erection, making him moan.

"Oh, sorry," I say, and in the same breath proceed to untie his pants. "It's only fair given I'm topless." I slap his hand away as he tries to palm my breast.

He opens his mouth to protest, but his words die a sudden death when I lower his pants, wrap both hands around his girth, and pump my hands downward.

"Fuck," he groans.

He was hard before I wrapped my hands around him, but there's no denying he's growing even more.

Abruptly, he picks me off the ground and deposits me on a patch of soft moss. He tears my pants off, then using his knees, wretches my legs apart.

"So fucking delectable," he says, then, in a quick assault, runs his tongue between my seams, tasting. He trails kisses up my stomach, pausing at the wound on my side.

"I am so glad you are all right," he murmurs, kissing around the spot.

His voice thrums with unexpected fervor, but it's not something I can deem real—not in a moment like this. He may just be glad he gets to fuck me. He continues kissing his way up until we're face to face.

"This time," he says, "I want to feel your tight heat around my cock."

At first, his dirty talk alarms me, but then I realize it's all part of the game, the excitement of it all. I may be inexperienced, but I'm a fast learner.

"I'm so wet for you," I say in a sultry tone.

He seems to lose all control then, and pressing his tip to my entrance, he pushes in, letting out a moan that is met by my own whimper of pleasure. Slowly, he draws his hips back while I curve into him, eager for more. As he slams into me, I bury my face in his neck, fearing he will split me in two.

I feel every inch of him, gliding in and out, the ridge around the swollen head of his shaft rubbing me in just the right way with every thrust. Our bodies rock in unison at a perfect pace. I cry out as he pauses then slams into me again as if he can't have enough. The exquisite sensation inside me is all-consuming.

Savoring the feel of his slick skin against mine, I cling to him like a lifeline until I climax violently. Moaning, I contract around his shaft, waves and waves of pleasure spiraling until I'm left limp and totally satiated in his arms.

He takes his pleasure a moment later, his face buried in my neck as he goes tense, muscles taut and trembling. There's power in owning him like this. Because he can't deny it. Right now, he's utterly mine.

41

VALERIA

"If you pronounce the words, the world will hold its breath. I will teach them to you, son, as you will soon take my place."

Faolan Theric – King of Tirnanog – 1878 DV

I stand at the edge of the plaza, my head spinning and my body tingling all over.

Rífior is walking away from me. He uses his wide shoulders to cut through the crowd. He's gone off to find drinks. On the other side, there's a cart selling orange juice. He offered to get me some, said I must be thirsty. His cheeks are flushed, and his eyes gleam. Stranger yet, the ghost of a smile touches his lips. He looks so young, so content, and if I didn't know better, I would say he's eager to please me, eager to do something nice for me.

Not that he didn't do that already.

Saints and feathers! He turned my world upside down and, from now on, nothing will be the same. I thought I knew the power of sex, but I've only scratched the surface. Is there more? I can't wait to find out.

Yet, it's this small act, this modest bit of attention, that is making me feel a strange warmth inside, making me wonder about this other Rífíor I've barely glimpsed at, a side that he officiously keeps hidden from everyone.

Gods! It scares me. I don't want this other side to be real. If it is, it might be my doom. This desire I feel for him is already more than I can handle, more than I should feel. But if he can please more than my body, if he can soothe my soul with a simple smile, I will forget what he has done to me, and I will fall, fall, fall . . .

My heart feels fit to burst as I follow his strong shape cutting through the crowd. If only—

Something imperceptible happens. It is negligible, a slight disturbance, a split-second pause in the crowd, an overall change of mood. My breaths speed up.

Rífíor's head snaps in my direction, his eyes locking with mine, his gaze flashing a dire warning.

My ears ring. My heart hammers.

Is there danger nearby?

My instincts flare, heightening all my senses. The din of the crowd echoes in my ears. The twirl of the dancing couples fills my vision with rainbows of color. The smell of hot bodies, food, and smoke from the bonfire overwhelm my sense of smell. And yet, despite the warning, I react a second too late.

"Valeria! Behind you!" Rífíor shouts across the distance and over the bodies that separate us.

Just as I'm about to turn, an arm viciously wraps around my neck, cutting the airflow. I buck, nails digging into flesh as I fight to get free. Instead, the hold tightens, strong muscles bruising my throat. A wall seems to press against me. I attempt to plant my feet squarely on the ground to lean forward, but I'm lifted clean off until my legs dangle.

Through blurred vision, I watch Rífíor cutting through the crowd, shoving people aside and sending them reeling off balance. He calls my name as my assailant pulls me back into the woods, the thick canopy throwing deep shadows over me.

I thrash and claw, but I can't get free. A couple kissing nearby startles and runs away, shrieking.

"Be still, princess," a female voice sneers in my ear.

A chill shoots down my spine. The wall of muscle is Calierin.

Gods! I should have killed her.

Hoping against hope, I send out my awareness to make a connection with The Eldrystone and to use espiritu to repel her. But as I feared, Niamhara remains elusive, failing me yet again.

"You little human bitch," she says. "You thought you could get away from me?"

Her free hand paws at my neck, reaching for the amulet.

I clench my teeth, struggling for air, fighting as hard as I can to stop her from taking it. She grabs the chain and pulls. It cuts into my skin, then snaps.

Calierin seems frozen, as if surprised that she finally has it. Taking advantage of her momentary distraction, I buck again. The motion brings my feet to the ground, though she doesn't let go. Undeterred, I stamp my heel down on her toes.

Calierin, a seasoned warrior, barely loosens her grip. Desperately, I twist my head and tuck my chin. She attempts to regain her hold, but her efforts falter as a body collides with us, sending us tumbling to the ground. My bones rattle. My elbow slams into a rock and pain shoots up my arm. I cry out. Grunts and growls fill my ears as Rífíor pulls Calierin off me, finally setting me free.

With a quick shove, he sends me rolling over the ground, down a slope. My head spins. When I come to a stop, I spit out dirt. Holding my side, I roll to my knees, blinking to clear my vision and reclaim my bearings.

Rífíor and Calierin fight at the top of the incline, punching each other viciously.

Calierin is as strong as any fae male. She's fierce, and on top of it all, she has espiritu, which she might use at any moment.

"I should have killed you when I had the chance," Rífíor says, landing a punch that knocks Calierin to the ground. Jumping on top of her, he proceeds to strangle her. "I have told you enough times that you will never beat me in hand-to-hand combat."

I start up the slope, the wound in my side pulling.

Calierin struggles under Rífíor for a moment, trying to get free. But she seems as helpless as I was against her. As I reach the top, she braces her hands against Rífíor's chest, and I know it's coming.

"Rífíor!" I warn.

Espiritu blasts from Calierin's hands—a blinding flash of violet sparks between their bodies that sends Rífíor flying through the air.

Something glints in his hand as he hurtles away, and I realize it's The Eldrystone. He took it back, but his grip is tenuous. The amulet slips from his fingers, soaring through the night sky. Its iridescent opal winks as it travels. Briefly, it seems suspended in midair, and then gravity takes hold. With a sudden drop, the chain snags on a branch, leaving the jewel hanging like a pendulum, just out of reach.

Knowing I must do everything I can to retrieve it, I sprint toward the tree at full pelt. Rífíor writhes in agony, his chest smoking from Calierin's blast. I do my best to ignore him. As I reach the tree, I scramble up the trunk, clutching at the rough bark and trying to reach the lowest branch. I manage to gain some traction, but quickly lose momentum. I fight to hold on, but my side is on fire, and a couple of my fingernails tear off their bed. I cry out, then helplessly slide downward. The bark ripping away under my weight, I tumble to the ground and roll to a crouch.

A growl of frustration escapes me. I shoot a glance over my shoulder.

Calierin is back on her feet and straddling Rífíor, this time with her hands around his throat, though I doubt she plans to simply strangle him. There's still espiritu left in her, and she's not stupid enough to underestimate an opponent like Rífíor. I might not have been a problem for her, but he's a whole different story.

Panic surging, I look back to the amulet and mentally reach for it.

Blast her! I order.

The Eldrystone swings, mocking, useless.

Niamhara, why did you bring us this far just to let us fail?

Cursing the capricious goddess and her trinket, I do the only thing I can. I charge, fists clenched. I aim for the sorceress, hoping I can knock her down before she kills Rífíor.

Calierin jerks her head upward, and her violet eyes lock with mine. She grins, hands beginning to glow.

No!

I'm only a few steps away, but I know I'm too far, too late. Every fiber of my being screams it, yet I press on, hoping against hope.

The sorceress turns her attention to Rífíor again, bearing down on him, her espiritu intensifying.

Whizzing and barely audibly, Rífíor speaks. "Let the whispers . . . turn to screams if you dare defy me."

Calierin's eyes widen at the words.

"My crown demands obedience. My blade demands respect," he goes on, his voice clearer as Calierin seems to lose her resolve and the pressure around his neck diminishes. "By the will of Niamhara and my people, I am your ruler! And in their name, you will stop."

The words reverberate through the forest. This realm and all the others hold their breath, stilling at the powerful command. The trees stop swaying, and no insects chirp or owls hoot for leagues.

I realize I'm not running anymore. I'm at a standstill, my lungs paralyzed as I stare in disbelief.

Calierin, cruel and terrible Calierin, is rooted to the spot, unblinking, espiritu dead on her fingers. To my utter bewilderment, she slides away from Rífíor and stops several feet away, one knee on the ground, her head bowed.

Rífíor coughs and struggles to a sitting position, hands to his throat, scorching marks of espiritu still smoldering on his chest. Blistered skin bubbles beneath his shirt, outlined by the singed imprints of Calierin's hands. Rubbing his neck, he finally stands. His chest rises and falls visibly as he struggles to catch his breath. He glares darkly at the sorceress.

Slowly, Calierin holds her hands up in surrender. "Forgive me, my king. Forgive me," Calierin begs. "I did not know."

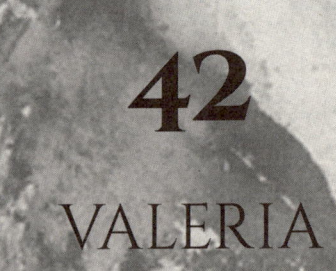

42

VALERIA

"Loyalty burns brighter than any blade."

Tuathacath Proverb

I tremble as I regard the strange tableau: Calierin kneeling in front of Rífíor, her vicious expression folded inside out and replaced by incredulity and shame. And Rífíor... tall and unwavering, looking more commanding than ever.

"Forgive me, my king," she said.

My king.

My king.

My king.

The words echo in my ears, and I think there must be something wrong with my hearing because this can't be true. Yet, here is more than what Calierin said swimming in my mind.

"Let the whispers turn to screams if you dare defy me. My crown demands obedience. My blade demands respect. By the will of Niamhara and my people, I am your ruler! And in their name, you will stop."

I know these words. I learned them from a story Mother told me. She said that in a realm where espiritu reins, anyone with enough power can usurp another's identity, even the king's.

"That is why," she explained, *"our wise goddess devised a declaration that only the rightful king can intone. No one else, no matter how hard they try, can issue the same statement. So if these words ever grace your ears, my little pixie, know that you stand before the true Fae King."*

Rífíor is Korben Theric.

Korben Theric is Rífíor.

Slowly, he turns to face me, his expression uncertain.

The Eldrystone still hangs from a branch right above his head. I peer up at it and then down at him.

"It really belongs to you," I whisper. That's why he never seemed afraid of it.

He doesn't answer, but the look in his eyes seems to say *I told you it did*.

"You're . . . Korben Theric."

Tears blur my eyes.

"Let's talk about Loreleia Elhice," he said three hours ago. *"She stole The Eldrystone from me, Valeria. I know you doubt it, but it is the truth."*

My mother stole from the Fae King, barring him from his throne, his people—all along hiding the key to his return.

The meaning smashes into me like a relentless hammer, delivering blow after blow, each one a different truth threatening to shatter me. There are his new lies and betrayal, but the worst . . . the dawning horror that the fae have been without their ruler for over two decades.

I try to envision Castella without Father at the helm for all that time, and I can only picture chaos.

The initial reaction would have been raw panic. First, the desperation to find the missing king, hoping to unravel his disappearance. As the days went by, fear would have gripped the kingdom, whispers of abduction and murder swirling in the air. Then those bound by loyalty would have fiercely guarded his throne, clinging to the hope of his return. But as that hope dwindled, a grim reality would have set in, and the question of "*if he comes back*" would have morphed into "*who will succeed him*?" Ambition would have raised its ugly head then, and at last, power struggles would have erupted, the rightful heir's claim challenged by those consumed by greed.

Father did his best to keep us in the dark about the Theric dynasty, and I never understood his reasons until now. From the scant knowledge I was able to acquire before we left Nido, I know that Korben Theric was unwed and had no heirs, which means the fae throne would have become a glittering prize for power-hungry nobles. And then what? Infighting, cruel alliances, murder, anything to seize control.

I can only imagine his desperation and impotence at the thought of his kingdom unraveling at the seams in his absence. It would have been a torment he couldn't escape.

Yet, despite understanding what he has been through, it is his betrayal and lies I feel more keenly along with the questions that still stand unanswered even after everything we've been through.

He tried to explain, Valeria. He did, but . . .

Calierin's voice cuts through my thoughts. "Forgive me, my

king. Never in my wildest dreams could I have guessed who you truly are. I wish to atone for my mistake. Please accept me as your humble servant. I am a Tuathacath warrior, and my order has always served our realm proudly. From today till the day I die, you have my loyalty and my sword."

Rífíor says nothing—no, not Rífíor. Every guise he has worn required a different name, a different lie.

King Korben Theric says nothing. He only regards Calierin with magnanimity.

Calierin moves suddenly, jumping to her feet and walking toward the tree where The Eldrystone hangs.

"No! Let it be," I command, but she doesn't listen.

Instead, with a powerful push, she launches herself off the ground, using the tree trunk as a springboard to propel her even higher. Soaring effortlessly, she snatches the amulet, unhooking it from the branch, before landing gracefully in front of Ríf . . . Kor . . . No! I can't think of him with this new name. I simply can't.

Bowing, she cradles the amulet in both hands and presents it to her king.

Rífíor's jaw twitches as he regards her and the amulet with a mixture of emotions I can't decipher. At last, he takes it with a curt "Thank you."

Once more, he turns his attention to me. "I was going to tell you."

Head still bowed, Calierin takes several steps in retreat, then disappears silently through the trees, leaving us alone. I barely notice her.

"But you didn't," I say.

I look down at The Eldrystone, the chain hanging from his clenched fist. Just moments ago, it had felt so rightfully mine. I'd thought that once I reached the other side, I would find its rightful owner to hand it back, but he was here all along, playing me for a fool. I want to snatch it from his fingers, and it takes every ounce of my will not to do it.

He must see something in my expression because he takes two steps forward and presses the amulet into my hand.

"Will you still help me?"

I want to deny the relief that washes over me, but it's impossible to ignore. I've become used to its weight around my neck. I want to place it there, but it's broken, so I only grip it and tighten my hold around it.

The words that come out of my mouth don't match the way I feel. "But it truly belongs to you, *King Korben*."

He flinches as I say his name, at the reminder of all his lies.

How many times did he laugh at my naïve pursuits? Korben Theric is two hundred and twenty-one years old—I learned that much before I left Nido—he must think me nothing but a naïve child.

"Valeria, everything I did was for my people."

I shake my head and hold a finger up. "Before you say more, there is *one* thing I want to know."

His nostrils flare and an invisible shield seems to appear in front of him.

"You know what it is," I say.

The shield only seems to thicken.

"Fine, I'll ask." I pause and feel the chasm that stands between us open wider. Still, I need to know. "Why did my mother curse you? What did you do that drove her to such an extreme?"

He takes a deep breath as if in need of strength.

"And no more lies, please. I just . . . I just can't take anymore, Rífíor . . . Bastien . . . Korben . . . whoever you are!"

Anger flashes in his eyes. "Yes, I lied," he says so quietly that I barely hear him. "What else did you expect from me?"

"Nothing more and nothing less than I expect from others," I reply with just as much anger, then throw the next word in his face like a slap. "*Honesty!*"

"Why? Because it's what others have given *us* in abundance? People like your mother? She deceived you, too. Don't be naïve, Valeria. Of course I had to hide my identity. Loreleia was willing to let your father kill me, even knowing who I was."

I shake my head, ears ringing, heart hammering. He's right. Mother lied to me. Father, too. The knowledge tears me apart.

"Simón Plumanegra may not have known my identity at that precise moment, but I'm sure she told him who I was eventually. And did he come looking for me then? Did they try to fix the mess they made? No, they did not. Instead, they holed up in their fortress and let my people suffer."

"You keep pointing fingers," I say, "but you're still not answering my question."

"Yes, I lied," he repeats forcefully. "I lied because I'm—"

The earth beneath us quakes, a monstrous wave rippling through the woods. I fall, hands and knees scraping the rough ground. Rífíor, reflexes sharper, manages to fling his arms wide and stay upright. A second wave hits. He lurches sideways, grimacing as he collapses to one knee.

"What in all the hells?!" he spits.

I realize the ringing in my ears and the accelerated beat of my heart has nothing to do with our argument.

"Danger," I whisper.

Calierin appears to the right, staggering and cursing under her breath. "The guards and that fucking for-hire sorcerer are here. We have to run."

43
RÍFÍOR

"I had to see for myself, and now I have. The veil is truly gone. Ironically, my homesickness has redoubled. Before, I could go back if I dared. But now, I'm truly barred."

Galen Síocháin – Fae Sorcerer – 0 AV

We stumble to our feet. I brace myself for a third wave, and when it does not come, I grab Valeria's arm.

"Come on! We have to go." I pull her and turn to leave, but she remains rooted to the spot. I glance over my shoulder and find her expression etched in doubt.

"Hurry!" Calierin urges. "We can still outrun them."

As Calierin's voice cuts through the air, Valeria recoils, extricating her arm from my grip.

Shaking her head, she says, "She almost killed me, and you . . . I don't know what to think of you. I have no idea who you are."

"Valeria, we can talk about this later. Right now, we *have* to leave. We have to do what we set out to do."

"No," she replies, and there is only resolve in her tone. No doubt left.

Once more, the ground shifts, but this time it is different. The earth churns, dirt swelling, then erupting and birthing what looks like tentacles. They slither up and tower high above, undulating as if tasting the air. One of them seems to sense me and lunges down.

Unsheathing my sword, I slash and cut it in half. No, not tentacles. Roots.

To my left, Calierin's magic hits a second tendril and burns it to a crisp.

"If she will not come, leave her," Calierin shouts, releasing two consecutive blasts of magic at a pair of newly erupted roots.

My gaze locks with Valeria's, entreating her to come, but she does not move a muscle, appearing indifferent to the churning ground and the looming roots.

The anger that flickered in her gaze moments ago has dwindled to a faint ember. Now, disappointment and uncertainty take its place, as if the path she so meticulously mapped to bring us here is slowly disappearing right before her eyes. Ever so slightly, she shakes her head, a silent confirmation that she will not be joining us.

"But you . . ." I trail off.

She is meant to wield The Eldrystone and reopen the veil, at least that was the plan. Except it was never a promising idea, was it? She is concerned with preventing Amira from making a mistake that will unravel Castella and create an environment ripe for political turmoil and social upheaval. That is Valeria's true battle.

"Give me The Eldrystone then." I put out my hand, not

without difficulty. I thought I would see this journey to an end in her company, but it will not be.

At my request, her eyes widen, and she takes a step back, clutching The Eldrystone tighter.

A familiar crushing sensation settles over my heart, and I realize, belatedly, that it was always going to end up this way.

This was your plan all along, was it not, Niamhara? To play another joke on me.

"The Eldrystone?" Calierin echoes behind me. "Of course!" She comes closer, cutting a root at the base with a quick flick of her wrist. For the first time, she realizes we are not dealing with just any amulet, but Niamhara's conduit itself. She joins my side. "That does not belong to you. Give it back to its rightful owner, *thief*!"

A wave of color rises up Valeria's neck at the word. She is hesitant for a moment, as if she is considering returning it. That crushing sensation in my chest eases a little. Naturally, she will return The Eldrystone. She is different. She—

All of a sudden, the ground beneath Valeria cracks open, and a monstrous root erupts at her feet. Coiling with unholy speed, it ensnares her ankle and surges skyward, dragging her screaming.

"Valeria!" I raise my sword to hack at it, but before I deliver the blow, I find myself ensnared too. The root hoists me upward, slamming me with immense force against a tree. Pain blossoms across my back and side. My grip on the blade loosens, and it falls to the ground.

Through blurry eyes, the world looming upside down, I watch

as a handful of guards rush the small clearing, led by a cloaked figure outlined in a red glow.

"Galen," I rasp, reaching out a hand.

I would know the red sheen of his magic anywhere.

Calierin thrusts her hands forward, violet magic building. Her face is set in rage, her features sharper than any weapon. With a battle cry, she releases her attack. It sails directly toward the for-hire sorcerer.

With confidence, Galen marches straight into Calierin's assault. She smirks, thinking she has won, but she has no idea who she is dealing with. Galen keeps on walking even as her magic hits him square in the chest. Calierin gapes, then starts preparing another attack.

With a nearly imperceptible flick of Galen's fingers, a root appears behind Calierin and twines around her waist. She struggles, but as the root begins to glow—matching Galen's shade of red—her body goes rigid, only her eyes swiveling wildly as she tries to comprehend the turn of events.

My head spins as I dangle. A trail of agony burns along my spine, and my side throbs. I fear my ribs may be broken. Below me, Galen turns and peers up at me, hands on hips.

"Well, well," he says in that careless tone of his that always irritated me, "I thought I'd imagined you. I told myself *Nah, there's no way Korben is trapped here with the rest of the rabble*. So I had to come and make sure I wasn't crazy. And lo and behold, my eyes didn't deceive me." He chuckles. "Here you are. Though," he frowns, "how come you haven't shifted? Shouldn't you have wings and be trying to peck my eyes out by now?"

"Fuck you, Galen," I manage as a wave of sickness rolls over my stomach, and I vomit on the sorcerer. Or at least, I would have liked to, but he is too quick on his feet.

He looks down at the vomit with disgust. "Now, that's not the way to welcome an old friend."

Galen is *not* a friend. He was once my court's Master of Magic and, indeed, a friend, but that was a long time ago, before he betrayed me and left Riochtach over fifty years ago.

Now, he's just another enemy trying to keep me from the only thing that matters.

I open my mouth to curse at him, but the pain in my ribs sharpens. I groan, then vomit again, my consciousness slipping away even as I fight to hold on.

44

VALERIA

"It is worse than I feared. Saints forgive us."

Bishop Benedicto Brasa – Bishop of Castellina – 21 AV

Blood spews from Rífíor's mouth, spraying down as his body goes limp. He has passed out. Something must be terribly wrong with him if he's vomiting blood. Concern fills my chest, a feeling that I'd like to deny, but that is as real as my anger at the fucking, smug sorcerer that did this to us.

Down, I think, clutching The Eldrystone tightly in my fingers. The opal flares hot against my palm.

Finally!

The pressure around my ankle vanishes. For a terrified moment, I think I'm going to crash on my head, but I clutch the amulet and wish for a smooth descent. Espiritu warms my chest, and with a sickening flip, the world spins right side up. My stomach lurches. Propelled by the amulet's espiritu, I float down effortlessly and land gently on my feet.

The guards circling us raise their swords, but the for-hire

sorcerer, Galen, gestures for them to stand down. They don't sheath their weapons, but remain in place, watching me warily.

Galen regards me with a raised eyebrow and quickly puts both hands up in a pacifying gesture. The hood of his cloak is down, and for the first time, I take a good look at his features. He has sun-streaked, long brown hair held back from his face by braids. His brow is strong, and three-day stubble covers his face. He wears an olive-green cloak that matches his warm skin tone too perfectly to be a coincidence. He appears to be five to seven years older than me, but I doubt that's his true age.

"Hold your fire, Princess Valeria!" he says. "Peace! Let's not have a repeat of that whole statue situation, shall we? It wasn't exactly . . . pleasant, and besides, I'm just following orders from your lovely, but slightly terrifying, sister."

Behind Galen, Calierin's eyes reveal an internal battle as she's surely attempting to free herself, but it seems her opponent's espiritu is more powerful than hers.

Ignoring the sorcerer, I run to Rífíor's side and drop to one knee. I inspect him for wounds, but the only blood present dribbles down the corner of his mouth. He's still and pale. With trembling fingers, I check his pulse, and I'm relieved to find it.

Galen approaches and speaks casually. "He has a punctured lung. Broken ribs." He waves his hand in an esoteric way that is slightly comical. "I can sense them," he adds in an outlandishly mystical voice. The male seems to be some sort of jester, one of those people who never takes anything seriously.

Furious, I straighten and glare at him. He's a full head taller than me, but he takes a step back, gaze falling to The Eldrystone clutched in my hand.

"Then do something about it!" I growl.

"'Fraid healing isn't part of my . . . repertoire."

I have no idea if he's telling the truth, and I—

"But *you* can take care of it. After all, you're the one with," he leans close and whispers, "The Eldrystone."

Feeling stupid for not realizing it, I glance down at the opal, then at Rífíor.

Heal him, I think, waiting breathlessly for a sign that it's working, but he remains still, lifeless.

I search Galen's face for an answer.

He frowns. "Maybe put your hands on his chest or . . . something."

The bastardo doesn't seem sure, but with no better idea of my own, I must try. I go to hand the amulet around my neck, but it's broken.

Galen waves his hand, and it's suddenly whole again. I don't question his actions and put on The Eldrystone, kneel next to Rífíor, and brace both hands against his ribs.

Heal! This time, my thought is forceful, a command.

As if lightning has struck him, Rífíor sits up, dark eyes wide, blood spraying from his mouth as he coughs. A wave of relief washes over me, and I lean back, trying not to show it. I blink in awe, noticing that the burns on his chest have also healed.

Breathing hard, he glances all around, taking in the situation. When his eyes meet mine, he seems confused. Blinking, he runs a hand down his side and inhales deeply.

"Thank you," he mouths.

I stand. "I couldn't let the Fae King die in this *godsforsaken* realm." I turn my attention to Galen, vaguely noticing my torn nails have healed too, and all pain in my side is gone. "What now?" I ask, expecting him to have an answer because I sure don't. I don't know what to do next.

My plan to reopen the veil doesn't seem half as sound anymore—not when one of the most vengeful people I know is Tirnanog's king *and* the owner of the most powerful object in existence.

I had hoped to approach King Korben Theric, entering his palace with his lost jewel in hand. I imagined he would be grateful for such a gift, and after that, everything else would have been easy. He would have agreed to an arrangement that would result in a peaceful, civilized transition. There would be no retaliation for any injustices we might have committed against his kin. He would understand it was a sad and natural reality that two different races can't coexist without tensions arising, for surely, the humans stuck in the fae realm have gone through a similar experience.

But now, how can I reason with him? How can I trust him when he won't tell me exactly what led to the veil's collapse?

"What now?" Galen repeats. "Well, I would say you're under arrest but—"

A fist strikes the sorcerer across the jaw, and he goes down like an anvil, hitting the ground with bone-cracking force.

"Arsehole!" Ríffor shakes his hand, glaring at the fallen sorcerer.

The guards, who up until now have stayed at the fringes of the clearing, close the circle, swords pointed at us. They look terrified but are following orders, nonetheless.

Thankfully, Calierin is still ensconced in Galen's espiritu, even if he's unconscious. She's too volatile and would only complicate things.

Rífíor goes for his discarded sword, ready to start a fight.

I open my mouth to tell him to stop, but my words are cut off by the arrival of more guards, and the last person I ever expected to encounter during this journey: Don Justo Medrano.

"No one move a muscle," he says, squaring his shoulders and facing Rífíor and me. "If anything happens to me or anyone else in my party," he glances down at the fallen sorcerer and makes a gesture to indicate the fae doesn't count, "something *unfortunate* will befall a certain cousin of yours, Dear Princess." He smiles crookedly and coldly, sending a shiver down my spine.

Gods! He has Jago.

45
VALERIA

"Should something unfortunate happen to Valeria and Jago Plumanegra, my betrothed will become second in line to Castella's throne. Ah, the wonders of the world!"

Don Justo Ramiro Medrano – Master Mason – 21 AV

"Hand the amulet over." Don Justo extends a hand in my direction, still smirking.

Rage with the force of an earthquake courses up my body. I clench my teeth to stop me from trembling, to clear my mind and erase any thoughts of killing this bastardo on the spot. I have to make sure Jago is all right. I have to lay eyes on him, and then . . .

"Give me the amulet," he repeats, a rumbling threat in his voice and a hand raised to grab me.

With a rumble in his own chest, Rífíor joins my side. "Touch her, and it will be the last thing you do."

The ferocity in his voice makes Don Justo pause, though he doesn't appear intimidated, only quizzical, like a good commander assessing the threats before deciding on the best course of action.

"If I don't return promptly *with* the amulet," Don Justo says, "my men have instructions to slit your cousin's throat."

"Hijo de puta. Perro!" I curse him, dragging both him and his mother through the mud. "You will regret this."

Don Justo tenses.

Reaching for The Eldrystone's power, I think of Jago safe and sound. Warmth spreads through my chest, and I think it must have worked, but can I be sure without seeing it with my own eyes?

Bring him here. Now.

I wait for my cousin with his full head of tousled dirty blond hair and mischievous smile to appear in front of me, but only Don Justo's frigid blue eyes stare back at me, while Jago's warm honey-colored gaze remains absent.

With an almost imperceptible exhale of relief, Don Justo makes his demand once more. "Hand over the amulet, unless you don't want to see your cousin's insipid face again."

I exchange a glance with Rífíor. I may not want him to have the amulet back, but Don Justo is an even more unpalatable choice. Still, I can't risk Jago's life.

Slowly, I reach for the chain around my neck.

Rífíor shakes his head. "Don't," he whispers.

I'm sorry.

I can't bring myself to say the words out loud, but I'm genuinely sorry. I understand his desire to return to his home. I do. Many times, when he thinks I'm not looking, his dark gaze seems to go blank, the way Mother's used to whenever she thought of Tirnanog. How many loved ones did he leave behind? How many nights, in the past twenty years, has he lay awake homesick and aching to set foot on his beloved realm?

Yes, I can nearly feel his pain. Yet, I have a duty to my own family, my own realm.

Sick with disgust, I pull the chain over my head and dangle the amulet in front of Don Justo.

Like a snake striking, Rífíor lifts a hand and attempts to take it from me. Just as he's about to snatch it, an invisible force hits him squarely in the chest and he flies through the air, hits the ground, and skids to a stop ten feet away.

"No, you don't!" Galen stands, dusting himself with one hand while with the other he shakes a finger at Rífíor as if at a naughty child. Quickly, he spares a look toward the amulet. A flash of surprise crosses his features, but it's gone in an instant.

Rífíor sits up, looking dizzy. "You fucking—"

"Subdue him," Don Justo orders his men.

Four guards run to Rífíor. Two point their rapiers at his neck while the other two proceed to tie him to a nearby tree.

I hesitate and nearly pull The Eldrystone back, but Don Justo quickly snatches it away. My heart lurches forward as I mourn its absence. Gleefully, I wait for the amulet to burn him, the way it did Amira, but he's able to hold it without trouble.

Dammit! I was counting on his inability to handle it.

He turns it this way and that, examining it. His brow furrows as if he's concentrating on something.

Gods! He's trying to use it!

I brace myself for . . . I don't know what . . . Rífíor's and my sudden deaths?

As if from a distance, I hear the guards curse at Rífíor as he fights them. A cold breeze blows through the clearing, carrying the smoke from the bonfire. And an owl hoots somewhere deep in the forest.

Disappointment curdles Don Justo's features as The Eldrystone vanishes into his jacket pocket with a flick of his wrist. My shoulders slump in quiet gratitude. I can only hope Niamhara is still on my side. Though, I inwardly curse her for allowing this turn of events. Whatever game she's playing is far beyond my comprehension. I can't rely on her. I have to ensure Jago's safety and get the amulet back. I don't know how I'll accomplish either of those things, but I need to think of something. Quickly.

"Make camp," Don Justo orders, rubbing the back of his neck. For the first time, I notice circles under his eyes. He must have traveled nonstop to catch up with us, and now that he has reached his goal, he suddenly appears exhausted. "You," he points at a man wearing the Royal Guard uniform.

In fact, now that I pay closer attention, I realize they're all members of Nido's guard—the most highly trained and decorated graduates from the Academia de Guardias.

The young guard stops in front of Don Justo and salutes. "Yes, sir."

Don Justo looks him up and down with indifference. "You're in charge of the prisoners. Watch them at all times until I relieve you. Understood?"

"Yes, sir." Another salute, though his obedient expression falters as soon as Don Justo turns away. It's clear he doesn't like taking orders from someone who isn't a superior, someone who never attended the academy. Regardless, he walks in my direction, rope in hand.

"I'm sorry, Your Royal Highness, but . . ." he says, holding out the length of rope.

"I know you," I say. "You're Enrique."

He was under Bastien's command when we went to Alsur and fetched me when Rífíor locked my sister in her room. I shake my head, thinking of how strange it is to think of the same male as two different people. Actually three, now. Four if I consider I once thought of him as River. He's worse than a chameleon.

"Yes, Princess Valeria," Enrique says in a whisper. "I don't want to tie you down, but I have to." He glances uneasily over his shoulder.

I blink at the guard. He has no idea I wasn't shaking my head at him, but at my foolish thoughts. "It's all right, Enrique. I know you're following orders." I hold my wrists out.

Without touching me, he guides me toward the tree next to Rífíor's.

"Let me know if the rope hurts your wrists too much," Enrique says apologetically as he bids me sit at the base of the tree and begins to secure the rope. He's gentle, tightening the rope just enough to impede any slippage.

As he leans closer to test his knots, I ask, "How's my cousin?"

A frown cuts across his forehead, and he's quiet for an instant, then he says, "He's fine."

"Where?" I ask in a rush of breath.

"He—"

"No talking to the prisoners," Don Justo's voice booms across the clearing, causing Enrique to hurry and quickly move away to stand off to the side. He clicks his heels, back as straight as his rapier.

I sigh, trying to be grateful. Jago is safe. Now, I just have to figure out how I'll get out of this tight spot. Surreptitiously, I peer up at Enrique. Perhaps he will help me.

Biding my time, I watch as guards mill about setting up a tent and avoiding Calierin's frozen shape in the middle of the clearing. I have a feeling this is going to be a long night.

46

RÍFÍOR

"I could not have asked for a better Master of Magic, my dear friend."

Korben Theric – King of Tirnanog – 1951 DV

The arsehole disappears inside the tent the guards set up for him. I strain against the ropes that bind me, trying to slip my wrists out, but the guard standing on watch places a hand on the hilt of his rapier, eyes flashing a warning. I relent. For now.

This turn of events is entirely unexpected. We should be on our way to the veil, but Calierin . . .

It is her fault we were captured. I glance at her frozen figure, hoping she stays like that forever. Despite her oath, I can't trust her. I fear for Kadewyn. Did she kill him? I shake my head, dismissing the thought and praying to the gods he is all right.

What now? How do we get The Eldrystone back?

"Why did you give him the amulet?" I demand, throwing a sidelong glance at Valeria.

She doesn't answer. She only glares.

"Because, unlike others," Galen answers for her, strolling in our direction, a blade of grass in his mouth, "she holds family in high esteem, don't you, princess?"

Valeria's mouth twists, her displeasure clear.

Of all people, why did it have to be Galen with his smug face and eternal carefree façade to ruin everything?

"Came to gloat?" I ask.

He crouches, throws away the blade of grass, and points at the guard. "You, go get something to eat. I'll watch them for a spell."

The guard appears uncertain.

"Go!" Galen insists, his tone brooking no argument. His skillful command of magic has always lent him a great deal of authority wherever he goes. No one would like to end up a smear on the ground.

"Once a traitor, always a traitor," I bite the words out.

"Get over yourself, *King Theric*." He whispers the last part, as if to make sure no one else can hear him call me that.

Next to me, Valeria watches our interaction with deep interest.

Galen rubs his stubbled chin. "Imagine my surprise when I realized I wasn't chasing Rífíor of the Veilfallen but *you*." He extends a hand toward me in a demonstrative gesture. "I could hardly believe my eyes. But then, the princess turned us to stone and when I was able to undo the spell, I wondered if I'd imagined it all. You'll have to understand, I had to make sure."

"Is there a point to all of this?" I demand, wishing my hatred for this male was capable of reaching across the short distance that separates us to knock him out once more.

"Only that I'm glad to see you." He grins widely, irritatingly.

"Fuck you, Galen."

"Nah, you already did that to me for over fifty years. Not a pleasant experience. Though, I must say . . . it brings me pleasure to no end to find that you're just as thoroughly fucked as me." He throws his head back and laughs. "To think that you have been trapped in Castella for twenty years. It's poetic justice."

I strain against my bindings, and I swear if he comes any closer, I will bite his face off.

He lifts his chin theatrically, and I know he's thinking of the next inane thing to say, but before he opens his mouth, Valeria voices a question.

"Who are you? And why are you . . . bothering him?"

Galen turns his attention to her and scans her up and down. He never misses anything. He plays the fool, and people assume many things about him—none of them true. He is as shrewd as they come, which made him an excellent Master of Magic. It was also what caused his downfall.

"He hasn't told you about me?" Galen asks.

Valeria shakes her head.

"I used to be his Master of Magic until he exiled me." He looks satisfied with delivering this news.

I huff. "Why not tell her *why* you were exiled?"

"Would you be surprised if I tell you, it was because of his precious amulet?"

Her eyebrows go up, and she does a slow blink that clearly delivers the message: *No, I'm not surprised*.

"You tried to steal it and use it against my will," I snap.

"To end a war, Korben."

"A war that *you* made worse," I shoot back.

"Exactly the reason why I was trying to put an end to it."

I shake my head. "And at what cost?" I feel my anger mounting, so I rein it in. "Never mind, it seems you have not changed one bit."

"I could say the same about you."

"Then do it and leave me the hells alone." I glance away at the distant darkness between the trees.

"I take that back," he says. "You're worse than before." When I say nothing, he turns to Valeria, hooking a finger in my direction. "He's worse."

"Oh, you mean he was less of an asshole before?"

He makes a weighing motion with his hands. "Give or take, I suppose."

Great! All I need is both of them colluding against me.

Galen scoots closer to Valeria, looking right and left as he lowers his voice. "So . . . that was The Eldrystone you handed over to that miserable dunghill. I had no idea that's what we were after."

I cock my head to the side to better see and listen.

"What are you saying?" Valeria asks. "That you wouldn't have taken my sister's gold if you'd known?"

Galen shrugs. "Depends."

"On what?"

"On . . . why you were running away."

Valeria remains quiet, likely weighing up every nuance of our situation, wondering whether or not revealing our purpose is a good idea. I wager it is. Galen would be as eager as any fae to see the veil restored. He may be exiled, but that is quite different from being physically barred.

"We were on our way to reopen the veil," Valeria answers at last.

It seems she came to the same conclusion as me. Mayhap she hopes revealing the truth will procure Galen's sympathy and, perhaps, his help. Or am I reading too much into her straightforward answer? I fear it is the latter. She changed her mind about going through with our plan, after all, and only seemed to care about keeping The Eldrystone to herself.

Except . . . she gave it up for Jago, a part of me reminds me. Though a crushing realization follows . . . *She would not give it up for you, Korben.*

"Were you really?" Galen leans closer to me now.

"We were," I reply, without looking at them.

"And why did *she* have it? What could she possibly have done to make you part with it?" He pauses, thinking for a moment. "W- wait, wait, wait a minute, you're in love with her."

"Quit being an idiot," I snap. I do not miss the way Valeria's face turns away at my words, but I cannot focus on that right now. "You have no idea what brought us here. So either help us get the amulet back or leave us alone."

"Well, well." Galen stands, dusting his hands. "It seems I have lots to think about tonight. Sleep tight." He leaves.

Our guard returns to his post. He never took his eyes off us, waiting at an out-of-earshot distance.

Galen strolls as if he does not have a care in the world. He feigns disinterest, but I know better. He is not so cavalier as he would have everyone believe. The question is: will he take The Eldrystone for himself as he once tried to do? Or will he bring it back to me? I suspect I will know the answer before the night is over.

The irony does not escape me. I once banished him from Tirnanog for coveting the very thing I would gladly let him have now, for I would rather see the conduit in his hands—a fae who would use it to restore access to our realm—than in Don Justo's, a human who would use it for ends I cannot begin to fathom.

I glance at Valeria, a mixture of emotions crowding my chest. I do not relish the sensation. For years, I have felt nothing but emptiness, and now I feel too much, too keenly.

When I took her earlier tonight—ecstasy fogging my thoughts, her body supple and willing in the circle of my arms—I dared believe forgiveness was possible, dared hope her mother's curse could be broken. I thought Niamhara had decided it was time to end my suffering.

It took mere minutes to disabuse me of that half-witted notion. One more truth revealed—the least harmful of all—and Valeria's scant trust shattered.

Even if she had learned my true name from my own lips, it is the still-unanswered question that really matters. And once she learns the answer—the reason why Loreleia stole The Eldrystone—trust will never be a possibility again.

I did something horrible, something I should regret but I do not. Perhaps, seeing my lack of remorse, Niamhara has led us to failure. Perhaps this is just another penance. A meticulously crafted torment designed to raise my hopes before dashing them to dust once more.

The Goddess mocks me, her cruel hand moving me about like a piece in a game.

Father passed The Eldrystone to me over a century ago before he crossed to the Glimmer, the day I turned one hundred years old. The amulet fell heavily upon my chest, a responsibility I did not want, but could not escape. Despite the years of instruction on the duties of the conduit keeper, I felt unprepared.

My own magic was strong. Like my ancestors before me, I was a raven shifter, capable of all the forms: corvus, dreadwing, scatter, and chimera. Not only that, but I could also control the darker powers, something few in our line have ever been capable of. I felt no need for more. I was content as a prince and dreaded the weight of the crown upon my head as much as The Eldrystone.

It took me a few years to come to terms with it all. To my surprise, I found that my work as king was deeply rewarding. My days were filled with the orchestration of many projects that made Tirnanog a better place. Seeing my people prosper filled me with pride. There was peace under my rule as I swiftly stamped out any sign of rebellion with the help of the amulet I once dreaded.

The Goddess created us in her image, giving us control over the forces of nature. But not all fae aim to use their powers for good. Some seek to do evil, and as the keeper of The Eldrystone, it was my duty to maintain a balance.

And so I did, for seventy years.

Until Morwen the Mistwraith sprouted out of nowhere.

That's when the true trials began.

As her name suggests, she came like a phantom in the night, unknown and unseen. With a viciousness that augured a deranged mind, she began instigating old rivalries between neighbors, causing accidents, terrorizing villages with clandestine attacks, and more. During every onslaught, she seemed to spring out of the air when least expected to quickly disappear in the same fashion.

We searched for her, using every resource available to us, but she eluded us at every turn, disappearing like fog in the presence of the sun. It was the first time The Eldrystone was powerless against a foe.

Thirty-five more years crawled by, and my kingdom remained haunted by her ghostly presence. To the north, war festered like a plague sore, erupting between two feuding clans, one Galen called his home—hence his misguided attempt to steal The Eldrystone.

The penalty for his actions would have been death. It is what the council advised, but in the end, the decision was mine, and I chose exile. He had been my friend, almost family.

Our troubled existence continued for thirty more years after his departure.

Needless to say, I had my hands full. Marriage was not something I sought, rather it was thrust upon me. The Royal Mate Rite had to take place. I had reached my two hundredth birthday.

Females came to the capital from all around the realm. It is our way for males to find a mate at this age, and the king is no exception. On the contrary, I was to choose a queen from amongst my people and thus keep our blood diverse, strong.

Worries about the war gnawed at me, threatening to break my concentration from the rite, but it was Saethara's presence that proved far more distracting and pulled my attention from what really mattered.

Saethara.

When I close my eyes, I can still see her beautiful face, her devastating, sensuous body. From the first moment all the candidates were presented, it was she who drew my complete attention. I went through the motions, meeting with every candidate, waiting for a turn with her. There were banquets, dances, private meetings, and tests.

It was these tests that worried me. I feared she might fail them, and then I would be heartbroken because I was in love with her. Each female received a different test, but they all consisted of giving the potential brides access to The Eldrystone. Or more accurately . . . a replica of it.

Greed to possess the amulet has corrupted gods know how many people since its forging. It is part of the rite for kings in my family to ensure that the final candidate is free of such covetousness.

A few of the females were tempted and took the fake amulet, but Saethara . . . she showed absolutely no interest in it. It was all the proof I needed. I had found the perfect bride.

We were wed immediately. No male in the realm was happier than me. Then, on our wedding night, after I thought I had reached the Glimmer in her arms, she stabbed me in my sleep and took the amulet. I only survived because my innate magic helped me heal. She left me for dead while Tirnanog still celebrated our marriage.

Mad with grief, I grabbed my sword and went after her. She had fetched Loreleia, her childhood friend and Valeria's mother. They had come together to the rite from a small village called Nilhalari. Saethara had dragged Loreleia with her. As I confronted them, I thought them accomplices. I thought they had planned the deception together, like hungry spiders lurking in their webs.

"Saethara, why?!" I demanded.

She was surprised to see me on my feet, healed. Yet, she was not afraid—not with The Eldrystone in her possession. Releasing a cackle that froze the blood in my veins, she revealed her true self, her contempt for me.

"You fool. You weak fool. You do not deserve to be the keeper of such power." She held the amulet aloft. It glowed with her evil intent, but I did not care. The possibility of death only seemed like an escape from the ravaging aching in my heart.

Oblivious of any danger, I roared and rushed toward my treacherous wife, sword held high. A chilling vision flickered before my eyes—a twisted tableau of us both dead, intertwined in a final, gruesome embrace. A fitting end for our blackened hearts.

But Loreleia, taking advantage of Saethara's distraction, snatched the amulet from her hand. Saethara fell to her knees at the force of my blazing rage, a plea on her lips. I could have stopped, I think, but I did not even try. Instead, I gritted my teeth and ran her through with my blade.

It was not enough. My fury was not satiated. They had come from far away to deceive and betray me. They were harpies, born from malice and bred to be pure evil.

"I will destroy every trace of you," I swore. *"I will raze your wretched village to the ground along with every person who lives there. Nothing good can come from a place that spawns such monsters. Everything and everyone responsible for fashioning such vile creatures will meet its end."*

"No! You are mad," Loreleia said, her voice trembling.

"Give me back my amulet!" I demanded.

She shook her head and retreated.

I meant to kill her, too. She deserved the same death I had devised for Saethara, and it would have been so if not for Vonall, my best friend. He intervened, giving Loreleia the chance to escape, to run and search for refuge in the human realm.

Yet not even Vonall could hold me for long, and I caught up with Loreleia. She had crossed the veil already and had encountered Simón Plumanegra. What transpired afterward... two decades of torment, a life sundered in half.

Until I met Valeria.

Through narrowed lids, I steal glances at her, hoping my interest will escape her notice. She is furious at me, and rightfully so. I owe her the truth after all the ways I have hurt her.

A part of me clings to the notion that our first night was a misstep, a lapse in judgment after years of solitude. But our time in the wagon... and tonight... each encounter reveals more. My resolve crumbles when I am near her, her allure greater than any I have ever known—for no male seeks the flames willingly when memories of the past still sear his soul.

She is no misstep.

I am conquered.

Walls I erected, shields forged from pain itself—none of it mattered. Her courage, her kindness, the very things that drove me mad with frustration... they were her weapons against me. Her wit, her beauty... they were my undoing. I fell for all of it, every last irritating, endearing bit of it. And now, how am I supposed to confess the truth? How, when every word will be a wedge driven between us, pushing her away?

47

VALERIA

*"It is time to cross to the Glimmer and leave my burdens behind.
I am glad my son is strong enough to inherit them."*

Faolan Theric – King of Tirnanog – 1879 DV

My shoulders hurt. I push with my feet to get closer to the tree trunk. It relieves some of the pressure.

Rífíor sits quietly, lost in thought. I avoid his gaze and focus on the activity around us, the guards sitting by the fire they built. They're preparing food, some looking pleased their mission is over, others casting glances this way. Do they wonder why I've betrayed my sister? Do they care?

For the first time, I realize this is a different group of guards than the ones we encountered a few days ago. I don't remember all of them, but I'm sure Teniente Coronel Eva Toromayor is not here.

"Enrique," I say, glancing sideways at my guard, "what happened to the first group of guards that was sent after us? They were led by a woman, Teniente Coronel Toromayor."

He seems reluctant to answer my question, but after a moment, he says, "They are . . . statues, Your Royal Highness." There is accusation in his voice, though he tries to hide it.

Lowering my head, I press my lips together to stifle a sob. I'd hoped Galen had undone the spell for everyone, but maybe he was only able to save himself.

One careless thought, and I killed them.

Perhaps it's for the best I don't have The Eldrystone anymore.

"I would rather *you* have it," Rífíor says in a barely audible voice, as if he has read my mind, as if he knows exactly what I'm thinking.

"I killed all those people."

He nods once, acknowledging what I did, not dismissing it. "It was an accident. The amulet is powerful. You have much to learn."

"I'm sorry," I say, the words jumping from my mouth before I can stop them.

Rífíor's gaze darts my way. He frowns. "You have nothing to apologize for."

"Don't I?" I blow air through my nose, feeling disappointed in myself, my anger toward him quickly souring into regret. "I told you I would help you reopen the veil. Now, I don't know if that's the right thing to do anymore. I don't make a habit of going back on my word."

He looks pained at my apology, as if he realizes all his wrongs outdo mine, and he's the one who owes me not only an apology, but an overdue explanation.

Taking a deep inhale as if to draw strength from the air, he opens his mouth to speak.

"Pardon me, Princess Valeria," Enrique interrupts. "It's not that

I'm eavesdropping—I don't really have a choice—but is it true that you planned to re-open the veil?" His tone is cautious and hushed.

I nod.

"It really is possible?" he insists.

"Yes." I've never felt so certain, which is stupid since I don't even have The Eldrystone with me anymore.

He appears troubled by my answer.

"What is it, Enrique?"

Uncertainty etches his features.

"You can trust me," I say. "Please . . . what's on your mind?"

His uncertainty morphs to concern, and deep worry lines form across his forehead. After a moment's hesitation, he takes a few sideway steps, coming closer. His back is ramrod straight, and he stares ahead, the perfect picture of a Guardia Real.

"I was born in Castellina," he says. "On the west side."

He lets that sink in. The west side is the poorest area of the city.

"Growing up, my best friends were fae," he goes on. "They are good people and, pardon me for saying this, but they don't deserve what your sister is doing to them."

A knot forms in my throat, and next to me, Ríffor releases a breath along with a deep sound of anger rumbling in the back of his throat.

"What . . . has happened?" I ask, terrified of the answer.

"I've always been proud to be a Castellan, but after what I witnessed . . . Well, I don't feel so good about it anymore."

Tears prick the back of my eyes. *Oh, Amira!* I fear what she has become, fear she will never be the same again.

"Keep going, Enrique," I say, because I need to hear this, and Ríffor does, too.

"The queen sent Castellina's Guardia in the middle of the night. They pulled fae folk from their beds at sword point, even children, all of them born in Castella. Those who dared resist were cut down without mercy. I don't know how many were killed."

A strangled gasp escapes me, and I don't dare glance at Ríffor.

"They emptied the old Monasterio de San Corvus de la Corona," he continues, "herded them there like cattle, and locked them up. They call the place *La Haderia* now. They're offering gold—a reward for those willing to point a finger at their fae neighbors who ran and hid."

We're quiet for a long time. Horrible images dance before my eyes: brutal hands shoving people out of their homes, terrified cries echoing in the night, the glint of steel cutting down parents as they try to protect their children. It's a nightmare.

"I'm sorry, Princes Valeria," Enrique clears his throat, "but I thought we were better than that." A pause. "I kept wondering why the queen sent us after you, but I understand now. You oppose her." It's not a question, but a statement that I don't need to confirm.

Enrique cracks his neck and rolls his shoulders, as if working up resolve. Setting his jaw, he pulls his dagger from his belt, crouches, and saws at the rope that binds me.

"Open the veil, Princess Valeria," he says. "I will help you."

The tension around my shoulders gives, and my wrists are blessedly free.

"Thank you, Enrique," I say.

He smiles sadly, then his eyes widen as someone wraps an arm around his neck and drags him back, pulling him into the darkness of the trees behind us. I scramble backwards, kicking, and nearly end up on Rífíor's lap. He struggles to get free, alert to the danger. Panic snaps down my spine as a figure moves in the dark, approaching.

"Boo!" Jago says in a mock whisper as he peeks from around the trunk.

I nearly jump out of my skin from relief. My teeth clamp down on my lower lip, stifling a cry of joy. Quickly, he proceeds to cut Rífíor's rope.

When he's done, I wrap my arms around his neck. "You're all right!"

"It was the damnedest thing," my cousin says. "My handcuffs just came undone, the wagon's door sprang open, and *no one* was watching. I practically strolled out of the camp."

"The guard." I peer with concern into the dark.

"He's fine. He might wake up with a headache, though," Jago says. "Here, take his rapier."

"This is a very pleasant reunion," Rífíor says, "but we best get moving before they notice us."

Just as he finishes saying this, one of the guards by the fire does just that. He jumps to his feet, going for his rapier and sounding the alarm. "The prisoners are escaping!"

With the knowledge that my cousin is safe, I lunge into an offensive attack, meeting the first guard as he charges. Our rapiers meet, the metal singing. I shuffle to the side and jab again. He parries the move, offering no counterattack. He seems hesitant, unsure of whether or not he's allowed to stab the princess. That's his mistake. I don't hesitate. A quick thrust of my blade finds its mark, slipping through the intricate guard of his rapier. With a flick of my wrist, his weapon spins away, clattering to the ground.

Four more guards charge. Jago faces one, and I another. The other two go for Rífíor who is unarmed. I thrust and parry, barely keeping my opponent at bay. My attention is split, drifting to Rífíor, who is outnumbered. Though my worry is misplaced because he easily disarms one of the guards, slamming him head-first into a tree, then deflecting the second guard's blade right before it slices open his middle.

The three of us defeat our opponents in unison. I'm careful not to deliver a killing blow, and I'm gratified to see that even Rífíor refrains from such violence.

More guards are running in our direction. Don Justo is now out of his tent, screaming orders. There are over a dozen guards and only three of us.

"Let's get out of here!" Jago grabs my arm and pulls me toward town.

I hesitate. We need to get The Eldrystone back, but we won't be able to do that if we let them capture us again. Rífíor also hesitates, but in the end, he nods, agreeing with Jago. Running at full pelt, we disappear under the trees' shadows.

"Catch them!" Don Justo shouts, his angry voice cutting through the night.

We run, Rífíor guiding the way and urging us to go faster. He finds a clear route, taking us across town, weaving in and out of allies until we reach the burnt remnants of a building. No one roams the streets, the celebrations surely cut short by the presence of the Guardia Real and the ensuing commotion.

With the senses of a burrowing creature, Rífíor spots a passage between charred and fallen logs. Nearly crawling, he enters the battered structure. Moonlight easily seeps through the cracks, illuminating our way. With Jago quick on my heels, I go in, fearing the wreckage will collapse atop our heads. Rífíor finds a set of steps that lead us down to a musty cellar, which remains fairly untouched by the inferno that devoured the building's flesh and left only scorched, broken bones.

Our agitated breaths are loud in the cramped space. We sit still for several long moments, listening for signs of pursuit. We hear running footsteps and voices around us. Someone takes a close look at the ruins, then announces it's all clear, which feels like a miracle. The noise dies down by degrees until we're left in utter silence.

Jago heaves a sigh. "It's been quite a day. What about you two?"

Neither Rífíor nor I say anything.

"That good, huh?"

Rífíor grunts.

"As talkative as ever." Jago shakes his head, a strand of blond hair shining in a stray ray of moonlight. He peers at me, his honey-colored eyes nearly black. "I'm so relieved you're all right." Reaching across the space, he squeezes my shoulder.

"Me, too. Don Justo threatened to hurt you if I didn't give him The Eldrystone. I used it to wish you to safety, but I didn't know if it'd worked."

He nods slowly and deliberately. "So that's what happened. Makes sense. Thank you for not selling me out. It's nice to see I'm still worth more than that damnable jewel to someone."

"Of course you are," I say. "You're my favorite cousin."

We both laugh, our amusement laced with nerves.

"What about the troop? And Cuervo?" I ask.

Jago grins. "They're here. After you left us, Esmeralda and I made quick work of the couple of guards who stayed back to watch over us. We figured we should continue on and ran into . . . an interesting sculpture display."

I'm mortified by the comment, and it's hard not to let in the image of all those petrified faces staring blankly into nothingness.

"I thought you might rejoin us," Jago continues, unaware of my internal conflict, "but when you didn't, it was clear you'd also continued on. Your bird drove me crazy, by the way. He kept asking where his *friend* was. He flew ahead several times, and I thought he wouldn't return, but he did. At any rate, we got here late last night and camped right outside of town. I was asking around if anyone had seen a pretty princess and three grumpy fae, when Don Justo spotted me and put me in chains." Jago nods at the grumpy fae present and gives him a salute.

"We need to get the amulet back," Rífíor says. "I will go. You two stay here." He moves to leave.

I grab his wrist. "Wait! We need a plan. We can work together."

He looks down at my hand.

I let him go. He's so close, his shoulder only an inch from mine. I feel the heat radiating from him and shiver as his dark eyes rove over my face.

"I can easily evade anyone patrolling the city," he says, his deep voice traveling over my skin making the fine hairs on my arms stand on end. "I can track Don Justo, isolate him, and—"

The rubble above us groans, ashes and small pieces of debris raining down on our heads.

"Shit!" Jago exclaims. "I knew this was a bad idea."

Rífíor arches his body over mine and pushes me toward the exit. We scramble like rats, ashes stinging our eyes and clogging our noses. The air itself seems to groan under the weight of the collapsing building. I squeeze my eyes shut, picturing the heavy wooden beams pinning us like insects. Then something shifts, a disturbance that seems out of place. I peek with one eye and watch as the blackened skeleton lifts up and floats away, the silver light of the moon splitting the darkness, exposing us.

A dark figure stands above us, one hand lifted toward the hovering pile of rubble, red espiritu flowing from his fingers.

Galen huffs. "Well, don't just sit there gaping at me. Hurry!"

48

VALERIA

"On the charge of treason, you are hereby exiled from Tirnanog until the hells devour you."

Korben Theric – King of Tirnanog – 1971 DV

As soon as we dash out from under the wreckage, Galen lets the charred bulk drop. I flinch, expecting a deafening crash, but the sorcerer waves a hand, and there is barely a sound as the weakened beams snap and the rest of the building collapses into the cellar that served as our hiding place.

So naïve of us to think we could hide from his espiritu. It was only a matter of time before he found us.

Rífíor squares his shoulders, stepping protectively in front of me. Galen smirks, dusting his cloak. He doesn't look the least bit intimidated.

"For our people's sake, Galen," Rífíor says, "help us or get out of the way."

"Who is this guy?" Jago leans in to whisper in my ear.

I ignore his question, trying to think of a way to escape, but I don't see one.

"Help you?" the sorcerer asks, as if it were the most foreign concept he can imagine. "Help you, how?"

Rífíor's fists tighten, but they'll be no match for espiritu. If only we had our fae-made blades, but Rífíor's is lost in the forest and La Matadora is back at the inn, reclining against the wall.

Galen sticks his hand under his cloak. Rífíor tenses, his entire body coiled to spring. The sorcerer pulls something from a hidden pocket and holds it out for us to inspect.

The Eldrystone!

As if frozen by espiritu, Rífíor stands mutely.

I step from behind him, driven by a slight glow of the opal. Seeing it, I realize how much I've missed its weight around my neck, its warmth over my chest. Mechanically, I lift a hand and reach for it. When Galen pulls it away, my heart lurches and anger fills me. It takes all my strength to rein it back in, but I prevail.

"Nah ah ah." He shakes a finger. "I have conditions for the king." His sharp green eyes drift over my shoulder to Rífíor.

"The king?" Jago echoes. "Puta madre! I have a feeling I missed a lot."

"Anything." I turn to Rífíor. "Right?"

I sense his disappointment at my thoughtless answer. I haven't the faintest idea what history exists between them, and what the sorcerer could possibly want from the Fae King. It isn't for me to decide if Galen's conditions are met. Yet, we're talking about The Eldrystone. Surely, Rífíor will agree to any demands.

"What do you want, Galen?" Rífíor asks.

"You know what I want."

"You already have it in your hand, do you not?" Rífíor's tone is heavy with contempt.

"The damn thing refuses to work for me," he complains. "Also, you could show a little gratitude. I took the amulet back from that dolt, and I diverted their attention in the wrong direction."

"Thank you," Rífíor says, but it sounds more like *fuck you*.

The sorcerer crosses his arms and presses his lips, looking like a stubborn child who refuses to talk unless he gets the sweets he has demanded.

Rífíor runs a hand through his hair, an ocean of frustration in his sigh. "Fine. Your exile is lifted. You may go back to Tirnanog."

Galen perks up. "Aaaand?"

"I do not know. What more could you possibly want?"

"My old post back."

"What?!" Rífíor asks incredulously. "You think I would bring a known traitor back into my inner circle?"

"And I also want you to stop calling me that."

What the male is asking doesn't seem unreasonable—not considering the reward.

I step forward to take control of the situation. "And if he does what you demand, you will give us The Eldrystone?"

Galen raises one eyebrow. "I will give *him* The Eldrystone. He's the rightful owner, milady. Not you." He bows with exaggeration.

"The rightful owner. The Fae King," Jago whispers in awe. "Saints and feathers!"

Ignoring Jago, I nudge Rífíor's arm. "He isn't asking for much. Considering."

"What a smart princess you've got there, *Rífíor*." Galen mocks the name.

I can't bring myself to call him Korben. Or King Theric. Or whatever else he goes by. So Rífíor it is.

"Fine," Rífíor growls with irritation. "You can be the Master of Magic again."

"And?"

"And I won't call you a traitor."

"You swear?"

"Why are you being such a child?!" Rífíor demands.

"Do. You. Swear?"

"I swear. For fuck's sake!"

"Very good. You can have it." Without warning, Galen tosses the amulet. It sails through the air, the chain trailing behind like a comet's tail.

I'm tempted to snatch it out of the air, but I press my hands to my sides and refrain. Rífíor catches it, and as his fingers close around it, his expression seems troubled rather than relieved.

Galen dusts his hands. "Now that's settled . . . let's go. No time better than the present to open the veil. Faoloir's bollocks! I can't wait! The first thing I'll do is drink twenty bottles of feyglen." He points at Rífíor and winks. "Wanna join?"

Rífíor shakes his head and places the amulet around his neck, hiding it under his shirt. It is *his*, however, and when he asked for it back, I didn't give it to him. Of course he doesn't trust me now. A bitter pang shoots across my chest. Something occurs to me: What if he has regained access to The Eldrystone's power? Has

Niamhara decided to return her favor to him? That bitter pang intensifies, but there's another feeling that overshadows it.

Fear.

Fear of what he might do after what he heard from Enrique.

The events the guardia recounted are nothing short of a nightmare. Deep down, I still hoped Amira's conscience would reawaken once faced with the final decisions of her cruel plan, but she has truly lost her way. What she's doing is unforgivable. The veilfallen have been at war with us for a lot less. I shudder to think what horrors their leader might be concocting in his mind at this very moment, a brewing tempest of vengeance. A part of me fears his wrath, another part wonders if we deserve it.

Yet, my loyalty lies with my people, not his.

"I think we should rest," Rífíor says.

"Rest?" Galen sounds as if Rífíor has suggested self-immolation.

"Yes," he says in that authoritative tone he has—the one that makes him sound like someone used to being obeyed . . . a king. "Valeria is recovering from a mortal wound."

"Mortal wound?" Jago puts a hand on my shoulder and peers into my face. His expression is both worried and appalled. "Why didn't you say something?"

I huff. "When? Between the sword fight and running for our lives?"

"Rífíor is right," Jago says. "You need to rest. You look pale."

"And you sound like Nana." I shake his hand off. "I'm fine."

"So are those huge circles under your eyes," Jago puts in. "Mighty fine."

Rífíor turns toward town. "We have a room in the inn. We'll go there."

"Are you crazy? They'll find us." I shake my head. "Let's join the troop instead."

"Galen will take care of it. Your betrothed won't find us," Rífíor says.

The sorcerer makes a face, affronted by the implicit order.

"What?" Rífíor gives him a once-over. "Do you want your old post back? Or not?"

Galen raises his eyes to the sky and rubs the back of his neck. "For now, I guess. I may have to reconsider later."

"Please do." Rífíor begins walking, headed in the direction of the inn.

I catch up with him. "Don Justo isn't my betrothed anymore."

His gaze flicks to mine, and I swear I see relief in his expression, but it quickly turns to indifference.

"Are you sure Galen will keep Don Justo from finding us?" I ask.

"Yes," he responds dryly.

"Walking in the open is unnerving," Jago pipes in from the side, glancing back at Galen, who is a few steps behind.

"Yes," I agree, feeling as jumpy as he looks.

A few people have ventured back outside now that the commotion has passed. They glance tentatively in all directions, but their inquisitive gazes seem to pass right over us, as if we're not there.

"It's like we're invisible," Jago whispers.

"No need to whisper," Galen says in a perfectly audible voice. "They can't see us, *nor* hear us. Stealth spells are one of my specialties."

There is something about Galen that makes me nervous. He is too self-assured, too . . . I can't put a finger on it. He seems carefree, but something about his exchanges with Rífíor makes me think it's all an act, a barrier he puts up to hide his true self. What is with all these fae and their unknowable personalities? I thought I knew about their kind because of Mother and my half-fae blood, but the more of them I come in contact with, the more I realize I shouldn't assume.

Perhaps it's impossible for a human being to understand a race with lives as long and vast as the fae.

Living for centuries may grant them profound wisdom that a shorter lifespan cannot afford. On the other hand, it may also dispense heartbreak that would cripple a human spirit.

Time erodes and time hardens.

I don't have to guess what it has done to Rífíor.

Either way, who am I to tangle with him? I'm decidedly out of my depths.

We're across the street from the tavern when a dark shape swoops down and lands in front of me. I'm startled only for an instant because I immediately realize it's Cuervo.

"Friend, friend, friend!" he croaks, jumping from one talon to the other.

"Cuervo!" I crouch to rub his neck. "I'm so happy to see you."

"Stupid chicken! You're going to give us away," Jago hisses.

"No, it's fine," Galen says. "No one can hear him. He's within our aura of silence."

Galen crouches next to me. "He yours?"

"No, he's not *mine*. He's my friend." I glare at him.

The sorcerer stretches to his full height and huffs. "Women."

"Let's go inside," Rífíor urges.

"I'll see you later, Cuervo. I missed you." I wish he could go inside, but I doubt the owners would like it.

The inn's tavern is quiet with only Francisca and her husband standing behind the counter. He rests his chin heavily on his hand, looking bored, wiping the counter with his free hand, going over the same spot over and over. Next to him, his wife sews a pair of old pants while she hums a tune.

We walk in, the thick wooden door whining on its hinges. They don't look in our direction and continue with their tasks none the wiser.

The steps creak as we climb.

"Damn guardias!" the man harrumphs. "They ruined business on one of the best days of the year."

"At least no one's dead," his wife replies.

"Yet," he puts in.

We enter the small bedroom. It is as we left it.

Jago glances around. "There's only one bed. We can't all sleep here."

"We'll make do," Rífíor says.

"I've been sleeping on the ground for two weeks," Jago protests. "Tonight, I plan to sleep on a bed *and* on a full stomach. I've had quite the day as I mentioned. Anyone else with me?"

"Now," Galen says, "a man after my own heart." He thumps my cousin's back.

"Galen," Rífíor complains.

"Don't worry, *Your Majesty*," the sorcerer says. "This entire inn has been erased from existence. No one will disturb us."

"Fantástico!" Jago exclaims. "This guy is like Gaspar imbued with strength from San Christopher."

Galen throws an arm over Jago and starts leading him out the door. "I think you and I are going to get along. Jago, right?"

My cousin grins and nods.

"Besides, I have a feeling these two have *a lot* to talk about." Galen hooks a thumb over his shoulder, pointing at us.

"You have no idea," Jago says.

I want to smack him. He's supposed to be on my side, and instead, he's making friends with the fae sorcerer? Traitor.

Not that Galen is wrong. Rífíor and I have to talk. A momentous decision lies ahead of me. If he still needs my help, is it wise for me to reopen the veil? Or should I refuse and protect my realm from his wrath?

In the end, Jago redeems himself. "If you hurt her again, fae," he tells Rífíor over his shoulder, "you'll answer to me."

49

VALERIA

*"You have no right. Let her go. Do not touch her.
My child is Castellan. She was born here!"*

Naeror Qhen – Fae Outcast – 21 AV

After Jago and Galen leave, Rífíor closes the door, making the room feel even smaller.

I'm alone with the Fae King, I think in disbelief, then quickly realize this moment is meaningless compared to so many others. I've insulted him, sparred with him, slept with him.

Oh, gods!

"How do you feel?" Rífíor asks, pointing at my side.

I press a hand to the wound and feel absolutely nothing. "It's . . . fine. I feel fine, as if nothing happened." I'm reminded of something Francisca said. "The innkeeper, she said that you paid the price to make me better. What did she mean?"

He shakes his head as if it's of no importance.

I raise an eyebrow and wait for an answer. I'm tired of his reticence. I understand it now better than ever, but I'm done with it.

"I would like you to explain," I say in a tone that brooks no argument.

He sighs. "The healer was a dwarf."

"Aaand?"

"He was from a clan known as the Nightmend. Their magic is rustic. They must draw the energy for their spells from somewhere, so he drew it from me. That is all."

I incline my head to one side. "What do you mean he drew it from you?" Slowly, he lifts his shirt and shows me his abdomen. A scar mars his side that wasn't there before. Realizing something, I lift my tunic and confirm that it matches mine perfectly.

"He used my pain to heal you," he explains.

"What? I've never heard of such a thing."

He takes a seat on the chair in the corner. "Nightmends are few, even in Tirnanog. I am grateful he was here." He pauses. "Even as you lay dying, The Eldrystone ignored my wishes. Without him, you would have died."

He stares at the floor, looking so tired, as if all the things he's been running from have finally caught up with him, and he's decided to give up the fight. Watching him like this makes me feel for him.

"Thank you," I say. "For saving my life even though . . . it cost you."

"It was nothing." He shrugs.

"Not . . . to me."

He looks up and meets my gaze. His throat bobs up and down.

"Or to me," he admits, surprising me. "I would . . ." He shakes his head and looks away.

I want to finish the sentence for him, fill it in with the words I would like to hear, but that would be like dreaming awake, so instead, I ask, "You would what, Rífíor?"

His jaw tightens. "My name is not Rífíor. My name is Korben."

"I don't know Korben."

And I don't know Rífíor either. He's a lie upon a lie. Yet, I wish he was real, as real as his touch and the way he shudders in my arms. Rífíor . . . I can hold close, and maybe one day, let into my heart. Korben is a male in history books and encyclopedias, a mystical shifter of untold power, victor in ancient battles, no more real than a fictional character.

In one fluid motion, he stands in front of me. "You do know me, Valeria. In here," he taps his chest, his black eyes intense as they drill into mine. "I have always been the same. I was always true to my people, my duty. Everything I have done has been for them. I am ashamed because I failed them. In Tirnanog and in Castella. This is all my fault. And all I have been trying to do is fix the pain I have caused them. It is the reason I sowed chaos with the veilfallen, the reason I stole, the reason I lied to them . . . to you."

The words don't come easy to him. I don't think he's used to this type of honesty. Was he always this way? Or did something change him?

"Perhaps that is true," I say. "Yet, there's more about Korben Theric that you don't want me to know."

He turns his face to one side, his eyebrows drawing together. I'm tempted to caress the line of his sharp jaw, grab his chin, and tell him to kiss me, but he feels so distant right now, a true stranger. And there's still so much anger in me.

Knowing I have to do everything in my power to understand him, I push against what may be the final barrier between us.

"Why did my mother take The Eldrystone from you?"

He takes a step back, putting some distance between us. "I was a different person before I met your mother."

I brace myself. His next words may shatter anew the pieces of my heart that have been able to find their way back into place. If he and Mother . . .

Air lodges in my throat, and I can't swallow.

"She came to Riochtach for the Royal Mate Rite," he continues.

Tears prick behind my eyes, and I feel the room closing in on me. "Please, stop!" I blurt out.

I don't want to hear it. I *can't* hear it. He and Mother were involved. *Oh, gods!*

He scans my face, swiftly closes the distance between us, and seizes my chin in his hand. "No, no! It was not what you are thinking. She only came because her friend, Saethara, dragged her there. Saethara was the one who wanted to be part of the rite. Not your mother."

A broken sob of relief escapes me.

Rífíor's eyes fill with tenderness as he looks at me, and my knees go weak. He's never looked at me this way. His gaze lowers to my lips, but an instant later, he pulls away again, retreating to the other side of the chasm that always seems to separate us.

He clears his throat. "I was . . . your mother . . . um." He hangs his head, eyes closed.

I reach out and take his hand, and it feels like such a bold move.

Up until now, we've only touched each other when our passion left us no other choice. So many times, I've wanted to reach out and caress him to offer comfort, to trace his handsome face, to connect us, and that door always felt closed. Except, he just threw it wide open by taking my face in his hands to soothe me from my dreadful thoughts.

"You can trust me," I say, interlacing his fingers with mine.

He extricates his hand, slamming shut the door he just opened. I retreat, hugging myself, feeling the sting of rejection.

"There is no easy way to tell you what happened. I will not make excuses for my actions, so I think the facts will suffice." He pauses, swallows thickly, then continues. "From the moment I laid eyes on Saethara, I knew I would pick her. Barely a week after the rite began, we were married. On our wedding night, she stabbed me in the chest in my sleep and took The Eldrystone."

I gasp, pressing a hand to my breastbone as my heart leaps at the horror he's describing. "That's awful. I'm so sorry, that—"

He cuts me off. "My shifting magic saved me, and as soon as I healed, I went after her and took my revenge. I killed her, ran her through with my sword."

His black eyes are cold shards of obsidian as he looks straight at me, unwavering. His jaw is set, and I can tell the fury of that night still boils in his veins like an incurable disease.

Gods! He killed his wife.

Rífíor continues. "Even as I held my sword, dripping with her blood, I was not satisfied. I wanted others to feel the pain I was feeling, so I vowed to destroy the village and the people who spawned her."

Legs trembling, I sit at the edge of the bed and let out a hot rush of breath filled with anguish.

"And I would have done it," he adds coldly. "I would have razed Nilhalari to the ground, if not for Loreleia. Because she took The Eldrystone from Saethara and ran. So, there you have it, princess. The entire truth."

Only the sounds of my quivering breaths fill the heavy silence that hangs between us. My heart lies in ruins at the bottom of my chest.

"You wanted to know," he says. "And now you do."

I cover my face with my hands and take a deep breath, managing to stave off the tears that threaten to show him I'm undone. Flexing my fingers, I place my hands on my thighs and inhale deeply.

Tentatively, he kneels in front of me and touches the tips of his fingers to my leg. "Say something, Valeria."

I meet his gaze. His onyx eyes have lost their edge and are now filled with the warmth of candlelight. His expression is soft, pleading. I can only imagine how hard it was to confess the dark deeds that lead him here, how fiercely he has guarded his heart after that vile creature tore it to shreds, destroying his ability to trust and forcing him to build barrier upon barrier.

But what can I say? What could he possibly want to hear from me?

He killed his wife, the woman he loved.

I can almost see the vivid crimson of her blood on his blade. Yet, I can't blame him, nor could anyone else. Most people, me included, would have done the same. She used his feelings against him. This Saethara was a monster consumed by greed, who used him for her own gain.

Of course I understand him, and maybe that is what he wants me to say. It's just . . . he isn't the person I wanted him to be. He's precisely the enemy I feared.

"I would have razed Nilhalari to the ground, if not for Loreleia."

His words play in a loop inside my head. My mother stood in his way to protect those she loved. And not only that, she did it despite the pain and loss it brought her. Is it my hopeless fate to do the same? Or will it be possible to carve a different destiny?

Nana, what do I do?

I can't help him reopen the veil. Aiding him now would be a reckless gamble, a risk that could mean the destruction of my beloved Castella. Instead, I should take The Eldrystone from him and never give it back.

RÍFÍOR

"I need time to think," she chokes out, her eyes refusing to meet mine, *"Korben."*

The sentence hangs heavy in the air, punctuated by the unexpected murmur of my true name. It's a bittersweet moment, and the weight of it settles upon me, a chilling premonition that from now on, everything between us will be a cold formality, a clean break from any warmth we have shared.

"I will leave you then." I stand and walk away. I take my time exiting, hoping she will ask me to stay, but as I close the door, I see her sitting on the bed, staring at the same spot on the wall.

Downstairs, I find Galen and Jago, sitting at a table, four tankards between them. They turn to look at me, but wisely let me be. I would find no refuge in weak human drink or in the conversation of these fools. I sit in a shadowed corner, lost in the pain of my unearthed memories.

Part of me waits for Valeria, but I know she won't come. For the briefest instant, I thought she could be mine, but it seems I am condemned to deceive myself.

Hours pass. I feel their slow passage like a wheel slowly grinding on my nerves. The Eldrystone around my neck feels foreign, a weight that used to be part of me now a bothersome splinter that keeps calling attention to itself, reminding me of its twenty-year absence.

I was right to never want the amulet when Father passed it down to me. And if I had known the suffering it would bring me and others, I would have renounced my right to the throne, Theric dynasty be damned. Since Saethara's betrayal, destruction has been the only word the amulet has whispered in my ear. How did my father remain pure from its influence? How has Valeria? She grows stronger to its effects every day, using it wisely even as our quest turns more precarious.

Struck by a realization, I rise to my feet. I glance toward the stairs and hesitate only for an instant before I climb them two at a time and knock on Valeria's door.

"It's Korben," I say when there is no response.

"I want to be alone," she replies.

"Just one thing and then . . . I will leave."

I hear rustling, then the door opens a crack. Her face is pale, and I fear she's lying about being fully recovered. My lips part as I prepare to speak, but my words get lodged in my chest, crowding it, making it feel as if a thousand bees are stuck between my ribs.

"What is it?" she asks, impatient.

Actions have always served me better, so I take The Eldrystone and pull the chain over my head. Reaching between the door and the jamb, I take her hand and press the amulet to her palm. When she only stares mutely, I bend her fingers around the jewel and let her go.

"It is yours," I say. "You may do with it as you wish."

Her eyes waver, and she shakes her head, uncomprehending.

"It should have never been mine," I explain. "Before I became king, I did not want it. In fact, I feared it. I was wiser then than I have been since." I inhale sharply and glance away. Scrubbing at my chin, I let out a derisive laugh. "Anyway, that was all I wanted to do. Good night." I turn to leave, but she grabs my arm.

I glance down at her delicate fingers around my biceps as if they are all I need to find salvation. She misinterprets my look and pulls her hand away, leaving me adrift.

"What are you doing?" she asks, narrowing her eyes.

Her question takes me aback. Does she know me that well?

"Just what I should have done a while back."

Valeria shakes her head. "That's not what I'm asking."

I push air through my nose in tired amusement. "I am leaving," I confess. "I have been going about *everything* the wrong way, and in my blind pursuit, I have caused much pain. I was given the power to shape the fate of so many, and I grew arrogant and callous. I did not understand the responsibility that was set upon my shoulders. Go and use the amulet as you wish. I am sure you will do better than me."

Grabbing a lock of her hair, I rub it between my fingers, enjoying its silkiness. "I am glad I met you, Valeria Plumanegra. Goodbye."

VALERIA

"I am glad I met you, Valeria Plumanegra. Goodbye." Korben walks away, his shoulders straight, his steps firm.

I glance down at The Eldrystone, the true culprit in all of this, Niamhara behind every action *and* inaction.

And Korben?

Only a victim, a victim willing to erase himself from what's to come next. He doesn't want to destroy Castella.

"Wait!" I look up.

His head swivels, though not quite enough to meet my gaze.

"Stay," I say. "Stay and figure this out with me."

His breath hitches, and he turns his head again, facing completely away from me. His shoulders rise and fall visibly. I walk over to him, go around, and stand in front of him.

A silver line wells in his eyes, unshed tears from a male I thought was cold-hearted beyond repair.

I press a hand to his cheek. His eyes close as he leans into my touch. Feeling as if I can finally rest after an interminable journey, I lay my head on his breastbone, wrapping my hands around his neck.

He presses his cheek to the top of my head and lets out a sigh. His strong arms envelop me, and a sensation of safety descends on me. When I broke him out of Nido, he was a threat I had to constantly watch. My goal seemed impossible, little more than a treasonous action against my sister. But here in his arms, with his heart beating against my ear and his utter surrender at my feet, I think we can make this work.

We can free his kin and help them return to their homes. We can convince my sister there's a better way, and broker peace between our people.

Taking his hand, I lead him back to the room and gently close the door behind us. When I turn to face him, his expression makes him almost unrecognizable. The lines around his eyes and mouth are soft. His lips are parted, tremulous, as if he's afraid of something.

I think I know what it is.

"I would never stab you in your sleep." I let that sink in, then add, "Watch out when you're awake, though."

He sputters a laugh. His hands shoot out, grabbing my waist and tugging me against him. The press of our bodies is heady. Heat radiates through the fabric that separates us.

"That," he murmurs, his voice husky, "is not what I am worried about." He's still vulnerable, a trait I want to hold on to because, for the first time, I have a glimpse into a part of him I've yearned to see, something I need to guard.

"What are you worried about then? That you'll fall in love with me?" I laugh nervously and immediately want to take back the words.

He shakes his head. "No, princess, that already happened."

A thrill runs down my spine, and my universe seems to shrink to the pinprick of his pupils only to explode and expand into a million possibilities. He just conceded he's in love with me. It seems impossible that he would ever let anyone through his barriers, let alone admit it. *Oh, gods!*

He gently strokes my cheek with his thumb. "What I am truly worried about is that I have allowed you to burrow so deeply within me," he murmurs, pressing a forefinger against his chest and making a twisting motion, "that if you were to reject me, my very soul would crumble."

If his admission of love hadn't sobered me up, this certainly has. He doesn't ever seem to do anything in half-measures, even love. It's both terrifying and exhilarating.

He leans his forehead against mine. "Do you want me, Valeria Plumanegra?"

"Y-yes," I confess in a rush of breath. "I want you, Korben Theric, Rífíor, Bastien. I want you in all your shapes and forms. I want you even though I'm terrified of what comes next. I want you. I want you."

He laughs then, and I don't think I've ever heard such a genuine sound of happiness from anyone. And knowing that it has come from him—this male of glacial glares and surly grunts—makes me reevaluate everything I know.

Korben holds my face in his hand as if I'm made of crystal. His smoldering gaze falls to my lips. "May I?"

I nod once.

The side of his mouth lifts to form a wicked grin. He wets his lips, and carefully, so carefully, kisses me. It's nothing but a whisper, the touch of a feather. Yet, a wave of desire crashes against my core. Eager for more, I lean closer and capture his lower lips between my teeth.

His large hand comes around and cradles my rear, pulling me until I feel his erection against my abdomen. His tongue slips into my mouth and a moan—an undiluted sound of desire—escapes me. Taking this as his cue, he sits on the bed and hauls me into his lap.

He kisses my chin, my jawline. "You taste like feyglen, intoxicating."

His hands steal under my tunic to find more of me. He cups my breasts, finding them unbound, my undergarment lost somewhere in the woods.

A groan of pleasure rumbles from his chest. He pushes the tunic over my head and throws it to the floor. The Eldrystone's chain jingles in my hand, catching his eyes. He reaches for it, and I hold my breath in a moment of panic. I imagine it was all a trick, and he didn't mean to bestow the amulet upon me. When he hangs the chain around my neck and the opal falls heavily between my breasts, I feel terrible for doubting.

He kisses one of my nipples and then the other. They tighten in response, and he chuckles, satisfied.

"You are so beautiful." His hands run up my sides, lifting my arms above my head, then caressing downward, slowing as they pass the curve of my breasts. He lies down on the small bed and pulls me along, setting me right on top of his hardness.

I shiver at the pressure.

"Ride me, Valeria," he says. "I want to see you."

In awkward jerks and shoves our pants come off, then I'm

poised over him, my knees on either side of his hips. Holding his gaze, I lower myself and take him in, my lungs seizing as he fills me completely, pushing deep against my inner barrier.

Head thrown back, I rock my hips front to back. A whimper pushes past my lips. He breathes heavily with every thrust, his eyes drinking me in, never closing.

I lift my hands, fingers splayed, and he takes them in his, our fingers interlacing. Now, instead of front to back, I move up and down, taking him out to the tip, then lunging back down until tears fill my eyes, and I'm biting my lower lip to avoid screaming. His body goes tense, and he can barely keep his eyes open as pleasure builds. I keep a steady pace, enjoying the way his powerful body shivers underneath me.

When he spasms, throwing his head back and sighing in full-body relief, I can't believe *I* have done that. *I* reduced him to this defenseless creature completely at my mercy.

My heart feels ready to burst. I lie on top of him, sweat slick between us. His heart is hammering fast and hard. He wraps me in his arms as if he'll never let me go and kisses the top of my head. We only rest that way for a minute before he flips me over, ending on top of me.

"Your turn, princess," he says, then begins to kiss his way south.

50
VALERIA

"Now, our dear home is a prison. How shall this horror be undone?"

Hermano Jacinto – Monasterio de San Corvus de la Corona Monk – 21 AV

Early next morning, Korben retrieves our horse from the stable he hired to take care of it and buys three more mounts. Jago takes one and rides to inform the troop of our plans. He didn't want to leave without telling them and without paying what we owed them for their services. I suspect he also wanted to see Esmeralda.

We head out of Badajos, trotting easily down the main road, in view of everyone.

I hold my breath as we cross in front of two royal guards standing on a corner and surveying the area as they clearly look for us. It's disconcerting to pass unnoticed by everyone.

Jago sticks his thumb between index and middle fingers, makes the fig sign, and waves it at them. "The fun I would have sneaking up on Esmeralda," he says with a mischievous grin.

"Esmeralda, huh?" I tease.

He twists his mouth to one side, then says, "The Fae King, huh?"

My cheeks grow hot, and I chide myself for inviting him to tease me and making it so easy.

Korben throws me a sidelong glance, looking amused. He wears La Matadora on his back. I try not to think what Father or Amira would think of that.

"Do you trust him?" Jago asks later when Korben isn't listening.

"I do."

He raises an eyebrow and purses his lips asking, *Are you sure?*

I nod, no doubt in my heart.

Jago sighs. "Then I guess I'll have to trust him, too, but if he hurts you again, I'll hang him by the balls."

"And I'll help you."

We both laugh.

Soon, we're out of the small town, Cuervo's shadow skimming over the ground as he flies overhead.

The border with the territory once known as Portus is only two days away. I have never visited this far west, but I've read that Portus died out when the veil first appeared over two thousand years ago. With all trade routes gone and cut off from the rest of the continent, I imagine they slowly found it harder and harder to thrive.

Many who rather believe in grimmer things say that as Tirnanog took its place, Portus shriveled away under its presence. It is said that no Castellan travels beyond that border, fearing the veil's abrupt reappearance and a death sentence if the fae lands settle anew. Most people believe Tirnanog exists in a different plane. Nonetheless, anyone on Portus's side would find themselves cut off from their homes, so I think it wise not to travel there.

I could never have imagined my traveling partners at the end of the journey. I'm only glad Calierin isn't here.

Korben and I talked for a long while last night. We crowded together in the narrow bed, wrapped in each other's arms. I asked him what he wanted to do, and he said it was my decision alone. I told him my fears.

"Learning your true identity," I said, "made me doubt our goal. I thought you would go to Tirnanog and return to Castella bent on war."

"I was willing to destroy everything when you gave me the amulet in your sister's bedroom. Twenty years taught me nothing. They simply served to enhance my rage. But these last few days, I've come to realize how much I relied on The Eldrystone. How dependent on it I became. That conduit has been the source of all my pain. You showed me that, Valeria. You . . . with your restraint in the face of so much power. For a long, long time, Niamhara was quiet, and The Eldrystone seemed to be a tool she bestowed upon us and then forgot about. But now, she is quite present, with you directly in her sights. You are young, yet you have displayed wisdom beyond your years, resisting the amulet's allure far better than I ever managed once it took root within me. That is why I think you will be a better keeper than I ever was."

My fingers trailing down his smooth chest, I said, "I . . . I'm not as immune as you may think." It was hard to admit it, but I needed to acknowledge it. "At times, when I didn't have it in my possession, there was this strange feeling in my chest, a sort of desperation that made me want to rip it from your hands, Amira's hands, Calierin's hands. It took all my strength to control the urge."

"And yet, you did. I can't say the same thing."

"I . . . tried to kill you."

"I'm still here."

"You wore it for years, Korben. I've only just . . ."

"*Shh.*" He smoothed my hair, light fingers moving along its length, then trailing down my back, making me shiver. "You do not give yourself the credit you deserve. You are so strong."

I grunted noncommittally.

"You must hate Amira," I said, still afraid of what he might do.

"She is not my favorite person," he admitted, "but I understand her. I hate to say this, but when Francisca brought Thoran here, I showed my own lack of acceptance. I judged him based on my ignorant ideas. Yet, he saved you, and you are here thanks to him. I learned something valuable. Your sister, like me, has been dealt a difficult hand. Mayhap, there is still hope for her. I did not think I could change, but here I am."

I caressed his face. "Thank you for saying that."

With a smile stretching his chiseled mouth, he took the white streak in my hair and pulled it up. "Did you always have this?"

Shaking my head, I buried my face deeper into his chest. This is one of those things I don't like to talk about, but no barrier exists between us anymore.

"I got it the night Mother died," I say, my voice growing thick. "I was wearing The Eldrystone, playing and pretending to be

Mother. The amulet helped me save Father from Orys, but I was too late to help her. Afterward, I had this."

"How old were you?"

"Eight."

"Like I said, you are strong, ravógín."

I pushed up on my shoulder to look at him. "What does that mean?"

He smiled crookedly. "It means little raven."

Resting back on his chest, I hid my smile. I liked it. "Tell me about your espiritu, your shifting magic?"

Aching sorrow seeped into his voice, a hollow echo of the emptiness he feels without his raven skills.

By the end, I was in awe. Before the veil fell, he possessed the ability to shift into all the forms of a formidable raven shifter. Corvus, a regular-sized raven akin to Cuervo. Dreadwing, a colossal bird with talons the size of a house. Scatter, an unkindness of ravens capable of darkening the sky. Chimera, a creature with a blend of raven and fae characteristics. He also confessed to other, darker powers, but chose to end the conversation there, deciding it was too late.

"You will be able to do it all again when we reopen the veil," I said, stifling a yawn.

"Mayhap you are right, little raven."

Now, I smile as I look ahead between my horse's ears. Petting the animal's neck, I feel optimism sparking in my veins for the first time during this journey.

Everything will be all right.

Two days later, my optimism has taken root. We haven't run into any trouble. Galen's espiritu is as Jago called it: Gaspar imbued with strength from San Christopher. Unfortunately, Korben doesn't seem to share my good cheer, and the closer we get, the more somber his expression becomes.

Overgrown brush blocks the path, a testament to the lack of travelers. Galen uses his magic to clear our way. Korben's gaze dances around as if he expects trouble to jump from behind each bush. My cousin has picked up on it and is doing the same, hand tight around the hilt of the rapier he took from Enrique.

"We are close," Korben announces after an hour of silent riding.

We have left the path and entered the forest which, without Galen, would be impassable.

"Yes," Galen agrees. He cracks his neck and scents the air like a hound. Can he sense the veil? My eyes rove all around, and I see nothing, only massive trees covered in vines and moss. The forest is so thick, it is hard to see past it.

Abruptly, Korben brings his mount to a halt and leaps off the saddle. He walks over to a tree as wide as five men and runs a hand over the bark. He steps lithely over the gnarled roots and rounds the trunk.

"Here," he announces.

"How are you so sure?" Galen asks.

"Because of this." He points at something we can't see on his side of the tree.

We all dismount and go around to find a large gash scarring the trunk.

"I left this here as a marker when I passed through," Korben explains. "I don't know what made me do it." He frowns and looks down at the ground.

"Perhaps your instincts told you something bad was about to happen," Galen says.

Korben shrugs. "Mayhap."

They both look at me expectantly.

"Um, all right, how do I do this?" I ask.

Galen frowns at Korben. "How does *she* do this?"

"Yes, Galen. Valeria will do this," Korben answers in a tired voice.

"Why?"

Korben ignores the question.

The sorcerer thinks for a moment. "Of course, you have no magic. That's why you can't shift. That's why we're trapped here."

"Brilliant as always."

"But how? Why?"

Korben crosses his arms. "That's not something you and I are going to discuss."

Jago puts a hand up. "I want to know, too."

They both get death glares from Korben.

I clear my throat. "Again, how do I do this?"

Galen huffs in frustration. "Just wish it open. I'm sure that's the extent of what you can do with the amulet, isn't it? You don't yet know how to weave spells?"

"Weave spells?" I glance over at Korben.

He looks chagrined. "There is much more to know about how to channel The Eldrystone's power than merely asking it to do your bidding."

"Hmm, interesting how you hadn't mentioned that." I narrow my eyes at him.

He only looks smug and says, "There is much you still need to learn, ravógín."

"What is this *ravógín* nonsense?!" Jago demands. "The veilfallen leader is to the level of using pet names? Simply discussing."

"Shut up, Jago, or I'll turn you into a chicken," I threaten, tugging the amulet from under my tunic.

"Chicken!" Cuervo croaks from the branch where he's perched. I don't think I've ever heard such a delighted tone from him.

My cousin glares up at Cuervo. "Then I'll finally look just like you, buddy."

Cuervo hops on the branch, flapping his wings in annoyance.

"What's wrong with that bird?" Jago asks no one in particular.

"Nothing," Galen replies. "He is a perfectly normal Runescribe Raven. My family used to raise them. They're counted amongst the smartest animals in Tirnanog."

This is surprising information, and I want to know more, but I save my questions for later. Clearing my throat, I grab hold of the amulet, holding my hand tightly to my chest, and I wish for the veil to reopen.

Nothing happens.

"Did . . . you do it?" Jago asks.

"I did."

"Try harder then. You have always been such an underachiever."

I send a death glare his way but avoid glancing in Korben's direction. I don't want to disappoint him. We have come so far, and failure isn't an option.

Planting my feet firmly on the ground, I close my eyes and concentrate. Before I tell The Eldrystone what to do, I say a little prayer for Niamhara.

Please, Goddess, let us find a path into Tirnanog. Let all these people, your children, go home. They have suffered enough already. Open the veil.

"What am I looking for here?" Jago asks. "Maybe she did it already and we just can't see it."

I sigh, opening my eyes and registering the disappointment in Korben's expression.

"Trust me," Galen says. "You would see it. It's not something you'd miss."

"It shimmers," Korben murmurs, his head hanging.

The next hour, I wish for the veil in a thousand different ways, but nothing works. At some point, my prayers turn into one-sided arguments with Niamhara, and I'm sure that if I ever make it across the veil, she'll smite me as soon as I enter Tirnanog. She hasn't done it yet because she's enjoying my frustration too much.

After my thousandth and one attempt, I growl in frustration and have to bite my lip not to scream at the heavens.

"Come take a break, cousin." Jago—as well as the others—is sitting against a tree, munching on dry bread. "Get something to eat, then try again. I bet it'll help."

Letting my anger build certainly isn't helping, so I sit next to him, snatch a piece of bread from his hand, and take a bite.

After a moment of sitting in silence, Galen scratches the side of his head. "Um, it's beginning to look as if . . . this is a failed endeavor. Perhaps it's time to count our losses and decide what to do next."

"I won't give up so easily," I shoot back, retransmitting every ounce of the anger his defeatist attitude reignites in me.

He throws his hands up in the air. "Just a suggestion, princess."

"Can anyone think of something I could try?" I ask.

"Stand on your head?" the sorcerer suggests.

"Galen." Korben growls his name in a clear warning.

I jump to my feet. "I don't need you to defend me, Korben. You know well I can hold my own. Maybe Galen needs to learn that, too."

"I believe he does," Korben agrees. "I suggest a rapier duel."

Glancing at him sideways, I smirk. "Great idea."

Korben says, "Naturally, magic is forbidden."

"This seems quite unfair." Galen begins picking pieces of grass off his pants, looking disinterested.

Korben stands. "I am your king, sorcerer. I have every right to set rules of combat for one of my subjects."

"I want to watch this." Jago rushes to the horses and retrieves the rapiers. "Here you go, cousin." He tosses the weapon, and I snatch it out of the air and strike first position, pointing at Galen's face.

"En guardia," I say.

Galen sighs and laboriously gets to his feet. Jago tosses the second rapier at the sorcerer, who fails to catch it. The weapon hits the bushes and embeds itself in their tangled branches.

"I have told you time and again that your big mouth will be the death of you." Korben sounds amused, and I can't help but wonder if he's using this as a distraction from my failure.

"Pick up the sword." I slash my rapier through the air, making it sing.

Galen disentangles it from the bushes and looks at it as if it's an unknown device never before seen by human or fae eyes. Looking as dexterous as a newly hatched bird, he raises the weapon and attempts to imitate my pose.

Gently, I touch my blade to his and slide it down its length. The hissing sound sends a thrill up my back. Sparring has always been invigorating to me.

"Prepare to—"

A loud croak from Cuervo cuts me off.

"Treasure," he says shrilly, leaping from the branch and flying downward.

When he's halfway to the ground, he does something strange. He hovers in midair for an instant, using short, powerful wing flaps. At the same time, he scratches the air with his talons as if he's trying to snatch something from nothing. Did he see a bug he wants to eat? I begin to think that's what he's doing, when he lands on the ground and begins walking in circles while he looks up, turning his head this way and that.

There's a sudden glint in his eye. He jumps into the air again and performs the same maneuver.

"Now you have truly gone crazy, chicken," Jago says. "Couldn't you just get a hound like regular people, Val?"

It's unlike Cuervo to ignore Jago's jabs, but he is too intent, flying at the same spot over and over again and clawing at it as if he has, indeed, gone mad.

I put the sword aside and approach Cuervo. "Hey, what's the matter?"

He flutters to the ground, looking exhausted and frazzled. "Treasure," he offers as an explanation.

"There is no treasure here, Cuervo." I crouch and pet his neck.

He peers at me sideways and insists, "Treasure." His dark beady eye shimmers as his membranous eyelid opens and closes. I pause. There . . . that shimmer again. What is that? I glance over my head, squinting at the air, feeling as crazy as Cuervo.

Then I see it, a small glimmering light like a tiny star hanging at waist level. I stand and, as I blink, lose track of it.

"Where did it go?" I ask.

"Where did *what* go?" Jago starts circling the spot with me, mimicking Cuervo and me, flapping his arms like wings.

I shove him. "Stop being ridiculous and help me find it."

"I promise," he says solemnly, "I don't know where your sanity went."

"I see it!" Korben exclaims, walking in from the side.

I take a position slightly behind him, mimicking the tilt of his head to follow his gaze. There it is again. I stare at it mesmerized.

"What is it?" I whisper.

"I . . . it is said that Aldryn Theric, my great-grandfather, stumbled upon a tear in the fabric of our realm." His dark eyes rove all around, the speed of his thoughts apparent in his expression. "He didn't open or create the veil. He simply widened that tear."

"You think this is . . ."

"Yes, yes!" Galen exclaims. "Korben is right. I remember reading an account of the events." He starts pacing behind us, trying to spot the anomaly. "I see it too."

He shrugs Korben and me out of the way, gingerly moving closer to the glimmering spot. "If that's all that needs to be done, maybe I can . . ." He kneels, squinting, then raises his hand, a red espiritu outline around his fingers.

"I don't think you should—" Korben doesn't finish his sentence because as soon as Galen touches the spot, there's a loud sizzling sound, followed by a blast, and the sorcerer goes flying backward.

Korben approaches him, looking concerned for a moment, but then Galen groans and lifts his head, dazed.

"Perhaps I shouldn't have touched that," he says, shaking his head as if to clear it from the impact.

"You always have the brightest ideas," Korben puts in.

"I still don't see it," Jago complains, stomping his foot like a child.

I grab his shoulders and position him just so. "Squint your eyes a little, search about two arm lengths away from you, then try to unfocus your eyes."

"Would it help if I stick out my tongue too?"

I swat his arm. "You don't take anything seriously."

He laughs. "I already saw it, Val."

"But of course."

"All right," Jago says, "so if this tiny star is a tear in the fabric between our realms and the sorcerer there," he points at Galen, "only managed to get zapped, are we supposed to assume that Val won't because she has The Eldrystone? And in fact, she will open it?"

"That's how it worked for my great-grandfather," Korben says.

"So what exactly did he do?" Jago puts his arms up and swings them from side to side. "Did he dance a little jig?"

"Unfortunately, I don't know what he did." He turns to Galen. "Did you happen to read anything about that?"

Galen looks up from his hand, which he's slowly flexing. "No, I didn't."

"Fantástico," Jago says sarcastically.

"All right, let me try." I stand in front of the tear, holding the amulet.

This time I think of the spot growing taller and wider, enough to let us through, but I receive the same result as before, which is to say none.

I try several more times, but it's useless.

A faint buzzing begins in my ears, like thousands of insect wings beating. My vision tunnels to the anomaly, and I see a rainbow of colors flicker in the air. It's very pretty. I reach out to touch it.

"What are you doing?!" Jago grabs my hand and pulls me toward him.

I crash into him, feeling dazed. Everything is turning around me, and I have to hold on to my cousin to keep my footing.

"Are you all right?" he asks.

"I am. I just . . . I thought I heard something." Slowly, I pull away from him, and once my head is clear, I take a step back.

"I think I have to . . . reach inside." I don't know where the idea comes from, but it sounds right.

Jago shakes his head. "Val, I don't know. What if it hurts you?"

I glance at Korben questioningly.

He shrugs, his expression saying, *it's all up to you*. He trusts me.

"Galen's still alive," I tell Jago with a smile.

"Barely," the sorcerer calls from his spot on the ground, where he still sits licking his wounds.

"I'll be fine," I say.

Jago twists his mouth in disapproval. "How do you know?"

"I have a feeling."

He runs stiff fingers through his dirty blond hair and whirls around, frustrated. "This damn quest is going to get you killed or worse."

I guess there are fates worse than death, but he's exaggerating.

Bracing myself, I approach the spot once more—one hand on the amulet while the free one goes through the tear.

51
VALERIA

"Bring me my sister. No one will be safe until she's captured."

Reina Amira Plumanegra (Casa Plumanegra) – Queen of Castella – 21 AV

O pen.

The buzzing sound grows deafening, and the light expands to envelop me, swallowing me whole. For a long moment, there's nothing else but the overwhelming distortion of my senses, and I fear I've gotten stuck in between the fabric of the realms, like a bug in a spiderweb.

A restless energy builds in my veins as I cling to The Eldrystone, a steady chant in my mind.

Open. Open. Open.

Blindly, I stumble around, my free hand guarding my eyes from the piercing glow. I want to scream. I want to leave this place.

I don't want to be here!

The buzz and the light stop abruptly, and I find myself standing in an entirely different forest than before.

The air shimmers with multicolored dust dancing in a haze all around me, extending past the thick canopy overhead. Towering, twisted trees unlike anything I've ever seen reach for the sky, their bark a kaleidoscope of emerald green, sapphire blue, and a startling violet that seems to pulse with an inner light.

Vines as thick as my arm writhe between them, some glowing faintly with an ethereal luminescence, others bristling with thorns that warn off intrusion. The silence is broken only by the occasional chirp of an unseen creature, a sound that echoes strangely and seems to repeat itself.

As I take a staggering step forward, there's a soft crunch, and the vibrant green moss under my boot seems to ripple.

Even the sky, glimpsed in slivers between the colossal leaves, seems different. It's a canvas of swirling, iridescent clouds, tinged with hues of lavender, apricot, and the faintest blush of green. It's the loveliest twilight I have ever witnessed.

Gods! This is Tirnanog.

"She did it!" Galen exclaims behind me.

As I glance back, he appears out of thin air, pushing through the multicolored shimmering dust that hangs like a curtain and reaches upward and to the sides as far as the eye can see.

Gaze raised to the heavens, he falls to his knees, breathing hard, as if he's doing everything in his power not to weep like a child.

Jago comes through next, and for the first time in his life, I see him struck mute. He has nothing to say, all his attention is invested in gaping.

Next comes Korben, and the expression on his face as he lays eyes on his homeland for the first time in two decades is equal parts ecstatic and wary—the latter suggesting he fears this is nothing but a dream from which he doesn't want to wake up.

Slowly, an array of emotions shapes his expression, and it's impossible to believe that this is the same male I met as a frosty and indifferent Guardia Real. It's clear that he feels deeply, but hard lessons forced him to hide himself from the world.

I want to walk up to him and wrap him in a tight hug, but this moment is his. I can't begin to comprehend what he has been through. I'm only glad I was able to help him.

We did it. We're here! Everything is going to be all right.

The fae will be able to go back to their homes, and that will be one less worry in Amira's mind. I'll return to her and make her see why this was the only solution. Once the peace we're used to returns to our realm, she will understand that I didn't betray her, that I was only trying to do the right thing.

The light feeling of elation bubbles up from my stomach, filling my chest. A smile spreads across my face, and I think I'm going to—

My stomach twists violently. I press a hand to the wound Calierin inflicted, wondering if it's a side effect from the Nightmend's espiritu. The pain passes quickly, and I begin to think that it was just a random upset, but then it comes back, and this time it's accompanied by a wave of nausea that makes me bend over, threatening to spill the contents of my stomach onto the ground.

Noticing, Jago comes close and puts a hand on my back. "Val, what is it?"

I shake my head, unable to answer. Bile burns its way up my throat. My head pounds, and my skin smarts as if with a million needle pinpricks. The feeling is everywhere, my chest, arms, legs, face. I scratch my forearm so hard I leave angry red tracts running up its length.

"Valeria!" Korben is at my side now, sounding as concerned as my cousin.

I fall to my knees, crying out in pain.

"Galen," Korben shouts, "what is wrong with her?"

"How should I know?" he shoots back.

Crowing, Cuervo flies through the shimmering veil and lands right in front of me. He seems panicked, as if he was terrified of crossing, but as soon as he notices me kneeling on the ground, he begins hopping from leg to leg, making comforting sounds. He has joined Jago and Korben in their concern.

"G-good . . . boy," I manage, right before another wave of nausea hits me, and this time I do empty the contents of my stomach, groaning and falling to my side, twisting from the agony.

"Maybe something here is causing it," Jago suggests. "Let's take her back to Castella."

"Yes, you are right. That must be it." Korben kneels and begins to scoop me off the ground, but then he pulls back. "Oh!" He releases the small exclamation in a whisper, dark eyes roving over my face.

"What?" I ask, my voice shrill, strange, as if it's not my own.

"Ravógín, you are shifting."

KORBEN

My worry subsides. There is nothing wrong with Valeria. She is shifting for the first time in her life. I had wondered before if she had inherited her father's abilities, and it is now clear that she has. In Tirnanog, magic permeates the land and touches everything it finds. It's what she was missing all along. At last, she has what it takes.

"She is fine," I tell Jago, whose panic only seems to grow as small black feathers sprout along Valeria's neck.

"What do you mean she's fine?" he demands. "She's turning into a chicken."

"Not chicken." Cuervo hops all around Valeria, a loyal friend full of concern.

The process is slow and grueling. It is extremely hard to watch, and I wish I could do something for her, but she has never shifted before, and her body is not used to it.

"It will pass, Valeria," I say. "It will pass. I promise. Be strong."

"Saints!" Jago exclaims. "It's going to kill her."

"No!" I say. "It is not." I don't allow any doubt to enter my voice or my heart. She is going to be all right.

A strangled cry tears from her throat, ripping through the stillness of the forest and carving a shard of ice through my heart. She convulses. Tears well up in her eyes, her beautiful face laced with agony. Each shuddering breath seems like a struggle against an invisible tide ripping her apart from the inside.

Valeria's body shrivels, contorting. Bones crack with sickening pops as her spine changes shape, ribs rearranging to accommodate the emerging wings. Her hair morphs into sleek feathers that ripple down her body. Her fingers elongate into sharp talons, the nails black as night.

A primal scream escapes her lips, and it is not a human sound. The final change sweeps over her. Her features blur, her nose and mouth sharpening into a beak, her eyes turning perfectly round.

Then her entire form shrinks to her Corvus form.

On the ground lies not Valeria, but a small raven, her clothes and the amulet gone, swept away by her magic. Her obsidian eyes fill with a flicker of recognition and an ocean of pain. My throat tightens. The raven caws once, a mournful sound and a question.

"You are safe," I assure her.

Cuervo hops closer, cocking his head from one side to the other. "Friend?" he croaks.

Galen approaches. "That was excruciating to watch."

I glare at him, and he starts humming, appearing extremely interested in a nearby tree.

Arsehole!

Trying to decide what to do next, I stretch to my full height. The best would be for Valeria to shift back, and then—

"Who goes there?!" a male's voice demands, accompanied by the rustle of brush and snap of branches.

I turn to the sound. A moment later, three males appear. I scan their clothes in surprise. They wear the uniforms of The Oakheart Brigade, yet the emblems on their chest bear a coat of arms that does not belong to the Theric house.

At the sight of us, one of them, the leader, unsheathes his broad sword, while the other two nock arrows, fixing us in their sights.

It takes them a moment to realize what's behind us. The veil shimmers, connecting Tirnanog to Castella once more.

The leader opens and closes his mouth, unable to utter any words.

"Greetings," I say, taking a step forward.

"Hold it right there," the leader orders, raising his sword. "You are hereby detained."

"Detained?" I frown. This is not our way. No one is detained for no reason. "Under what grounds and authority?" I demand.

"You are under arrest for . . . breaching the veil. By decree of Queen Saethara, you are under arrest."

Queen Saethara?!

No. It cannot be.

VALERIA AND RIVER'S STORY WILL CONTINUE...

COMING SOON

DON'T MISS THE FIRST PART OF
VALERIA AND RIVER'S STORY . . .

OUT NOW

HE NEEDS MY HELP,
BUT HE'LL BE MY DOWNFALL.

OUT NOW

THE PRINCE WOULD CHOOSE
TO SAVE HIS REALM.
BUT THE BEAST WOULD FOLLOW
HIS HEART . . . TO ME.

OUT NOW

THE FINAL BATTLE LOOMS,
AND OUR LOVE HANGS IN THE BALANCE.

OUT NOW

FIND YOUR HEART'S DESIRE...

VISIT OUR WEBSITE: www.headlineeternal.com
FIND US ON FACEBOOK: facebook.com/eternalromance
CONNECT WITH US ON X: @eternal_books
FOLLOW US ON INSTAGRAM: @headlineeternal
EMAIL US: eternalromance@headline.co.uk